GW00459133

# THE VELVET GLOVE

## Alexandra Connor

PEACH PUBLISHING

Copyright © Alexandra Connor 2014

The right of Alexandra Connor to be identified as the Author of the Work has been asserted by him in accordance with the Copyright, Designs and Patents Act 1988.

This book is sold subject to the condition it shall not, by way of trade or otherwise, be copied, lent, resold, hired out, or otherwise circulated in print or electronic means without the publisher's prior consent in any form.

ISBN 978-1-78036-265-6

Except where actual historical events and characters are being described, all situations in this book are fictitious and any resemblance to living persons is purely coincidental.

Previously published as *The Houses of Razzio*

Published by
Peach Publishing

*This book is dedicated to everyone who has ever believed in, and fought for, a dream*

*The iron hand*
*Within the velvet glove.*

French proverb

# Book One

# Origins

# *One*

**1900. New Year's Eve**
**Minutes before the new century began**
**Liverpool**


He stood immobile, looking down past the dock buildings towards the oily waters of the Mersey. Lights from the moored ship flickered over the river, the echoes of men's voices coming over the listening night. A sudden splashing sound broke into the liquid stillness, then a loud, joint chorus of laughter lunged upwards over the water and slid up the cobbled street. The noise seemed to pool at Guido Razzio's feet, to take shape for a pulsating moment until the bells started.

They rang from all corners of the city it seemed, and in ringing, the residents of the houses came out into the dark street carrying lights and forming moving puddles of illumination under the luminescent stars. It was the moment of the turn of the year, the turn into the twentieth century, and as Guido watched, women came out of their homes, embracing each other, children borne high on men's shoulders, the shabby street suddenly filling with noise, the boat's lights making a gilded island on the Mersey beyond.

He stepped back, dipped into the doorway and watched for a moment before unlocking the door and moving into the house. Once inside, he struck a match and lit the lamp he carried, lifting it shoulder high. The hallway was cramped, hardly more than a yard wide, the room on his right dark behind a warped door. Guido walked in, shining the light around. The onion smell of bugs was chokingly strong, the black range which faced him mottled with old fat, a pan with a broken handle lying on its side. There was no floor covering, only flagstones, and the black mark someone had told him about only hours earlier.

"... it's a blood stain, or so they say. Scrubbed it after it happened – even had a go at it myself – but couldn't budge it. Blood. That's what it is ..." Nellan rocked uncertainly on his feet, a slop of beer spilling over the rim of the glass. "No one'll ever buy the bloody place, and that's a fact," he went on, wiping his mouth with the back of his hand. "It's unlucky."

Calmly, Guido asked the next question. He spoke slowly to minimise his accent – although having been brought up by an English mother he had been bi-lingual from childhood – still he spoke softly and slowly.

"*Why* is it unlucky, Mr. Nellan?"

The man had put his head on one side, trying to make out the stranger. Some foreigner, he was sure of that. Eyes too deep set, a little too self assured for someone without means. Maybe, just maybe, if he paid his cards right he could have a buyer here.

His eyes were suddenly sly: "I didn't say unlucky –"

"Yes, you did," Guido replied without annoyance. "But you didn't say *why* the house was unlucky."

The man was wrong-footed and irritated by his own stupidity. The young man had approached him in the 'Bell and Monkey' pub, the landlord having already pointed him out and telling Nellan that he was in boxing. Arranged the fights, he'd said. Didn't fight himself, just laid them on, like the one last Saturday down at the docks. He'd won a few bob on it, the landlord said, winking. This *Guido*, he'd baulked on the foreign syllables – or whatever his bloody name was – this *Guido* Razzio was worth knowing.

"You said it was unlucky," Guido persisted. "Why?"

"There was a bit of trouble there once," Nellan said grudgingly.

"What kind of trouble?" Guido prompted.

The older man paused. He wasn't sure about this at all, the man was too calm, too unhurried, too bloody cool for his own good. Nellan studied the stranger's wide cheek boned face, the unblinking eyes, the compressed mouth above the defined jaw line. The clothes he wore weren't expensive, but he made them *seem* expensive, wore them like he wore a hundred pounds on his back.

Discomforted, Nellan rubbed his greasy forehead with his hand. "There was a killing there."

"A murder?"

"You might say that."

Guido breathed in; looked away for an instant. "You said the house was on Cranberry Street?"

"You heard," Nellan agreed sullenly, certain that he had lost his chance of a sale. "… number 14."

"Who was killed?"

"Eh?"

"I asked you …" Guido said, turning his glance back to Nellan, "… who was killed?"

"Jack Holland's daughter. Some fella did her in. No one knew who, they never caught him. It was five, maybe six years ago. Her father found her in the kitchen. She was cut up bad." Nellan stopped, downing his beer and sniffing loudly. He'd gone and blown it again, bloody fool! Why hadn't he kept he mouth shut? When would he ever learn to keep his bloody mouth shut?

"Number 14?" Guido repeated softly, his eyes studying the sweating Nellan. "I want to see it."

"It's not a bloody museum!" the older man said belligerently, "I only show serious buyers."

Guido's voice dropped. "You haven't *had* any serious buyers for the place," he said calmly. "You know that, and I know that … I want to see it, Mr. Nellan, and if you've any sense you'll show it to me."

Nellan was befuddled with beer and openly hostile. He didn't like the man in front of him; didn't like the way he looked at him, or the way he talked to him. But he was right, no one *had* ever seriously thought of buying the house on Cranberry Street. Clumsily he reached into his pocket and brought out a key with a small slat of wood attached, marked with the number 14.

"You want to see it? Well, go by your bloody self!" he said, slamming the key onto the bar top next to them. "I'm not catching my death of cold out there just to keep you company."

A hour later, whilst the bells rang out over the Mersey and the surrounding terraces welcomed in the new century, Guido Razzio stood in the foul little pit of a kitchen at No. 14 and looked around him. The walls were dark with damp, an old tap dripping eerily against the outside wall, a yellowed sheet tacked up at the window. The air was fetid, dank with old cooking fat and the smell of mice. Above his head, a clothes rack with broken slats threw a black-grilled shadow against the mottled wall, and as he turned to move, the lamp caught the mark on the floor by his feet.

He stared. He remembered what Nellan had said in the pub. Blood? Yes, it was blood. There was no smell, no tell tale vermillion to prove it, only the *sensation* of the mark. It gave off a pulse, a heat, a power which emanated from the flagstone. Something *lived* in the mark, some memorial of violence and terror … His thoughts shifted instantaneously; he could smell mimosa, hot stone under a high sun. There were birds in a garden and a glass, fully filled, laid down on the bedside table. Below, a door banged, the liquid trembling for an instant, the water throwing off the sun and patterning the wall with light. The day was curling inwards, soon night would take down the last of the light and later, under a waning moon, he would flinch to hear footsteps in the corridor outside.

*Breath in, breath in, calm down, calm down,* Guido willed himself. *You got away. You're safe …* But his thoughts still travelled back … A peacock in the gardens outside mewled into the dry Italian air and there was blood drying on a towel at his feet …

Startled, Guido dropped the lamp, then bent down and retrieved it, relighting it and leaning for a moment against the door frame. The memory had gone, in its place there was only the stink of the room in which he stood.

But he didn't leave; instead he stayed and regulated his breathing, composing himself. Outside, a man's voice, hoarse with violence, ricocheted down the terrace, a woman calling pleadingly after him. Under the peeling of bells, a child cried and a cart clattered past, the horse's hooves clacking on the cobble stones.

In Italy Guido had had a horse called Seraphina, had ridden her in a field set well away from the house; and sometimes, in cool mornings, he had risen and gone down to the fields and watched as she came out from under the trees and walked over to him, her body steaming, her breath ivory smoke. She was vast and kind, terrible as a white dragon, and she smelled of August rain …

The candle flickered, Guido lifting the lamp higher, his figure throwing its own shadow across the wall. He knew that people talked about him, wondered. However much he kept himself removed, they talked. He had had little accent, and less money when he arrived in Liverpool two years ago. At first he had thought of going to London, but that was too obvious, too easy to trace. No one would think of Liverpool. Certainly not his father. All he would be told, and all he would believe, was that his beloved son had left. He would never understand – for there would never be any explanation offered. Guido had gone. His son, loved above all others, had left his family and his home.

There would never be the chance to ask *why? Why?* was the most dangerous question of all. *Why did you do it?* Required an answer, and the answer was too terrible to articulate. To even utter the words would be to expose the truth. *I left to escape. I left my home, my inheritance, my roots, because of ...* He could never say *why*. Could never confess. Besides, if he had done, his father would not have believed him: he would have asked questions instead and demanded explanations – and to what end? What possible ending *was* there apart from destruction? To tell the truth would have been to tear out the belly of the family and the house. All the shaded rooms, the laid grounds, the heady precision of their exquisite and envied life would have been peeled back and skinned. And in the end, for what?

It was better to say nothing, Guido realised. No one else was in danger, he had only to protect himself. But it still took him two days to leave; two days in which he paced his home and memorised, and touched, the myriad possessions he would never see again. It was hot, summer, skies without clouds, shadows long and cool – and threatening. He tempted fate; in staying he invited his own death, almost wanting it to happen ... but the forty eight hours passed and his leaving still came.

When he finally walked out of the grounds it was very early on a summer morning, just following dawn. Dry with anxiety, he went up to the field and called for Serphina, clicking his tongue, the sound echoing in the still air. She came down, warm from the trees, her hooves heavy in the moist earth. Gently he blew on her nose and for an instant she closed her eyes, dew freckling her mane. Then he moved away, imagining he could still hear her soft whinnying long after the field was out of sight.

Several days later he docked in Liverpool. His mother's English had not prepared him for reality and Guido struggled daily to understand the Scouse accent. Cultivated and sternly attractive, he provoked animosity and found it everywhere. The narrow cobbled streets and the frigid cold barked against his skin and although he had taken only his shabbiest clothes, his demeanour marked him out immediately. Friends were absent; but he found lodgings quickly, his room in a terrace only two away from Cranberry Street, and when he leaned out of his window he could see the boats gliding past the end of the street, coming in on the Mersey tide.

He was too empty to be homesick; too anxious to risk showing fear. He had made his decision, and must abide by it. But when he passed down the streets people stopped to stare at him, and when he walked into the pub the first time the drinkers turned their backs on him and the landlord refused to serve him.

"Why?"

"We don't like foreigners."

He was too reckless to be afraid: "You serve foreigners off the boats. What makes me different?"

The pub quietened. People listened. Waited. Watched him.

"They don't live here."

"I'm not doing anyone any harm," Guido said defiantly, standing up to the landlord. "I want a drink. Please, give me a drink."

His manner antagonised the man. Something unbeatable, something indefinable about him marked him out. They were all, in some way, awed by him – and resented it.

"Go on, lad, I don't want trouble."

"Neither do I," Guido said resolutely. "I just want a drink."

"Go home –"

"THIS IS MY HOME!" he bellowed, enraged. Immediately an onlooker moved over to him, roughly clutching his arm and trying to propel him to the door. "Let go of me!" Guido shouted, flinging out his arm and striking the man.

The silence swelled. In one infinitesimal instant the quiet engulfed and swallowed him. Faces all turned on him, they merged, pooled into one, two men approaching him, pacing their steps in unison. They expected him to back off, to retreat, but he was that most unstable of beasts – a man with nothing to lose and nowhere left to go. So Guido Razzio held his ground and when the first punch landed, his legs buckled under him and when the second pounded into his stomach he doubled up, vomit filling his mouth.

"Now, get out."

But he didn't. Instead he slowly, painfully, got to his feet and turned back to the landlord.

"I want a drink."

The third blow landed in his kidneys, thrusting the air out of him, the red blood of pain flooding his vision. But he kept his footing and turned, throwing out a wild punch, the two men joining forces and pulling him towards the door and out into the street. On the Mersey he could hear the sound of a boat's horn knifing the night tide and as they struck him he saw, out of the corner of his eye, a dog lapping water from a puddle nearby. The evening air cut into him, snapped at his wounds, thickening the blood from his lip as a fist landed on his jaw and sent him sprawling backwards onto the cobbles. Rain fell. Liverpool rain. Dog rain, coming barking into the dirty night. But still Guido didn't stay down, and panting for breath, got to his knees and then straightened up.

They knocked him down again. And he got up again. And he *kept* getting up. His clothes were torn, his face swelled, the sounds around him merging, cat calls, shouts, the callous echo of someone clapping coming through his ears and into his burning brain. But he wouldn't lie down, *couldn't* lie down. He tasted blood and vomit and gasped for air, but still struggled upwards, rising and rocking on his feet. The night watched him; the crowd watched him; and as the beating continued, several onlookers, shamed, turned and walked away.

He took it all, and he never stayed down. He took it all and below the blood and the pain, he saw Seraphina coming out from under the trees and the water shaking in the glass by his bed … Agonisingly slowly, Guido rose on all fours and then staggered to his feet again, facing his attackers. The men watched him disbelievingly, surrounding him, waiting for him to admit defeat, to beg.

But he didn't. Instead, Guido Razzio, virtually naked, stood on the greasy street, the rain coming over him as he threw back his head.

"*You can't hurt me!*" he screamed, a woman in the crowd biting her lip and turning away. "You can't beat me, because I'm already dead!" he shouted. "I'M ALREADY DEAD!"

The men stopped. Watched him, studied the bloody figure rocking on its feet in front of them. Guido's voice was thick, muffled, coming between bloodied lips, but they could hear what he said, and turned away from the screaming man who wouldn't lie down; and wouldn't give up. He shamed them under the Liverpool night, and as his voice howled out again, the dog started in fright and ran away, the low moon shining malevolently on the window panes.

They turned away from him and walked into their homes. They left him under the white moon and closed their doors on him, drawing their curtains against the ungodly figure in the street outside. For minutes afterwards, Guido Razzio stood under the rain and howled with fury and hopelessness; his voice rising over the Mersey and cursing the black tide. It slid under the closed doors and damned the occupants and it carried over the water to the boats and beyond; it rode the night and howled its pain and agony to God and it reached over the sea towards Italy – to a land abandoned and a home left forever behind.

*

Slowly, Guido's thoughts returned to the present. He turned away from the kitchen, the light swinging away from the stain on the floor and leaving it to the darkness. Step by step he climbed the stairs and glanced into the two upstairs rooms, then pushed open the skylight and felt the black air fall in on him. The bells were still sounding, soon the night would be quiet. On the morrow he would go down to the ruined church site, and, at noon, an opponent would take on one of his fighters over from Manchester. The bets were laid already, the man confident. It would be the first day of the new year. A new century; the twentieth.

Quietly Guido walked down the stairs again and opened the front door, breathing hungrily at the damp air. He had fought for his place here, fought for his peck of power and earned it. He closed the door of No. 14 and locked it, putting out the lamp and walking down the dark street. The house would be his first possession. It had cost him more than anyone would ever realise, and it seemed right for him. No one else would want it, no one else would visit it. It would be his little sanctuary, his place of safety. For others, it would be a fearful place, but not for him. He had nothing to fear any longer. Fear had gone out, any ghosts who lived there, would live with him. Any uneasy spirits would find, in him, a comrade in arms.

Guido turned at the end of the street and looked back. The house was blank, without lights, without life. I will buy this place, this crypt, and will bury myself here … The thought comforted him, and when he walked on, he was oddly and unexpectedly, at peace.

# *Two*

At noon, on the first morning of the new century, the two fighters stood on the flattened patch of dirt, eyeing each other up. The day was chilled, misted with drizzle, Ted Hagen coughing in the damp wind. He spat out suddenly, the glob of spittle landing a few feet in front of the other fighter's boots.

Slowly, George Slater looked at the spit and then glanced over to Guido. "When?"

"When what?"

"When do we start?"

Guido looked at his watch. "In a minute. Just hold on a bit longer, George."

He nodded, dipped down his head, although his eyes remained fixed on Ted Hagen. "I can beat him."

"I know."

Hagen coughed again, staring at the worn laces of his gloves, his head broad, his hair matted.

Guido had tried repeatedly to get a hall, some gym where they could hold the fight, but there had been nowhere available, and besides, it was only a sparring match, a way of seeing what George Slater could really do. Guido had heard about the man from a landlord: had been told that he was a docker who supplemented his income by fighting. Some man from Glasgow had even been asking after him, after seeing a couple of his fights. Some agent, the landlord said, Guido had tracked George down to one of the boats coming into the docks. He had been unloading fruit, walking precariously on the edge of the upper deck, his weighty body perfectly balanced, his head turning to the sound of his name being called.

He had four children and a wife, he told Guido. He needed money, and he needed it fast. There was little more to say. Guido wasn't one for talking, and George was not gregarious by nature; just determined to prove himself – and boxing was the only way he could. He was no one's fool, didn't believe in the bright lights and the wild stories about the money fighters made. Food he wanted, and enough money to stop worrying. I want to see you fight, Guido had said. Fine, George replied. When?

New Year's Day was the date fixed. On the old church site. Some Liverpool people thought it was unlucky, but that was mostly the Irish and they thought anything to do with God was naturally fearsome. Men shouldn't fight on hallowed ground; it wasn't godly, they said. But the site had been derelict for decades, a fire burning down the church, kids and weather destroying most of what had been left. Now only one side of the church remained, a grim ridging of stone which threw a lengthy shadow when the sun came out.

Not that the sun was out that morning.

Ted Hagen coughed again, George fixing his eyes on his opponent and then taking the nod from Guido to begin. The bets were minimal as the fight had been arranged quietly; neither boxer well enough known to draw crowds. But there were a few people watching, men in cloth caps making a rough circle, a girl hanging behind her man, her eyes pink rimmed with cold. The punches thumped into the air, Guido keeping time, following some vague ruling as he acted as the referee, Ted Hagen's 'manager' chewing tobacco on the sidelines.

He was a hard referee, but fair. When he told either man what to do, they did it, and as they fought an urgency came into George's manner. He wanted to win, Guido realised. No, not just to win, to win emphatically, to earn his purse. His punches were well aimed, his opponent's avoided, his head tucked down, his chin drawn into his chest. Good, Guido thought, that's good … He glanced over to the small crowd. They can sense it, he thought, they can sense something in the man, and they are responding to it.

George was not as quick at Ted Hagen, but he was calmer. He didn't panic if he was hit, merely rode the punch and waited for another opening. Guido watched him, found himself compelled to watch him, saw in him what he had been looking for – a fighter with intelligence. George might be fighting for money, for his family, but there was more to it than that, even if he didn't realise it yet. He listened to his opponent, heard his rate of breathing, watched his expression, the quick flicker of anxiety in the eyes, the almost imperceptible hanging back. As a boxer he read the other man as easily as a scholar would read a book – and Ted Hagen knew it.

The crowd knew it too. There was a little frisson of excitement, a low murmur which accelerated steadily, George's name being called out in encouragement. Ted Hagen heard it and was rattled, his punches less measured, his confidence dipping as he became over-eager to win. But if George heard the voices he didn't show it, he just continued, watching and weighing up his man, moving onwards relentlessly, his calmness palpable. Guido had seen many fights over the past two years, but this time his attention was riveted, a slow building excitement turning in his gut. At last he had found the man had been looking for. The golden ticket, the born boxer. This was the man he had dreamed about, the man he could promote and push to the top.

Under the heavy rain, on the derelict church site, Guido Razzio watched George Slater fight, and when a strong right hook sent Ted Hagen falling backwards onto the dirt ground, he moved over quickly and patted George once on the shoulder.

"You did well."

He was out of breath, steaming in the cold air. "Yeah … yeah …"

Guido threw a jacket over George's shoulders and walking a few yards with him before stopping again. "You could be a great boxer –"

"I need money."

Guido reached into his pocket and pulled out some coins, holding them in front of George's sweating face.

"You want money? Here's money," he said, pushing the coins into George's pocket. "But there's more. More money – and more to fight for. A name, George. You could make your name."

He was still breathing heavily, wiping his nose with the back of his glove.

"And you?"

Guido smiled distantly. "I said *your* name, George. I have no desire to be known," he paused. "I can manage your career, look after your interests, and get you a good purse for your fights."

George looked over his shoulder at the small crowd of people – and at his beaten opponent.

"I like to fight."

"So do I," Guido replied. "But the difference is – you fight inside the ring and I fight outside it. We could make a good team." He put out his hand. "So do we have a deal?"

George Slater looked at Guido Razzio for a long moment, shivered in the cold, and then tapped the Italian's hand with his gloved fist.

The crowd dispersed quickly, the bets paid off by Guido, the watchers trailing off into the wet day. Only one person remained – a young woman standing by the ruined wall of the church. She was tall, sombrely dressed, her head covered with a wool shawl, her face white against the dark eyes. It seemed as though she wanted to say something, but she never stirred from her position and remained motionless by the stone wall. Guido had already noticed her, but looked away. When he glanced back an instant later she had gone.

# *Three*

Jessie Worthington was stretching, her arms raised above her head, when her daughter walked in. "Hello, love," she said simply, leaning across the table and picking up some material. "Have you come home for dinner?"

"The shop's closed for the day because it's new Year," Mary replied, taking off her shawl and watching her mother. "Did you finish the dress?"

"With time to spare," Jessie replied, pointing to the gown lying on some brown paper, ready to be wrapped. "That'll bring us some good money."

Mary nodded, sitting down in front of the fire, the heat of the blaze warming her calves as she raised the bottom of her hem. Her mother had been widowed for eight years, during which time their fortunes had plummeted. When Albert Worthington was alive they had lived in a better street, worn better clothes, and had never needed to work. He had been an industrious man: a man who had kept his worries to himself. Neither his wife nor his daughter knew that the money was running out, and when he died unexpectedly in the 'flu epidemic, neither of them realised that their life would change so suddenly and so drastically. To lose a loved husband and father was agonising, but the fall from status which followed nearly destroyed them.

They coped because Jessie was a survivor and because she had a daughter to look after. Having always been able to make her own clothes, she exploited her talent and after searching for work for weeks, was finally employed by a dressmaker in Davies Street. Her skill was recognised and appreciated, and although her wage was mediocre it allowed Jessie to pay for the rent of the house and for necessities. At first she hoped she might be able to put some money away, but as the years passed it became obvious that survival was the most they could ever hope for.

So when Mary was sixteen she also went out to work, finding a position as a seamstress in the same shop; mother and daughter employed together, although a year later Jessie began to work from home, pleading sickness. The shop owner suspected something, but he never pursued it. If Jessie Worthington wanted to work from home, who cared? She delivered on time, and she was the best worker he had, all his customers asked for her – so why should he bother where she worked? The truth was simple – Jessie worked from home because there she could work her own hours. At the shop she had been confined to certain limited times, in Bridge Street she could work from early morning until night. There was no one looking over her shoulder, no limitation to her industry.

Mary tried to reason with her mother, but Jessie would have none of it. She had seen eight years pass and nothing to show for it. No money in the bank, no future. She didn't want to stay in Bridge Street; didn't want to see her daughter hobbled by poverty. It was all carefully worked out. If she could increase her outlay she could save, and in another eight years they might even be out of Bridge Street, and nearer to where they truly belonged.

So she nagged Mary and drummed good manners into her, and she made sure that she spoke properly and not like the other shop girls, and she criticised her and harangued her and drilled morals and principles into her – and she made her dream.

"We won't be here forever, Mary," she'd say. "Before long we'll be out of here." She stared hard at her daughter, noticed the serious oval face, the direct gaze, the steady calmness in the girl's expression. "You'll meet someone and marry them and things will be good for you. I promise you," she said fiercely, "it'll all come. But you have to believe it and work for it."

"Mum, it doesn't matter –"

Jessie's white skin flushed. "Oh, it *matters*! I don't want this," she shouted, gesturing to the kitchen, "and neither should you. There's more to life. I had more once, and you will. You will, I promise you."

Mary's hand covered her mother's. She could see the unflattering shadows of tiredness under Jessie's eyes, had watched her mother straining to sew in poor light, had heard her struggling into bed, even sometimes found her in the mornings asleep in the chair. She was killing herself – but she wouldn't accept help.

"Let me do something for you –"

"No!" Jessie snapped, pulling the material out of her daughter's hands. "Go to bed, get some sleep. You have to look after yourself."

"Why? You don't."

Jessie's eyes fixed on her daughter. "I know what's best for you," she said coldly. "Now go to bed."

"You'll get ill –"

"So I should let you help me? So we can both get ill?" Jessie replied furiously. "I should ask you to sit up and work with me? You're young, you're pretty, you can get out of this life. You can find something better. I'm working for you, yes. But I'm working for myself as well." Her voice dropped, all anger gone. "I'm not being a martyr, Mary, don't think that. I just want us to leave here – and this is the only way I can see us doing it. Money is power. Money is power, love. Without it you're nothing." She rubbed her eyes slowly. "Every stitch I see as a step away from Bridge Street. Every hem is a mile away, every dress takes us down the street and over the river and to a house with a garden," she paused. "The houses are still there, Mary. They won't fall down or disappear – we just have to get back there, that's all."

Mary remembered the conversation as she watched her mother wrap the dress and label it, then straighten up and put the kettle on the range. The fire spluttered suddenly, the day clouding over, making shadows of the two women on the kitchen wall. Thoughtfully, Mary turned to the window and glanced out. The street was empty apart from a man walking towards the corner. She leaned towards the glass – but it wasn't who she expected, and disappointed, she turned round.

Her mother would be furious to know that she had watched the fight on the old church site, Mary thought. Not that she had set out to go there intentionally; she had merely been leaving the shop and hadn't wanted to go straight home. So she had taken the long route, walking down unfamiliar streets, and had almost lost herself when she came across the gathering of people. Curious to see what was going on, she had peered over their shoulders then, realising it was a boxing match, was about to turn away.

But instead she saw him. And stayed. Guido Razzio was looking at his watch, his head down, his hair darkened with rain, his eyes shadowed, his mouth compressed with concentration. He was unlike any man she had ever seen; some quality marked him out, some difference, and she found herself staring at him. And she *kept* staring, not seeing the fighters, or the other onlookers, only watching the man in the dark suit, holding his watch.

Her shyness made her back away. But she didn't leave, only waited by the ruined wall of the church, and watched, and found herself dreading, and yet longing, for him to look up and see her. But he was concentrating on the fight, his eyes fixed on the boxers, his hair damp against his head as the mist turned to drizzle again. At last the fight ended, and she thought for an instant that he might glance over to her; but he didn't. He merely looked up and turned away – and only then did she leave.

"… pass me that cotton, Mary."

She turned back to her mother and leaned across the table, passing the reel to her.

"… what were you thinking of?"

The girl hesitated, unwilling to lie, but uncertain of the reception the truth might get. "I was wondering about the man I'll marry."

Jessie threaded the needle in one easy movement. "Marry someone who doesn't need you, and someone who doesn't want anything from you."

She stared at her mother, disbelievingly. "What?"

"A man who wants nothing from a woman, will give her everything," she said calmly. "Chose someone who wants to give, not take – and only a strong man can do that."

Mary studied her mother for a long instant. "D'you think I'll find him?"

"D'you think we'll get out of Bridge Street?"

"Yes."

Jessie turned back to her work: "Then I think you'll find him. Fear less and hope more, Mary. Fear less and hope more."

# *Four*

The bar was noisy, filled with smoke, the landlord calling over to Guido as he entered. He heard him, nodded in acknowledgement, and then glanced over to where he was pointing. Tucked away in the back of the Snug a man sat drinking a pint, a small terrier sitting on the table in front of him. He was absorbed, talking to the dog, the animal rearing up on his hind legs and begging.

"You're a lovely wee lassie," the man said affectionately, his accent betraying his Glaswegian roots. "Here you are, pet, here you are …" he poured some of his beer into an empty ashtray and watched as the little dog drank.

Guido lowered himself into the seat opposite. "Your dog?" he asked.

"Aye, she's mine. And she's a beauty," the man replied, taking the terrier off the table and tucking her into his coat. "Pleased to meet you, Mr, Razzio," he said, extending his hand. "I'm Cubby Lloyd."

Guido shook his hand, looking at the corpulent little man in front of him. He was small and very stout, his legs barely brushing the floor, his head as smooth as a boxing glove, his mouth wide and virtually toothless. A manager of sorts, Guido had been told by the landlord, a Scot down on his luck …

"I heard you were making progress," Cubby said, "you're getting a name for yourself."

"I have a few fighters –"

"– George Slater, for one," Cubby said, turning his attention back to his dog, "There now, you just lie still, lassie. Lie still."

"What exactly do you want from me?"

Cubby's blue eyes fixed on Guido with amusement. "Oh, I don't want anything from you – I was going to give you something."

"Why?" he asked calmly.

Cubby laughed, then signalled the landlord for two more beers. "The smoke makes me cough in here," he said, stroking the dog's head. "I wonder if it's not bad for her too – but what can you do? A pub's a pub." He took his pint and allowed Guido to pay for both. "So you don't want a wee favour?"

Guido shook his head; "Not without knowing why it's being offered."

"I might be a fair Christian."

"And I might be the Pope," Guido countered.

Cubby laughed again, swinging his stumpy legs. "All right, I'll tell you what it's all about. I've got a fighter – Ron Poole – and I want you to look at him, that's all. I'm too old for this game, you're up and coming. Just have a look at him, and if you think he's okay, then we can come to a deal."

"What kind of deal?"

"Like an introduction fee," Cubby said smiling. "Just a bit of money to say thank you. That's all." He stopped, his eyes taking on a look of helplessness. "I've had a wee bit of bad luck lately, lost money – you know how it goes." He glanced down at the dog, coughed again, and then wiped his mouth with his handkerchief. "I want to get home, Mr. Razzio. That's the long and the short of it. Back up to Glasgow. I'm too old for all this. Can't take it anymore." His hand shook as he stroked the dog's coat. "I just need the fare back to Glasgow. No more than that – It's nae charity; I'm nae asking for money without offering something in return. I just want to go home, get back to my roots … I don't suppose you can understand that at your age, but when you get older, it matters."

Guido glanced down at his pint. Give me enough money to get home, the man had said, I want to go home … He felt suddenly lost, helpless, adrift. No amount of money would ever buy him the chance to go home. However rich he became, however important, he could never return … The realisation winded him, left him silent, Cubby's plaintive voice cutting through the noise from the bar.

"… Look man, it's not that much. And you would be getting a fighter in return. He's a canny boy, Ron Poole. He is, honest …"

Guido struggled to his feet, anxious to get away.

"Please …" Cubby begged, grabbing the sleeve of Guido's jacket and clinging on. "I'm nae asking for charity. You get the fighter and I get home. That's all I'm asking – to get home."

Without uttering a word, Guido looked down at the round moon of the man's face and then dug into his pocket and handed him a wad of money.

Astounded, Cubby took it and then frowned.

"It's more than I need, Mr. Razzio," he said, struggling to his feet, the little dog wriggling under his arm. "I just wanted –"

"Go home!" Guido said sharply, turning away and crossing the bar, the little man hurrying after him.

"Wait! Wait!" Cubby shouted, pushing past the drinkers and following Guido outside. "Wait for me!"

Guido heard him, but hurried on, only stopping when he realised that Cubby was running after him into the street.

"Wait for me, Mr. Razzio! WAIT FOR ME!"

He turned reluctantly, towering over the breathless little figure as Cubby reached his side.

"You … gave … me …" he was panting heavily. "… too … much … money …" he paused, fighting for breath before carrying on. "I canna take it, Mr. Razzio. You gave me too much."

Guido sighed. "I don't think so, Mr. Lloyd. You can get home now, and that's what you wanted." He glanced away, keeping his voice steady. "Tell Ron Poole he can reach me at the pub most nights."

"I will, I will," Cubby said eagerly, peering up at the Italian and frowning. "Are you all right?"

Guido hesitated, for once tempted to confide. But he couldn't put his feelings into words and instead he extended his hand and stroked the top of the little dog's head.

"What's it called?"

"Oh, I don't have a name for the wee thing," Cubby said, smiling. "I call her all sorts of things. Darling, petal – you know, silly names."

"She's a good dog," Guido said quietly.

"Aye, she is that." Cubby hesitated for an instant and then rushed on: "D'you want her?"

Frowning, Guido shook his head. "She's yours."

"But I canna take her home with me," Cubby said shortly, lifting the little animal out of his coat and holding out towards Guido. "You've given me what I need, so let me give you what you need. She's only a dog, but she's company. A tough little bugger too," he rushed on, "aye, and a good ratter." He jiggled the dog gently in his hands. "Go on, take her – she'll be a friend to you."

Guido stared at the dog, and then looked at Cubby. His mind jolted backwards to Seraphina and for an instant he closed to his eyes.

"Go on, Mr. Razzio, take her … she needs a home."

His eyes opened as he heard the words, and then, without saying anything, he took the dog out of Cubby's hands and walked away.

# *Five*

Ron Poole came into the 'Bell and Monkey' pub at around nine thirty that night, walking in quietly, his physique speaking for him. At six feet three inches in height, and weighing over sixteen stone, he found his way to the bar miraculously unhampered, his progress as effortless as Moses' parting of the Red Sea. His eyes remained fixed ahead, his shorn head bristling with a half inch growth of auburn stubble. A thick, and incongruous parting, low down on the left side of his head was the remnant of a knife fight, and as he reached the bar a stooped, shuffling figure moved over to his side.

"By Hell, that looks a mean bugger," someone said, eyeing Ron Poole through the glass pane which separated the pub from the SNUG bar. "I bet no one waters his bloody beer."

"It's Ron Poole," his companion said, watching the boxer avidly, "and that's Fitting Billy."

"Who the hell's 'Fitting Billy'?" The first man asked curiously.

"Ron Poole's brother. He used to be a fighter up until a few years ago, a good one too – I know because I saw him myself a couple of times in Salford – then he had a real mauling with some mad bastard from London. Poor Billy was mangled, had that many knocks to the head his brain's about as much good as a whistle with a feather in it," he tapped his forehead. "He's simple now and he has turns too – that's why he's called 'Fitting Billy'. You should see him when the fits take him. I saw it once, and I never forgot it. He started fighting like a bloody madman, his arms everywhere, and then his eyes rolled back in his head til only the whites showed – just like a couple of hard boiled eggs." The man peered through the glass again, hurriedly shifting his position to get a better look and the fallen idol. "Billy Poole used to be a real flashy one too, real good looking once. He wore snappy suits, silk shirts, leather gloves, the works. And the women, Christ, they were queuing up lift their skirts for him … Poor bugger," he went on, looking at the shaking man by the bar.

"… if he hadn't come in with his brother I'd never have known him now – not from how he used to be."

"So why does … shit!" his companion snapped, nearly tipping off his stool as he strained to see the strangers more clearly. "… why does Ron Poole drag him around with him?"

"They're brothers," the first man said, rattled by the question. Quickly he lowered his voice; "and don't say a word about 'Fitting Billy' in front of Ron Poole or you'll find your bloody eyes looking up at you from an ashtray."

Fully aware of the interest they had provoked, Ron Poole leaned heavily against the bar and drank his beer, 'Fitting Billy' standing next to him, his hands, in worn gloves, shaking, the beer slopping over the toes caps of his shoes. Ignoring his brother, Ron carried on drinking, his dull-skinned, freckled face turned away.

"Ron?"

He turned to his brother: "Aye?" he said simply, watching Billy's hands shake round the glass, a spittle of froth spattering his greasy suede gloves.

"Can I show you now? Is it time?"

"Nay, not now, Billy." Ron said patiently, his voice low, indulgent.

Billy nodded reluctantly, his hands clutching the glass, his gloved fingers sliding down the smooth sides. His head suddenly juddered to one side, his hair falling long over his eyes, his mouth slack.

"Are you sure?" he whined. "Are you sure it's not time?" he asked again, putting down the glass and grasping his brother's sleeve. "Is it time, isn't it? Isn't it?"

"Nay, it's later," Ron said patiently, "A bit longer yet, lad."

Billy sighed, his hand reaching out again for the glass; but this time he missed it and knocked it off the bar top instead. It fell onto the stone flagstones with an penetrating crash, conversation ceasing instantaneously. The landlord turned, looked at Billy and frowned – then stiffened when he saw Ron Poole watching him.

"Another beer for m' brother," the boxer said calmly, leaning over the bar, his piebald face only a foot from the landlord's, his voice dropping to a whisper. "Don't shame 'im 'bout the glass, right? I'll settle up with you later."

Billy was just beginning his next beer when Guido came in at the side door of the 'Bell and Monkey', the little dog following at his heels. Immediately his attention was caught by the landlord, who pointed out Ron Poole and his brother to him. Curious, Guido watched them for an instant before walking over, sizing up Ron Poole's Mancunian bulk before turning his attention to the spare, juddering figure beside him. His head resting limply on his left arm, Billy was slumped forwards over the bar, his open mouth only inches from his glass. He was not asleep, in fact his eyes moved constantly as he murmured quietly and incessantly under his breath

Fascinated by the ill-matched pair, Guido walked over to the two men, his attention focused on the giant figure of Ron Poole.

"Cubby Lloyd said you'd be coming to see me."

Ron turned at the sound of his voice.

"Is it time?" Billy mumbled softly behind them.

The big man sighed and smoothed his brother's hair away from his face: "Not yet, Billy. Not yet." His voice hardened as he turned back to Guido, "Cubby said you wanted a fighter."

"I want a good fighter, yes."

The boxer's expression flickered with surprise, his freckled skin colouring as he looked down at the Italian. He noticed the dark, steady expression in Guido's eyes and the solid confidence – and immediately regretted his belligerence.

"D'you want a drink?"

Guido nodded. "A beer, thanks." His eyes turned to Billy, watching the man's lips move unceasingly whilst his eyes remained fixed on his brother.

Ron responded immediately. "'e's Billy," he said simply, lifting his brother upright on the bar stool. "'e was a grand boxer once. A real champ. You'd have been taken with 'im then, Mr. Fazzo, you would that."

"Razzio," Guido corrected him.

"Razzio," Billy mumbled softly.

Guido glanced briefly at Billy, watching his gloved hands shake as Ron passed him a glass – then he noticed the shattered remains on the floor. More than one glass, certainly two, if not more. Above the shattered remnants, precariously perched on the bar stool, Billy nursed his beer. The liquid slid around the glass, lipped the rim, dribbled over the edge and made a humiliating dark patch on the front of his trousers.

"Careful, lad," Ron said gently, "they all go thinking you wet yourself." He turned back to Guido, leaning his weighty bulk against the bar again. "I can box good. I'm strong, and I don't give up easy."

"I have to try you out, see for myself," Guido replied calmly. "I'll match you against one of my fighters."

"George Slater?"

Guido nodded. "Maybe. Have you seen George fight?"

Ron Poole grimaced, his mottled skin creasing around his mouth, his tone arrogant; "I'm better than 'e is."

"I doubt it," Guido said coolly.

The boxer flinched: as startled by the remark as by an unseen blow; his skin flushed darkly under the blotchy freckles, his neck reddening around the collarless shirt.

"Listen, I'm the best –"

"That's for me to judge," Guido said, interrupting him curtly. "I make up my own mind, Mr. Poole. Nothing you say will convince me to accept you or reject you – only your fighting will do that."

The boxer watched him, his irritation obvious, "You a foreigner?"

Guido nodded, unperturbed. "Yes. I'm Italian."

"So what you doing 'ere then?" Ron persisted meanly.

"Making money, Mr. Poole," Guido replied calmly, his eyes fixing on the boxer. "Which is what you could do – if you'd learn to control your temper."

Ron winced, banging down his glass viciously on the bar top.

"Is it time?" Billy asked suddenly, cutting into the uneasy atmosphere between the two men. "Well, is it?"

Irritated, Ron turned to his brother: "Hush, now, Billy. Hush … We're talking," he said quickly, his eyes flicking from his brother back to Guido, his anger intimidating.

But it had no effect, Guido simply glanced away, studied 'Fitting Billy' for a long instant, and then looked back to Ron Poole.

"What's the matter with your brother?"

The question, coming from another man, would have been deadly, but Guido's tone of voice wrong footed Ron Poole. He realised instinctively that the Italian was genuinely interested in his brother; not curious, not sneering; but interested.

"Billy had a bad fight down in London," Ron said harshly. "Some bastard nearly did for 'im. We 'ad a East End manager then, some snot nosed kid who said 'e knew everyone; said 'e'd take right good care of Billy. 'e was a right liar. M' brother's bin fitting and silly since then."

"Is it time now?" Billy said fretfully, his eyes widening, his gaze moving frantically between the two men who flanked him, his gloved hands drumming on his narrow thighs. "*Is it time?*"

"Nay, not yet. Not yet …" Ron said, his voice catching, his eyes narrowing. "Billy were supposed to get a good purse for that fight; supposed to be matched with some lad his own age. But it were crooked, fixed. That man were much older and harder than Billy. 'e bloody near did for 'im," Ron said savagely, his eyes bleak with anger and betrayal. "'e made 'im like this. It weren't the fighter, I don't blame 'im, it were the manager, that bastard Tunny did this to our Billy." His voice dropped, soft, almost tender. "But I caught up with the bugger in Birmingham." He stopped, his eyes fixed on Guido's, holding the Italian gaze. "… 'e weren't so clever when I'd seen to 'im. Nay, Tunny weren't so clever then."

There was a long pause, Guido watching the Mancunian's face, feeling the heat of his rage as it sweated out of him. Their attention was so intense, so concentrated, that neither had noticed Billy slip off his gloves and move suddenly.

"NO!" Ron shouted, reaching out and catching hold of his brother's arm. But Billy had been too fast for him and had already driven his right fist into his mouth, biting hard into the thin white flesh. The blood came fast, pooling down his chin, his eyes rolling back as he bit down harder, the nearby drinkers backing away hurriedly.

"Come on, lad, stop it," Ron said hoarsely, tugging at his brother's wrist.

But the hand remained fixed in Billy's mouth, his teeth biting down into the skin. "Drop hand, drop hand!" Ron said fiercely, his voice punching into the silent air as everyone watched him. "DROP HAND! DROP HAND!"

Then suddenly his eyes rolled forward again, the pupils reappearing, Billy gagging violently on his fist as Ron pulled the hand out of his brother's mouth. He vomited automatically, a frothing of spittle and blood bursting from the dark slack gap of his mouth, the bile mottling the front of his worn checked suit.

"There, there … good boy, Billy," Ron said quietly, "Drop hand, drop hand." He glanced at Guido, "'e needs some air. I 'ave to get 'im out of 'ere."

Nodding, Guido walked over the door and stood back for the two men to pass. "I'll settle with you tomorrow," he called to the landlord. "Mark it up on the slate."

They walked down the street together, the three men and the little dog trotting at Guido's heels. Apparently having forgotten what had happened in the pub, Billy recovered within minutes, although he repeated the same question interminably in his child's voice:

"Is it time? Is it time? Is it time?"

Guido frowned: "What does he means, Ron? Time for what?"

The man shrugged. "Don't egg 'im on, Mr. Fazzo –"

"Razzio."

"Razzio … it's just a fancy of 'is, nothing else."

Guido paused, watching Billy intently: "It seems more than that. It seems worries him, Ron. Why?"

The huge man stopped walking and reached for his brother's hands, pulling Billy under the gas lamp, his palms turned upwards.

"Look, Mr. Razzio, get a *good* look," he said, turning Billy's hands over. The skin was covered with bite marks, the scars deep, some white, old scars from years earlier; some scabbed, fresh bitten scars; some still bleeding from the attack that night.

"Look at this too … You want an eyeful, we can give you that. Oh, aye, we can give you that, aright." Ron yanked up his brother's sleeves and turned his arms under the light. The skin was wired with bites, cross hatched with teeth marks. "'e bites 'is legs too," Ron said quietly, surprisingly so. "Once 'e hit a vein in his calve, ripped at it with 'is teeth. There were blood everywhere. Like a bleeding abattoir it were."

Silently Guido stared at Billy's arms and legs and then he suddenly reached out, pulling back Ron's sleeve, his eyes fixing on the single ribbing of teeth marks.

Ron shook him off angrily. "It were an accident."

"They're fresh, Ron," Guido said quietly. "They're recent."

"It were an accident," he insisted.

Guido held his ground. "What does your brother mean when he asks 'if it's time'? What does he mean, Ron? What?"

"I don't know," Ron said sharply, pulling down his sleeve and watching Billy run ahead down the narrow street towards the River Mersey at the end.

Guido persisted. "You know exactly what it means. Don't try and deceive me."

The boxer turned clumsily, oddly, lying with his body. "I don't know … honest I don't."

"You *do*," Guido insisted. "Listen, Ron, I can't take you on unless you're straight with me. I can't be looking over my shoulder, wondering about you. I have to know about my fighters. I have to know about their pasts, their families, their problems. I insist on knowing."

"You don't 'ave to worry about me, Mr. Razzio, and I can take care of Billy," Ron pleaded. "I know 'im. 'e wouldn't hurt anyone now."

Sighing with impatience, Guido glanced ahead. Billy was wearing his gloves again, clowning childishly in the darkening street, the little terrier running after him. He stopped suddenly under the gas lamp and called to his brother, pointing excitedly to the lights on a ship moored on the river at the end of the street. His voice skimmed like a pebble over the evening tide, his eyes shaded, hidden under the heavy fall of hair.

Guido turned back to Ron Poole: "I can't take you on unless you're straight with me. No secrets, I want to know everything."

"Billy's aright, they said 'e were aright," Ron blurted out helplessly, sitting down heavily on the kerbside, the hobnailed soles of his boots flat on the cobbles, his bristly scalp ugly under the lamplight. "Billy's okay now."

"Is it time'?" Guido said evenly, "What does it mean – is it time?"

"'e were in hospital for a long time, Mr. Razzio … " Ron began, reaching into his pocket and rolling a cigarette. He then spat loudly into the gutter, the gob of spittle landing in a puddle of old rain. "… they patched 'im up in the body, but 'e were gone in the 'ead. I knew that, knew 'e were odd. But 'e were quiet like, not violent, never 'ard to look after. A bit like your little dog, sort of tame an' friendly. Good company really … But trouble were that 'e got to thinking 'bout that man, our manager, Tunny. 'e kept thinking 'bout 'im and fretting and then Billy suddenly 'ad all kinds of nonsense going round in 'is 'ead. You know, like Tunny were a devil or something … Well, 'e were a bad bastard, and no mistake, but he weren't no devil. No more than any other man. 'e were just greedy, and cruel …"

Ron paused, the lighted end of his cigarette burned in the thickening night. At the end of the street Billy stood watching the boat, the terrier at his side, a couple passing by, giggling softly.

And Ron Poole talked on: "…'e had a right weird idea that Tunny had put thoughts in 'is 'ead, things to drive 'im crazy. It bloody near did too. Poor Billy, 'e went from bad to worse dead quick. 'e wet the bed and 'imself all the time, threw up, wouldn't eat, wouldn't do anything, just banged 'is 'ead 'gainst the wall day and night. Made marks, dented 'is skull, dented the bloody plaster. Knocking, knocking all night … We got thrown out by the landlady in Salford. She said 'e were 'disturbing her other tenants' – crazy old sow, *What other* tenants? No one else would live in that bug riddled shit hole …" Ron drew on his cigarette, then rubbed one hand over his face. "… It were my fault, I know that now. But I were so mad, so bleeding angry. I shouldn't 'ave gone on and on 'bout it. But the doctor said 'e were passed it, said Billy couldn't understand what anyone said. I talked 'bout that bloody Tunny over an' over again. Got like a bloody fixation with me. I should have known better, but I were so angry, looking at Billy an' thinking 'bout how 'e used to be …" Ron's eyes glanced down towards where his brother stood, now only a black shape against the boat's lights. "'e were 'andsome. Dead 'andsome. Like someone out of a book … Women loved 'im, chased 'im …'is posters were the biggest 'cos 'e were so good looking. 'Bonny Billy' they called 'im. 'Bonny Billy' … but not when 'e were banging 'is bloody head against the wall day and night. 'e weren't Bonny then. Nay, not then …"

"I searched for that bloody man Tunny, asked about him all over the place, til someone told me 'e'd gone to Birmingham. It took me a long while, but I found him …" Ron paused, spat out again, then dragged hard on his cigarette. "… I'd kept telling Billy that I'd find Tunny – 'In time,' I'd say, 'In time'. Well, it caught on with Billy; and soon he were asking – 'is it time? Is it? Is it time?' – they said 'e didn't understand, so I couldn't see the 'arm in it. They said 'e were past it, daft in the 'ead. So I kept talking 'bout Tunny, almost to myself. You know, the way you do."

"Only Jimmy understood every word. Them doctors were wrong. Bloody fools. 'e'd heard and understood everything and so when I went up to Birmingham to get this bastard he knew why we were going, and for what …'e were dead quiet that day. Still as you like, calm, and when I got 'im into this boarding house 'e just watched me go out without saying a word … But 'e followed me, Mister Razzio. 'e followed me to where I found Tunny and when I'd worked the bugger over I went back to the boarding house for Billy. Only 'e weren't there …"

"I don't know what tipped me off, a hunch maybe, but I went back to where I'd left Tunny … and Billy were there, sat on a wall outside, swinging 'is legs like a kid with nought on his mind …" he glanced at Guido quickly, furtively. "You've seen 'im bite. Well, 'e started that night … I went into the club and I found Tunny …" Ron stopped, tossed the cigarette stub into the puddle and rubbed his eyes. "…'e were bitten all over. ALL over, Mister Razzio." He looked up, held Guido's gaze and then glanced down again. "… I thought a dog 'ad got Tunny at first …'is clothes were ripped and 'is neck was torn open at the side, blood everywhere, pumping out of 'im like a stuck pig …'e made gurgling noises, and bubbles come up from 's mouth, and all the time 'is legs were jerking and 'is hands were drumming on the floor next to 'im …"

Ron stood up suddenly, blocking out the lamplight and turning the puddle into a dark and fathomless hole.

"I got us out of there quick as you like," he went on hurriedly. "I threw away Billy's clothes and washed 'im and I never asked 'im 'bout it – not ever – and 'e never mentioned it … They put what happened to Tunny down to dogs. At least that what I heard. No one would've believed the truth anyway, and who'd tell 'em? Who COULD tell 'em? Me? Nay, ever … If they'd found out, Billy would've been taken away," he sighed in, caught at a breath. "Billy's no harm to anyone, Mister Razzio. 'e just punished Tunny for what 'e did to 'im. An eye for an eye. That's fair, innit?" he turned, suddenly panicked. "Jesus, that fair, innit? Tunny turned Billy into that …" Ron pointed to his brother standing at the end of the street. "… Billy just paid 'im back for what 'e did, that were all. It were justice, that's all."

Guido's voice was expressionless. "He killed him."

"No."

Keeping his tone steady, Guido stared at the huge man in front of him; "Your brother's dangerous. Think about it, Ron. You look after him, but he's bitten you –"

"– only when he had a fit!" Ron snapped, towering over Guido as he stood on the raised kerbside. "'e only bites me when he fits, otherwise 'e's no trouble. You can trust 'im. Honest you can. I stake my life on it. Besides, I'll watch out for 'im. I always have and I always will."

"I *can't* trust him, and you know it," Guido said calmly but coldly. "You can't be with him every minute, Ron. There will be times when he's alone. How can you expect me to trust him?" he asked incredulously. "He's a murderer."

Ron dropped his voice: suddenly it was metal edged, sharp in the cooling night: "'e didn't kill Tunny."

"You told me he did."

Ron shook his head: "No, I told you how I found 'im, Mister Razzio."

A chill swept up from the Mersey, engulfed Guido, and sucked the breath out of his lungs. But he held his ground, his voice steady.

"What d'you mean?"

"Billy didn't kill Tunny," he said hoarsely, "I did." A light went out in the window behind them, a door banging closed and echoing in the silence. "… I stood there listening to that gurgling sound and the drumming of 'is fists on the floor and I knew 'e wouldn't live … Think about it, Mister Razzio. If I'd gone for help, Billy would've been shut up somewhere, prison, hospital, asylum – how could I do that to 'im? How?" he moved forwards, jumped down from the kerbside, landed softly on his feet, the sound surprisingly muted. "'e's m' brother, m' blood. I don't regret what I did. I'd do it again, no bother. I did it for Billy because 'e's had more trouble than any man should 'ave …" he glanced at his brother, tiny, brittle in the dark. "The strong protect the weak, Mister Razzio – I killed for m' own reasons, but they were the right reasons, and I'll face God 'imself with a clean conscience."

I killed for my own reasons … Guido stared straight ahead, seeing nothing of Liverpool any more. Instead he saw a woman walking towards him, a silent woman leaving a shadow under the noon sun … he swallowed suddenly, suppressing the memory and then turned, studying Ron Poole. He'd killed, and yet Guido knew there was nothing to fear from him. He knew it without thinking, without consideration, he simply knew it. But what of Billy?

Guido's gaze wandered ahead, searching, and then he whistled suddenly for his dog, the terrier running towards him, lighted intermittently by the gas lamps as she passed under them. She reached his side and he lifted her with relief, tucking her under his arm as he stared at Billy Poole, walking slowly towards him.

There is something about you, Guido thought, struggling with a feeling of pity and some other suppressed emotion. Fear? No, that was too definite; this was something finer, crueller perhaps. Billy was flawed, or was it that Billy would flaw those around him? Do I take him in for pity, or for perversity? Will he maim others, or will others maim him? Guido wondered … And onwards Billy Poole came; onwards, walking towards him and smiling benignly under the mustard colouring of the lamps. His skin looked greenish, a drowning man on dry land, thrown gagging from the sea …

Guido's skin prickled, his mouth parched. I have seen this look before, only then it was in a woman's face … He wanted to be gone then, to turn away from Billy Poole and from the memories of his mother. But he didn't; instead Guido faced the oncoming man and took him in. He held out his hand and took Billy's, feeling the knotting and creasing of scars on his skin as he looked into the shaded, idiot eyes.

But there was nothing there; no intelligence, no gratitude, no savagery. There was nothing – only his own reflection looking back.

# *Six*

"There she goes – the Flirter and Darter."

The girls on the workbench stretched their necks over towards the window on the second floor, above 'Elizabeth Dray's', the dressmaker's. Mary was one of the nearest, seeing quite clearly the skittering figure pause on the kerb on the opposite side of Davies Street. She was alert even whilst stationary, her head darting from side to side, her eyes, upward tilted, matching the curve of her mouth and the sudden and impressive escalation of her nose. In short, every feature of Miss Drew's face defied gravity. In her forty second year, her expressionless was sky-bound, her hair swept upwards, even the hem of her dress flirting and darting with some unseen energy. She seemed, as she stood on the kerb, to be agitated within a vortex of seething activity, her every expression and movement crackling with some weird, unexplained life force.

"Who is she?" Mary asked the girl next to her.

"I've told you – the Flirter and Darter," the girl sniggered evilly. "Really she's called Miss Drew," her voice puckered with derision, "the daughter of our employer. His only daughter, who's never been married –"

"– and doesn't look like she ever will be," someone else cut in.

Another voice, older than the others, added: "Oh, she'll marry all right. Old man Drew's going to leave her nest well feathered one day and that enough of a reason for her to find a husband. Besides," the woman added slyly, "no man sees the fireplace when he's poking the fire."

There was a chorus of laughter, Mary ignoring the other girls and leaning further towards the window. The Flirter and Darter was still hovering on the kerbside.

"Why does she have that nickname?"

"Because she spends all her time going from here to her uncle's shop across the street – that the tailor's, Michael Drew's." The woman bit off the end of her cotton and started to sew again. "She flirts with the men there, and then darts over here to tell us what's wrong with our work. If a man's flattered her, she'll be all right; if she's been ignored, God help us. You wait, Mary, give her another minute and she'll be up."

The Flirter and Darter was true to her reputation and arrived shortly afterwards, her dress crackling with energy as she swished through the narrow space between the workbenches. Everything she wore rustled; she talked quickly and her dress accompanied her like an unseen Greek chorus, her every syllable echoed by the rise and fall of a skirt or sleeve. The Flirter and Darter was, in all her upturned, gravity-defying appeal, a rowdy dresser.

"Oh, so you're the new girl," she said, bending loudly over Mary and peering at her embroidery. "Nice, very nice," she said, then frowned, pulling down her escalated face momentarily. "Oh, but this should be daintier," she said, lifting the fabric and peering at it, her tone as high pitched as her forehead. "A little more light handed, I think."

Mary bit her lip in irritation. Her work was good, precise, after all, she had been taught by her mother and Jessie Worthington never let anything sub-standard pass.

Stung, she was about to reply, but was warned off by a look from the supervisor, and fell instead into silence, grimly watching the Flirter and Darter as she moved round the room, interfering with everyone's work and making inane comments. She left ten minutes later, with a triumphant rustle on the stairs, Mary walking over to the window to watch her leave. The woman had irritated her intensely, and she realised, with a guilty jolt, that she was jealous. But what right had this idiotic creature to come and pass judgement over her work? To criticise, to pick at her skill? She didn't have to graft for her living, she spent her time aimlessly, an idle, ageing laughing stock, who would, no doubt, still find a husband for all her faults.

Mary sighed, her eyes fixed on the departing figure on the street below. Some misguided, unsuspecting widower would be collared, she thought grimly; or some impoverished long term bachelor, seduced not by the Flirter and Darter's uplifted features, but by the tempting promise of an uplift in his financial status. Mary watched the woman avidly from above. Tucked into a house outside the grime of Davies Street, she would never worry about money or status, never have to lay awake on Thursday night thinking of how to find the rent for Friday morning …

Mary leaned forward suddenly, her elbow nearing knocking off a pot of geraniums on the narrow window ledge. From out of the tailor's came a familiar figure, the man pausing by the shop window and adjusting the fob watch hanging from a chain on his waistcoat, his little dog waiting patiently by his feet.

"Come on," the supervisor said sharply. "There's work to be done."

"Please, just a minute –"

The woman's tone hardened. "Mary Worthington, if don't want this job, there's plenty who do. Now, get on with you work."

Reluctantly Mary moved away, but not before she had seen Guido Razzio glance towards the end of the street where the church bells peeled out the hour. He paused, listened to the chimes of eleven, then set his watch and tucked it back into his pocket.

The watch had pleased him. Heavy and solid in his hand, it had felt weighty, an object of real substance. At home in Italy Guido had been surrounded by expensive possessions, his father reminding him constantly that he would inherit every one. This will be yours, and this … he would say … I worked for this so that you could have it one day, and then leave it to the children who come after you … The collection of possessions, the passing of them hand to hand down the generations like memories. Feel this, take this, treasure this … his father had said, his pride sleek with feeding, ignorance making his dream seem feasible, easily within reach.

But Guido knew even then he would not inherit. From being young, very young, he had some premonition that all the things which surrounded him were on loan. I will never own them, he told himself, they will never be mine. Later he knew why, later the reason was obvious, as was his need to leave Italy; but he had known instinctively as a child that his home was poisoned, that the beauty was sour, that the furniture and paintings his father so admired, so enjoyed as decoration, were, to Guido, only so many threatening shapes casting shadows against bleached walls.

He weighed the watch in his hand as the church bells stopped peeling. The day was warm, the dirt in the street drying, puddles sucked up by the late morning sun. A boy ran past waving a paper, a bill flapping idly on a nearby tree. Curious, Guido walked over and read the lettering, then frowned. So Jack Dudley had come up from London, had he? Jack Dudley, an ex-heavyweight boxer who had had gone forty three rounds with an champion before knocking him out on a dirt patch of earth down by the World's End in London. The under dog made good. Jack Dudley, going deaf, with a paralysed right hand, always dressed like a fairground barker, his twin sons following him round the country like a pair of Guardian angels. Guido smiled, thinking of the boys. He had a theory, unproven but more than a little likely. Dudley was a clever man, and a great publicist, he knew that people turned out to his fights to see him and bask in his legend – just as they turned out to see his boys.

But were they boys? Guido wondered, staring at the fading bill poster with the two cherubic heads framing their bruiser of a father. Boys? No, more like girls, Guido thought, smiling suddenly. But which man, even a boxer, would take two girls around with him to the fights? Which man would take them to the spit and shit fights? the pubs? Which man would let them mix with the whores who flocked round the fighters after the match? No man – not even Jack Dudley. But he could take two boys, especially two ethereally lovely boys who would draw the crowds as much as the fighters did …

Oh yes, Guido thought, Jack Dudley was real competition. He had a few good boxers too; but then, so did he. In the eighteen months since Guido had come to Liverpool he had built up his string of fighters – George Slater, Ron Poole, Mick Leary and Bryn Davis – all good boxers, all hard men, and the 1901 Bill which recognised boxing as a legal sport in England had helped his progress. The fighters were grateful to have a good manager and all were easy to handle because they respected Guido. Only 'Fitting Billy' gave him any trouble, shadowing him, following him, watching him. Ron tried to keep him out from under Guido's feet, but Billy hung around him constantly, fascinated by something in the Italian's manner.

"I don't know how the shit you can stand him," Mick Leary said to Guido one night, "he's always just one bloody step behind you – like a bleeding ghost."

He *was* a ghost; like the ghost of Guido's past; and that was why he tolerated him. Fitting Billy reminded Guido of Italy and of the reason he had left; he reminded him of his mother; he was his ever present anxiety, the dark spirit on his shoulder, a reason to wonder, to fear. In the eighteen months since Guido had bought 14, Cranberry Street no one had visited the place. It was shunned, a soiled house with a dirty past. Yet he had moved in and felt at home there immediately. Why? Because he liked to test himself, to push himself, to see if fear increased or decreased. If you surround yourself with darkness, did coping with it become easier? he wondered. Or did you take on the darkness yourself, and then wonder why others shunned you also?

He bought sound furniture for the house and a rug to cover the mark on the kitchen floor. A woman called Mrs. Lyman came to clean and soon stripped the dirt and dead fat off the range and set the kettle humming. A domestic sound, built into many a child's memory – but not in Cranberry Street. There the kettle's whistle sighed round the dark and narrow house; it whimpered on the stairs and it crept under the door of the front bedroom where Jack Holland's daughter had died.

Night came dark there; dark and long. Guido slept in the back bedroom, and for a time listened for sounds from the room next to his. He wanted to be punished and to feel fear; he wanted to feel something. But there was nothing. No voice in the dark, no sounds in the worn hours, although the little dog skirted the bedroom uneasily and never once lay on the rug on the kitchen floor. The house took in the outsider; the front bedroom slept fitfully; and in the back, Guido turned over in his sleep and dreamed of Italy.

In the morning he woke to the sound of women calling and men banging doors, boots clattering early on the cobbles, the rain making inroads into the cold drizzle. The sky was heavy and it thickened throughout the day, curls of grey-yellow smoke coming from chimneys, the boats hooting eerily from the end of the street, the sound cheerless in the unseeing smog. Cold and unsettled Guido rose, washed and dressed himself, and began his day, the dog following him.

No one ever came to see him in the house in Cranberry Street – until Fitting Billy. He came. He came a knocking one night, wet, shivering, standing on the step with his hair dripping over his eyes.

"I were passing," he said, "I thought I'd come and see ya'."

Guido paused. He didn't want the man inside, didn't want him there at all. But then, suddenly, he stepped back and Fitting Billy skittered past him, almost running into the dim kitchen beyond. The kettle hummed morosely on the black range, a gas lamp giving little illumination, Fitting Billy throwing an uneasy shadow on the wall behind.

"Were it aright, me coming?"

"Fine," Guido said, gesturing for him to sit down.

Billy smiled. His teeth were yellowed, pitted, and when he sat on the wooden stool in front of the grate he tucked his gloved hands under his knees and leaned eagerly towards the red glow of the fire.

"Where's Ron?" Guido asked, making two mugs of tea and laying one down next to Billy.

"Sleepin'."

"Where?"

"At t' house," Billy said flatly. His fringe dripped water into his tea.

"He'll be worried about you," Guido said, leaning against the table and studying the man in front of him. "You should have told him you were going out."

Billy glanced up at him, his eyes dark in the dim light, his mouth slack.

"I'm not mad, ya know."

"No, Billy."

"Ron thinks I am, but I'm not," he hiccupped suddenly. The sound made him laugh, a thin, tin laugh. "'e thinks I'm daft."

"He cares about you," Guido said calmly.

Billy nodded. The tea slopped over his gloved hands and ran over his trouser legs; but he never moved, just kept nodding to himself. "...'e thinks I'm rite daft." His eyes strayed. "What's it called, that little 'un of yours?"

Guido glanced at the terrier sitting by the fire, watching Billy.

"Tita."

"Daft name."

Guido smiled. "It's Italian."

Billy nodded slowly. The gesture was lose, his head hanging forward idly.

"What's it like?"

"Where?"

"Italy," Billy said, suddenly leaning towards Tita. She sniffed his hand and allowed him to pet her.

"It's warm, Billy. Warm and sunny and it … it smells of flowers."

His attention wandered suddenly.

"We friends, aren't we?"

Guido nodded. "Yes, friends."

"Like before?"

"Before what, Billy?"

"Long time before …" he frowned, losing his train of thought. "You and me … I mean, I knows ya, don't I?" He laid his right hand on the table, the gloved fingers drumming. "… You and me … we know each other … that's rite, innit?"

"Yes, we know each other. Your brother's one of my boxers –"

"Nay!" Billy snapped, suddenly angry. Tita backed away into the corner, Guido stiffening. "It were *before* that. It WERE!"

His voice was loud; it bolted through the kitchen and made a threatening echo on the stairs.

"Drink your tea, Billy."

He paused and looked at Guido, his eyes focusing for an instant, his expression cunning. His fringe had stopped dripping rain water, now only a line of yellow mucus ran from his nose to his top lip.

"Drink your tea, Billy," Guido repeated.

But his fingers continued to drum on the table top, Tita growling softly under her breath.

"Billy!" Guido said sharply, "Drink your tea."

He stopped drumming at once, his eyes turning off, the crafty animation gone. Obediently he picked up the mug and began to drink, Guido startled by a sudden knock at the door.

Breathing heavily, Ron Poole stood on the step, clothed only in a collarless shirt and a pair of trousers, his feet bare.

"Mister Razzio, is our Billy 'ere?"

Guido nodded. "Yes, he's here. Drinking tea."

"BILLY!" Ron shouted loudly, then looked at Guido again. "I'm rite sorry, I fell asleep and when I woke, 'e'd up and gone." He called out again, "BILLY! Get out 'ere! Now!"

"Come in, Ron, you're soaked," Guido said, standing back. The rain was sheeting down, bouncing on the cobbles, wicked shafts of water flashing against the gas lamps. "Come in, you haven't even got your shoes on."

"I were worried," Ron said, stepping into the tiny square lobby. He filled the space, dripping water on the cold flagstones. "… you know, with our Billy wandering. I don't like 'im wandering. BILLY, git out 'ere!" Ron dropped his tone and leaned towards Guido. His body steamed. "Were 'e aright? I mean, were 'e bothersome?"

"He was fine," Guido said, turning as he heard footsteps behind him. Billy stood sheepishly at the kitchen door, his eyes moving from Guido to his brother and back again.

"I meant no 'arm. Honest I didn't."

Ron took his hand. "I know, lad, but you shouldn't come bothering people. 'Specially Mr Razzio."

"We 'ad a talk."

Ron nodded, pulling him towards the door. He squeezed past Guido, his body surprisingly tense.

"… we talked … d'int we?"

Guido nodded. "We talked."

"… and we'll talk again …" Billy said quietly, turning from his brother and looking hard into Guido's eyes.

He held the look and stood up to it, until Fitting Billy finally glanced away. But there was something in the look which drummed into Guido's consciousness and later, into his semi-consciousness. That night, as he slept, Fitting Billy came into his dreams, his fingers drumming incessantly on the table top, his eyes shifting backwards and forwards between cunning and stupidity.

"… we'll talk again …" he said. "… we'll talk again …"

Guido remembered the dream as he stood looking at Jack Dudley's poster and making a mental note of where his next fight was to be held. If the two of them got together they might be able to arrange another match, with a good purse, maybe hold the fight in some decent hall and make the whole thing a bit more respectable. They was money to be made, Guido knew, just like the money he had made over the last eighteen months, money invested wisely, No 18, Cranberry Street and No 5, Lemon Street being added to his growing list of properties. He rented them out at fair rates, and he kept them well maintained, although he had the intelligence to get one of the boxers to collect the weekly rents. No one argued with Bryn Davis – the Welshman as smiling and black haired as a devil – and no one bothered to offer excuses either. They just paid, on the day, to the last farthing. Bryn wasn't an unreasonable man, but he wouldn't take no for an answer, and even the Liverpool hard men wouldn't stand up to him. In sixteen fights he'd won all but three by knockouts, his reputation fearsome. Smiling and affable, dapper, and proud of his unmarked face, Bryn Davis swaggered down the cobbled streets, calling at the terraced houses for the rent.

"Good morning, Mrs. Ladsky, how are you on a lovely morning like this? You know what I've come for."

She was full of mock remorse, "Oh, Mr. Davis, my husband's gone for the money but he's not come back yet. I can't pay you today. Sorry."

Bryn smiled luminously and leaned against the door frame, humming under his breath and rolling a cigarette, his cheap straw hat tipped back on his oily hair.

"Well, you won't be minding my having a little smoke whilst I wait?"

Mrs. Ladsky's eyes widened. "Oh, but my husband might be gone all day."

Bryn breathed in the warming air, summer was coming over the Mersey, soon the water would be rank.

"Well, I've nothing else to do with a day like this. I'll wait," he said easily, kicking a child's football with the top of his boot.

Bryn stayed all day until dusk when Mr. Ladsky finally re-emerged. He had enjoyed himself immensely, had talked to all the wives and all the passing girls, had eaten all the meals and titbits they offered him, and had sung to all the kids, revelling in his role and behaving like a visiting potentate. The women loved him and spoiled him and wouldn't have minded if he's spent a whole day with them every week – but the men did. The rents after then were always paid on time; Bryn's charm had frightened the money out of them.

Guido smiled to himself and turned his steps towards the hotel where he knew Jack Dudley would be staying; the hotel he always stayed at when he was visiting Liverpool. Expensive, in the middle of the city – a central position where everyone could come and pay homage to the master up from the Smoke. Well dressed and composed, Guido walked in and asked for Jack Dudley at Reception, the uniformed manager smiling fleetingly.

"Mr. Dudley is in his suite."

"Tell him Mr. Razzio is here to see him."

He winced at the foreign name. "Razzio?"

Guido nodded. "Razzio. Mister."

Pointedly he looked at Tita. "We don't have dogs here, sir."

"She isn't a dog."

"She looks like a dog."

Guido's face was a blank. "And you," he said quietly, "look like a wise man … now tell Mr. Dudley I'm here, will you?"

A few minutes later Guido was shown into a suite overlooking St. George's Square, the sunshine making sleepy patterns on the fringed settee where Jack Dudley sat smoking a cigar, a red macaw chattering in a cage placed next to him. Seeing Guido he smiled and lurched to his feet with his left hand outstretched, his right arm hanging uselessly by his side;

"Razzio."

"Dudley."

He laughed, his voice loud, his failing hearing obvious.

"What the hell is that?" he said, pointing at Tita.

"My dog."

"Some dog – it looks like a rat."

Guido smiled. "Looks are nearly always deceptive."

"JESUS!" Jack said loudly, waving his good arm about. "Always riddles with you … So you heard I was in Liverpool?"

"The whole city heard," Guido said calmly, sitting down. "You've got a good fight laid on tonight. I wondered if we could fix something up ourselves later in the year? I got some good boxers now."

Jack paused, concentrating, running the words through his brain to check that he had heard them right; "Yeah, I heard. You're doing well – for a foreigner." He laughed, then was suddenly serious again, "When d'you want to hold the fight? And with who?"

"What about George Slater? In August?"

"August's too hot," Jack said loudly, the macaw screeching in its cage beside him. "I HATE the heat. I went away last year – over to your neck of the woods. Christ, it was hot there. Italy."

"Italy's a big country," Guido said evenly.

"I was in Florence."

"Florence is beautiful."

Jack laughed. "Okay, so be a cagey bastard, I'll not push it. You don't want to tell me where you came from, that's fine by me." He jammed some cut apple into the bars of the cage; the macaw eyed it suspiciously, the fruit making a dark, crescent-shaped shadow on the floor. "I like George Slater, Guido, really I do – but I also heard some good things about this Irishman you've got, Mick Leary."

"He's not ready."

"I heard different."

"I'm his manager, Jack," Guido said calmly, "and I say he's not ready."

"What about Ron Poole?"

"What's wrong with George Slater?"

Jack shrugged. "Nothing, nothing at all. I just heard you'd got Poole now," he leaned towards Guido, his paralysed right arm hanging heavily against his thigh. "How's 'Fitting Billy'? I heard some rumours he was mad. Barking."

"He's simple," Guido said coolly, "but he's not that crazy."

Jack lost interest quickly, sighed noiselessly and then leaned back and rapped on the wall four times. Almost instantaneously two boys appeared in the doorway of the adjacent room. Unnerved, Guido stared at the twins, perfectly matched, perfectly replicated copies of each other, moving in complete unison. They were wearing pale azure suits to show off their white blond hair and heavy lidded blue eyes, their feet small in matching spats. Slowly, languorously, the sat on either side of their father.

"These are my boys," Jack said, beaming and glancing from one to the other.

Boys? Never! Guido thought, staring avidly at the mesmerising heads. They're girls. They have to be.

"… they're the most handsome boys who ever lived, and they're mine," he boomed. "Who'd have believed that an ugly bastard like me could sire these?" He nudged the boy on his left, "Well, greet our visitor."

"Welcome. I'm pleased to meet you."

Jack watched Guido for his reaction, knowing full well that the voice would allay any suspicions in the Italian's mind. It was a full voice, deep – and seemingly male.

Expressionless, Guido inclined his head. "I'm pleased to meet you too," he replied, his eyes moving down to the creature's throat. But a high white cravat prevented him from seeing any Adam's apple and he glanced back at the impassive face. There was no hint of a beard either, he thought. Oh yes, the hair was short enough and the voice was male enough, but a girl could be taught to pitch her voice low …

"You're staring," Jack said, smiling widely. "My boys make everyone stare. My angels," he crooned, then moved suddenly, leaning forward towards Guido. "Okay, I agree on George Slater – but not in August, in September."

"And your challenger?"

"I'll come back to you about that. Maybe the lad fighting tonight – if he wins." Jack rose to his feet suddenly, taking Guido's hand again, "We'll talk."

"I want a proper fight, in a proper venue," Guido said firmly. "A classy fight."

Jack was eager to agree: "Sure, sure ––"

"I mean it," Guido pushed. "I want a good fight, one people will remember. I want my fighters names to be known."

"And yours?"

"No, not mine. My boxer's."

Jack frowned. "You like to keep to the background? Well, I admire that in a man. Myself, I like a front row seat, but …" he trailed off, walking with Guido to the door. "Don't tell me you don't want to get on – in your own way – even if it *is* on the quiet. You're ambitious. I understand that. We both are. After all, ambition and money make the world go round." He glanced over his shoulder at the silent twins, then squeezed Guido's shoulder. "Ambition and money – ain't that the long and the short of it?"

# *Seven*

And love. That too made the world go round. That made Davies Street and Bridge Street go round for eighteen months. They pivoted on the axis of one girl's hopes and danced on the edge of her expectations. Thoughtful, Mary leaned back against the pillows. She had seen Guido Razzio again that morning, going into Michael Drew's, the tailor's, and coming out in a new, light-weight summer suit. He seemed always to stop outside and set his watch to the chiming of the church clock – but he never looked up at the window on his left where Mary watched him.

She wondered how to make herself known to him. Coincidence wasn't feasible, Mary was too reserved to affect a collision on the street. Besides, what if he ignored her? How could she cope with the public humiliation of that? So instead of confronting him she set to finding out everything she could about the Italian – and people were eager to talk. He had a string of boxers, they told her; and property, dozens of terraced houses in Liverpool. He had money; he had a past; he had a secret; a wife? … No! Mary thought, I don't believe that. Not a wife. He has no woman, no children, this one is a loner. This one likes being alone. She understood that; she liked being alone too. Knew how to live in her head, just as he did. So maybe they weren't suited, Mary thought suddenly: maybe two loners needed to stay alone. No, she consoled herself, loners may want their own piece of the world – but those pieces might, at times, be shared.

She leaned forwards, pushing open the window by her bed and trying to fan in some hot June air. The smell of cooking onions came in rank and greasy, a dog barking in a nearby street. Next door, a baby cried and below her, in the dim light, Jessie Worthington stitched her way out of Bridge street and over to the tall houses with their cool summer gardens by the park. Hot in the airless room, Mary sat thinking of a man she had seen only a few times; she thought of him and when she dreamed she took him with her to the future she longed for, and when she awoke, she waited.

# *Eight*

"George, how's your wife?" Guido asked the fighter the next day.

He looked up, drying under his armpits with a piece of old towel.

"Grand."

"And your children?"

"Another on the way."

Guido nodded. "I want you to fight one of Jack Dudley's men in September," he said calmly. "It will be a fair fight, and a good purse. You certainly need the money."

George looked down, unable to articulate his thanks.

"Aye, and I'll give him a run for it."

"Yes," Guido said simply, "I know you will."

He was pre-occupied when he walked out, passing Fitting Billy and Ron Poole, and stopping for a word with Bryn Davis. Only the previous week Guido had bought an old church hall and turned it into a gym for his fighters. True to form, in Liverpool there had been an outcry, people complaining about God's house being used for the devil's work. What the hell was everything coming to? they asked. A church used as a fighting pit! And run by a bloody foreigner as well! ... The antagonism was so intense that they banded together and sent a priest to see Guido one steaming August night.

"I'm Father Raymond ..."

Guido turned; didn't take in the face, only the clerical garb and the church smell, sunk deep in the priest's skin, like a colouring. My mother's priest smelled this way, he remembered blackly; smelled of the odour of ignorance and ritual.

"... I came to have a word with you."

"Why?"

The priest was wrong-footed.

"People are worried –"

"Have their women been bothered, or their children hurt?" Guido asked coldly. "Have their houses been destroyed or the food taken from them?"

"Mr. Razzo –"

"Razzio! RAZZIO!" Guido snapped, his voice for once raised.

Alerted, Ron Poole emerged at the entrance to his employer's office.

"D'you need 'elp?"

Guido sighed, then shook his head; "No ... no ... thank you, Ron."

He moved away from the door, Guido turning to the priest again.

"Get out."

"But I –"

"Get out," he repeated quietly. "I've no quarrel with you, and you should have no quarrel with me. I run a business, a good business which gives my fighters a living. I run a clean business, and the houses I own I rent out at fair rates – which is more than the church ever does. Before you criticise me, look at your own record. What are you doing for the homeless, father?" his eyes were colourless with anger. "When did you last throw open your church and take the poor in? What about 'Fitting Billy'? You've no time for him, or for others like him, have you? You've no time for any of us – until someone wants to use one of your churches for something other than a Mass. I made it into a gym. A gym!" He was bitter with contempt. "I set up a godless business in God's house. Well, who said that fighters weren't God's children too?" he walked towards the priest, his tone threatening. "I know you; I know each of you men – you priests. I know what goes on under the black coverings; I know how you hide and pray your way out of life. I know you."

The cleric was panicked, thin-voiced with fear, "Now, listen –"

"No," Guido said coldly, edging the priest to the door. "Take yourself – and your smell – out of here."

"I am here on God's business –"

"God has no business with the likes of you!" Guido shouted. "You have nothing to do with God. You mock Him by your stupidity and your cowardice, and you lie to Him – just as you lie to the people who turn to you. I know you, I once relied on your kind for help – and you turned your backs on me." He stopped, unwilling to give himself away. "Get out. Now."

"But –"

"Get out. Now."

The priest left.

Unsettled, Guido immediately snatched up his coat and walked out, passing Ron Poole and George Slater without saying a word. Angrily he walked down the hot streets, loosening his collar and fanning himself with his hat. The heat was unusual, out of place in Liverpool; this was Italian heat, heat which should come singing over the sea and lingering in gardens; heat which should glow on skin and ripen peaches; heat of the kind measured out in months over an Italian summer.

His head ached suddenly, his tongue thick and dry in his mouth. What had Jack Dudley said – ambition and money were the only things which mattered? Was it true? Was it? … Guido flicked a bluebottle away with his hand as he passed a wet fish shop, a sudden wedge of flies swarming over a slab of cod. The fish's eyes were open, exposed, but shiny still, a passer by casting a fleeting shadow over the blank pupil. Money and ambition – no, there had to be more, Guido thought, it wasn't enough otherwise.

Unusually sombre, he hurried down the street, keeping to the walls, trying to find some sweet slip of coolness. But there was none; the heat swamped the city, drew smells from the gutters, and bloated the rubbish on the Mersey tide. Children cried out irritably, a small boy relieving himself against the side wall of a bread shop as a dog snapped half heartedly at the shadow of a passing bird. The city swum dizzily under eighty six degrees, it smelt and rotted under the sun, the alleyways steaming, the step of the butcher's sticky with drying blood.

And the smells grew, sprawled, spreading everywhere. Human smells, animal smells, river smells, come rotting and rising on the tide. Guido staggered on, for once unsteady on his feet, his heed aching, his eyes unfocused. If I can just get back to Cranberry Street, he thought; it's cool there, and quiet. Always quiet in Cranberry Street … Dodging the hurrying footsteps and the occasional misaimed kick, Tita scuttled behind her master, panting from the heat and the reckless hurry. She swerved with him through the crowd and as they rounded Lemon Street she caught up with him, keeping close to his side.

He was almost home, almost at Cranberry Street, almost away from the heat and smells and the thought of the priest. Madly, Guido drove himself on, his eyes blurring, his heart banging unnaturally in his chest, Tita barking in panic by his side as she weaved her way next to him. Only a little way to go, Guido willed himself, only a little way … But it was too far, he knew suddenly, as his legs buckled, his body dropping heavily onto the paving stones, Tita barking beside him.

The sun swallowed him; took him up, cradled him, steaming and burning, and turned him home to Italy … His mind wandered, slipped from reality, and the only thing he knew for certain before passing out was that someone was kneeling next to him, and that a girl's white hand lingered on his forehead and bought down the healing night.

# Nine

"Ssh …" Mary said, rising to her feet and walking over the bed.

The curtains were drawn, sunlight coming filtered into the cool bedroom at Cranberry Street. She turned to Mrs. Lyman and smiled.

"Can I have some more water?"

The older woman nodded brusquely and walked out, Mary turning back to Guido. His forehead was skimmed with sweat, his hair damp to his head.

"The doctor said you'd be all right. You had a fever," she paused; he was watching her avidly.

"How long have you been here?"

"On an off for three days," she replied, suddenly diffident.

After Guido had collapsed, Mary had helped him home, knowing where he lived, Mrs. Lyman answering the door at Cranberry Street and both of them taking him upstairs. Mary hadn't looked whilst the older woman undressed him, she had merely drawn the curtains and then, when Guido was laid out in bed, she had wiped his face with a cool flannel. He had moaned, slipped back into sleep. And she had stayed. And she had lied to her employer and her mother. Guido needed nursing, and he needed constant care – so, without considering the consequences, Mary stayed off work and told everyone she was ill. During the day she stayed at Cranberry Street and only returned home at night. For two days she got away with it, until someone from the dressmaker's bumped into Jessie in the street and asked how her daughter was.

That night Mary returned from Cranberry Street to find Jessie, white faced, waiting for her. The flat was unwelcoming, no meal on the table, the sewing machine silent.

"Where have you been?"

She had the grace not to lie. "I stayed off work –"

"I KNOW THAT!" Jessie snapped, "I want to know where you've been instead."

"I've been looking after someone."

Jessie blinked. "Who?"

"Someone who's ill –"

"WHO!"

"Guido Razzio."

Jessie sat down heavily, one hand going to her throat. "Guido Razzio," she repeated disbelievingly. "Are you mad?"

"Mum, listen –"

"No!" Jessie hissed, turning away. "Nothing you could say could excuse your behaviour. I trusted you, your employer trusted you, and you lied to both of us," she turned back to her daughter and rose to her feet. "I can only imagine that you've lost your senses. The man is a foreigner, a boxing promoter." Jessie paused, her voice was white hot with fury. "What possessed you, you stupid girl? Whatever possessed you?"

Mary glanced down at her hands. "I did nothing wrong. Honestly, I didn't do anything I shouldn't have –"

"It doesn't matter what you did – it's what you *appear* to have done!" Jessie snapped. "Nice girls, respectable girls, don't go off nursing men who aren't they're relatives or their husbands. Dear God, what were you thinking of? The whole town's talking about it," her eyes narrowed. "Just what is this man to you?"

Mary hesitated. "A friend."

"'A friend!'" Jessie repeated violently. "A nice girl doesn't make friends with the likes of him!"

"He's a good man!" Mary snapped, then paused, both of them stunned by the fury of her reaction.

Jessie looked at her daughter for a long moment, realisation unfolding.

"Are you in love with him?"

Dumbly, Mary nodded.

"Have you …" Jessie paused, "… have you been to bed with him?"

"NO!" Mary retorted hotly, her face crimson.

"Well that's one thing – although I imagine that most people will think you have."

"I was looking after him, that's was all," Mary said, her voice dipping, tears close to the surface. "Nothing else."

Jessie regarded her daughter thoughtfully. Shy Mary – who would have believed it? She studied the fine head, the pretty face. You could have had anyone, even without money you could have married well, and yet you had to got and do this, ruin your chances; become the focus of gossip. No decent woman even passed the time of day with the boxers, or their manager. And as for Guido Razzio – the stories were legion. Stories about his arrival in Liverpool. Jessie frowned, some said he had had to leave Italy – why? Why did a man have to leave his home? Because he was a criminal or worse … Jessie shook her head incredulously. There was only one solution, they would have to move away, go somewhere where no one had heard about this episode, where Mary could find herself a husband. Jessie stared at the silent girl in front of her – her behaviour had been so unexpected, so out of character, so unlike her. Whatever had possessed her? What power had this man over her to make her act this way? She had always been a loving child, obedient, gentle – never headstrong, never duplicitous.

"We'll leave Liverpool."

"No," Mary said simply, "I won't leave. I won't leave him."

Jessie was taken back, "You'll do as I say!"

"No," Mary repeated. "I have to go to him," she turned, moving to the door.

"Come back!" Jessie snapped, moving towards her.

But Mary had already left and was hurrying down the street, her shawl over her head. She passed several women talking and felt them watching her, her face colouring. But she didn't turn back and when she reached Cranberry Street, let herself in with the spare key.

She took the stairs hurriedly, walking in and looking down at the figure in the bed. Oblivious, Guido slept on, his eyes closed. Oh God, Mary thought, sitting down, what am I doing? What am I doing? This man has never said he loved me, but I've risked everything for him. She thought of Jessie and put her hand over her mouth, fighting tears and remembering how they had banded together after her father died, and all the unending, unyielding work Jessie had undertaken to sew them into a better life.

I've disappointed her, Mary thought brokenly. I've let her down … beside her, Guido stirred and then opened his eyes, fixing his gaze on the young woman sitting by his bed.

"Mary?"

She smiled, touched his forehead. "The doctor's pleased with you," she said quietly, "he said that your illness was mostly due to tiredness and over work."

He nodded, but there was more to it than that. He had a soul sickness, a soul weariness, his heart beating for too long without rhythm to his mind. Ambition and money, he thought endlessly – ambition and money – Was there to be nothing else. Was his whole life to be encapsulated within three words – Ambition and Money. And what was the purpose of it anyway? What amount of ambition would lead to a loss of memory? What amount of money would buy his way home? Nothing he ever did, nothing he ever earned, could change reality or secure his return.

All that was offered in his new world was the pinnacle of the materialist's dream – ambition and money. It wasn't enough to live for, Guido had thought wretchedly the previous night. It wasn't enough to leave his bed for, and the realisation of that fact left him winded on a narrow cot in the back bedroom. There is nothing to fight for, he thought blackly, nothing of value left. Except her. He had opened his eyes in the dark, thinking of Mary, and slowly, as the fever left him he realised how much time she had spent with him – and what that meant. Oh God, he had thought then, it can't be, it isn't possible. It has to stop … but when he slept he dreamed of images. Lemon cool, lemon clean, lemon clear like the ribbon she wore to tie back her dark hair. Lemon, like the colour of mimosa. She had walked into the heat of that Liverpool summer and cooled him, tracking Guido's dreams like a calm angel … And yet he knew that there was a strength in her, a quality he needed and lacked – a stability – and in that stability she offered reason for his ambition; a purpose for his money making … and yet, and yet, it couldn't, mustn't happen. He couldn't fall in love … he closed his eyes … he couldn't fall in love? He was in love.

"What are you thinking of?" Mary asked gently.

He stirred, a shadow falling across his face as a bird passed the window.

"Mary … thank you for all you've done."

She smiled slowly. "I wanted to help you."

"I should be up and about tomorrow," Guido said tentatively. "I'm feeling a lot better …" He had to back off, for her sake as much as his own. But she was looking at him so tenderly, and her eyes were so dark-shaded, that he faltered, as terrified of losing her as he was of keeping her.

"Mary … Mary …"

"Ssh …" she said simply. "Go back to sleep."

He slept for an hour, Mary sitting by his bed, listening for the knock on the door, waiting for Jessie to arrive. Dear God, she thought, what if I'm wrong, what if this man doesn't love me? Tentatively she glanced over to him, pulling her shawl around her shoulders. I love you, she thought, rightly or wrongly, I love you … The hour unwound and then another followed, darkness coming in. Go home, she told herself, you have to go home.

But she couldn't, and when he finally woke the room was in semi-darkness. He woke immediately, alertly, turning to look at her – and she looked back at him. They said nothing, but in that instant both of them felt a love which was almost tangible – a love coupled with despair.

A knock on the door broke the spell, Mary hurrying downstairs to find Jessie standing on the step.

"Come home," she said coldly, walking in and closing the door behind her. "Dear God, girl, come home. It's not too late."

Mary shook her head. "I can't," her hand extended towards her mother's. "Please, understand –"

Jessie shook her off, wrenching open the door and walking out into the street, Mary following.

"I love him," she said quietly.

"You're such a fool!" Jessie snapped, keeping her voice low. "Dear God, I don't know why I'm whispering, everyone knows what's going on. After all, you've having been keeping it a secret."

Mary caught hold of her mother's arm. "I've done nothing wrong –"

"Then come home!" Jessie pleaded. "We'll make a new start –"

"I don't want a new start. I want him."

Jessie's face was chalky. "Then go to him!" she shouted. "I've worked for you, done my best for you, and now you let me down. You've made yourself look like a cheap tart, running after a common man that no one would cross the street to talk to," she was hoarse with distress. "D'you want to be some whore running around with fighters? A woman no one decent would respect? – and if – IF – he married you, what would your children turn out to be, Mary? Outcasts, that's what they'd be. With a foreigner for a father – and worse, a man in one of the most despised trades in the world."

"He's a good man."

"How do you know!" Jessie snapped. "WHAT do you know about him? About his past? About his life?" She grabbed her daughter's arm. "Why did he have to leave Italy, Mary? *Why?* Oh God, think girl. You're innocent, naive, you've not been brought up to know about people like him. You've been protected from life, shielded –"

"Perhaps I shouldn't be any more," Mary said quietly.

"Don't kid yourself! You're not tough enough to take on someone like him." Jessie replied, her voice deadly. "You're too gentle, too kind. The world eats up women like you." She glanced over to the doorway of 14, Cranberry Street, "He'll eat you up too. He'll use you and leave you," her voice softened. "Come back now. Come home with me, it's not too late. Please, Mary, don't do something which will ruin your life."

"I can't," she said softly, "I love you … but I can't do what you say."

In the dim street Jessie faced her daughter: "Come with me now – or never come home again."

Mary looked at her mother helplessly, her breathing shallow. If she chose to leave, she could never return; she would have cast herself off forever. Did he love her? she wondered desperately. Did she dare to test him now? The chose she made would set the pattern for the rest of her life. Could she reject the security of her mother's set of values for the unknown?

"I love him …" she said at last. "I'm sorry …"

Jessie took in her breath, then, after another moment, she walked away.

Guido was standing at the top of the stairs when Mary walked back in.

"Who was that?"

"My mother," Mary said quietly.

"Were you arguing about me?" he asked, walking downstairs and facing her. He was white with the exertion, hollow eyed, troubled.

"She wanted me to come home," Mary said simply, bowing her head. "I've been very stupid."

He stared at her face, struggling to know what to say to her. "I never thought … I never realised what it meant, your coming here. I never realised how people would talk." He frowned, trying to marshal his thoughts, "I was selfish, I'm sorry. I should have known."

She touched his hand, then turned, her forehead leaning against the door.

"I can't go home."

"What?"

Her voice dropped, her embarrassment and anguish overwhelming; "I won't stay here," she hurried on. "I never meant to do this … to force you … to …"

"Mary," he said gently, "I can't – *we* can't – let this go on."

She took in her breath.

"… there are reasons. Good reasons, why I can't. It's not that I don't care for you," he touched her shoulder. "I do … I love you, Mary."

She sighed, tears rolling down her face.

"… but I can't marry you – or anyone."

Her head rested heavily against the door, her eyes closing.

"… If I could marry, it would be you," he went on. "I would chose you, no one else. But I can't marry."

Her voice was hardly audible; "Why not?"

"There are reasons –"

"What reasons?" she persisted gently.

"My past."

She nodded, still turned away. "Are you married already?"

He turned her round to face him. "No."

"Then why not?"

"I can't explain," he said quietly, drawing her to him, her head resting against his shoulder. "If I married you, I might put you at risk. Any children we would have would be at risk. I can't have children, Mary. I have to stay alone …"

She wept against his shoulder.

"… it would be a risk no man could take. I can't endanger you. It could tempt fate."

"Only 'could?'" she asked, "If there's a chance it might not, we could risk it. I would, for you."

He shook his head. "But I wouldn't risk you," he replied. "It wouldn't be fair, or honourable."

"I don't care about fairness!" she said defiantly. "I care about you. I'd risk anything, go anywhere, take on anyone – man or God – for you."

He drew back, looking into her face. "Oh Mary, you don't know what may happen

–"

"I know I won't live without you," she replied. "I would rather risk anything than lose you."

He stared into her face, into the dark eyes: "Courage comes in two forms, Mary – the courage to fight, and the courage to walk away … If you stay with me, you might be punished for it."

The words hung over them, pressed down on them, bearing the full weight of a threat.

"Do you love me?" Mary asked finally.

He nodded. "Yes."

"How do you love me?"

His eyes fixed on hers. "How do I love you? How do I breath? I love you for what you are, and for what you could be, and for what you will become. I loved you the first moment I saw you and the last moment I will see you – and all the moments in between. I love you utterly, totally, completely, and I know that if I lost you I would walk into hell alone."

"Then tell me, Guido," Mary said softly, her eyes filled with tears. "Do you trust me?"

He nodded. "With my life."

Tenderly she touched his cheek: "Then trust me when I say that nothing will ever hurt you again. I won't let anything, or anyone, harm you. I will always be there for you – until the end."

Cranberry Street seemed not to unsettle her; she disturbed no ghosts, neither did she see or hear anything to startle her or keep her away. Poised within her own world, she walked away from other people's existences and seemed complete. But not quite, he realised, not quite … Her nursing was simple, without much talk; food plain and nourishing, nothing more. She read to him in the evenings, bringing her own, well used books and settling herself by the window where the light was good. He remembered nothing of the novels, only her voice, even, the quality of it steady, her head tipped downwards as she read. She was tall, he reasoned, and measuring out the length of her back and arms, calculated that she had to be over five feet eight. Yes, he decided, height would suit her, would carry that strong dark head properly. She had to be tall.

She told him her name was Worthington, Mary Worthington, pronouncing her surname in syllables WORTH-ING-TON, and then she smiled, as though she had given him something. He told her his name then, but she didn't repeat it, indeed she seemed familiar with it, almost as though she had run the foreign syllables over her tongue before. Guido Razzio … she said, smiling that dark deep smile … it's fine name, now rest …

He did, and as he slept he took her with him and together they went back to Italy, and then strangely, slowly, easily, Guido found he no longer dreamed only of his home country, now he walked with her in Liverpool. In his adopted country he paced the city streets, and in his sub-conscious he rehearsed his speeches and lost his reticence, becoming adept and easy with her. His instinct, which had warned him and helped him so many times before, came like a companion between them and it prompted him. It walked like a well-loved friend with them in his dreams, and before many days were over Guido knew that this girl, this dark and solitary girl, was the woman who offered him completion. A wholeness, and a place in the heart.

Jessie was not pleased by the turn events had taken;

"Are you mad!" she hissed, flinging down a half worked dress and turning on Mary. "Is *this* what I'm working for?"

"He's doing well –"

"Guido Razzio is a boxer."

"No, mother," Mary said firmly, "he runs a string of boxers, he's a manager – and he has property."

Jessie picked irritably at the tacking stitches round the dress she was working on, her mouth ridged with frustration. "What kind of work is *that*? Boxing? Running them or boxing them, it's all the same. He'll never be respectable, *never*."

Mary was cool, resigned. She had watched Guido Razzio for a long time and had waited. Now she was with him, and no one, not even her mother, was going to make her give him up.

"He's a fine man, a good man. If you met him –"

"I don't want to meet him!" Jessie said fiercely, "and I don't want to see you throw your life away on a foreigner."

"Mother, he's going to do well; he is ALREADY doing well. Believe me," Mary said calmly, "I know he'll go far."

"He'll do well, will he?" she countered bleakly. "In what way, Mary? How will be earn money? Mixing with the likes of Jack Dudley and Cubby Lloyd? How *can* a man do well like that?" she sighed, laid down the dress again; her skin was shiny in the heat and her breathing was laboured. "I know of these people, I know the type they are. Believe me, you were born for something better than this. You could have a nice young man, someone respectable."

"I know," her daughter said simply, glancing away, "but I want him. I'm supposed to have him. He's the man I was supposed to meet and the man I was supposed to marry."

Her calmness astounded Jessie and, defeated, she rose to her feet and walked over to her daughter.

"I told you once to hope more and fear less," she said softly, "now I tell you that again, because it's important and I want you to remember it. If you marry this man you'll have to take on all his troubles, and fight all his battles with him. He's a foreigner and an outsider; he has a past you know nothing about; he's had a life you know nothing about." Her voice lifted, her eyes seeing past the rooftops to the park beyond, "Little problems can ruin a marriage, Mary, but great ones can make it."

Her daughter looked up, her eyes fixed steadily on her mother.

"You mean –"

"I mean only this – hope more and fear less. Be strong, because if you marry this man, you'll have to learn to be stronger than you ever thought possible. You will have to be everything to him, his mother, his family, his wife, his inspiration. I don't doubt Guido Razzio can go far, I just want to be sure that his destination is the same as yours."

# Ten

At first, Mary found the life tough and was frequently ill at ease, even, at times, afraid. They married only months after meeting, Jessie reproachful, Guido stern, his fighters dressed up in their best clothes and sitting at the back of the church, Fitting Billy rocking himself back and forwards in his pew and joining loudly in the Amens. Jessie refused to look round and kept her eyes fixed on her daughter, Mary tall and white skinned in a ivory dress made from silk scraps culled from the dressmakers. Her hair, dark as a liquorice, was gathered at the nape of her neck, her eyes disturbingly still, fixed on the altar in front of her, and then later on the wedding band on her left hand. She didn't smile or cry, she merely lifted her veil and, fully exposed, turned round to face the men who would share her life from now on.

She had not realised what that life would mean. The smell in the gym was unfamiliar to a woman, a toxic mixture of sweat and heat, the windows running with condensation in winter, and thrown open wide in summer, the men steaming from their workouts, the bald trainer, Morrie Gilling, cursing and spitting as he chivvied the fighters. Yet gradually, as she travelled round with Guido, her confidence increased and little by little Mary found the courage to move away from his side and make her own way. The boxers were uncomfortable around her at first; if they were married, their own women were at home, and the boss's wife added an unwelcome restriction on their behaviour and their language. But Mary's appearance was her greatest advantage; she looked and sounded assured, she dressed stylishly, but darkly, and the implacable expression in her eyes protected her from any threat of interference. She had a good memory too, and a strong curiosity about her husband's business, listening to the fighters tales and Morrie Gilling's reminiscences. At first they excluded her, but, after a while, the men began slowly to confide.

They trusted her instinctively, as Guido had done, and they were surprised to find themselves easing around her, the familiar tall figure emerging after fights to attend to the less serious injuries, her dark head bent over, her voice controlled, firm.

"You fought well, George."

"I should have floored him. Finished him off early," the fighter replied, his left eye closing. "Sorry, Missus Razzio," he mumbled, his left eye closing, a cut the length of a forefinger running along his cheek bone.

Hurriedly Mary rolled up her sleeves, glancing over her shoulder and beckoning to Fitting Billy.

"Be quiet now, George," she said, reaching into the bowl of water and wringing out a cloth. "You fought well. You should be proud of yourself."

Guido had always been fair, but his concern for the boxers lay mostly in securing them good purses and clean fights; he had limited idea of medical care although he was never slow to call in a doctor to attend to the worse injuries. Sensing a real need, Mary began attending every fight, watching over the boxers and supervising each injury. Meticulously, precisely, she made notes of their condition and the length of healing, adding additional details such as weight gain or weight loss. If a man was off his food, Mary knew it; if he was distressed, she knew it; and if he was in pain, she was the first to hear of it because he would tell her. Not Guido. No, none of the boxers would have dared to let down their guard with their boss, and all would have been ashamed to admit weakness to him. No man showed vulnerability to Guido Razzio because every one of them knew about the beating he had taken when he first came to Liverpool. They were hard men, and their boss was the hardest of all. Guido Razzio they could rely on for business, but in other matters, they turned to Mary.

Not that any of them every tried their luck with her. She was no trollop, and besides, she conducted herself in a way which prohibited familiarity. That was the very reason they could talk to her; knowing that she would keep their counsel and always give sound advice. Even Bryn Davis – who could never resist a woman – was in awe of Mary Razzio. But if she had nothing to fear from their fighters, some of the outside boxers were suspect, and after a long argument Mary insisted that Guido gave her some protection.

In the end he did – a small Italian hand gun which she tucked into the pocket of her skirt. Both of them knew she would probably never use it; just as both of them knew it wasn't loaded; but to Mary it was her safeguard, a way of standing her corner if she was ever seriously threatened. And more than once over the months to follow, her hand strayed to the little gun in her pocket, her fingers closing tightly over the mother of pearl handle.

"I don't want you coming tonight," Guido said one December evening. "It's going to be a rough fight."

"I'm all right. I can cope, Guido," she said coolly, refusing to argue.

He studied her, his gaze travelling over the heavy striped dress she wore, and the thick coil of her hair at the base of her neck. She was handsome, he thought admiringly, and strong.

"I don't want to you coming with me, Mary –"

She turned quickly on the balls of her feet, the black eyes steady. "I've got my bodyguard," she said smiling coolly, her hand tapping her pocket. "Fear less and hope more, Guido. Fear less and hope more."

At that time most of the matches were held in clubs, bars, or halls, a back room usually laid aside for the boxers to change and recover, and here Mary went after that December fight to find Ron Poole. Guido was settling the bets in the tap room, but after waiting for him for a while she had grown impatient and had decided to see to Ron herself. Walking into the temporarily changing room with Fitting Billy following, she realised too late that the room was occupied with a group of unfamiliar fighters in various stages of undress.

Pandemonium broke out as they saw her, Ron Poole lying unconscious on a broken door several yards away, the boxers jeering and making obscene gestures as Mary stood rigid on the threshold. Unwilling to be cowed, she drew in her breath, her hand sliding into her pocket as the men surrounded her. Their faces were lascivious, taunting her as she tried to make her way towards George, Fitting Billy hanging back, afraid.

"Let me pass," she said, her tone imperturbable.

"Let me pass!" they chorused back, one man reaching out and touching her face.

45

She recoiled, but kept her voice steady as she pulled out the handgun and pointed it in their direction. "I asked you to let me pass … now, stand back."

The jeering stopped immediately, each man's eyes fixed on the chilling brunette in front of them, then slowly, one by one, they stood back to let her pass.

The legend of Mary Razzio was born.

# Eleven

"Pregnant – I don't believe it!"

Mary nodded. "The baby's due in four months," she said contentedly to her mother. "Guido says it'll be a boy – and you know he's never wrong about the future."

"He should have foreseen a house for you by now," Jessie said sourly. She wanted to dislike Guido, but couldn't help admiring the man. He had accumulated over twelve houses in Liverpool and had a string of boxers who were getting famous enough to have their pictures in the paper. Even wily Jack Dudley from London was running scared, they said, his last fighters knocked out cold by Bryn Davis and Ron Poole. Oh yes, her son-in-law was up and coming, but for how long? How long could you dodge and duck people like Jack Dudley? How long did boxing promoters survive?

She had seen a definite change in her daughter over the last three years; there was no hesitancy in Mary now, no holding back. Her place was assured by her husband's side and by God, she was going to hold onto it. Not many other women would have wanted it, but she did. Mary loved Guido, and in her cool, detached way, she loved the fighters. Hers was the last voice they heard before they went into the ring, and hers was the first voice they heard when they left. She never flattered, never made excuses for them, but she cared for each of those men – and each of those men knew it.

Guido Razzio fought for their purses and got the money to feed their families, but Mary Razzio fought for the men's honour and soon she could be seen at every fight, sitting by the ringside, silent, her vast unfathomable eyes taking in everything. She learned about boxing, about the moves, about the weights, about the men's previous fights. She memorised their histories as she memorised their problems: studiously vetting the referees and the seconds. And Guido encouraged her. As he organised the fights she watched over his boys; as he fixed up the deals, she listened to the gossip and tipped off her husband to a suspect promoter or a fighter who might throw a match.

As a team they were unbeatable, both at work and at home. And where was home? Why 14, Cranberry Street, where else? Others might be afraid of the house's reputation, but Mary wasn't. She had little imagination and could only understand what she could see. Not that she sneered at Guido's premonitions or his lapses into introspection; she didn't understand his ways – but she didn't dismiss them either. Her loving was coolly complete. She took on her husband as the man he was, and she never tried to question him about his past, or intrude into the areas he held secret.

He respected and loved her for it, and in return, he left Mary to dwell sometimes in her own solitude. They were two solitary people living two solitary lives which intermittently combined. The marriage, for them, was very nearly perfect.

"You'll have to move now," Jessie said flatly, amazed that her daughter would want to stay in Cranberry Street.

After all, with Guido's help she herself had long since moved out of Bridge Street. She wasn't yet back in one of the houses by the park, but she would be soon. Which was all the more reason why she couldn't understand Mary's reluctance to better herself. A house on the park was well within reach for her daughter, the Razzios had the money to buy a good property now.

"You'll need more room."

"We're fine in Cranberry Street," Mary said, with a tone of voice which implied that the subject was closed. "The baby should be born at the beginning of December. Guido wants a lot of children."

"Yes," Jessie replied dryly, "all men do. It's because they don't have to give birth to them."

"December …" Mary repeated again. "A Christmas child."

But it wasn't a Christmas child. On the last day of October, Mary was sitting by the side of the ring at a fight, Mick Leary battling against one of Jack Dudley's finest heavyweights. The man was good, in fact he had even challenged the Champion, and he fought as though he had something to prove. Sitting on the opposite side of the ring, Jack Dudley was sucking on a cigar, his boys sitting beside him, their beatific faces blank. He was concentrating, his glance repeated flicking over to Guido was stood behind his man's corner with Morrie Gilling.

There was an atmosphere about the fight, something out of balance, the hastily erected marquee juddering uneasily in the high wind. Several times the gale caught at the door flap and wrenched it open, Fitting Billy sent to tie it back in place, the whole edifice sighing and groaning from the onslaught outside. And inside it steamed and sputtered under gas lamps, the ring erected on a patch of rough ground, the sparse grass cold underfoot, the seated part of the crowd pressed from behind by the standing onlookers.

The mood was nasty, something disturbing in the air.

"What's amiss?" Bryn asked Mary, leaning towards her.

She sat with her hands over the swell of her stomach, apparently perfectly at ease.

Bryn glanced round again, his eyes raking the swelling bank of faces. "Don't you feel it, Missus?" he asked. "Something's up."

"Relax, Bryn," she replied calmly, "just watch the fight."

But he didn't like it and couldn't rest. He had been asked by Guido to take special care of Mary, because even heavily pregnant, she refused to miss a fight. Firmly Guido had stressed that if there was any trouble or disturbance, Bryn was to get her out of there immediately. There was a rest tent off the main marquee for the fighters, but there was a portion partitioned off where she go. Remember, he said to the Welshman, if there's any trouble, get her out. I hold you responsible.

Which was way Bryn was anxious. He glanced round once more, then looked up and caught the expression in Morrie Gilling's eyes. The trainer looked anxious, and Morrie seldom looked that. If he was spooked, then there had to be a reason for it.

"I think you should leave," Bryn said to Mary suddenly.

"No."

"Please, Missus Razzio –"

She sighed briefly, turning to him; "I'm staying here, Bryn. If you want to go, please do."

In the ring, Mick Leary knew he was tiring; he wasn't the favourite and realised that most of the audience wanted Jack Dudley's man to win. He had a reputation and a colourful past – which was more than the red haired Irishman had. Doggedly he fought on; he was used to being the under dog, but as the fourteenth round progressed, Mick became aware of something different about the mood of the spectators.

Guido noticed it too and when the round came to an end he called over the ropes to Bryn.

"Get my wife out."

He had to shout over the cat calls and the slow clapping.

"SHE WON'T GO!"

"GET HER OUT OF HERE!" Guido repeated, exasperated as he was dragged out of the ring by Morrie Gilling before the next round began.

Jumping off the ringside, he moved over to his wife, his eyes fixed on the growing crowd who were pressing on the seated front row.

"I want you to go, Mary. Please."

She was immovable. "Guido, leave me be, and look after Mick," she replied equitably. "He needs you at the moment. I'm all right."

Guido caught hold of her hand, her expression for once fierce: "Something's very wrong here –"

"Imagination, Guido."

He snapped, startling Bryn.

"No, not imagination! There *is* something wrong and I want you out of here." There was a roar from the crowd, a sudden pushing forwards from the back and then Guido realised that there were more spectators still piling into the marquee.

He jerked Mary to her feet and turned to Bryn. "GET HER OUT."

Neither of them argued further, the Welshman hurrying Mary towards the open tent flap which lead to the outside, jostling past the heaving crowd, his body going first to take most of the weight off her. She moved behind him quickly, clinging to his left hand, her face contained, although her heart was racing and the creaking of the tent overhead made her look up suddenly, the wind making a hard dash through the open gap of the exit.

Bryn tugged her through and then turned. The gas lamps inside made shadows of the crowd, the men's heads bobbing against the tarpaulin sides, the edifice moving uneasily. He realised then, with horror, that the marquee was unsafe and let go of Mary's hand, moving back into the tent and calling after him:

"Go to the other tent, Mary. GO NOW!"

"Bryn!" she shouted, the word hardly out of her mouth when the wind caught at the high sides of the marquee and wrenched several of the guy ropes out of the earth. She stumbled back, her hands folding over her stomach, torn between wanting to go to Guido and wanting to protect her unborn child. In the bitter wind she stood for an instant paralysed – and then gasped in pain, doubling over.

The marquee creaked again, it shifted, it tipped over several feet, a hoarse chorus of panic coming from the inside, the silhouetted figures hurtling towards the open tent flap in panic. Grimly Mary staggered towards the smaller tent, her waters breaking, her legs juddering, her hair pulled lose by the wind. She reached the second tent and turned – and in that instant the marquee collapsed. There was a second's silence, a holding of breath, a cessation of the wind, and then a screaming set up and the first animal cries of fear scuttled over the darkening field. The gas lamps which had lighted the fight were not all extinguished: some smashed and lighted the tarpaulin, the flames licking round the hem of the marquee as men began to fight their way out from under the collapsed tent.

In terror Mary stood watching, screaming for Guido, and then, knowing that she was in labour, she forced herself to lie down in the tent, her legs drawn up, her eyes close against the horror outside. The pains came fast, and then faster; she heard the sound of movements, horses, and smelt the cold scent of water dousing some of the fires. But the screaming continued, the sound of moaning and of names being called echoing through the dark and being carried cruelly on the unending wind.

She tugged at the sleeve of her dress and began to bite down on the material, relaxing only when the pain subsided for a while.

"We can't move her, the baby's coming," she heard someone say, and looked up into Morrie Gilling's face. He was holding a lamp, his arm held high to throw as much light as possible onto the scene.

"Guido?" she asked softly.

The man turned his bald head away and called: "I need a doctor, get a bloody doctor here!"

Mary closed her eyes, the contractions starting again:

"Is …" she struggled to talk. "Morrie, did Guido get out?"

He avoided her eyes, then – incredulous – she felt the baby coming and shouted to him: "Get out, Morrie. Get out. I want. I want you out of here …"

"I can't leave you."

She waved him away. "Then go on the other side," she insisted, pointing to the canvas partition. "I'll tell you what to do."

The wind picked up suddenly, the tent juddering around her, Morrie's shadow making a evil black shape against the canvas partition. Biting down hard on the wedge of material Mary gathered up her skirts, feeling the baby's head come. Panting, she pushed the child into the world, the dim lamp light making the blood look black.

"Get me a knife."

Morrie heard her voice from the other side of the partition and stiffened.

"What?"

"I need to cut the cord. Get me a knife – and clean it."

Morrie slid his hand into his pocket, passed his knife through the lamp flame, then handed it to her, his head averted.

Wincing, Mary cut the umbilical cord and then wrapped the baby in her shawl. "I need a blanket, Morrie. Get one from the trap."

He returned with it hurriedly, keeping his eyes averted as he passed it to her. Suddenly, softly, a baby cried.

"Oh, God, Missus Razzio …" the old man said, "It's alive."

His hand shaking, Morrie lifted the lamp and looked at the child in her arms, the illumination lighting a mark on the left side of the baby's forehead. Mary saw it in the same instant and frowned, touching the dark patch. It was about the size of a little finger, and as she stroked it the baby opened its eyes.

"It's so quiet," she said, staring at her child.

The old man knew she wasn't talking about the baby. Outside the screaming had stopped, even the wind had died down, and only the acrid smell of burning remained. He knew how many people had escape, just as he knew that the people in the centre of the marquee had come off worst. The fire had begun there and spread – even if they weren't burned, most of the people who had been there would have been crushed or suffocated. Morrie had seen them come out; and he'd seen the ones who hadn't; he seen some running; some staggering; and he's seen the shapes still lying, immovable, under the wreckage. He knew who had come out – and he was sure that neither Mick Leary or Guido had been one of them.

Silence hung on them, Mary waiting for news. Afraid of the answer. Guido had known, he had *known,* and she hadn't believed him. The child moved in her arms, and then slowly and haltingly, she sat up.

"Take me home, Morrie."

He nodded and helped her to her feet, holding back the flap of the tent to let her pass.

The field was dimly lit, only the occasional lamp remained to help the police and the doctors. Looking straight ahead, Mary walked towards the pony and trap, her grip tightening around the baby. The burning smell stung her nostrils and reddened her eyes as Morrie helped her into the trap.

"I'll take you home."

Mary nodded.

"What about Bryn?"

"No …" Morrie said simply. "He didn't make it."

She closed her eyes against the thought, a picture of the Welshman flashing into her brain. Dark haired, full of life, his hand holding hers as he pulled her to safety. Another picture, one more unbearable than the last, followed. Guido bending over the ropes, calling to her, his dark eyes fixed. Something is wrong, something is very wrong … Guido as he had looked that day outside the tailor's, composed, prosperous in a new suit. Guido, with his little dog, lifting his hand to her as he came home to Cranberry Street.

She had wanted him the moment she had seen him, had waited for fate to move him into her world, had nursed him, loved him, accepted what he was and who he was without question; the outsider, the foreigner. Born under a different sky, carrying an unknown history, a man far removed from the run of Liverpool men. A special man, an unusual man, her man. But not now. She had been stubborn and refused to accept what he had said. She had ignored his warning and now she had lost him. If I had stayed, Mary thought blindly, if I had stayed there I would have gone with him … I would be with him now …

The baby moved in her arms and she looked down. But if I had stayed his son would never have been born. She expected the thought of the child's survival to comfort her, but it didn't, instead she stared ahead blankly, hearing the running footsteps approach the carriage. Morrie would drive her home now. He would drive her back to Cranberry Street. The footsteps came closer. She would go back, and then what?. Closer and closer came the running feet, Mary rigid in her seat, the man's shadow falling on the rough ground beside the carriage. Numb with shock, she stayed motionless, waiting for

Morrie to get in; never turning, never moving, hardly breathing.

He hauled himself into the carriage and buried his head roughly against her neck, Mary drawing back in surprise until she realised that it wasn't Morrie and that the man next to her was Guido ... The surprise was so intense that she found herself paralysed, unable to move. Her voice failed her and she thought for one instant that she was imagining him; that she had, in the fierceness of her grief, drawn her husband back from the dead.

But he stayed next to her and she knew then that he was alive. Unable to talk or even touch him, she merely rested her head against her husband's and watched as he reached out, their hands meeting, clasping, and then lying protectively over the sleeping child.

It was the first and the last time she would ever see her husband cry.

# Twelve

They christened the child Drago a month later, the ceremony coming soon after the service for the dead. On the night of the 29th October 1905 both Bryn Davis and Mick Leary had died, Bryn lingering for a few hours before dying from his burns. True to form, poor Mick Leary remained the underdog even in death, the Welshman being missed far more than the red haired Irishman. What the hell, said Morrie, the poor little bugger would probably have seen the joke … Neither man left any family, although Bryn's funeral was attended by two young women, both weeping and both believing themselves engaged to the fighter.

The boxers kept his poster on the wall of the gym. They had no poster of Mick, but someone found an old sketch and tacked it up, and for a long time when the men went out to fight, they touched their pictures for luck.

Morrie had miscalculated in thinking that the people in the centre of the marquee would necessarily be killed. When the tent collapsed, the wooden caging snapped but fell at an angle, forming an air pocket over the ring. Mick had died from being struck by a wooden strut, the first row of the spectators caught under the tarpaulin. Many burned there; but not Guido. He had been in the air pocket, Fitting Billy next to him. Fitting Billy, Silly Billy – not so silly that night. He had been the one with the knife – the weighty hunting knife he kept hidden from his brother – and he been the one who had cut through the tenting, making the hole through which many people escaped. People like Jack Dudley, and his boys. Old Jack Dudley crawling out into the smoky night, his sordid angels following.

"You were responsible for the marquee," Guido had panted, catching hold of Jack's collar and shaking him. "YOU were responsible. You knew about the wind, you knew! You said it would be safe."

The promoter had been blank-eyed, his boys beside him, their hair jerked away from their faces by the wind.

"You bastard! " Guido had snapped, letting Dudley go and walking away, his eyes taking in the rows of covered bodies; "Oh God," he said repeatedly. "Oh God."

Fitting Billy had run after him; "I were a help, weren't I?" he asked, his eyes wide with excitement. "Dinna I help?"

Guido had nodded stiffly.

"Yeah, I were a help," Billy had repeated, tugging Guido's jacket and forcing him to turn. And there, wriggling under Billy's arm, was Tita.

"Thank you, Billy," Guido had said, taking the little dog and pushing her into his jacket. "Come on, help me!" For another hour Guido stood holding up the canvas, standing in the gale force wind and helping the panicking people to safety, Fitting Billy giddy beside him, his gloved hands banging against his thighs rhythmically.

"It's a fire!" he said idiotically. "A fire!"

It had been a fire, and in that fire Bryn had died – but not before he had told Guido that his wife was safe.

Which was why they remembered him every day.

The baby was strong, but as he grew the mark on his forehead never faded, just corresponded exactly to the mark on Guido's forehead where he had been struck by a piece of metal when the marquee went down.

Morrie was amazed: "I'd never have bloody believed it unless I'd seen it with my own eyes," he said to Mary, "the same mark, the same bloody mark on both their heads", he peered down at the baby. "Uncanny."

Maybe, she thought, but for some reason the mark pleased her. It made the child even more of his father's son, and it singled him out. A child born to do great things. An heir come fighting into the world. They christened him Drago, much to Jessie's displeasure.

"A heathen name –"

"An Italian name," Mary corrected her.

"This is England, the boy will have to grow up here," she persisted, "Life is hard enough without having a foreign name."

Mary repeated the conversation to her husband later that night.

"She's right, life here *is* hard enough without a child having to carry an Italian name."

"But Drago won't always live in England," Guido said simply, his hand bent down over a pile of account papers. "He'll go back home."

Mary frowned. "You never talk about Italy … Why?"

He leaned back in his chair. A clock chimed in the front room next to them. Ten o'clock in Liverpool and all's well.

"I was unhappy there."

"Why?"

He blinked slowly, tempted to confide. But was now the right time? Now? Yes, perhaps. His wife had more than proved herself to be a match for him. She had given birth to their son in circumstances which would have destroyed another woman. The strength she had was awesome – and he relied on it, on the power she had. But he still couldn't confide.

"Mary, forget it … it's in the past."

Her eyes held his. He nearly faltered, the accusation in her expression was so fierce, but he resisted . There was no point, no one needed to know anything; he had taken nothing from his family, and he needed nothing from them – and neither did his son. *He* would provide for his child, and he would see to it that his son never became an outcast.

"We need new boxers," Guido said suddenly.

The subject of Italy was closed, and Mary knew it. Sighing, she raised her eyebrows: "So soon?"

He nodded. "I have to replace …" he bit down on the word, "Bryn and Mick. I need more fighters or we'll lose ground."

"Ron was talking about some man he'd seen in Manchester," Mary suggested tentatively. She too found it difficult to talk of replacing the dead men. "He said that his name was Jem Adler. He's from Israel."

Guido glanced up. "That's a long way away – I wonder what brought him to

England."

"What brings any man to England?" his wife asked calmly, rising to her feet and taking her son up to bed.

Ambition brought Jem Adler to England, ambition and wit, and a lucky pair of gloves. Well read and articulate, he had arrived in Manchester only months before, his luggage filled with books, a fiddle strapped to the outside of his bag. At first people thought he was a gypsy, his long, almond shaped eyes and forelocks making him the butt of stares and jokes. But Jem never got annoyed outside the ring – why fight for nothing? he said.

Oh yes, he told Ron Poole one night, he'd had it rough to begin with. He gone over to Dick Fancy's school outside Dublin at first, thinking to pick up some tips. Oh, he'd picked up tips all right, like the time he'd been winning in Belfast and his opponent had put turpentine on his gloves. Almost blinded him, Jem said matter-of-factly. Luckily he'd had a smart second who knew what to do, and had washed out his eyes, and then – why then he'd nearly killed the bastard.

"… 'e's heard 'bout our bad luck," Ron said to Guido, his freckled face only inches from his boss's. "… I reckon 'e might do 'ya. 'e's not that tall, granted, but 'e got a look about 'im …" Ron struggled to put his feelings into words. "… a dog look, if you take my drift, Mister Razzio. Right mean about the mouth."

Jewish Jem, as he christened himself, looked anything but mean when he met up with Guido in the 'Bell and Monkey' pub later that night. In fact, he looked like an exotic minstrel playing ballads, his slight build emphasised by a long velvet frock coat. Amused, Guido leaned against the bar, listening, Morrie behind him.

"Jesus wept, he looks like a bloody Jessie."

"You've no ear for music," Guido teased him.

"Not from the likes of him, I've not," the trainer replied sourly.

"You play well," Guido said when Jem came over a few minutes later. "I'm surprised you want to risk your hands in the boxing ring when you can play like that."

"I don't fight bare knuckled," he responded, "and I'd heard that none of your fighters do. Was I wrong?"

Guido admired his candour.

"No. All my men fight gloved," he assured him. "What weight are you?"

"Middleweight –"

"That's settled it," growled Morrie, his bald head appearing over Guido's right shoulder. "We don't want a middle weight."

"But I heard –"

Guido raised his hand: "Don't listen to Morrie," he said, smiling. "He has no subtlety. I'd like to see you fight. Spar."

"No trouble," Jem said evenly, "I bought my sparring partner with me."

He wasn't lying, he had bought his partner along. Only his partner didn't come from Israel, he came from Mississippi. He came in at six feet one inch, and weighing seventeen stone, black from head to toe with a tight beard and a silver earring in the lobe of his right ear.

"Bloody hell," Morrie said simply. "Those two ought to get married."

"I want to see what they can do –"

Morrie's face was incredulous: "Oh, so do I."

"Now, come on," Guido said warningly. "Just keep quiet and watch. They might surprise us."

They did, but not in the way either of them expected. Ron had been right, Jem *did* have a dog look, his convivial gentility fading as soon as he settled into the fight, the American, Leo Willard, keeping his distance then moving in fast with a series of body punches which would have floored many opponents. At first dismissive, Morrie found himself leaning forwards watching the two men, wincing when Willard landed a punch, and then grimacing when Jem Adler ducked out of the reach of the taller man.

"God, he's fast," Morrie said admiringly.

"And Willard's got a right hook which could give some trouble."

"Only to the opposition," Morrie said, shouting suddenly at the American. "GET YOUR GLOVES UP, YOU DOZY BASTARD. KEEP 'EM UP. UP!"

Intrigued, Guido folded his arms, watching both his trainer and the two new men sparring in the ring. He was slow in forming a judgement about the pair; Willard looked tougher, but he had a suspicion about Adler — there was a viciousness about his fighting which was unexpected and needed controlling. He had to admit that they could both box, in fact, unless Guido was much mistaken, Adler might even have the makings of a champion. And yet … and yet.

"What do you think, Morrie?"

The old man spat on the floor in disgust. "That darkie's sloppy with his left hand, and the girlie one's too busy dancing round to get on with it."

Guido stared at him coldly.

"Okay, okay," Morrie said, grudgingly. "They both have some skill. They could be good." He paused. "But that Jew bothers me."

"You too?"

Morrie nodded, his watery eyes fixed on the slightly built boxer in front of him. "Something's not quite right about him, Mister Razzio. He needs bloody watching."

Mary felt the same, Guido irritable as they talked in the gym later that night, Jessie looking after the baby. Unsettled, Guido paced the floor, thinking aloud.

"I don't know where I am with these men," he said flatly. "Willard's all right, a bit twitchy, a bit touchy, but all right. But Adler …" he frowned. "There's a meanness about the man, a spite about him."

"It might make him a better boxer."

"I don't know, I've never gone along with the idea of the 'killer instinct,'" Guido paused, "a cool head usually wins, in and out of the ring."

"But all fighters can't be the same," Mary replied, leaning against the ringside. Beside her, a sack filled with sand swung from a hook in the ceiling, a pair of worn gloves lying on the ground by her feet. She had grown to love the gym, the familiar smells and the way the men welcomed her — but that had been before the accident, and now two of her favourites were dead. No Mick Leary, no Bryn Davis anymore. New men were coming in, foreigners from strange countries, different names and faces. Unknown, untried men.

She glanced over to the pictures on the wall. Bryn smiling broadly from his poster, 'The Demon Davis': poor Mick looking out warily from the sketch above.

"I knew where I was with Bryn and Mick," Guido said, as thought reading her thoughts. "I knew those men."

"Not when they started," Mary said, walking over to her husband and resting her head against his shoulder. "Give them time to settle in, Guido. Give them time to adjust."

"It's Adler," Guido said suddenly, moving away and nudging the punch bag as he passed. It swung heavily in the still air of the gym. "He's suspect."

Mary stiffened. She knew too much of her husband's premonitions to scoff. "So don't take him on."

Guido turned. "I could be wrong."

"You usually aren't."

"Oh, I have been in the past," he admitted. "I was always wary of Fitting Billy, always looking over my shoulder, wondering about him, suspecting. I had reason to, after what his brother told me – but it was something else, a hunch about him which made me nervous," he paused. "In the end I was proved wrong, Billy didn't harm me, he saved my life."

Mary said nothing. The night was dark outside, the gas lamps indoors popping occasionally, the sound lonely as it echoed against the vaulted ceiling of the old church.

"If you're worried about it, don't take Adler on," she said simply.

"But we need him. We need fighters. Good fighters."

"Yes," she agreed, "but we don't need trouble. That we've had plenty of."

# Thirteen

The old church hall became famous throughout the North of England, the one gym people could put a name to – The Roman House. No one knew if Guido came from Rome initially, but it was the one Italian city everyone had heard of, and so the nickname stuck. In time The Roman House became a landmark, and the fame of Guido Razzio's boxers spread – as did his own. Everyone knew he was a fair and honest promoter. He couldn't be bought and in 1906 Guido had finally settled an old score with Jack Dudley.

Knowing it was Dudley's fault Bryn Davis and Mick Leary were dead, Guido had plotted his revenge, and had secured it by coaxing Dudley's best boxer away. Under his new management, Potter Doyle went on to win the Middle Weight Championship of England that autumn. Dudley was too old and too sick to fight back, and when several of his other boxers were defeated by Guido's men, and his London gym was closed down by the police, he capitulated. Six months later, Dudley was brought up on charges of fraud, and one of his 'boys' married a well known tenor. The last event provoked so much laughter, a rumour circulating that Dudley had welcomed prison to avoid the humiliation. True or not, he escaped permanently six months later when he died after having a heart attack.

Hearing of his death, Guido felt no remorse. He had been to see Jack Dudley several times, asking for him to accept responsibility for his part in the marquee disaster. He didn't want money, he wanted the man to stand up and be counted – which was the last thing a crook like Dudley would do. So Guido took revenge his own way.

"You're ruining me, you bastard!" Dudley shouted one night when he had travelled up from London to face Guido. "You can't buy up my fighters –"

"I can. It's perfectly legal."

Dudley had been angry and short of breath, his right hand hanging uselessly by his side, his voice raised louder now that he lost virtually all his hearing. Behind him, his boys had hung back, looking sullen, their outfits not as pressed, not as pristine as before. Going swiftly to seed.

"I want you to stop," Dudley had hollered, his eyes bulging. "I'll pay you to stop. We could split the business between us, I get the South, you get the North –"

"I already have it," Guido had replied phlegmatically.

"THIS IS JUST REVENGE FOR THAT BLOODY TENT!" Dudley roared.

Guido's eyes had fixed on the blustering figure in front of him. Two men had died under that tent; two friends. "Yes, it's revenge for the tent. And in my country people of any breeding take their revenge cold."

"What the shit is that supposed to mean!" Dudley roared.

"Watch and see," Guido had said, turning away. "Watch and see."

Dudley died soon after, and by 1907 Guido had bought five further properties and a derelict hall on the outskirts of Liverpool, a venue where he could ensure that his fights were safe, that the bets were legally made and legally settled, and from where he could control his rapidly expanding empire. He liked to control, and only one other person was allowed to share his power – Mary. Her skill and her support made her a valuable ally, her strength of will growing with her confidence.

He knew soon after the birth of Drago that he had married any exceptional woman, but how exceptional was not apparent until later. Her practicality counter balanced his impulsive and intuitive approach. Mary offered facts, he offered hunches; he settled scores, she never forgot a slight and remembered everything. And she was the only person who could stand up to him.

The others were afraid, all except Fitting Billy who wasn't afraid of Guido and who lovingly looked after Tita. Otherwise the boxers held their boss in awe. Jem Adler might talk to Guido about music or books, but he never dared to pry into his manager's past: Tom Poole, the oldest and loyalist boxer, worshipped Guido, but was afraid of him; and the American had little in common with his employer. Only George Slater came close to Guido, because they were alike; two men of few words who had come up the hard way. With George, Guido could talk about his son and listen to the stories of George's five girls; with George he could reminisce about their first fights – but even George could go too far and one night, reading the signals wrongly, he talked about the time Guido first came to Liverpool and the beating he had taken.

George had meant the story to be a tribute, but Guido was disturbed by it and cut him off, walking away without another word.

George was mortified. "I meant no harm, Missus Razzio," he said, bewildered.

"I know, George," Mary replied, tapping him briefly on the back of his hand. "Don't worry about it. It's just that certain things still disturb him."

"I never meant to upset him."

"And he didn't mean to upset you either," she said practically. "Forget it, George."

She could have tackled her husband about it, but she decided to leave well alone. Since Guido had been told that Mary was going to have another baby, he had changed, his reluctance to talk about his past suddenly lifting. Curious, Mary wondered why. Was money and status making him feel more secure? Or was having a family giving him emotional security?

And so Guido began to tell his wife portions of the past, in his own way and in his own time. Mary never pressed him, allowing him to reveal what he wanted, when he wanted. But it was difficult for her. She had no trouble imagining the wealth from which her husband had come; it had always been obvious to everyone that he was cultured and well bred; but other things confused her. References to his mother were always curtailed, explanations begun and never finished. Yet when he spoke of his father there was love in every word.

So she let him talk on, and she walked down the gardens with her husband, and, sitting in The Roman House, Mary listened to him talk of the taste of fruit picked fresh from garden trees, and the long and listless summers. She heard in her own mind the insects humming and the soft whinny of his horse in the field beyond. Guido spoke of a view which looked out over a warm sea, of a house which was cool inside, the outer walls white under the sun. She saw his childhood, and heard footsteps echo down marble corridors and the clicking of shutters on the cooling night.

But when he spoke of his mother he paused, and repeated only two images – the silence around her, and the soft shudder of water in the glass by his bed.

"Is she still alive?"

Guido looked up. "I don't know."

Mary showed no surprise at the admission. "Do you want to see your parents again?"

"I can't."

She took a moment to respond. "Is there anything I can do?"

He stood up, suddenly remote. "Let it be, Mary. There's no point going back." Quietly he walked over to the bed where his son slept. Drago was nearly five years old, a child whose every expression gave away his Italian origins. A still child, serious for his years. Proudly, Guido studied his son.

"His Italian's already good," he whispered, "soon he'll speak it as well as his father." Guido leaned down, stroking a hair away from his son's cheek. "It's good to have another language, another culture. One day he'll go to Italy, and he'll be a success there."

Getting to her feet, Mary walked over to him. Her mother's wish had been granted, they had moved from Cranberry Street and now owned a house on the edge of the park. A red brick house occupying four floors, a staff of two maids living in the attic, a cook ruling the kitchen in the basement below. What Jessie Worthington had dreamed of for her daughter had come true – almost. Mary had the house, but not the respectability. She had the husband, but not the social entree to her neighbours homes. Her standing was uncertain. Guido was wealthier than the doctors and solicitors who lived nearby; but he was a boxing promoter and as such he was shunned. As was his wife.

The snubs which would have crucified Jessie, only amused her daughter. Mary had no time for the snobs who surrounded her; in fact, if it had been left to her she would still be in Cranberry Street. Her major achievement had not been to marry money, but to marry Guido Razzio. The renegade streak in her temperament which had been dormant before her marriage, had steadily uncurled. Her stubbornness made her reject the dictates of society and, as time went on, she revelled in her bizarre and picaresque role as 'the boxing manager's wife,' and 'the woman who mixed with the fighters.' By marrying an outcast she had become one.

Mary knew her reputation went before her; knew that her son was already treated with suspicion because he was half Italian. But she also knew that Drago was strong enough to be able to withstand anything. But what of the baby to come? Would it be another boy, or a girl? And if it was a girl, how would she cope with the upbringing in the Razzio home? Mary frowned, moving towards the desk in the bay window of the drawing room, her hand lingering on the walnut surface. Money had brought her possessions, rooms mapped out with antiques, curtains lined and fringed. A house of careful good taste; nothing gaudy, nothing brash, nothing expected from a foreigner, a man in the boxing world. Her fingers drummed on the wood lightly, her thoughts moving to Fitting Billy.

A man was judged by the company he kept, Jessie had said only the other night. Well, thought Mary, what kind of company was Billy? She had tried to accept him for her husband's sake, but she had been uncomfortable with Billy's slavish adoration of Guido, and then, a little later, she had admitted that she was jealous of him. She flushed with the thought. It was a low emotion, jealousy, but one she was often plagued with. Years earlier she had envied the Flirter and Darter. But then her luck had changed. She had married Guido and the memory had faded – until the other day when she had suddenly seen the woman on the street and had felt an immediate judder of envy as powerful as it had ever been.

Guilt and shame followed immediately. What had she to envy anymore? She was a rich, securely married woman now, a mother; but as she watched the Flirter and Darter make her crackling way down the street, Mary still could not rid herself of the feeling of envy. It was the same feeling that swelled in her throat when she was out with Guido and she watched the attention he attracted. Women admired him, were fascinated by him. With good reason, he had an unusual appearance and accent, and he was known. Mary should have been proud of her husband's prominence, and she was – but only up to a point – some trace of insecurity remained and with the birth of Drago and the imminent arrival of their second child, she felt increasingly vulnerable.

Mary's looks had not faded, but she had lost weight, her height making her appear thinner than she was. The first delight at having money to spend on clothes had faded. Now she dressed well, but with little interest. In tune with her coolness of personality Mary shaded her wardrobe; favouring blacks, browns and dark greys instead of the lyrical pastels. Her austerity suited her; it made her more the icon her legend suggested. And besides, there was a practicality to her dress. In the gym, and amongst the boxers, there was no room for trimmings or light colours. There was always spit, sweat and blood after a fight; the floor scuffed with sawdust, bandages: and the lotions in their dark brown bottles had odours which clung all too easily to fabric. It was not the place for silk. Mary had to move easily, tempering her femininity to demand respect. And respect she had in plenty.

Suddenly Mary's fingers stopped drumming on the table top, her eyes fixed on the figure moving up to the house. Ron Poole was slightly stooped, almost embarrassed, the alert little shape of Morrie Gilling skipping and hopping besides him, his bald head red as a beetroot from the heat of an unexpected sun. Mary sighed. It was Sunday and she didn't relish the thought of Guido being disturbed. For a moment she toyed with the idea of sending the maid to say they were out, but then relented. Guido would want to see his men, talk tactics, discuss the forthcoming fight.

It was his business, after all. She was suddenly piqued. His *family* was also his business. For over six months, Guido had seldom played with his son or spent time with his wife, the boxing occupying him from seven in the morning to late at night. Once or twice he had even slept at The Roman House. Unsettled, Mary heard the sound of running feet overhead. Drago was playing with his nurse, calling for her, but in a moment he would run down to his mother.

*His mother* … Mary took in a steadying breath. That was what she was now. A mother. Obviously life *had* to be different. Her place was now primarily in the home. Her time with the boxers was limited, and although she still insisted on attending the fights, she had missed several when Drago had been ill and needed her. Torn between her husband and her son, Mary found herself having to relinquish the position of which she had been so proud. No woman had infiltrated the boxing world so thoroughly. She had enjoyed the notoriety, the acclaim, the envy – even the outrage. It had stimulated her, forced the best out of her, toughened her, and then, when her place was secure, she had given birth.

Mary loved her son, and she knew that she would love her next child, but every call from the nursery took her further away from the boxing world, and from her husband. She had been Guido's confidante, his partner in every sense until she had become a mother. Now who did he turn to when she wasn't there? To Ron Poole, Morrie? Jem Adler? *Who?* she asked herself, anger rising with her jealousy. They all spent more time with him than she did, even Fitting Billy. Yellow toothed, silly, drooling Billy.

Her husband was surrounded by his cronies, his permanent following of men. But what if, some day, Guido was away at a fight and he saw a woman? Mary thought suddenly. Someone unattached, young, free to devote their life to his life? No, she thought helplessly, he loves me. He loves me … But when I'm not there. When I'm out of sight, am I out of his thoughts? What power have I here? Cosseted in a house I never wanted? By a park I never walk in? … Mary felt an unexpected panic. Soon there would be another child, another reason to stay at home; to see my husband intermittently, to lose, hour by hour, the status I once had. Segregated from society by her lifestyle, Mary could only look ahead and see the coming decades as a life filled with childbirth and childcare – and I was not what she wanted.

"Mary –"

She jumped, turned quickly to see Guido at the door. He was pulling on his coat. "I have to go out, apparently Willard's refusing to train and he's got a fight next week."

She said nothing.

"Mary? Are you all right?" he was gentle with concern, his hand resting on her stomach. "Is the baby coming?"

For an instant she wanted to catch hold of him, to cling to him, to be dependent. To beg him, bribe him, entice him, to stay with her. But she couldn't. Instead she looked him in the eyes and said: "Go to the gym and sort it out," Then she turned, trying to keep her voice composed. "Do you want me to come with you?"

"No, not in your condition. You have to look after yourself."

She nodded, still keeping her head averted: "Well then, you go. I'll see you later … be careful."

The door closed behind her a moment later and then she moved, running hurriedly to the window and leaning out to watch her husband walk down the drive. He was striding out between Ron and Morrie, his head down, as it always was when he was thinking, his left hand tucked in his waistcoat pocket. She knew that in another moment he would pull out his watch, check the time, and then listen.

And from far off a church bell would ring out the hour for him.

# *Fourteen*

"A girl!" George said, grinning idiotically at Morrie. "… a little girl …"

The trainer's bald head was bent down over a bucket as he threw up for the fourth time. "Jesus, Mary and Joseph!" he cursed, wiping his mouth with his shirt sleeve, "I never thought I could puke so bloody much and still live."

They had been out celebrating all night, the news of little Misia's birth being carried all over Liverpool at one in the morning. The pronouncement had caught Guido unexpectedly, the baby coming a week early. Hearing the news, he had jumped down off the side of the ring in The Roman House, the messenger standing breathlessly in front of him.

"… doctor sent me …" he gasped, "… ran over … soon as a could …"

Guido tipped the boy generously and grinned."Mary's had the baby. A girl!" he shouted delightedly to the boxers.

"She has them as easy as shelling peas," Morrie replied. "No bloody trouble."

The noise in the gym had stopped as soon as the boy delivered the news, Jem Adler leaning against one of the ring posts, his gloves by his side, Ron poised, transfixed, in front of the sand-filled punch bag. A baby had been born, a girl, a clean new creature come into their steaming patch of earth. It was more than Mary's child, more than Guido Razzio's child – to the boxers it was their child. All bachelors, apart from George, they responded sentimentally to the birth, and the birth of a girl touched them far more deeply than the birth of a boy. A girl was something fine, something delicate, something which caught their imagination in unison and touched them with a neglected, and unexpected, sense of hope.

Guido was unusually loquacious, almost giddy; "She's going to be called Misia –"

"*Misia!*" Morrie replied teasingly. "What kind of a bloody name is that?"

Guido turned to him, his dark eyes fixed on the trainer. "A special name, a name to live up to," then he glanced away. "This will be a wonderful child, a wonderful woman. I know, I know these things." He fiddled with his coat, turned the brim of his hat in his hands, fumbled with his watch. Unseeing, unhearing, locked somewhere in the safety of future optimism, and the promise of a child not yet seen.

Even Morrie was moved by the emotion in his words and patted him hard on the shoulder. Misia Razzio was twenty five minutes old then, and already loved.

"We'll drink to her."

"No," Guido said, snatching up his coat and hat, "I'm going home."

Then he turned at the door. Jem Adler had picked up his fiddle and had begun to play, the sound melancholy on the still Liverpool night. In the cool wind Guido stood listening; the notes trembled, shuddered on the air, the sound rising to the vaulted roof and coming back like a memory, half forgotten. Adler played with his head bent over the instrument, his black hair oiled, his eyes closed; he played so lyrically that the other fighters also bent their heads, forced to a tribute; he played from the heart of all hearts, Fitting Billy crouched by the side of the ring, his gloved hands tucked under him, spellbound. The music filled up the seconds and swelled, taking the minutes away, and when the last note died, it faded slow, continuing long after in the listening men.

"Thank you," Guido said simply.

Jem nodded, the dog look around his mouth disguised in the dim light. "Jews believe that you should play a child into the world. Give them a tune to dance to."

"She's called Misia," Guido said unexpectedly, offering up her name.

"Misia …" Jem repeated, nodding. "May Misia be blessed."

# Fifteen

She was. From her cradle Misia Razzio was blessed and beloved, the chosen one, the child who captured her father's heart entirely. It was apparent immediately, the bond between the two. Guido shortened his time away from home, and when he went to the gym he took the baby, Mary following.

"She's still being breast fed. Do be reasonable."

But he couldn't, wouldn't, be parted from her. "Can't you cope?" he asked his wife.

Provoked by the challenge, Mary responded as she had always done – practically – and from then on there was always some area made available for her where she could feed the baby in private. Besides, the inconvenience was a small price to pay.

Little did Mary realise how much the birth of her second child would strengthen her marriage. Guido loved his son, but Drago was a distant child, and on the few occasions he had been taken to a fight he had been fretful, tremulous at the boxers' attention. He preferred his grandmother Jessie; preferred her petting, her clean house and ordered mealtimes. Her regular routine comforted him, and, being a reserved child, Drago gravitated towards Jessie more and more, leaving his parents free to lavish their attention on their daughter.

And Misia was a fighter born. In the blood, Morrie said.

"Look at her, look at her watch them in the ring, look at her hands go …"

She came to The Roman House only months after she was born, and easily withstood the poking and prodding of the fighters, and the lusty cradling George Slater gave her. Compact, oval faced, dark eyed, she was passed like a automaton from fighter to fighter, and when her father was busy she was put in a basket laid cross two seats – and placed within sight of the ring.

By ten months old she was walking – Mary holding her hand – to a round of indulgent applause. Surprised by the arrival of this feisty newcomer, Mary loved her daughter, and was fulsomely grateful to the child for leading her out of exile and back into the world she loved. Yet although they lavished so much attention on Misia, there was no guilt about Drago. He was happier with Jessie, and the time he *did* spent with his sister was limited; his solemn, doleful face eyeing the baby with detached curiosity. He would play with her, but would bore quickly, walking away when he had had enough. Willing to give his toys, but not his time. At only five years old, Drago had measured up his sister and decided how much of a part she would play in his life – and it was limited.

Misia had neither the time of the inclination to feel rejected. If her father had been the only person in the world to love her, she would have been indulged; as it was she was surrounded by men and endlessly petted. Not that she took such attention for granted; she seemed to possess from the start a form of emotional judgement; what she received, she returned. Her affection was spontaneous; she had none of her mother's jealousy or coolness; she had none of her father's reserve; she was wide in the heart and giving – without ever judging whether or not the recipient was worthy.

Already entrusted with the care of Tita, Fitting Billy took on Misia with the same enthusiasm. He watched her endlessly, mesmerised by her, understanding much of her baby talk before the others did. But he never touched her. The American, Willard, might rise long enough from a sour mood to nurse her, and George spent all the time he could playing with her; but not Billy – his role was to listen to the diminutive god-child, no more. He would never have dared to touch her, would never have presumed to pick her up – he merely shadowed her, listened to her, and watched her.

He was, quite simply, obsessed, and transferred his affection ruthlessly, dismissing Guido for his daughter overnight. Always eager to amuse Misia, Billy would dress up in bizarre costumes culled from his landlady's attic, coming into the gym and bowing like a gallant. Oblivious to the cat calls from the men, he would grin with his pitted teeth, his eyes round, the whites a pale crescent under the pupil.

"Billy's not had a fit for months," Guido said to Ron one day.

He nodded, relieved. "Nay, not fer a long time," he cocked his head to one side. "'e having trouble with 'is teeth though. Gums bleeding like you wouldn't believe. I caught 'im running them on 'is sleeve only yesterday."

Billy was more than a little resistant to examination, his gloved hands clapped over his mouth.

"Let me look," Guido said patiently.

He shook his head.

"BILLY!" Guido repeated, "let me look."

His hands dropped, his lips parting fractionally.

"Wider, Billy. Wider."

Grudgingly Billy opened his mouth. He had lost several back teeth and most of the side molars were chipped, one jagged and catching the side of his tongue as he talked. The front teeth, always yellow and pitted, were blackening, his breath sour, the flesh around the gums puffy, blood smeared, infected.

"He needs to see a dentist," Guido said, turning to Ron.

Billy's eyes dilated suddenly, his hands beginning the unearthly tapping on his thighs. He lost his understanding totally, his confused mind, so frightened by the thought of the dentist, reverting automatically to another terrifying episode.

"Is it time?" he asked, panicked. "Is it time?"

Ron's voice was horse: "Nay, Billy," he said, holding onto his brother and staring into Billy's face. He had begun to shake, his head lolling over to one side.

"Quick, Ron!" Guido shouted. "He's going to fit."

Ron reacted quickly. Billy's hand had already begun to move up to his mouth, but his brother stopped him, struggling to push his arm away.

"Billy, stop it," he warned. "BILLY! DROP HAND, BILLY, DROP HAND!"

But he was strong and he panicked, fighting back, pushing Guido and Ron away and falling onto the floor, his gloved hands repeating the eternal rhythm on the floorboards, his mouth moving incessantly:

"IS IT TIME? IS IT TIME? IS IT TIME?"

He was quick too, and as Ron and Guido reached out for Billy he rolled away from them, moving his body rigidly as though it was bound with ropes, his legs ramrod straight, his arms tight to his sides. Only his hands moved, persistently drumming as he rolled over and over on the floor of the gym, the dirt and sawdust smearing patterns on his back. His voice rose hysterically, echoing in the vaulted ceiling as he kept rolling, his head jerking madly as Guido and Ron ran after him.

Then suddenly Billy stopped and blinked, staring at the little creature sitting in front of him.

Misia looked back calmly.

"Billy …" she said, grinning, then added less clearly. "…"Itting Billy.'"

He smiled slowly, his mouth closing, his limbs unlocking, his gloved hands clasped together as he crossed his legs and sat in front of her, mesmerised.

"Billy …" Misia repeated easily, without fear. "… 'lo, Billy."

# *Sixteen*

The Great War was over, Guido had returned to England, as had Jem Adler. George Slater had been reported missing, and Leo Willard had been last heard of returning to America in 1915. Seventeen months later, in Spring 1917, Potter Doyle, Guido's unbeaten Middleweight Champion, was gassed and invalided out of the Army, coming back to England labelled unfit for service; and Ron Poole, the first and bravest of them all, was killed in France only four days before the war ended.

Of all the boxers who had been taken on by Guido Razzio at the turn the century, only one remained. Two had been hospitalised, another was missing, and yet another was dead. It was a roll call which rocked the boxing world and which left Guido bereft; he mourned for them as he would have mourned for his own children, and missed them. When he returned to Liverpool, he went home, but stayed for only a little time, making his way to The Roman House alone. As he stood on the bare floor, the damp smell came up from the Mersey tide, pitching through the broken windows, a draught scuffling the posters on the pock marked walls. Many had faded, names worn off, initials missing. Others were jaunty, sadly so, Bryn Davis smiling out still, his hands tucked under his chin, young, terribly young.

Were we all that young once? … Guido turned away, his eyes fixing on the boxing ring in front of him. Time and the weather had damaged it, the ropes hanging broken in places, threadbare in others, and Morrie's old stool lay discarded, a broken three legged reminder of a man who had died almost six years earlier. *All I ever wanted was enough money to get a pub, Mister Razzio. After all, there's a bloody pub on every corner in Liverpool, so there has to be one with my name on … doesn't there?* Did there? Guido wondered. Morrie never got his pub, never had money enough or luck enough. Whatever it was, he never had enough.

The sounds of the gym filled Guido's ears suddenly: ghost sounds, old sounds, turning back down the years. George Slater punching the sand bag repeatedly, rhythmically, wiping his forehead with the back of his glove; Willard landing a punch on a sparring partner brought over from Salford. The man had stood silent by the ring for nearly an hour before the American was ready; he was quiet, his eyes betraying nothing, only a constant swallowing giving him away. The sparers couldn't show fear, or they began at a disadvantage; they couldn't think of the beating they might take, of the punch to the head or the busted ear drum. They couldn't dwell on the thought that they might be knocked out, or humiliated. They just waited, cool, hardly daring to breath, until they were called up into the ring.

Guido remembered the smell too. Young fighters sometimes: old, beaten fighters often. A smell of something worse than fear, hopelessness. He had seen them come looking for work – *I can spar, I've sparred with the best* – but he never took them on. Some were only trying to make a living, support a family, some were bumming for money for a night's drinking. All were too old, too sick. He had learnt how to tell them at a glance; pupils dilated, or tremors in their hands, or an unfocused look, and that smell … He'd had men over sixty trying to get back in the ring. Men half blind, deaf, one even lame. It made no sense, but it was the only work they knew, so they kept coming. Guido never hired them. In some ways he wanted to, knowing that they might end up badly mauled in a booth somewhere, or used as a piece of meat for a young boxer learning the ropes. But he had his own men to protect, so instead he gave the old boxers food – never money – and a drink, and sent them away. Some didn't want to fight. Not really. They just wanted to sit in the hot steamy atmosphere of the gym on cold nights, wanted to talk about the old days, the glory days, when they were young.

Guido winced. Only one boxer remained, Jem Adler, and he wasn't boxing any longer. He had come back to Liverpool after the war ended and never settled down. He never played his music again, or trained, or worked. In the year which followed he turned into a drunk, fighting in bars. He could have been a champion, Guido thought, a king in the ring, but now he was a champion brawler, an alley scuffler, a bully-boy, corrupt, cheating, lying, vicious with disappointment. For an instant Guido could see him in 'The Bell and Monkey' all those years before, slim in a velvet top coat, forelocks framing the aquiline face. He had known then something of the Jew's fate; had suspected the destruction he carried within himself. And he had been right. For all his talent and his skill, the dog look around the mouth had given away the true man long before his actions did. Jem Adler was no more; all that was left was a puffy-eyed drunk, serving time for assault.

What was the purpose of it all? Guido wondered helplessly. Why did Jem Adler survive the war just to waste his life afterwards, when George Slater had had a family and home to return to? It made no sense, no logic. Guido shook his head in disbelief. What was the reason for all the work, the ambition? The striving? To what end did it come? Disappointment and death, nothing more … Guido sighed, ashamed of his feelings and of his bitterness. He had a family, and he had come home to them. He had reason to be hopeful … But why him? Why had he survived when the others died? Why him, and why Jem Adler? Why not Ron Poole? After all, he had his responsibilities, he had Billy.

Only a short time earlier they had met up on leave, had had a couple of beers and talked about anything but the Army. He had been in the trenches, Ron said, then changed the subject and began walking down the street, Guido beside him.

"… only one thing frets me …" Ron said. "… our Billy." He squinted into the dying light, "'e couldn't cope on his own. Oh, I know 'e's helping Missus Razzio, I'm grateful to you for that –"

"It's only odd jobs here and there," Guido said quietly.

"Well, be that as it may, it keeps 'im busy in the day, an' the landlady watches out for 'im at night. Keeps a right good eye on the lad, she does."

Guido said nothing, he knew how much Ron worried about his brother and that was why he had made sure the Billy had enough work to keep his mind off the fact that his brother had been called up. Always eager to be useful, Billy swept the gym, did errands for Mary, washed the windows, tended the horses. Kept busy, busy. But it wasn't enough, Mary had told Guido so. Billy missed his brother, she said simply, and lately she had been worried about him starting to fit again.

"… I don't want 'im put away …" Ron continued, turning his huge, freckled face towards Guido. His hair was cut almost to his scalp, the scar as white as a bone. "I know you can't have 'im in the house with your wife and kiddies, I weren't expecting it, but I fret about 'im fitting again when there's no one to 'elp 'im. I wonder what would 'appen if 'e were on 'is own and 'ad a fit." Ron breathed in sharply, then rolled two cigarettes, passing one to Guido. "You and me, we go a long way back, Mister Razzio. You knows things 'bout me and m' brother no other man on earth knows. 'bout Tunny …" he inhaled deeply, steadying himself. "When I get back after the war, it won't be a problem with Billy. I've got a bit of money put by, and we'll do just grand. But while the fighting on, I fret 'bout 'im managing … I told Billy I 'ad to be away, told 'im that if 'e felt a fit coming on 'e had to stop himself. Calm down like …" he paused, struggling to go on. "I don't want 'im put away, Mister Razzio. If I weren't to get back from the war –"

"Ron."

"Nay," he said softly. "'ear me out … if I weren't to get back, I don't want our Billy shut up someplace. Not with mad folk. Not like that … 'e feels more than you'd give 'im credit for, Mister Razzio. 'e's dim witted, I know that, but 'e die if 'e was put away in one of them places. 'e would, I know it." He turned slowly to face Guido, "Don't let 'em put our Billy away, Mister Razzio. I know you're a man of honour, I know if I ask you, you'll see to it that Billy's does right by. Don't have 'im locked up – I'd rather 'e was dead."

"You'll come back, Ron," Guido said evenly.

The big man nodded. "Aye, mebbe I will, and then again, mebbe I won't." He ground out his cigarette on the cobbles, his voice firm, "But if I don't, think on what I said. Billy would be better off dead, than put away."

It took Guido nearly a year to settle back into his home. He had seen too much and lost too much and was suddenly unsure of himself. To see his empire brought to its knees unnerved him; it seemed that everything, no matter how important or how treasured, could be destroyed. He had fled Italy for a new life, and through work and faith he had had created it. Luck had been on his side too, at times; fortune had put Mary Worthington into his life and his two remarkable children. Both Drago and Misia were handsome and intelligent, the boy now fifteen, the girl ten. To an outsider, Guido had little to worry about, but inside he felt a longing and a helplessness he had never felt before. The war had torn up his roots again, death had come back into his life: it had stalked him, walked with him, and sometimes, at night, he had imagined himself back in Italy.

He was going to die, he had thought one evening around midnight. After all these years he was going to be killed, at last. But not by his mother, by some unknown man, some soldier. Someone he might even had liked, or known once – if he had gone to Germany instead of England in 1900. It was all so random, Guido thought wretchedly, life and death, the beginning and the end. We are born, we die, and the manner by which we die is irrelevant. He wondered then why he had run away from his home; why he had wanted to live so much. The survival instinct? Maybe, he thought, but why am I almost ready to go now? Now, when I have a wife and family? Because you have

70

done your best, he answered himself. Mary and the children are well provided for. They have the house and money, their lives will be insured, protected from poverty. It was his last gift to them. His bequest.

But Guido Razzio didn't die. He lived through the Great War and came home and much as he tried to disguise his anguish there was no pleasure in his return. The others were gone, and it seemed that he had no fight left to begin again. All the strong men, the hard men, all the men he had loved in his own way, had gone. It seemed an apt tribute to a terrible war that of all of them only Fitting Billy remained.

He came looping towards Guido the day after he returned. He was going grey, and with a jolt, Guido realised that he must be approaching fifty.

"Lo, Mister Razzio …" he said, putting out his gloved right hand.

"Hello, Billy," Guido replied, shaking hands with him and dreading the question which was bound to follow.

"… I swept the place."

Guido frowned.

"You knows," Billy said chidingly, "I washed down walls too … Got soap from Missus Razzio."

"Good," Guido said tentatively.

"… I put board over the windows …" he stopped, his eyes looked confused. "Mister Razzio?"

Guido looked Billy full in the face, dreading the next words. "What is it?"

"… in the gym …" Billy said hesitantly. "… they came round, looking for you …"

"Who did?"

"Boys."

"Which boys?"

"Fighters," Billy said grandly. "Like out Ron …"

Guido looked away, his voice low. "Billy, I've got to tell you something." He turned back to face him, "Ron's … he's not coming back."

"'E said 'e were," Billy said dismissively.

"He wanted to," Guido went on. "… but he couldn't. He was killed, Billy."

"Nay," Billy said disbelievingly. "Ron were too big to get killed," then he picked at the cuff of his glove, frowning.

Guido expected at any moment for him to start banging his hands against his thighs in that awful rhythm and waited for the inevitable screaming to start. He tensed, his head humming, a filming of sweat skimming his forehead as he prepared himself for the fit which was sure to follow.

"… are you coming?" Billy asked finally.

Guido's voice was hoarse. "Where?"

"The gym, to see the fighters."

Guido thought for an instant that he might scream, that he might grab hold of Billy and shake him until his head lolled over and his breathing stopped. The air was thick with insects, clogging summer air, coming low over the park. Bloody parks, he thought desperately, what good was a park when the men who had once walked in it were dead? His eyes blurred, out of focus, Fitting Billy's head only a vague black shape against the sun. He had no right not to understand, Guido thought madly, he had no right *not* to feel and suffer.

"Billy," he said again. "Your brother is dead."

"We have to see the fighters …" he said stubbornly, stupidly, his mouth slack.

The air was full, thick with flies, black flies, full of pus, making the day sour; and blue-bottles, bloated, come over from France and Germany. Blood flies.

"He's dead," Guido repeated harshly. "RON IS DEAD."

Then suddenly Billy moved, turning away, his face coming back into focus as he moved out of the sunlight. He was crying.

"Oh God," Guido said, touching his shoulder. "I'm sorry." His shame was complete. In his own confusion and bewilderment he had struck out the man who was least able to understand. His cruelty winded him. "I'm so sorry."

Billy nodded, his hands by his sides. Limp, useless.

I've injured him, Guido thought, had I beaten him I couldn't have hurt him more. I've been unkind, brutal – he thought of Ron and burned with shame – and I've betrayed my friend.

"Billy …" he said quietly. "I don't know what to say to you."

Pathetic under the unkind sun, pathetic, and broken and alone, Billy held Guido's gaze.

"…'e were a fighter."

Guido nodded. "Yes, he was."

"… a good 'un."

"The best I ever had," Guido said honestly. "And the bravest."

Billy glanced down at the hot gravel, kicked at it. The dust puffed upwards in the heat shimmer of the day.

"… and he were my pal," he said simply. "… my pal."

# Seventeen

Guido saw the boys; saw them waiting at the doorway of The Roman House, hesitated, and then walked in. He meant to tell them it was over, that his days as a boxing promoter were finished. He had accumulated a tidy fortune in property, he had no reason to continue in the fighting game. Besides, he had had enough of blood and had lost his taste for combat.

But they were insistent, and Fitting Billy nudged Guido on, pushing him towards the doorway and into the old church hall. Once they were inside, he ran ahead, beaming, taking out his handkerchief and lying it on the side of the ring for Guido to sit on. Amused, he smiled, leaned back and folded his arms, then studied the young men in front of him.

"I'm not sure that I want to go back into the business now –"

"But you were the best," someone said at the back. "You took on my uncle in the old days."

Guido strained to see where the voice was coming from: "What was his name?"

"Bryn Davis," the youth said, pushing towards the front and then standing squarely in front of Guido. A small young man, a light weight, bright in the eyes, belligerent. "I heard him say you were the best."

Guido paused. "Your uncle was a good fighter –"

"I am too!" the youth replied hotly. "My name's Lenny Davis, and I could do well, Mister Razzio. If you'd take me on I could do really well."

"Listen," Guido said steadily. "I have no fighters left. If I wanted to promote again, I'd want a string of boxers of the calibre I had before. I'd need heavy weights, middle weights, light weights. I'd need a trainer," he paused, why was he even bothering to talk about it? The dream was over, he had accomplished it once, there was no point trying to reactivate the past. "I'm not going back," he said finally, straightening up, about to leave.

"But if you were the best, you could be again –" the boy persisted.

"I don't have to prove myself."

"Oh, you're all the same!" Lenny Davis snapped scornfully. "All the men who came back from the war are the same – gone soft," his tone was full of contempt. "You don't want to try again, Mister Razzio, and that's the truth. You're finished because you've lost your guts."

Slowly Guido walked over to him and then looked into his face for a long instant. At first the youth held his gaze, and then dropped his eyes, intimidated.

"I've nothing to prove, Lenny, to you or to anyone else," Guido said quietly. "If you want to succeed, I wish you well, but don't try to goad me into taking you on."

The lad shuffled his feet, embarrassed. "I just wanted –"

"Your own way," Guido finished for him. "Well, the first thing a boxer has to learn is that things seldom go his way in the ring. You've got a temper, Lenny, that's a waste of energy; and you're arrogant, that's a weakness," he looked at the other boys standing silently, listening to him and then shook his head. "What do you want from me? What do you think the fight game is going to give you? Money? Women? Your face and name on a poster? Your photograph in the paper?" he moved in amongst them. "You want power? And you think punching another man will give you that?" he smiled ruefully. "Well you're wrong. Power comes from here," he said, tapping first his heart and then his head. "Power is inside the body, not outside, not in these," he turned, snatched up Lenny's hands and then balled up the fists. "You can punch, that's good. But you have to learn to think, to look ahead, to gauge your opponent's strength. You have to be quick on your feet *and* in your head," he let go of the youth's hands. "You have to learn to be beaten before you can learn how to win. Your uncle knew that, he was a humble fighter, but a great boxer." He stopped talking; the boys were mesmerised, transfixed. "What do you *want* from me? *Why* are you listening to me?" his frustration exasperated him. Why should he start again, take on new fighters, young fighters, coax them, carry them, nurse them? Why? And then he remembered Mary, and the night of Jack Dudley's fire, and he remembered waiting and plotting to get his revenge. And after he did, Guido promised he would do everything to keep the boxing game clean and fair. All my men are honest, he said repeatedly to reporters, none of us steal from the other, or betray the other. We help our own.

*We help our own.*

"Lenny."

The boy moved over to him. "I want you to clean this place up first, and I mean clean it. Billy will help you." Guido turned to the group of hopeful young men who were watching him. "And all of you can line up against the wall over there so I can get a good look at you. Don't ask me questions, don't try and impress me, and don't lie. I want your name, height and weight. We'll take it from there."

# Eighteen

A year passed, Guido taking on eight boxers in total, four from the delegation who came to The Roman House that night and four others from various clubs around the North West. When news went round that Guido Razzio was back everyone in the fight game came calling at The Roman House, trying to do deals, or beg to be taken on. They all found him changed. The dark haired, dark eyed, high cheek boned face as impressive as ever, but there was a wariness which had not been there before. Guido Razzio had never been an outgoing man, he had inspired respect, not affection, but the war had changed him and now there was a sense of a man forever looking back and finding no comfort, only loss.

Mary felt it more than anyone. She was spare-boned now, her eyes as magnificent as they had every been, but shadowed underneath. The love that had brought them together was more powerful than ever, but unspoken, unmentioned on both sides. Guido knew his wife loved him; Mary simply did not need to be told. The only real affection Guido extended was to his daughter – but Drago, now seventeen, was as remote as a young man as he had been a child. Strongly built, in looks more Italianate that his father, he was full-lipped, his eyes heavy lidded, and when he moved he was slow, almost indolent. Yet he was fiercely intelligent – and critical.

He welcomed his father home from the war in his usual detached fashion, but when Guido began to rebuild the boxing empire, Drago was enraged.

"I don't see why he does it," he complained to his sister. "It's such an foul business."

Misia turned to look at him, her eyebrows raised. "Oh Drago, you are such a *snob*!" she said laughing, her small head turning away. At twelve she was tall and thin. Her body suited her personality, the rangy, boyish planes of her face corresponding perfectly with her easy, outspoken nature. But her hair gave her away, the light brown mass pinned back into a bulky plait.

"I hate this hair!" she said repeatedly to her mother. "Can't I cut it off?"

Mary was coolly patient. "You're a girl, Misia, and girls have long hair," she looked at her daughter steadily; "You don't want people thinking you're a boy."

Oh, but she did. She wanted to be Drago, seventeen years old, top of his class, destined to do great things. Drago, built like a dray horse – like the boxers at The Roman House. Misia had missed the fighters during the war, missed Ron Poole and the sullen American, Willard. She missed the gym too, and when Fitting Billy took her back there one night she had had to bite her lip to stop herself crying. It was cold, a white moon crossing a broken window pane, a scuttle of rats moving dark shadows against the blond tarpaulin of the empty ring.

She hadn't cried, of course. Only girls cried and she didn't consider herself a girl. Girls couldn't do so many things, and she wanted to do *everything*. At night Misia even dreamed of disguising herself as a boy. She could run away then – just like her father had done. But it hadn't happened, the war had come instead and all the fighters had gone, and there was no more going to the gym or being petted and carried on George

Slater's shoulders. It had all finished – and she missed it.

"I want Papa to get some new boxers," she said, turning back to Drago. "I like them."

His expression was dismissive. "You're only a little girl, what do you know about it?" he asked, reaching languidly for a book and placing it amongst the pile in front of him. The study was warm, the fire established, the lamps silk and heavily fringed. On the mantelpiece was a valuable Wright clock, the Champion Middleweight plaque Potter Doyle had won years before, and a poor, amateur painting of Tita, done by Guido only months before she died.

"Papa said that Billy used to be a fighter once –"

Drago cut his sister off; "Oh, be quiet!" he said irritably.

Angered, Misia slumped down into the buttoned settee and watched the flames of the fire. Her thoughts wandered, Drago's pen scratching on the page behind her, the doorbell ringing distantly. If her father did build up the boxing it would be like it used to be, she could go to the fights with her mother again, she wouldn't have to act like a girl and do girly things. Drowsy, Misia shifted in her seat and closed her eyes.

If she was Drago she wouldn't spend all her time reading – even if she had been as clever as him. She wouldn't want to go to University. Misia repeated the word in her head. UNIVERSITY. She didn't like what she had heard about the place; somewhere where lots of people read and studied all the time in order to get more and more clever. She frowned, her eyes still closed. What was the point of that? If she'd been Drago she would have been a fighter, someone no one could push around. She would fight and fight until she got really tough – and then she'd win a wonderful gold trophy like the one on the mantelpiece.

Misia jumped when a hand touched her cheek.

"Sorry, sweetheart," her father said quietly. "Did I startle you?"

"No, Papa," she said tucking her legs under her and making room for him to sit down. "Did you get a new trainer?"

He nodded; "A man called Nathaniel Nayton –"

Misia rolled her eyes.

"– apparently we can call him Nat," Guido said, leaning back and folding his arms. "He comes from America. Texas."

"I can't work whilst people are talking!" Drago snapped, slamming a book shut.

Calmly, Guido glanced over his shoulder. "You have a room of your own, you could go there to work."

"There's no fire upstairs."

"If you want a fire you just have to ask the maid."

"But I like it down here," Drago persisted, his tone deliberately goading.

His father sighed. "I've been working hard all day, I'm tired. We have no reason to quarrel. You are welcome to stay here with us, or, if you prefer, you can go to your own room to work. There's no need for unpleasantness."

He was tired, and it showed in his voice. Over the years Guido's accent had all but disappeared, but when he was weary it slipped back into a measured speech, giving his voice a peculiarly lyrical, hypnotic quality.

Drago was grudgingly cowed: "Sorry, Father."

"I know," Guido said simply, putting his arm around his daughter and drawing her to him; "I know."

For several months Mary had been anxious about her husband's condition. She didn't think he was ill, but there was an alteration about him she did not fully understand. After his initial lethargy when he returned from the War, he and worked avidly and, it seemed, contentedly. The boxers were coming on and the new trainer seemed ready to bring fresh life into the fight game. But there was something absent, and that alarmed her. A spark had gone out in him. At which precise moment, she did not know. Maybe on a battlefield; maybe later when he returned and found out that all his men had gone. Maybe it simply left him one night when they were apart, a tiny speck of his soul losing its hold. And what other losses would follow? she wondered, surprised by her anxiety. Would he gradually erode, his personality wearing out, his character losing its footing? Would words from his vocabulary disappear? Expressions thrown off? Affections lost? Was he to die over decades, casting himself off over months and years?

The thought terrified her, and as usual, she reacted practically. A doctor was called for.

"He's is perfectly well, Mrs. Razzio," the man explained. "In sound health."

"Are you sure?"

He nodded; "Your husband's in fine shape. There's nothing to worry about."

On the outside, she wanted to shout. On the outside, maybe – but what of the inside? Can't you see the loss under the skin? If she had been a different type of woman, Mary would have tried to talk to her husband about her fears: but she was unable to articulate her feelings and so, reluctantly, she let the matter rest.

But Guido sensed her anxiety. He knew that there had been a change in him, but he could not explain it. It was simply one of his feelings, a sudden realisation that something dark was tracking him. He did not think it was death, somehow that would have been preferable; instead it was a sensation of dread which was intangible, inescapable, and at times, consuming.

He had been sensitive since childhood; his perception had saved him then, and later, it had guided him to his wife and prevented him from making many a mistake in business. The genie that sat on his shoulder had often tipped him off about people, Jem Adler for one. Guido had known long before his downfall that the man was marked. But he hadn't always been right, Fitting Billy had alarmed him at first, but not now … Guido's thoughts wandered, looped around themselves, memories intermingling. I am merely tired, Guido decided, tomorrow I'll set the new trainer to work and I'll be busy. Tomorrow will be better.

But the feeling of lonely disaster dragged on him and as he held onto his daughter, Guido shivered for an blasted instant in front of the blazing fire.

# Nineteen

It took some of the fighters a while to get used to Nathaniel Nayton's way of training them. His Texan accent didn't help, and the way he insisted on singing out the instructions left the boxers standing dumbstruck the first time they heard him.

He stopped singing, mystified. "What's the matter, boys?"

Fitting Billy started sniggering on the edge of the ring, crouched behind the corner post.

"Well, what's the problem?" Nat drawled.

The boxers were too stunned to reply, Fitting Billy answering for them: "Your singing," he said, smirking. ".that's daft."

"It's the way we do it back home," Nat responded evenly, pulling his trousers up over his beer gut. "Always worked well enough before," his drawl rose. "In my state, the men sing to their horses –"

The boxers exchanged glances, Fitting Billy swinging his legs with mirth.

" – it's perfectly natural," Nat went on, moving over to Billy and looking down on him, his irritation palpable. "What the living hell are you laughing at?"

Billy kept laughing, unable to stop, his head thrown back, the top of his mouth exposed. Braying like an ass, he rocked backwards and forwards, the Texan finally losing his patience and knocking him off the side of the ring. He fell heavily, striking his head on the floor, a look of injured shock coming into his eyes, his mouth slack.

"We've got work to do, boy," the Texan said, helping him to his feet and then turning away. "No time for fooling about."

It was a small incident and one that Guido didn't hear about for a week. When he did, he confronted Nat and told him that if ever touched Billy again he would personally see to it that he returned to America without the full use of his legs. The Texan thought at first it was a joke, but soon realised that Guido Razzio was in deadly earnest. From then on he treated Fitting Billy with respect.

But Billy reacted badly. For some reason he held no grudge against the American, but seemed to be angry with Guido instead.

Misia noticed it too. "He's acting oddly," she said to her father one morning in early June.

The sun was already warming up, a hot day promised. The gym was full of noise; voices; the sounding thump, thump on the leather punch bag; the noise of feet being scuffed in the sand tray. It was going to steam that day.

Guido frowned, turning to catch Billy watching him, a look of solid dislike in his eyes. "I don't understand. Maybe he's not well."

Misia shook her head. "He said he felt perfectly fine," she replied, frowning. She had known Billy since she was a baby, had grown up with him, trusted him, understood him. Until now.

"Maybe I should have another talk to him."

She shook her head. "I don't think so, Papa, I think he just wants to be left alone."

Billy mumbled his way around the gym that morning, and then, about lunchtime, when the fighters ate, he suddenly began to call out for his brother, his voice a high-pitched whine. Alarmed, Misia ran to the office, Mary looking up from the account books.

"What is it?"

"It's Billy," Misia said, trying not to cry. "He's gone funny. He's calling for his brother. And Ron's dead."

Mary rose to her feet and walked into the gym. Billy was in the middle of the ring, turning frantic circles, round and round, his head flung back, his eyes blank. Around the ring the boxers stood watching him, the American trying to convince him to come down.

Calmly, Mary walked over to the ring; "Billy," she called. "BILLY!"

He stopped spinning, blinked, and then dropped to his knees.

"Billy," Mary repeated again, reaching through the ropes, her hand extended towards him. "Billy, what's the matter?"

It seemed as though he was about to say something, but then he shook his head, and slowly clambered out of the ring – on the far side, away from where Mary stood.

Mystified, Misia looked at her mother: "What's the matter with him?"

Mary shook her head. "I don't know. But I want you to run and get your father for me."

Deep in thought, Mary moved back to the office and sat down, then she unlocked the right hand drawer and looked at the gun lying there. Her hand went out towards it and she picked it up, feeling it heavy and comforting in her palm. Carefully she checked that it was loaded and then she hesitated, a moment passing before she put it back in the drawer and locked it again.

When Guido came back to the gym he talked to Billy for a long time and when he finally left it seemed that he had settled down. He was even humming to himself. But back in the office, Mary was still anxious and tackled her husband as soon as he walked in.

"I know what you're going to say – but Billy has to be put away somewhere safe."

"I can't to that –"

"He's not normal, Guido," she said, her tone cold. "I know you care for him, but you have to think of other people too. I don't know if Billy was injured more seriously that we realised by Nat, but something's happened to him." She clasped her hands and sat down. "I don't often ask you to do anything for me, do I?"

He shook his head. "No."

"But I'm asking you to send Billy away. For his own good and everyone else's." Her voice rose suddenly. "What if he attacked Misia? What then?"

Guido paled. "He wouldn't, he loves her, he's never even touched her."

"He might not be able to help himself. He isn't acting rationally anymore."

"He's sick," Guido said coldly.

"I know, and that's what worries me," Mary replied, her voice hard. "Billy's not getting better, he's getting *worse*. He needs help, and he needs to go somewhere where people can look after him –"

"I promised Ron that Billy would never go into a home," Guido said firmly, the old fighter's words coming back into his head. Better dead than in one of them places, Mister Razzio, 'e'd be better off dead.

"I promised Ron."

"Is your promise to a dead man more important than protecting your family?" Mary said sharply. "Ron Poole's not here to tell you his wishes now, and if he were I daresay that he would agree with me –"

"HE WOULDN'T!" Guido roared, suddenly, violently angry.

Mary stepped back. He had never shouted at her before and his anger startled her.

"I gave Ron Poole my word …" Guido said, his voice dropping. "… I promised him that I would never put Billy away."

Mary sighed: "So you won't do anything about Billy?"

"No," Guido answered. "But I swear that Billy Poole will never hurt you, or our children. I swear it."

The afternoon smouldered on, the heat sticky, thick, so heavy that it was scarcely breathable. The fighters sparred listlessly, sweat running down their backs, their shorts mottled with damp patches, perspiration dripping from their noses and chins. Punches were conducted in slow motion, the sounds of them falling full and sodden in the boiling air. For several hours no one knew where Billy had gone, but later, as the day faded, he came back to The Roman House and spent a while in the bath house, sitting on the floor in a patch of cold water, his head on his knees.

The evening burned on, doors in the Liverpool houses left open onto the streets, the Mersey at high tide bringing in the driftwood and a bloated ocean smell. There was not a shudder of air anywhere. Leaves hung down vertically, not a ripple moved on the water, and over the Liver Buildings the Union Jack hung breathless in the leaden night. Talking was difficult, too much of an effort, the dogs lolling against the flagstones with their tongues hanging out.

Mary had returned to the house early with Misia, Guido following later, around ten. The drawing room was hot, even with the windows open, the hum of a trapped wasp coming from behind a velvet curtain. Unsettled, Guido walked into his study, closing the door behind him. The air was stale, dim, and hurriedly Guido opened the French doors onto the garden, standing smoking for a while, his eyes fixed on the gate at the end of the lawn.

Before he could resist the sensation, his mind drifted to another gate, a gate in Italy, a gate through which he had gone as a child, a gate through which he had run away from home … A shadow moved across the garden and Guido jumped, unusually nervous. But there was no figure there. Only a cat or a dog making its listless way home … his mind drifted again. Then the dread dull sensation he had carried intermittently for a year came back.

The sense of danger was so intense that he dropped his cigarette on the flagstones and moved inside, fumbling for match to light the gas. He was suddenly clumsy and dropped the matches, then scrambled for them, jerking to his feet and striking one, the light spluttering for an instant before going out again. The room was darkening, dim, shaded, shapes indecipherable, unclear.

But he saw him. And in that instant, Guido knew.

He could have run, could have tried to escape, but he stayed and faced Billy instead.

Then softly, faintly, damningly, he heard the familiar drumming sound. Rhythmic, regular, the noise of his gloved hands on his thighs: der, dum, der, dum, der, dum …

"Billy?" he said hoarsely.

No reply.

"Billy?" Guido repeated, straining to see his face in the semi-dark. "Billy?"

*"Is it time?"*

The words chilled him, a real, biting terror swallowing him whole. Billy's voice was soft, childlike in the hot air. "Is it time?"

Guido fought to keep his voice calm: "No, Billy. Not yet."

He moved slowly, keeping up the rhythm, beating his thighs. A muffled, suffocating sound. "Is it, isn't it? … Isn't it time? … Ron, you said it were, you said … Ron, it's time, isn't it?"

It was then that Guido realised Billy was insane and knew in the same instant that he wasn't talking to him. He didn't even know Guido was there. He was talking to his dead brother instead, holding the conversation they had had many years earlier – on the night they killed Tunny.

And this time, Guido was Tunny.

"Is it time?" Billy asked once again, and then, almost as though his dead brother answered him, he jumped, landing only a yard in front of Guido before scrabbling to his feet and hurling himself towards him. They fell backwards together, Guido's head striking the side of the desk, his scalp split with the blow, his focus blurring.

Keep awake, he urged himself, don't pass out. Keep awake.

The pain in his head was agonising as he tried to roll over, Billy pressing him back, his mouth bearing down, his breath foul as Guido tried to push him off. But he was violently, madly strong, and with one sudden vicious movement Billy bit into Guido's neck, tugging dog-like, at his flesh. He screamed in pain, his hands fixing on Billy's face, but he was by then only semi-conscious and Billy was too strong for him. Kicking out desperately, Guido made one last effort and pushed his thumbs into Billy's eyes. Howling in pain, Billy bit him again, his teeth fixing on one of Guido's hands.

The pain blinded him, punched the air out of his lungs, his focus blurring – and then there was a sudden explosion, followed by a sensation of weight pressing down on him … Barely conscious, Guido blinked against the light, his eyes clearing long enough for him to see Mary at the entrance of the French doors.

She had come from the garden, had seen the men fighting and had, without pausing for an instant, shot Billy through the back of the head.

# Book Two

# The Benning Brothers

# Twenty

Portland Benning had been to see 'The Blue Angel' at the cinema in Leicester Square, and was still singing one of the numbers when he paused and lit a cigarette. A cafe on the street opposite invited him in: the night was a chill one and he was looking for company, any company. Hurriedly he walked in, the warmth burning his cheeks as he slid into a booth by the doors. The night outside was black, his face reflected back at him in the pane glass window; a wide face, the skin thick, with a deeply ingrained tan and wrinkles around the eyes which gave away the entering of his third decade under an Indian sun.

Glancing away, he ground out his cigarette in the cheap tin ashtray in front of him. A waitress came over immediately: "Can I help you?"

He smiled and she returned the gesture, feeling, as everyone did, an immediate liking for the man: "Have you got a menu?"

She laid on down beside him, eager to please, her pouter pigeon chest bending down towards him. "Do you want a snack or a meal?"

Portland looked up into the slack middle aged face with its froth of hennaed hair. "Does it matter?"

"Oh no, dear," she said eagerly, "you have whatever you fancy."

There was nothing he did fancy, and he passed the menu back to her with a smile, ordering coffee instead.

She seemed to take his loss of appetite as a rebuttal. "But you should eat something," she pressed him, "fine strapping young man like you needs his food."

His submission was complete, a gargantuan piece of apple pie arriving moments later, the pastry breaking down under the loading of heavy cream.

"Enjoy it, dear," she said happily, walking off.

He knew that she was still watching him from behind the till, even though he never once glanced in her direction. Her scrutiny crossed the floor to him with all the clarity of a whistle, and for an instant he had an urge to make a run for it: force the waitress out into the freezing night in her white apron, her hot hand waving his bill in startled fury. He didn't, of course: he finished the pie instead and drank his coffee and lit another cigarette, idly folding and unfolding a scrap of paper someone had left on table beside him.

The cold was the hardest thing to come back too. Not the English voices or the stinging, classical squares, not the underground or the London buses, jauntily red, flirting with the traffic. No, it was the cold which creased him, made him crouch into his coat, forcing his burly figure into the outline of a smaller, older man. Moma had warned him. Portland smiled. Moma. His aunt's real name was Una, but he had never been able to pronounce it as a child and his version had stuck. She was now Moma forever, the mature Moma giving way, after widowhood and malaria, to old Moma.

Oh yes, she had warned him; told him that he would find England very cold. Chill enough to bark your skin, bitter enough to rip away several decades of Indian sun, cold and damp enough to send anyone's thoughts home. Well, you could send your thoughts home all the time, but your body stayed where it was sent, and he supposed that after a while you forgot the sounds and smells of India, the heat, the white sun, the sound of water being trickled into copper bowls, and the bells that rang mournfully against the soft necks of the street cows, their haunches flecked with flies. He supposed that you forgot. But he doubted it.

Having folded and unfolded the piece of paper several times, Portland tossed it to one side, suddenly irritated, the newsprint leaving ink stains on his tanned figures. Tomorrow had would go up to Liverpool on business, and then later return to London and his legal chambers. Portland sighed, leaning back in his seat, his legs stretched out under the wooden table. The waitress was still watching him, he knew that, and wondered why. People did stare at him, they always had, just as they talked to him, openly, greedily, somehow expecting … what? Interest? Attention? Solutions? Portland didn't know, he just accepted the fact that he drew confidences as a jam tart drew flies.

It was invaluable in his profession. He smiled, wondering what the waitress would imagine his job to be. He could never had been cast for his role in life. His part, had it relied on looks, would have gone to another man. Someone autocratic, with refined features, someone grave. A barrister was supposed to have gravitas, he wasn't supposed to look like a tanned vagrant who had wandered into court by mistake. It was no better when Portland put on his robes; whilst the garb effected miracles on the less distinguished counsel, the black cape, winged collar and wig made Portland's heavy, mahogany coloured face even more unexpected. From the back, he was ideal, but from the front he had the look of a man who had stolen someone else's clothes.

The thought amused him and he smiled, the ridges around his eyes deepening. He hadn't known his parents, so he couldn't remember them, he relied on Moma's recall instead, and she remembered plenty. Her version was that Portland's mother had been loud, sociable and emotionally cruel, whilst his father had been a nervous, ugly man with a gimcrack personality and an obscene fortune. Unable to settle in England, they had moved to India to live off the family business and had bullied their way to the top of the ex-patriot social circles. They had bludgeoned everyone with their money, and battered everyone into extending invitations or taking them on as club members. They took from everyone – and then resented anyone asking for a return on their investment.

"I hated my brother, your father …" Moma said for the hundredth, hundredth time. "… he was a creeping Jesus of a man."

Portland had heard it all before and remained silent. Moma was far too sick to be alive and her skin had dried up in patches, giving her the look of someone sitting under a tree in summer, her face puddled with blotches of sunlight. She had never been a beauty, had never had a legend to protect, but she was inordinately vain and even the servants never saw her without a veil. In all the Indian heat, Moma had her face covered, her voice, with its gun-cocking jerkiness, filling up the night hours.

She had insomnia and couldn't sleep. When Portland was a boy she had been married and had kept her husband awake, but when Portland reached twenty four, Moma's husband died and so, from then onwards, her orphaned nephew sat out the nights with her. They played cards, or talked, or sometimes she tried to paint, making a birdie, clicking sound with her tongue as her hand moved over the paper, her brush trailing water snakes of colour which glistened under the lamp light.

"I have no talent," she said once.

Portland had looked at the work, his expression unreadable: "It's –"

"– poor!" she snapped, striking him lightly on the side of the head. "I taught you not to lie, Portland, so don't start now." She picked up the watercolour and crumpled it into a ball, tossing it through the window, where it had caught on a bush outside. "Your father was a liar and I promised myself that you'd never grow up like him."

"Didn't he have any good points?" Portland asked, leaning back and looping his leg over the arm of the chair.

"None," Moma had replied emphatically. Slowly she then rattled to her feet, a set of seven ivory bracelets clanking forwards and wedging against her fleshless wrist. Her weight had gone unexpectedly. It seemed one day that she had been in full flesh and that the next her body had been sucked out, her skin dry as a cricket's.

"I'm ugly," she had said, turning to Portland, "and you're ugly too." A smile had been winched gradually into place as she stroked the side of his face. "You're ugly like Caliban, or Lucifer. Ugly in a wondrous way." Her eyes were the only part of her well watered, the blue orbs moving easily in their lubricated lids. "Real ugliness is as powerful as beauty, Portland, remember that. Many people will look at you and see something crude, but they will keep looking and see something fascinating, and then" she had bent down to him; a pulse beating softly in her neck; "then, because they cannot place you, they will think you a god."

Light-headed, he had heard the words and allowed them to make magic in his head. She said nothing else for a few minutes, simply moved back to her chair and ducked away, out of the lamplight, her feet the only part of her still lit. Slowly, she had allowed the room to work for her – the still, dark corners, the candles burning next to a bowl of perfumed water, the quick, uneasy breathing of an old clock. Beside her, the window had been open, net curtains casting a ghost's shadow over the garden beyond. Feet had passed on the terrace outside; native feet, sure in the darkness, and from the village beyond, a boy had begun chanting under a gibbous moon.

"Many years ago …" Moma had begun. The room seemed to lean forward to listen to her, "there was a dog. It was a poor dog and belonged to a poor man," she paused, her voice had caught like a fish in a net. Portland could have still been a child. The story had been an old one, repeated many times over the years. Moma's way of loving him; as another woman would have caressed her nephew and held him, she had spun out her words and syllables and, with them, drew him to her. "When his master died, the dog was beaten and ill treated and finally, starving, and almost dead, it was left by the side of the ocean so that when the water rose, it would be drowned …" Moma had paused, the lamp light flickered, outside Portland could almost hear the whimper of the dog. "But that night, as the water rose, a girl came to the side of the river and saw the dog. She waded forwards and tried to lift the animal, but it was too heavy for her to move, then, as she was about to get help, the dog spoke to her …"

With one quick movement, Moma had moved her arm, the seven ivory bracelets sliding down, one by one, like beads drawn along an abacus. "… the dog asked her to leave him alone and let him die because death, although cruel, would be better than a life in which he was crippled, without a master. But the little girl was determined to save the dog and she waded in further and further, trying to lift him out of the water. But she couldn't, and finally the dog begged her to leave him or she would be drowned too …" The quick catch, the sudden hoarse inflection in her voice had made Moma pause. "The little girl was pretty, young, healthy, but when the tide came in, she kept clinging to the old, crippled dog until the water slid over her head. And she drowned."

The boy had stopped chanting outside; there was silence; except for the echo of water sounding in Portland's ears.

"Why did she do it?" he had asked, knowing the answer already.

"Because she was supposed to. It was her *Fate*," Moma had answered. "But the ghost of that little girl comes out every year on the anniversary of her death, and she calls for the dog."

"If she died with the dog, why does she still call for it?"

Moma had smiled, then leaned towards the lamp light, her face mottled snake-skin, her neck drawn out tightly from the ivory collar of her dress. *"Because the dog got away!"* she explained, laughing. "Now, Portland, let that teach you never to trust anyone. The girl died trying to help the dog, and the dog got away."

"I *never* liked that story," he had said dryly.

"You weren't supposed to like it," Moma replied, "you were supposed to learn from it. Never be deceived by what you see, or what you hear." She picked up a pack of cards and shook them onto the table in front of her, cutting them into four piles. "Now, amuse me, Portland," she had said, smiling, sly as an old cat. "Make me think."

That had always been her command; make me think. Having a piercing intellect herself she had demanded stimulation, and after her husband's death, it fell to Portland to provide it. He was not, nor ever had been, afraid of Moma. The native servants might think her a witch, their neighbours might go in awe of her, but not him.

"Portland, talk to me!" she commanded.

"About what?"

"Magic!"

"And where do it get the magic from?"

"THE MOON!" Moma had replied, her voice jerking on the double OO, her mouth a tunnel through which other worlds poured.

Portland jumped suddenly, the waitress materialising, unheard, by his shoulder. "D'you want anything else?"

He shook his head, still disorientated; "No, no thank you. That was fine."

"Sure you don't want some more pie?" the woman went on, smiling encouragingly. "It's good. Everyone says so."

Moma had died in the night, whilst they had been talking, around three fifteen. She had been telling him about her first home in Ireland when suddenly she began to count her bracelets, over and over again. One, two, three

"No more coffee? Go on, it'll do you good."

She couldn't get passed three … even though the bracelets were all there, all seven of them … she couldn't get past three.

"Well, what d'you say?"

Moma had counted them all in the end, let out a great sucking, roaring breath, then she had put both hands on her knees and let go. He had thought that he felt her spirit pass him. Even now, seven months after her death, he could sometimes sense her passing …

"You sure you don't want more pie, love?" the waitress urged.

"No, thank you," Portland replied, his mind snapping back to the present. Collecting his things together, he took his bill and paid at the door, then turned and retraced his steps to where the waitress was clearing his table. He coughed and she turned. Her face had been limp, tired, but she smiled when she saw him.

"Your tip," Portland said.

She looked at the money disbelievingly. "Oh, sir, it's far too much."

He knew it was, but something about her had reminded him of the girl in the story, the same silly helplessness had touched him, left him cold with pity. Embarrassed, he turned away, but he knew that she would watch him leave – and that she would save the tip and never spend it.

# Twenty-One

If everything was disorganised, Drago couldn't concentrate. His rooms off the Strand were noisy, but he could work with noise, it was untidiness he found intolerable. At the age of twenty seven he was qualified, the best in his year at medical school, destined for a consultancy and the medical square mile. Drago looked at the clock, then moved towards it, turning it slightly so that it was exactly central to the mantelpiece. Besides it, on either side, were candlesticks, and on either side of those, bronze heads brought back from a recent trip to Athens.

He prided himself on his erudition and his cultured, sophisticated surroundings. In London he could choose who to entertain, choose who came back to his flat, choose who were the fortunate few who might even be allowed to look at his books. Frowning, he studied the rows and then pulled on a pair of cotton gloves before rearranging two volumes on the second row. Grease marked leather, he knew, and bacteria could cause unending problems. He had the same fastidious attitude in the hospital: although there the brittleness of his nature was not immediately apparent. Indeed, the patients saw a tall man with sensual features, an amply-lipped mouth and slow, almost lazy motions. They thought he was handsome, they even thought that the mark on his forehead somehow added to his appeal; a flaw on the marble. He appeared, within his lush and languorous aura, to be amiable, a person with whom one could relax.

They misjudged him. He was hideously, bleakly cold. The cool jealous nature of his mother Drago inherited, without her balancing courage. The dark introspection of his father he inherited, without the judgement and strength. Although Drago knew nothing of his father's past, he seemed to take on Guido's unknown history and suffer for it. His bitterness was profound, acute and lasting; he remembered every slight, every inflection of voice which might carry an insult. His world spun on an emotional axis so fine that any minute imbalance would send him into himself for days, his suppurating wounds dressed and redressed in the privacy of his own flat.

His work never suffered from his moods. Drago could, almost instantaneously, segregate himself – and that ego he treasured so assiduously – from the task in hand. And he worked without heart to achieve what he most desired – a reputation. The Razzio name shamed him; marked him out as an Italian, a foreigner, an outsider. Liverpool was intolerable to him; it worked like a worm in his gut, taking the goodness from his food, undermining him, making him sicken, until finally, he left for Cambridge, and University.

There is a story of a land once used as a burial ground, over which no animals will pass or birds will fly. Drago carried the same sense of deadness, and people often shied from him. In work, it was different, he was a doctor, and he was a gifted clinician; but outside work, in the world which is governed by the loves and lives of men, he was able to form few friendships and inspired no love. Another man might had mourned for this, but Drago did not, his arrogance was fully-formed and consistent.

He did not miss his parents or his sister, he did not miss his previous life. He was ensconced in a world he could control. In his few expensive rooms Drago could cut his food into regular portions, fold his clothes symmetrically, lay his slippers by the side of the bed in perfect unison, with no one to remark on his habits. He would have only few friends – because only a few would accept his boorish, mental bullying; women, attracted by his looks, were soon repelled by the fixated, compulsive order of his life. Drago had no leeway in his ideas or opinions, he decided upon a thought and fastened it onto his existing intellect like so many warts on the back of a toad.

Shame was his closest companion; shame and fear that someone would discover his background, would find out that his father was a boxing manager, that his home was in Liverpool, that the people with whom he grew up where the likes of Ron Poole and Morrie Gilling. His mind could not fully absorb the shock if anyone discovered that his father owned The Roman House and worse. What of someone, by chance or by malice, should find out about the death of Fitting Billy?

Drago winced, rose to his feet, finishing the glass of sherry he had poured himself, then wiping his hands on a clean handkerchief. The room was not comfortable, every inch was arranged to impress, Turkish carpets laid under a heavy walnut table, two torcheres flanking the door. Drago's eye for detail was formidable, but the colours were sour, the pale walls too limply blue, the ivory silk curtains sickly; even the marble busts collected from his travels stood testament to the aridity of his personality. Drago's Grecian facsimiles had all the animation of perfection, of people who had never lived.

Bored and restless, Drago looked into the mirror, then, irritated, he adjusted his tie and rearranged his jacket. Finally satisfied, he touched the mark on his forehead and remembered the story of his birth. To be born in a *tent*, he thought despairingly, to be born at a boxing match … It didn't matter that his father's empire had paid for his medical education and for his trips abroad. It didn't matter that the boxers had, indirectly, carried Drago, unmolested and undisturbed, through life to his privileged position on the Strand. In fact, it made it worse. Drago owned them a debt; he had been financed by these people and by the money his father made in the boxing world, his rise to eminence had been dogged by the shadows of the fighters, of The Roman House, of the queasy terraced houses which were rented out. Yes, he had been helped, but at what cost? To be eternally looking over his shoulder? To be forever wondering who would expose him, and when?

To be forever waiting for someone, someday, to read the name Razzio. And remember.

# Twenty-Two

Summer came in quickly, then, as though she had exhausted herself too soon, she faded, and a long, limp July began. The sky, clouded over, seemed to rest on the roof of The Roman House, a cluster of pigeons cooing seductively in the moist air. The night before, Mary had been talking to Nathaniel Nayton, discussing the changes now that boxing had been put under the control of the Amateur Boxing Association and the British Boxing Board of Control. She had been as usual, composed, Misia by her side as they sat talking in the office.

Nothing had changed there for years: except the calendar and that was always similar – apart from the year, and photograph of a different fighter every month. Otherwise, nothing had altered, the same shelves were crammed with over-loaded files, the same few battered ledgers propped up against the wall of bubbled glass. On the dark wooden wall behind the desk hung an old sign from one of the boxing booths – *POTTER DOYLE* – *English Middleweight Champion, 1908* – its painted surface darkening under the varnish and cracking over the surname DOYLE. The desk was unchanged too, the leather top still waxed with polish, the pen set, tortoise and gilt, still lying where Guido had last placed it.

No one dared to touch it; no one would have risked Mary Razzio's wrath. Only she could touch his things and pick up his pen, and only she, on her own late at night, could take his photograph out of the drawer and hold it against her cheek. Sometimes, the slightly built figure of Lenny Davis would hover outside; she would see him and wait to see if he knocked. If he didn't, she would call out to him.

"Come in, Lenny."

He'd walk in, cocky in a new suit, his hair freshly cut, a graze over his eye from his last fight. "Missus Razzio."

"Lenny."

"I just thought I'd say hello."

He was trying to show off, to impress her, to make her see what a catch he was, and then, if things went as he expected, she might start to look at him as a future son-in-law. Lenny liked the idea of inheriting The Roman House one day, let alone all the houses on Cranberry and Lemon Street. It made him quite dizzy just to think of it. All he had to do was to pay court to Misia and he'd be home and dry.

Misia didn't seem to take to him though, and that was a problem. It confused Lenny, her lack of interest. All the other girls seemed to flock round him. They liked a boxer and Lenny had had his photograph in the paper only the other week. But not her. No, not her. She didn't act like a girl either; she was too quick, too flaming clever for his liking. Not that he could say Misia was spoiled; the boxers all thought the world of her, but they thought of her as a daughter or a sister, not as a girlfriend. She was too boyish in a way. Lenny frowned, maybe it was her figure, her straight, up and down form. Or maybe it was her hair, cut short onto her cheeks in the new fashion.

It was obvious that Misia was attractive, but she never seemed to want attention.

She had other things on her mind apart from attracting boys. Having been around men all her life, she was comfortable with them and had no need of feminine wiles. She swapped joke for joke and could handle herself very nicely, thank you. Which wasn't quite what Lenny wanted. A fluffy, silly bit of stuff would have been more to his liking. But still, no one had everything, and Misia *did* have money – if not now, at least in the future.

"How d'you think the fight went, Missus Razzio?"

Mary studied him for so long that he coloured. Was this really Bryn's nephew, she wondered, this cocksure little fool on the make?

"You did well."

He shuffled his feet. Mary Razzio was formidable, everyone said so, and besides, no one forgot what she had done to Fitting Billy Poole.

"I thought I might … I wondered if …" he gagged on the words. Outside it had seemed so simple, he'd just go in and ask if she'd mind if he asked Misia out. But now, now that he was looking into those vast black eyes, well, Lenny suddenly wasn't so sure.

"I'll be off then …" he blathered.

She didn't even blink. "Good night, Lenny."

"Yeah … well, good night then …" he said, backing out.

Breathing in, Mary closed the ledger she had been working on and walked to the door, crossing the passageway and moving into the gym. Only one boxer was still there, a young black lad from Preston way, Dan Whistler – WHISTLING DAN – as he called himself, living up to the name when he went into the ring, whistling loudly to prove that he had plenty of spit in his mouth and therefore couldn't be afraid. He was working on the punch bag, his steady thumping filling the air and making dull drubs against the walls. Mary felt old suddenly. She was only sixty – her character and bone structure holding back the years – but she felt old, and was glad of her daughter's help.

In the last seven terrible years Mary had come to rely on Misia; not to lean on her; Mary was not the type of woman to burden anyone, but she was grateful to have her daughter standing with her, shoulder to shoulder. There was nothing of the snob about Misia, she wasn't like Drago, ashamed of his past and his parents. Oh, he might deny it when he visited them, might pretend that he was at home in their house on the park; but his salt-dryness, his aura of superiority, he could not disguise. He had always kept away from the boxing business, even as a child he had never been curious; the fighters did not intrigued him – they repulsed him.

Mary was shocked by how much that fact upset her and automatically sided with the boxers. Drago was her child, the fighters weren't, and yet she felt protective of them, and angry that their courage was so lightly dismissed. Her son was gifted, but she wasn't proud of him – and he knew it. It rankled on him, just as Drago's pomposity rankled on her. So they shadow-boxed each other – throwing out jabs, a right hook, a sudden mental upper cut to the jaw – but neither won. There would never be a winner in this bout, and as time passed both felt something dislike for the other.

Many times Misia tried to act as a mediator; she talked to her mother, then she talked to Drago, but her efforts came to nothing. There was a deep, consuming gulf between them which opened a little further every day, and there was no way to span it. Drago, she was sure, was afraid of their mother; not physically, but spiritually. His behaviour crossed some boundary in Mary Razzio's morals. And for that, she would never forgive him. She loved Drago because she saw her husband in him; she loved him for the fact that he carried Guido Razzio's blood, but for no other reason than that.

"He's just different to us."

Mary's eyes were antagonistic: "Drago is a snob."

"Maybe," Misia conceded, "but he's done well. You know what he said the other week, he wants to be a surgeon," she leaned towards her mother, "you should be proud of him."

"I am more proud of you," Mary said, getting to her feet and putting her head to one side, listening. "Did you hear anything?"

Misia looked up. A new electric light hung from the ceiling, the glass shade modern, at odds with her mother's sombre dress. The house had been brought up to date, year by year, money invested wisely, a phone installed, as there was at The Roman House. It paid to keep up with your competitors, Mary said firmly, business was business. But although she accepted the new world and the new gadgets, she walked amongst them like a ghost, out of her time.

*"Did* you hear anything?"

Misia nodded. "Yes, the bell."

Mary moved to the door quickly and hurried up the stairs, entering the bedroom, her face relaxing at once, the tiredness of a wearying day lifting. Her steps were quick as she moved across the room, her voice shaded, intimate.

"My love," she crooned, leaning down over the bed. "How are you, my love?"

Guido watched her intently, his face without expression, his body immobile. Only his hand, his left hand, had any movement left, and in it he clasped a small brass bell. The one he used to summon her. Gently Mary stroked his hair, and his eyes closed, soothed by her touch. His body was stilled, rigid, wasted; but his mind was unimpaired. He wanted to tell her that it was not as dreadful as she imagined; that the seven years he had spent paralysed were not wasted, nor devoid of worth. He wanted to thank her for his life, but on the night she had killed Billy Poole Guido had suffered his first stroke and then, in the week which followed, he suffered another. All vocal communication had gone with the first; all movement with the second.

Dying, Guido realised, was not to be sudden for him. Humiliation he had come to accept, the daily washes, the mute agony of incontinence, the dreadful soiling of himself. A proud man, he had been made humble; as an independent man, he had been made dependent. It seemed that he had nothing left to lose, certainly nothing to gain. But in time Guido had found stillness, and he regretted, above all, that Mary did not realise it. Instead he knew his wife would grieve for him and imagine all the hideous restrictions that he would have expected to feel before his stroke. But she was wrong, and he couldn't tell her that.

He couldn't tell her that he lay in the bed and travelled; that all his ambition and fighting and struggling and wanting and escaping had come to this – this enforced settlement of the soul, this stillness, this rest. She saw him physically transfixed, and felt his humiliation – she did not know that hour after hour he moved about the world as he had never done before. Sometimes, at night, when the moon rose, he lay with his eyes open and thought of Seraphina, a white spirit come out from the woods; or of Tita, running besides him, barking at shadows; and then, sometimes, under a cold midnight, he thought of his mother and the long chill she had dragged morbidly over his life.

His body lifted with him in his head. Paralysis meant nothing, he was beyond movement, and he realised then that the soul travels on after death, and sometimes, to the lucky few, it travels a little way before. He was only surprised by the length of his dying. Seven years had passed into lifetimes: and yet as quickly as the space of an afternoon.

How he wanted to tell his wife that; to soothe her, to reassure her, to promise her that wherever he went, and whenever he went, he would go to make a way for her.

"My love …" Mary said softly, her breath sweet with pity. "Is there anything I can do for you?"

He opened his eyes and looked into hers and she understood. Gently, careful not to disturb him, Mary lay down on the bed beside her husband and turned his head to rest against hers. In the dim light, she then began to talk. And in his head, he took her home to Italy.

# Twenty-Three

**Three years later**

Portland had never been part of a clique, he had moved instead amongst a variety of circles, making friends wherever, and with whoever, he liked. He had come from a background which had fitted him to be either a recluse or a social hybrid; and he had chosen to be the latter. As a mongrel who went where he pleased, he needed no social qualifications and relied on his character to work as his entrance ticket; and it usually did.

Of course he had the advantage of wealth and talent; and was already in the fortunate position of being in demand. He had not truly struggled beyond the first few hiccupping years in Chambers, but he had never been blasé about his skill. Where another man might have abused his intellectual power, Portland did not; he took on difficult cases and tiresome clients; he defended the undependable and prosecuted the social or financial lions, making powerful enemies along the way. The fact that his appearance marked him out worked to his advantage. At first glance he had a villain's face, but when he began to talk, that melodious voice – with its spattering of quotes, its Indian references, and the lyrical rhetoric inherited from Moma – soon threw a potent spell over the court.

He worked with all his senses when he spoke to his clients. Extraordinarily, he could scent innocence. At first it was treated as a joke, but as time went passed members of the legal profession realised that Portland had a powerful advantage over them. Soon he was being watched in court, the great dark face immobile, the hand moving over the papers constantly. Some might think he wasn't listening, but he was, in his own way. He was drawing the words in, pushing them through a mental sieve; turning them over in his brain as though he felt and could squeeze the truth from them. He was impassive, a behemoth of a man who, when he stood up to speak, knew that every ear, and every eye, would be trained upon him.

Portland controlled people through seeking never to control them; and he remained faithful to the places and people he infiltrated. He asked not to be impressed or entertained, he asked to be accepted for whatever time he stayed, and if he wasn't accepted, he moved on. Life was a series of possibilities for Portland. He had no streak of melancholia, no maudlin introspection – he looked at the world as a place to explore, and as he amused others, he expected to be amused himself.

As Moma had amused him … Portland smiled. She would have adored Misia, would have found in her a fierce little ghost of herself. They were both similar, not in appearance, but in spirit. And Misia had a similar gift for story telling – a trait Portland, a lover of facts, had always found seductive.

Deep in thought, he was only half aware of his clerk walking in.

"Mr. Benning?"

Portland looked up; "Mr. Leamington," he answered, resisting a dreadful temptation to add, 'I presume.'

Leamington passed him a sheaf of papers, then stood, hands folded behind his back, waiting. He was a man of five feet ten inches, with greying hair cut short over his ears and a long concave face with an undershot jaw line, which made his bottom teeth close over his top. Nicknamed 'Hapsburg' for his unfortunate appearance, he lived with his four unmarried daughters, all of whom had inherited his looks.

Portland smiled at his clerk: "How are you today?"

Leamington thought the question over, searching for a way to introduce one of his offspring into the answer; "I'm very well, thank you, sir, but my second to youngest's not well. A nasal drip, they call it." He looked up at the ceiling as though Portland had suddenly levitated. "The nurse said she had to have drops. Very off-putting, sir, especially at mealtimes. Speaking of which, they wanted you at the prison this afternoon." The non-sequiter came as no surprise to Portland; the clerk, so meticulous in his duties, spoke in sentences which bore no relevance to each other. It was as though his mind was full of files, all of which had been thrown up in the air and jumbled, coming back to earth in no apparent order.

Portland frowned: "Wormwood Scrubs?"

Leamington nodded, his chin dipping down to his chest at a vicious angle. "And your wife rang," he added. "She said could you call her back in a hurry, sir? My second girl's like that, always hurrying, always wanting things done that moment."

Portland listened patiently. He knew that his clerk admired Misia, indeed he had once overheard Leamington likening her to his youngest child – an accolade beyond measure. He also defended his employer's wife against the verbal slights which circulated repeatedly, taking Misia's side whenever anyone made a comment about her background. Portland had overheard a number of such exchanges, seeing Leamington turn to rebuke someone, his hands always behind his back, his concave profile snapping out a chiding response.

He admired him for his loyalty and relied on him to report back anything of interest that happened in his, or other, chambers. Leamington was not slow to make progress in his new career. As a spy he was extraordinary adept and had an almost supernatural ability to uncover secrets. Papers had a way of attaching themselves to his hands as though magnetised; people had a habit of talking whilst he passed, sometimes relieving themselves – both physically and mentally – whilst he was undergoing his own ablutions. Together, Leamington and Portland made a formidable team.

Which was why Portland had no hesitation in telephoning Leamington later that afternoon to tell him that he would not be back in London that night.

"Nothing amiss I hope, sir?"

"Nothing, just a family matter."

"Ah, the ladies," Leamington replied, mesmerised. "What would we do without them? My third girl said only this morning –"

For once, Portland cut him off, glancing hurriedly at his watch. "I have to go, I'll phone you tomorrow."

The line went dead.

Thirty minutes later Portland had picked Misia up from The Roman House and driven her over to her mother's. The conversation between them had been short and terse; there had been no argument, Mary had simply informed her of what Drago had said to his father. For so long the peacemaker, Misia listened, her temper rising. She had endured her brother's arrogance for years, at times she had almost found his pomposity amusing, but this was unforgivable. He would have been wrong to talk to anyone in that way, but to talk to their father like that; to speak of his death in front of him; to talk about a loss which she found unbearable to contemplate for an instant.

Misia left the house hurriedly, running towards the car and getting in, slamming her door shut. Portland followed, sitting next to her and looking at her rigid face, yellowed from the streetlamp.

"I'm going to see my brother," she said finally, pulling the collar of her coat up around her neck. "I want to tell him what I think of him and then I want him to apologise to my father." She looked through the car window to the first floor of her parents house, to where a light burned. "How could he say such things? *How?*" her voice cracked on the last word.

Portland had never been close to his own father, so he couldn't fully empathise, but he could understand some of Misia's terror. Moma had been his bolt hole, his one certainty, the one reliable feature in his life. Whether he had been in India or London, he had, through all his childhood and adult years, known she was there for him. But when she died Portland was an adult, so her loss, bitter and dreadful as it was, was not consuming. Misia was only twenty two. Her mother was important in her life – but her father was her loadstone. If Misia had seen her father in terms of a religion he would have been her God and her Host – he was, and had always been, her Spirit. She idolised him in a way Portland found hard to understand, seeing him as he now was, paralysed and silent.

But something of the respect Misia felt, he also found in the boxers when they spoke about Guido.

"… you should hear about the first days, when he came to Liverpool, the beating he took. Not many men could get up from that, and stay up …"

Others spoke of his character:

"… he had a little dog for years – I forget what her name were – but she were like 'im, feisty, and if she got 'er teeth in you she never bloody let up. I remember Mister Razzio setting out to get that old bugger, Jack Dudley, aye, and getting 'im good. Taught 'im a lesson, he did that … What else can I tell you 'bout him? Well, he were quiet – not chatty. He were a man you'd 'ave liked to be seen with …"

Was Misia too close to her father? Portland wondered, waiting with dread for the day when Guido died; for that hideous parting, the cutting off which would leave her distracted. She had a husband now, but was it enough? he asked himself. Was any man enough to measure up against her father's legend?

"I want to see Drago," Misia repeated hoarsely. "I have to see him."

"We'll drive down in the morning –"

"NO!" she snapped. "I'll go by train if I have to – but I have to go tonight."

Portland was suddenly irritated. "Be reasonable, tomorrow I have to go back to London anyway."

"You don't understand, do you!" she snapped childishly. "I want him to know

*now* what's he done. Not tomorrow, not the day afterwards." Her hands dug into her pockets, fighting the February cold. "I know you don't understand, Portland, but I have to go now."

He reached over to her and touched the tip of her nose. It was cold, almost like touching a glass, with no sensation of blood flow beneath. Portland had never allowed himself to indulge his attractive, younger wife; he did not want to be a foolish husband and sensed instinctively that Misia – spoilt from birth – would manipulate him if he allowed her to. So he pushed her and expected much of her, treating her as though she was an older woman and in doing so, he deliberately divorced himself from the role of father figure. I will not take over Guido Razzio's function, he told himself, when he dies I will not take on his love, I will have secured my own.

"Is it so important to you?" he asked, turning to Misia.

She nodded; calm and still.

"All right," he agreed, "we'll go down tonight."

They drove through the evening and into the long cold night, stopping for petrol, Portland burly in his overcoat, Misia wide awake and staring out onto the patch of road lit by the headlamps. Around nine they paused by a roadside pub and ate dinner, Misia drinking a glass of brandy but leaving her food untouched. She wasn't hungry, she said, twirling the dark liquid around her glass, the lamplight shining over her shoulder.

Portland ate hungrily. Having been caught in a sudden downpour after parking the car, his hair was wet, his suit collar mottled with rain. He coughed several times, the sound husky, and then leaned back in his seat.

"You should eat something."

"I'm not hungry," she said, studying her husband, smiling back at him. "Sorry."

"For what?"

"Being unreasonable."

Portland leaned towards her, his tanned hands resting on his forearms. "M'lud, we see before us a poor wretch who has found herself caught amongst warring factions –"

She burst into tears suddenly, without making a sound, her eyes closed.

"Sorry …" she said, wretchedly embarrassed.

Portland took the glass of port out of her hand.

"… I'm not drunk …"

"I know."

"I just can't stop thinking how my father must have felt when Drago said all those things," her eyes opened quickly, like a doll hurriedly propped up in a high chair. "How could he talk that way – and in front of him?" her lids dropped again. Portland wondered if the drink was having a lethargic effect on her, or whether she was simply tired. "He never liked my father, never. He was ashamed of him," her voice was vitriolic. "After all he achieved, after supporting Drago through school and University, he *still* despised him." She picked up the glass with her other hand, draining it. Beside them, the logs shuffled on the fire.

Portland wondered if he should suggest staying there overnight, but even as he thought it he knew Misia would want to go on.

"Drago never supported my father, never by a word or a look did he ever seemed

99

proud of him. I hated my brother for that," she touched the side of her forehead as though a headache was imminent. "My father built up an empire from nothing. When he came to Liverpool he had nothing, no money, no family, he was completely alone. You never saw the best of him …" she said, glancing at Portland. Her eyes were luminous. "… when he used to put on the fights, how he used to struggle for the purses, make sure the boxers got their money. He never took on anyone who was punchy, never let anyone fight on too long. I've watched him step into the ring and stand between the boxers himself when the referee wouldn't call a halt," she seemed to see it all again. "The men respected him so much. They knew they'd never get a better manager anywhere. Do you know, when one of his fighters was killed in the war, my father looked after his family? Educated his kids, as well as his own? That was – that IS – the kind of man my father is. You never knew him at his best when he used to take me to the fights with my mother. I grew up in The Roman House. I grew up with the boxers – George Slater, Jem Adler, Ron Poole, Fitting Billy –" she stopped, rubbing her forehead.

"Go on."

"No … it doesn't matter."

"If it matters to you, it matters," Portland said quietly. "Tell me about Fitting Billy."

Another person might have missed it; the start, the almost imperceptible flinch of the muscles.

"He was Ron Poole's brother," she said simply.

"What else?"

"Just that."

"No, there's more."

Misia pushed back her seat, putting space between them; "I'm not in court, Portland, don't try and interrogate me."

"I didn't realise you had anything to hide."

Angrily, Misia got to her feet and stood in front of the fire. They were the only people in the room. A little way away they could hear drinkers talking, but within their few yards, they were alone. Picking up a log, Misia threw it on the fire, but it rolled back to the front of the grate, hanging over the rim precariously. Quickly Portland moved over and pushed it back with his foot; then he stood looking into the fire, Misia beside him.

"I don't want us to have secrets," she said, so quietly that he had to strain to hear her.

"Every man has to have his own secret, just as every man has to have his own grave." Portland remembered Moma telling him that the night before he returned to England to attend University. "Don't ever expect to know everything about anyone," she had gone on: "especially the people you love most. It's bad taste at the least, and dangerous at the worst."

"What is it?" Misia asked, watching him.

"I was thinking of Moma. She does that, you know – pops into my thoughts when I need her," he smiled, then his head bent down towards Misia's, his tone serious. "I don't want to interrogate you any further; because if I did, I might have to find you guilty and then you would been taken away from me," he looked at her intensely for a long moment and then touched her hair. "Do you suppose that when you're old, you'll still have this ridiculous little fringe?"

She laughed softly, moving towards him.

"… I do hope so," he said gently, "I really do hope so."

# Twenty-Four

It was night in London, not yet dawn. Deep in a four o'clock sleep, Drago never moved, his left arm thrown across his eyes, his breathing heavy. It is said that the highest percentage of people die in the hours between three and four in the morning, when the body is at its lowest strength; the pulse slow, the heart rate weak, the temperature cooled. Perhaps it is only a physical phenomenon, or then again, maybe it is more – a nightly rehearsal for death, a ritual opening of a door which is then closed again on waking.

Misia got out of the car first and walked up to the flats, pressing Drago's bell. The street was deserted and across the street, a light shone out above a closed restaurant. Locking the car, Portland moved over to his wife's side, and then knocked loudly.

"He might be out."

She shook her head. "No, I know he's there. My brother was always a heavy sleeper. Knock again."

Drago was dreaming of buying surgical instruments, pristine in their velvet lined cases, shiny and sharp. The man in the shop was ingratiating, flattered by Drago's interest in his wares, his hands pushing forwards more and more leather cases until the top of the counter was covered. In his dream, Drago asked him to stop, but the man kept bringing more and more instruments and piling them so high that they started to fall, making heavy metallic clacks as they hit the marble floor.

"What in God's Name!" Drago snapped, coming awake, the sound of the falling cases beating in time to the sound of the knocking below.

The knocking persisted as he fumbled his way in the dark and threw open the window. "Who's down there?"

"It's your sister. Misia."

"What the hell are you doing here?"

"Open the door, Drago," she called back; "I want to talk to you."

"I can't talk to you now, I have to sleep," he said petulantly. "I have to operate in the morning –"

"OPEN THE BLOODY DOOR, OR I'LL KICK IT IN," Portland shouted, his voice carrying on the still night air.

A moment later Drago was unlocking the downstairs entrance, muttering under his breath, then he turned without a greeting and moved back up the stairs, his silk dressing gown cord trailing the steps behind him.

"I can't think what the hell you're up to," he said, snapping on the light in the lounge and turning to face them. "If you want to stay, I'm sorry, but I don't have enough space," he was moving slowly around the room, as he always did, his heavy lidded eyes darkly shadowed underneath, his stubble dark. In the dim lighting he stood in his black and white dressing gown with his black hair and white skin and seemed to Portland, for one mesmerising instant, like a photograph in a magazine. A bloodless monochrome.

"I want you to apologise –"

"You wake me at some bloody silly time in the morning and you want me to *apologise* to you!" Drago hissed, lowering himself into a chair. Portland wondered if he moved as lethargically in the operating theatre, or if he worked at a different rate, like a film speeded up.

Misia was white with tiredness: "I want you to apologise to our father –"

Drago grinned: "'Who Are in Heaven' – but not quite yet."

She struck him with the flat of her hand, sharply, without either of the men having time to deflect the blow.

"I know why you did it," she said darkly. "You want him dead so that you can forget him, so you can forget the debt you owe him. You look at him even now and know – even now – that you could never match him."

Drago slumped further into his seat. He never touched his face, even though it was obviously burning. It was the only marking of colour about him.

"We've never got on," Drago said warily, "You know that, as does Mother. There's no point pretending my father and I were ever friends. If I went too far, I didn't mean to. I'd had a long drive. Anyway," he said, yawning widely, "Father can't understand anything. He won't have known what I was saying."

Misia was incredulous: "You know he can understand –"

"I'm the doctor!" Drago snapped, "I know more about these things than you do."

"You upset him," she hissed. "And you upset Mother too."

"She's always upset about something," Drago said smoothly, leaning across the table next to him and picking up an apple. As they watched. he bit into it, then chewed.

"I want you to apologise," Misia repeated.

"You can want all you like," Drago said, swallowing the chewed apple, "but I'm not going to. In fact, I'm not going up North again, I'm sick of the place. The city gives me a bad feeling, and that house," he bit off another piece of apple, juice running down his chin, "is just too creepy for words."

"We're wasting our time here," Portland said, taking Misia's arm. "Let's go."

"NO!" she snapped, jerking away. "I haven't finished. I came here to ask you to make amends, Drago. I thought, stupidly, that you might feel some remorse –"

"*Lasciante ogni speranaz voi ch'entrate!*"

"What?" Portland asked, frowning.

"He said: *'All hope abandon, ye who enter here.'*" Misia translated.

"Your Italian's very good," Drago said approvingly. "I often wondered if you'd kept it up."

"Yes. I'm just surprised that you did. I thought you hated everything about your background."

"I hate Liverpool, and the boxers," he responded evenly: "I don't hate Dante."

"But speaking Italian only underlines your foreign blood, Drago," she goaded him. "You should be careful, it won't impress your colleagues."

"*Varium et mutabile semper Femina –*" he raised his eyebrows. "Oh, do you know Latin as well?"

"*A fickle thing and changeful is a woman always.*" Portland translated, standing, arms crossed, by the door. "It's Virgil, and I'm afraid to say that it has little bearing on the matter in hand. Misia is neither fickle nor changeable."

"I would love," Drago said slowly, "to swap the Classics with you, Mr. Benning, but I must sleep. As I've already said, I have to operate later this morning."

Misia was flushed with rage: "You are the most hateful man I've ever known. I can't believe that you're behaving this way. What can you hope to gain by it, Drago?" she asked, leaning towards him, trying valiantly to understand: "You always were a snob, always were ashamed of the boxing −"

"The Roman House!" Drago snorted. "Who *wouldn't* be ashamed of that?"

"I'm not."

He finished his apple in silence, then laid the core in the ashtray next to him. "My dear sister, you and I are completely different. We have nothing in common except our parents. You see nothing wrong in being surrounded by the lowest of the low, you see nothing wrong in helping our mother to promote boxing matches," his voice lifted, incredulity in its tone. "Gossip, scandal, whispers − all mean nothing to you. Why should they? You have nothing to protect. Indeed, you wear your extraordinary position with pride! You seem to genuinely like the boxers, to enjoy mixing with them; their sweat, their injuries, their crude, working class ways." He crossed his legs, swinging his left foot. "You are at home with them. They are comfortable with you because you are comfortable with them," he paused, as though he was sorry to have to say such things. "But I never liked them or found them interesting, amusing or courageous. I do not admire men who batter each other for money. I don't like the smell or the sound of them. I am, as you so rightly said, a snob. I admit it. If that's the worst accusation you can throw at me, it does little to offend. My only crime is to want more from life. I have talent, a gift which can take me far. I intend to use it, to make money with it, to get myself a lifestyle I admire, amongst people I admire." He stopped swinging his foot, his tone was calm, serious, "My father wanted to make something of his life, well, so do I. It's hardly seems fair to blame me for choosing another route."

"Oh, I don't blame you for your ambition, Drago," Misia responded evenly. "I blame you for the price your ambition demands of everyone else. Our parents did everything to help you to succeed − you owe them gratitude, if nothing else," she stood up, towering over her brother. "You consider yourself educated. Well, I'm sorry but you're an ignorant bastard, and you'll pay for your cruelty."

She moved towards Portland, her head rigid, all emotion contained.

"Let's go home," she said simply, and then turned back to her brother, who hadn't moved. "Until you apologise to our parents I don't want to see or hear from you again." She was cold with anger and a sense of terrible loss. "For years I've made allowances for you, Drago. I've stood up for you, made excuses for you, and I've been the constant mediator between you and our parents. I am sick of you, tired of you, exhausted by you − and I can honestly say that you have never brought me any happiness, or offered any affection." She pulled on her gloves, pushing down the leather between her fingers. "I hope you find what you're looking for, and I hope that when you do, you won't discover that you gave away more than you gained."

Languidly, Drago rose to his feet and faced his sister, his hands deep in his pockets.

"That was quite a speech, Misia. Very articulate," he turned to Portland. "She must be picking up some pointers from you," he then turned his heavy lidded eyes back on his sister: "If you were trying to hurt me by your words, you failed. I won't apologise to our parents and I certainly won't ask for forgiveness from you."

She nodded, her eyes bleak: "Then from this moment on, I want to forget you, to see and hear nothing from you. I no longer consider you my brother."

Drago expression was unreadable: *"Non ragionim di lor, ma guarda, e passa,"* he said simply, turning away as Portland and Misia moved towards the door.

The air was depressing cold, the night coming thick and full of shadows. As they stood on the street outside, Misia felt her eyes fill and brushed at them hurriedly with the back of her hand. She hoped, and yet feared, that Drago would follow her, would somehow try to mend the fences they had so effectively shattered. But he didn't – and she knew then that he never would. Pride would stop him. He would climb without looking back, his eyes ever fixed on the sumptuous future the world held out for him.

The light still burned in Drago's bedroom overhead as Misia's thoughts went back. Another light, burning in another bedroom, well into the night. The house by the park, where Drago had studied and kept to his rooms. Then she thought of him as she had seen him once, coming in from swimming, his hair wet, his eyes alert. He had been, in that one clicking of time, the potent image of the brother she had wanted. He had freshness, humour, shaking his head like a dog, his laugh cracking in the early morning air. *That* was the Drago she admired; that damp limbed youth full of excitement, without affectation or cruelty. She had loved him that day.

But as though he had smashed it, or torn it, or burnt it, that picture of Drago had vanished. And nothing would ever call it back.

Gently, Portland put his arm around her. "What did he say when we left?"

Her voice wavered. "He said – "*'let us not speak of them, but look and pass on.'"*

"Give it time. In time all this will blow over, arguments always do."

She turned, looking at her husband with astonishment. "Oh no, Portland. This was the end."

# Twenty-Five

"So I said, what the blah-dee hell do you expect?" Alberto laughed, his head rigid, his shoulders jiggling with mirth. He had been well fed and was glowing warmly like a good angel under the candlelight, Misia leaning towards him, smiling. He stopped laughing and lit another cigarette, his pock-marked skin briefly illuminated as he leaned for a light towards the nearest candle. Some people, she realised, come into your life without any marker; they are simply there; have always seemed to be there; and without them, there would be an emptiness impossible for another to fill.

Silently, Alberto leaned back. No other man had ever enjoyed comfort as he did. Well fed, well wined, and well amused, he was at that instant, enjoying the silence of true contentment. Bespectacled Alberto de Brio, forty years of age, originally come over from Naples to study with Drago, a friend of both brother and sister. It was an achievement few could emulate; but he loved them both, and so, in his extraordinary way, he saw no hindrance to either friendship. He also knew that neither of them would ask him to make a choice between them, or press for details of the other, or beg for him to intercede for them.

He was safe and rewarded both of them by relating items of news, pieces of gossip or important events, always slid innocently into the conversation, his Italian accent only apparent in the occasional word:

"… so the nurse passed me the instrument and then howled, dropping it and bleeding all over the place. Poor baby. Of course, Drago would have banished her for that. He's happier, I think, in Italy. Rome has the climate for him. This nurse, though, I have to tell you, this bloody nurse has the face of a Carracci whore."

So Drago was now in Rome, Portland thought, refilling Alberto's glass and glancing over to Misia. Her face was as tranquil as a summer pond. She had given birth to Simeon early that summer, Mary coming over to help and staying for several week in the house they had bought on the outskirts of Liverpool. Not a spectacular house, but made fascinating by the accumulation of Portland's collection of legal prints and the imposing bulk of Indian furniture he inherited from Moma. Bewildering carved cabinets flanked ebony chairs, vast screens separating rooms and throwing webbed patterns in the sunlight, a series of graduating copper bowls filled with a plethora of tea roses. He could not sell anything that reminded him of India, so every silver sheaved knife and each piece of metal encrusted pottery was found a home, a massive portrait of Moma hanging over the fireplace in the dining room.

"You know," Alberto said, his hand running over the back of his chair, "the best ivory furniture has ivory inlay – sea ivory, not elephant ivory."

"Where do you get ivory from the sea?" Misia asked, drowsy with food, fine strands of hair clinging to her moist neck. The night was steamy.

"From walruses," Alberto said, waving his hands up and down like the creature making its way through the waves. "It's much the best, you know, because it never goes yellow." His fingers, tapering elegantly at the tips, ran over the ivory again. "I believe that ivory is called 'angel's teeth' it's so lovely."

Misia smiled sleepily and leaned back in her chair. Overheard they could hear the footsteps of Miss Gurney, the nanny, her feet moving idly from the nursery to her room on the top floor: and from the road outside a car braked as it rounded the bend. It was nearly eleven o'clock, the candles unmoving in the hot night, the light shimmering on the waste remains of fruit.

"Cosmetic surgery is the up and coming thing," Alberto went on. "But not like that English aristocrat who went over to Paris and had her nose injected," Listening, Misia smiled dreamily, "and the solution melted, made wattles under her chin." He sipped his wine, a drop lingered for an instant on his bottom lip. "I mean, the real future is in fine cosmetic surgery – surgery to make women heavenly."

"Women are already heavenly," Portland said, glancing at Misia and smiling that slow smile that comes when the light begins to fail and the loved one senses, rather than sees, the gesture.

"But plain women could be made magnificent."

"I'm not sure that the world is ready for perfection in everyone," Portland teased, suddenly serious. "Besides, there's so much else going on, Alberto. There's huge unemployment in England, especially up here, and it's spreading. In Glasgow, fifteen jobless men were injured when they clashed with police. It can only get worse. How can you think a woman's beauty matters with so much trouble in the world?"

"I think," Alberto said evenly, "that I have a duty to be frivolous. You talk about politics, Portland, but I don't want to think about such things. In this serious world of ours, with all its threats, there is also a lighter side. 'King Kong' was premiered in New York the other month, I saw it when I was over there."

"You went to America?" Misia asked, intrigued. "What was it like?"

"Some man had just tried to shoot Roosevelt, but he missed – so a little girl called Shirley Temple was on the cover of every magazine instead." He turned to Portland, "So much for your theories. People, unfortunately, have a natural disinclination to worry. They want to bury their fears – so they drown themselves in trivia." He whirled his wine round in his glass. "Some of us – however unworthy you think it, Portland, – have a duty to preserve beauty."

"For the rich."

Alberto was not to be provoked. He touched his left eyebrow with his finger and then turned to look out of the window.

"If I gave away everything I had, in a day no one would remember my fabulous generosity. But if I create something beautiful people can look at it, and admire it, and be moved by it, time after time after time. Real beauty kidnaps the imagination; it magics its way into the soul and lodges there in perpetua …" his voice was warm; it fluted on the still night. "I don't have the talent Drago has; I follow, copy," he breathed in then made a soft 'Oooooh' sound. Outside, a bird answered unexpectedly in the darkness. "I watch great talent and it makes me feel whole, truly alive. This is not an original thought, many others have experienced the same sensation, the admiration of the creation of beauty – 'He must be a god, or a painter, because he creates faces'."

"Shakespeare," Portland said, looking towards Misia.

She had cocked her head over to one side, listening. Far away, she could make out the faint sound of a baby crying, but it wasn't Simeon, and after another moment she relaxed, her chin resting on her cupped hand.

"But Alberto," she said softly, chiding him. "You love the boxing, you know you do."

"But that has a beauty of its own," he replied, taking off his glasses. His light hazel eyes were yellow as a cat's in the candlelight. "It has the beauty of two men, superbly fit, pitted against each other –"

"– and then mutilated."

"PORTLAND!" Misia said, feigning outrage. "How could you?" her head cocked over to the side again and then she stood up. "I think it's the baby," she said simply, "I'll be back soon."

Alberto watched her go, waiting until the door closed before turning to Portland: "This feud, is it really serious?"

He nodded, leaning back in his seat and nodding. "I thought it would burn out, these things usually do, but it's as bitter a battle as it was when it started."

"You know Drago got married?"

Portland leaned towards him; "No, when?"

"Last week."

"Bloody hell," Portland replied, "He never told Misia, or contacted their parents … who did he marry?"

"A woman called Catherine Clark," Alberto replied, "Her father is very wealthy, I believe."

Portland's expression was bland; his court face, giving nothing away. "Do you know her?"

"I've met her," Alberto replied, putting his glasses on again and looping the wire behind his ears. "She's a wistful, timid creature, not at all what anyone would expect. I think – I could be wrong – but I think she loves Drago too much to be happy."

Portland stared out of the window at the end of the room. He thought of Drago on the last occasion he had seen him, in a black and white dressing gown. Coldly unemotional, his flat clinically tidy.

"What about Drago – does he care for her?"

Alberto picked at the half eaten peach on his plate and then slowly and carefully he began to scrape the flesh off the discarded skin.

"He trusts her."

"Meaning?"

"Meaning that she will never become too clever, too demanding, or too judgemental. Meaning," Alberto continued, "that she has nothing of his mother, or his sister, in her."

"Then one can only hope he'll die of boredom," Portland replied wryly, getting to his feet and putting a record on the gramophone. A soft, drowsy jazz tune soon hummed on the listless air.

"You don't like him, do you?" Alberto asked, looping his arm over the back of his chair as he turned to his host.

"I can only judge by what I've seen of Drago, and what I know of him."

"A barrister's answer!" Alberto said chidingly. "Tell me the truth. Tell me what you feel."

Portland heavy features broke into a massive smile; "Italians always want to know what you *feel*," he replied, rubbing the back of his neck with his left hand. "Moma used to tell me to never reveal my feelings when I was asked – unless I was sure they were in line with the questioner's." He laughed, the room was slapped awake with the noise. "She said it – but she never lived up to it. She told everyone a story and had a different version each time; sometimes the chief character was a man, sometimes a woman. She thought it kept her anecdotes fresh." He looked up at the painting over the fireplace. "She was not beautiful at all, Alberto. Your skills would have been put to the test with her, I can tell you – and yet she was unforgettable."

"Strange, isn't it? The women we chose to love?"

Portland turned. "No, we chose a woman to provide the missing part of ourselves."

"So what were you missing?"

Portland tapped his foot in time to the music, smiling: "A family."

Alberto lit up another cigarette and kept his eyes averted: "Nothing more?"

"A sense of reason. I had no reason to be, to think, to feel. I am," he smiled with embarrassment, "an emotional man, and yet there was never an outlet. I felt, especially as I got older, that emotions felt and never expressed, never shared, were somehow dangerous," he sighed. "I can never express myself properly. Ask me to defend someone and I can articulate every thought with precision and sway a jury until they would let the man go and hang the judge instead – but ask me about myself and I fall at the first fence."

"But you know your worth."

"Oh yes," Portland said, "I know that I wasn't put here just to make up the numbers. And I don't say that with conceit. That's why, up to a point, I could understand Drago. He knew he had ability, but he couldn't separate his talent from his life. It was a choice for him – and he chose to forfeit his emotional security."

"Until now," Alberto said softly.

"Maybe," Portland replied. "But I don't think any woman who marries Drago Razzio marries a man. She will marry a force, an ambition, but not a real man. Drago forbids intimacy."

"Spoken like an Italian!" Alberto said, giving Portland a slow hand clap. "I wish Misia had the same judgement."

"Her judgement ceased the moment Drago turned his back on their parents," Portland said, "they will feud until they die, Alberto. You and I both know that."

Silence fell between them, and a moment later, the record drew to its close.

# Twenty-Six

Lenny Davis was sparring, his head ducked down, his chin tucked into his chest. A large throbbing bump bulged over his left eyebrow, his nose running as he dodged the next blow from Louis Mills. Things were not going his way; he had been knocked out in his last fight and now he was been looked over for some newcomer. The fist landed on the side of his head and made his chin snap back.

"You dozing up there, boy?" Nat drawled, bending over the ropes. "You tired of living?"

Lenny threw a quick punch and missed as Louis ducked.

"Call yourself a boxer? You couldn't hit the side of a cow with that punch."

Lenny stopped fighting. Breathing hard, he spat out his gum shield and walked over to the trainer.

Blank faced, Nat saw him coming. "I sure hope you can talk better than you can box."

"I can't do anything with you muttering on and on –"

"Hey boys!" Nat called, his voice echoing round The Roman House. "We have here a boy who's hearing is somewhat sensitive," he leaned across the ropes and tweaked Lenny's right ear. "We have here a delicate boy, a boy who does not like SHOUTING!" his voice roared, making Lenny wince. "Now, you look here, son, if you don't move your ass and start making some effort, you are in trouble. You are in trouble with *me*. You hear me, boy?"

Burning with fury, Lenny nodded.

"I am *so* glad that you and I have had this little talk. Now, get back in there and earn your keep."

"Problems?"

Nat turned, startled by the voice at his shoulder. "No, Mrs. Razzio, no trouble at all."

She folded her arms and watched the fighters, her black eyes steady. Guido had had a bad night, waking breathless, his breathing coming fast, his eyes closed long after ten. She had called for the doctor, but there had been little to report. Just a cold, he said, you had to expect this kind of thing now and then ... But he had been making so much progress, Mary had replied, he was even able to talk a little now.

A miracle had occurred. Years after the stroke, Guido had started to say a few words again. Mary had not believed her ears at first, and then she had turned and seen Guido's eyes wide open, and his lips moving, and she had run over to the bed and placed her ear against his mouth. His breath was hard, expelled hurriedly out of his lungs, the word coming short, urgent.

"Mary."

That was all; but it was enough. He had said her name after eleven years of silence. After eleven years in the bedroom which never changed, just let the seasons pass by the window. Snow, leaves falling, the first cuckoo come loud into the room when the window was lifted on a late Spring day. Dreaming, sleeping, being, living, Guido had laid in his bed for eleven years, turned like a corpse, cleaned like an infant, nursed and loved, and stroked in the long nights when he needed comfort.

And now he was speaking again, the delicate, tantalising communication which she had believed gone forever, opening up. Talk to me … she said, leaning towards him, seeing herself reflected in his eyes. Tell me about where you've been …

"Travelling," he said at last.

Four weeks it took him, but he said it. Travelling.

Where? she asked, laughing like a girl at the side of the bed. Where?

She missed the next word. Took her a week to interpret it, to shake the sense out of it. *Travelling home.*

Mary had gone to the libraries and the book shops then, getting everything she could on Italy, propping the books in front of Guido and watching his face. Expressionless to anyone else, it was readable to her, each tiny inflection, minute flicker, infinitesimal expression in his eyes telling her, guiding her. She turned the pages, pulling the lamp closer to the bed, the yellow light falling on the photographs of Rome and Florence, the script read and re-read, mentally dog-eared. He listened, she knew that, and when Misia came by with the new baby Mary watched her husband's face avidly. On the bed, Simeon lay beside his grandfather in the still room; the hot summer day coming in noisy with birds and the drone of a hungry bee on the window ledge. The child lay silent, his head turning slowly towards his Guido, his hands waving idly in the steaming air.

"… baby …"

*"What?"* Misia said, bending towards her father and then glancing back to Mary excitedly. "Dear God, did he say something? Did he?" she dropped onto her knees by the bed, her face on a level with Guido's. "Papa, talk to me. Say something. Papa?"

Mary watched him, her face expressionless, although her eyes were moist. It was too soon, she knew that, too soon for words and movement, but in time there would be both. In time Guido Razzio would come back to life and back to her. She pressed her hands together, her heart banging nervously.

"Guido, this is your grandson," she said, then leaned down towards Simeon: "And this is your grandfather – the bravest man who ever breathed," she touched the baby's head briefly. "You must live up to him," she said fiercely. "You must bring him back to life."

It seemed as though the child did; as though Simeon's birth re-activated something in Guido. In reality, it was just a wakening of resolve, a slow physical re-mergence, coupled with a phenomenal will, which dragged Guido back a little way into life. He listened as he had always done, but now he offered hints of his opinions when Mary talked about the boxers. A jerk of the head, a slow flicker in the fingers of his left hand.

"He'll never fully recover," the doctor said, "he might get a little more movement in his hand and some more speech, but you can't expect more. He's not a young man, after all."

Only sixty one, Mary thought, looking coldly at the doctor. How old are you? She dismissed what he said with irritation. Guido Razzio wasn't an ordinary man, he was the man who took a beating the whole of Liverpool knew about; the man who fought for his men and for his country. Guido Razzio was a legend, and legends had their own way of living.

From then on, Mary moved Guido out of his bed daily, propping him up in a wicker chair by the window, so that he could look out onto the garden and the park beyond. He could see the baby too, Simeon put out in his pram on the lawn, Misia running to the gate when Portland came home at the weekends. Other people began to visit. Alberto climbing up the stairs and sitting next to Guido, talking easily and endlessly about plastic surgery, the movies, the state of women's fashions; and he smoked, hanging out of the window, his glasses glinting blindly in the sunlight, his fingers picking at the peeling paint.

He never mentioned Drago; but he told Guido about the fights Misia had invited him too, and about the state of Italy: one afternoon lapsing into Italian by accident and then turning to see the expression in Guido's eyes. It was a look of hunger, a need to hear his own language spoken – so from then onwards Alberto came to visit with a copy of Dante or Boccaccio, his voice fanning out as he read their words, skimming through the summer windows and into the Liverpool air outside.

When Alberto returned from London he came back with records, Italian operas played loudly into the evening hours, Mary watching Guido for his reaction.

"He loves this part."

"Does he?" Alberto asked. "You remembered?"

"No," she replied calmly. "He's just told me."

The three of them listened to the music, Mary closing the curtains as the night came down, her hands making scuffing noises as she straightened the cushions behind her husband's back, her gold bracelet catching momentarily against the wicker seat. Guido sat rigid, his head heavy on the pillow, his hair growing awkwardly at the crown from years of being bedridden. When another person was there, Mary was composed, almost distant with Guido. Their affection was expressed only when they were alone.

"Here, just here, listen to that note …" Alberto enthused, waving his right hand around, the long grey line of smoke making for the ceiling above. "… enough to make you cry," he paused at the end of the aria, his slight body turned towards Guido, the collar of his shirt undone. "I come from Naples, and there they sing traditional songs …" There was no response from Guido; only the same still, bewitching stare.

Ah, but in his head, behind the stare, Guido was hearing his own music, music heard as a child, coming down warm streets with the dew on it. His father's music, whistled in the garden, accompanying his father's shadow, down the long stretch of grass. Notes, pauses, each well known, repeated phrases welcome as a breeze against his face. He remembered the birds too – then thought of Jack Dudley and his boys, and the way he had fed his macaw that day in the hotel in Liverpool, and the crescent shadow of the lemon slice falling as a black silhouette on the bottom of the cage.

"I saw Lenny Davis fight the other day," Alberto went on.

Guido's eyes turned to Mary: "You remember, Bryn's nephew?"

He remembered.

"… he's not sparky enough to win."

"He could be a good fighter," Mary replied, "but he hasn't the heart for it. He just wants to make money. To be well known."

Guido breathed in; he just wants to make money. Was that all there was – money and ambition? He smiled, the gesture edging at the sides of his mouth. He felt, rather than saw, Mary watching him. See me, see how I smile. You remember don't you? How ill I was that time; that time you came to Cranberry Street and nursed me and read to me, and then married me. What happened to No. 14 Cranberry Street? Guido wondered suddenly. Was it still empty, the only house no one, no matter how desperate, would live in? Was old Jack Holland's daughter haunting the kitchen still, waiting at the top of the stairwell? Creating her own little hell there; and was the house still dark and cold in amongst the warm homes of its neighbours?

Misia broke into his thoughts, coming into the room laughing, Simeon in her arms. "He wanted to see you," she said, putting the baby on her father's lap. "He misses you," her voice was light as she turned to Alberto. "You smoke too much, you'll be ill."

"I smoke to forget," he said extravagantly.

"Another broken romance?" Misia asked, sitting on the side of the bed, facing Alberto and her father.

"I have no luck with women," Alberto said, scratching his chin. "Who would marry a doctor?"

The question was innocent but it faltered, staggered, amongst them like someone mortally wounded. Automatically Misia glanced away, Mary looking at her husband as Alberto continued artlessly:

"Now if I was a barrister, I could have my pick of the most beautiful women in the country. Although I can't imagine why Portland leaves you up here all week on your own."

Good humour restored, Misia hauled Alberto to his feet and pushed him to the door. "Leave them alone for a while," she said, glancing back to her mother. "Look after Simeon for me, will you? I'll be back soon."

At the bottom of the stairs she stopped, tugging Alberto into the drawing room. The French windows – where Fitting Billy had been killed – were dark, the garden a shadow landscape outside. The scent of dust and lavender was suddenly overpowering.

"Drago got married."

Alberto nodded, lighting another cigarette. The tip glowed in the darkness.

"He never told us," Misia went on, her voice changed, sharp with anger. "He never told anyone. I think my parents would liked to have known."

"Misia," Alberto said, his face indistinct, his voice coming disembodied, remote. "You began the feud and Drago and you have continued it – how can I do anything to help you when you won't help yourselves?"

"You care for him."

He nodded. His head was a dark blur, without features. "Yes, and I care for you," he replied.

"I wondered if you if you would talk to him …" Misia stopped, dismissing the idea furiously. "No, don't! It would do no good, I don't know why I mentioned it. It was just that hearing about his marriage I wondered … He has a wife now and before long, children …" she turned, the movement was a shuffle in the semi-dark. "I wondered if he might have changed."

"No," Alberto said simply. "He's the same as he always was. Arrogant." He leaned against the back of the leather settee, his voice low. "Believe me, I understand how you feel, Misia. Perhaps I would have behaved in the same way as you did. I don't know, but you've made Drago into a monster a villain, without morals, scruples, honour –"

"He *behaved* without honour," she retorted hotly. "You have no idea how much he upset my parents. I'm sure my father's stroke worsened because of Drago's behaviour. He was cruel –"

"And yet he has feelings. He cares for his patients," Alberto interjected. "He's cold, unemotional. Yes, but he's the one who stays up at night to sit with someone distressed; he's the one who bullies the hospital administration into investing more finance into the care of the terminally sick. He has no sense of family, Misia, no sense of warmth. He cares by proxy; for patients, for people to whom he has no blood tie; for people who can never ask anyone of him other than professionally; for people to whom he owes *nothing*." Alberto walked to the French windows and opened them, flicking some cigarette ash onto the ground outside. "I've known Drago for sixteen years, and in all that time I've never been shown any kindness by him." He turned back to her, a talking silhouette. "But I've learnt how his kindness is expressed in his skill. I've watched his surgery, at first general operations, and then later, the beginnings of his work in plastic surgery. Men and women – grotesquely burned or mutilated – have gone to him, and he has helped them."

He waved his hand as though he was dismissing any contradiction: "I know other doctors say he experimented on some of his cases. He did, all doctors do. He didn't see them as people, only cases, patients." Alberto paused. "But does that mean he *didn't* help them? Perhaps we ask too much of our remarkable men, Misia. Drago is cruel, yes; he is pedantic, fastidious, obsessive, mean spirited, yes. But he's also remarkable."

"So is my father."

"Your father had the good fortune to marry your mother when he was young. He also had the advantage of being able to forgive," Alberto replied. "Drago is incapable of that – I have seen him react to a word or a phrase by shutting a person out completely. He might have been talking to them normally before, and then there is a closing off, a total rejection. A hateful, wounding abandonment. He hurts randomly, without thinking, but he hurts himself more." Alberto paused, again flicking ash on to the ground outside the French doors. In the distance a cat mewled softly. "He has no friends in the medical world, because he is afraid that they will steal his secrets, and he has no friends outside that world because he's contemptuous of the common herd –"

"You're his friend, Alberto, and you're in the medical world."

He laughed, pushed back his hair with one hand; it stuck up for a moment in silhouette and gave him the look of a startled bird.

"Drago has nothing to fear from me. We can be friends because I'm superficial, light hearted, the fool to his King Lear."

"You think so well of him," Misia said, her tone brusque. "He doesn't deserve it."

"I agree," Alberto replied, "but in time, if and when he finds power, Drago might become the man we both suspect he is. Someone who's no stranger to goodness."

"And you think his wife might affect this sea change?" Misia asked sarcastically, folding her arms.

"No, I don't think *she* will, but I think – I hope – a child might."

The silence fell over them again, complete and chilling. Misia watched him and then walked over to him, standing by the windows, looking out.

"Why the talk of a wife and family, Alberto?" she asked gently. "Do you want this for yourself?"

He laughed. The sound came out with his breath, warm, smelling of wine.

"I *am* married, my love."

She was shaken. "But you never said anything –"

"My wife is in Italy and we live apart. We love apart too," he said, throwing the cigarette butt through the windows. "I was very young when I married her, very poor, and she was very afraid of being a spinster. We married out of compassion; she for my poverty, me for her loneliness. She supported me through medical school and now we sleep together three times a year – in Naples."

"Oh, Alberto," Misia said smiling. "You really are terribly amoral, aren't you?"

He turned to look at her, the last of the light catching his glasses and giving him a sudden, sinister look.

"That is why I can understand Drago – and that is why I can tell you that he is not as sinful as he seems. I cover my tracks very carefully, Misia, to appear as I do. But inside there is nothing in my heart. It is a muscle, no more. And inside my soul there is a vacuum no one can fill."

The confession caught Misia off guard, but almost instantly Alberto was back in character. Smiling, he glanced up to the floor overhead: "I think your baby's calling for you."

She hurried to the door.

"Remember what I said, Misia," Alberto called after her.

She paused, her hand pressed against the wood. "Which part?"

He seemed surprised when he answered her: "About Drago. Who else were we talking about?"

# Twenty-Seven

**Four years later**
**1937 – London**
**Holland Park**

Nathaniel Nayton was a trainer with a mission. Absorbed with the gradual progress in Guido's condition, Mary was preoccupied for much of the time, and Misia, now the mother of three sons, spent most of her time at home. The house in Liverpool was retained, but now the family spent most of their time in Holland Park, Misia travelling up to Liverpool once a week to keep an eye on The Roman House. She needed to; Nat was a good trainer, but not capable of running the business, and Mary was having difficulties in finding a second trainer as good as Morrie Gilling.

The old order had gone; all the best known trainers were in London, and only a handful remained up North. Mary's grip (which had been formidable) was slipping, her appetite for the fight game reduced. She had made no conscious decision to draw back but Guido needed her; needed her company and her encouragement. The fighters did not. Or so it seemed.

So when Misia received a phone call whilst she nursed her third son, Vincent, she was totally unprepared for the conversation.

"We're losing our grip," Mary said, without any preliminaries.

Misia passed the baby to Miss Gurney. "What?"

"The Roman House isn't what it was. I don't like Nat Nayton in total charge and I don't trust Lenny Davis. We only held four fights this year, and the boxers are getting sullen and restless." Mary paused, her voice sharp. "Your father didn't build up this business just to let it go downhill. I feel I've failed him."

"Hold on for a moment," Misia said, gripping the phone. "You might be looking on the dark side –"

"I'm not!" her mother snapped. "If you'd been a boy, things would have been different. Don't misunderstand me, Misia, I'm not criticising you, you have a husband and a family, they have to come first. But to see the business faltering …" she took in a breath, trying to keep her voice low. "It's too much to bear. I do what I can, but I've been at fault, giving your father too much attention."

"I'm coming – "

"Don't be stupid!" Mary snapped. "What good would that do? We need a manager, a proper promoter, here, not a part timer. You can't have a family and run the boxers. It's not possible."

Misia was unreasonably annoyed. What was her mother actually saying? That the glory days were gone, that everything Guido Razzio had done and worked for, was dying? What that what was to happen to The Roman House? Left to drop into a ruin, the roof leaking, the old ring rotted, the fading poster of Bryn Davis left to peel off the walls? Was that to be the result of one man's dream? To see it decay before died?

Misia thought of her childhood; her cot laid across the seats in sight of the ring; her days with George Slater, and Fitting Billy, come silly in his costumes, to play with her. No more checking their hands, talking to the doctors, no more worrying about purses, about competitors, rival managers, rival fighters, rival cities. No more running to the printers with posters to be ready quickly …

*I need it for next week.*

*Too late.*

*Do me this favour, please. We have to have it tomorrow …*

And the smells, the scent of the crowd filling the hall in The Roman House; the sight of dressing gowns hanging on the back of doors, and the discarded gloves of a boxer who had lost.

Was *that* what it was for? The death of Mick Leary, of Bryn Davis? The war? The loss of George Slater, Ron Poole – all the good men gone, and what was left to stand as a tribute to them? Only the Razzio empire, which they believed would last forever. They had been caught up in an immigrant's dream, seeing a way of making money for their families, and more, a way of earning respect. They were proud to be Guido Razzio's men, proud to stand up in the ring and know that they were well managed, well thought of, well known. It had been a dirt track idea, and Guido Razzio had turned it into a mark of respect which each of them had prized. He had taken ignorant, brutish men and turned them into gladiators, and he had started a empire to see it flourish. Not to see it fold within his own lifetime.

Misia had given birth to three sons – Simeon, Harewood and Vincent. The Benning Brothers. In the next generation there would be men to carry on her father's work, a ready made continuance of the line. There was only a short period during which someone had to keep the empire afloat; to stand in as a Regent, until the baby King – which ever of the sons it was – could claim his throne.

"I'm coming up," Misia repeated. "Miss Gurney can look after the boys for a few days."

"But what about Portland?"

Misia smiled. Portland had wanted a wife and family, but he had been prepared to accept them on any terms. He had no need for conventions of any sort. It was not difficult for him to adjust to the fact that he and his wife lived apart. What other men would have found intolerable, he did not. In fact, he liked the time he spent alone when he could concentrate on his work; and he liked the time he spent with his family, when he could give his full attention to their needs. Misia and Portland did not think it odd that, as their family extended, they still lived separate lives, one in London and the other in Liverpool – it seemed a perfect solution. Portland's work was in London; hers was in Liverpool.

"… but it's not as though her work is important," Cyril Maxwell said to one of his colleagues at the Inns of Court. "Admittedly Misia used to run those boxers," he hedged around the word as though it might strike out at him. "… but now she's got children, she has to see things in a different light. I really can't think what Portland's up to. After all, is boxing really something you would want to brag about?"

Leamington overheard the conversation, his hands behind his back, his undershot jaw jutting forward. He didn't like Cyril Maxwell and knew that he owed his position in chambers to a favour procured by his father, not by his own abilities. Leamington had thought for some time that Mr. Maxwell should have his wings clipped, and that Mr. Benning should have more of a chance, and had assiduously succeeding in recommending Portland in preference to Maxwell. But this new piece of gossip aggravated him.

He thought that Maxwell was a whiney old fool, and his dislike dated back to the day he had overheard Maxwell referring to his four unmarried daughters as 'the Hapsburg Harpies'. The insult had gone deep and had swelled to gigantic proportions over the ensuing years. And now Maxwell was trying to discredit Portland, using a poisonous word here and there to pollute the bloodstream gradually, working his bile into the system to ensure a certain, if slow, death. Portland had a odd family life, Portland was eccentric, Portland wasn't the kind of colleague they were used to … Leamington could see it all with blistering clarity. They would band together and try to edge Portland out, and in his eccentric place would come another Maxwell automata.

Or so he thought … Leamington might only be a clerk, but he had seen the comings and going of the chambers for years and was quite certain that the best interests of all could only be served by keeping Portland Benning. So when Portland told him that Misia was going back to Liverpool for a while, Leamington was intrigued.

"Oh yes, sir, why is that?"

"Business," Portland said, pushing a brief across the table towards the clerk.

"I was saying to my second daughter only yesterday and she agreed with me that when women got the vote the whole world opened up for them. Take your wife, sir, look at the amazing life she has. Her sons – your sons – are flourishing and she runs the boxers too," he sniffed. "Lunch as usual?"

Portland nodded. "Lunch as usual," he agreed, then added: "I'm going to need your help, Leamington."

"You've got it, sir, you know that."

"My life might get a little complicated – and I would be grateful for any assistance you could give to me. I fully back my wife, you know that. But for a while she is going to be very committed to her father's business." He leaned back, crossing his legs. "She sees herself as a holder of the crown – until my sons are old enough to take over. She feels responsible for her father's dream. To hold it in trust, so to speak."

Leamington was moved by the confidence placed in him, and coughed slightly. "Like the new King, isn't it, sir?" he asked, "The outside runner coming in to save the day."

Portland smiled. "Yes, something very like that. My wife has a very strong sense of duty, and although she thinks she will only be involved for a while, I believe that she once she returns she'll never be able to give up her role. Until, as I say, one of our sons takes it on."

"Hold old are they now, sir?"

"Simeon's four, Harewood's two and Vincent's only a baby," Portland thought of the three boys; Simeon sickly and prone to solitude, Harewood protective and proprietorial, and Vincent, ah, Vincent …

Portland had never seen a baby come into the world laughing; he would not have believed it possible, except that the doctor told him Vincent came into the light – and grinned. Not a burpy smile, he insisted, an outright grin. He had grinned on and off ever since. Smiling out of his cot and his pram, his hair curly around his face, a burly pair of hands waving above his head.

"A fighter, by God," Portland had said, looking at him.

"A bruiser," Misia had answered, laughing.

Vincent was her favourite; he was everyone's favourite. Harewood might look solemnly at the new arrival and Simeon might stand warily beside his cot, but Vincent was without fear even then.

"He's been here before," Miss Gurney said firmly.

Really, Portland thought, was reincarnation true? He doubted it, always had, but something was terribly familiar about this baby's face, something mischievous, some lurking adult stuck in the mess of feed and nappies.

"Bloody hell," he said one night when he had been looking at his new son. "He reminds me of Moma!"

They had both looked at him again. And there it was; the unmistakable expression, the diabolical sense of ease with the world. Portland could, in that instant, see his son grown up, telling stories, eating lustily, his voice coming out with all the confidence of someone who knew they would be listened to. He would be thick set, massively boned, bearing the unmistakable brand of the Bennings.

He had would be the outside runner they were waiting for. Simeon was the delicate boy, the one likely to feel every pain of the world. Harewood would be serious, hard working: a lawyer in his pram. But Vincent – he was going to roll into his place in the world, fall into situations, pick himself up and laugh like one of God's angels at his own folly. He was the one. *He* was the one.

# Twenty-Eight

Misia arrived at The Roman House the following day, walking in to find Nat smoking in the gym, Louis Hills lounging against the corner post of the ring. The place had a lost and losing air about it, Lenny Davis reading a paper whilst Dan Whistler hummed softly as he strung on his gloves. None of them seemed interested, none of them seemed like boxers out to win. They looked and acted like amateurs – and when Nat saw her he jumped to his feet, startled.

"Hey, there, Mrs. Benning, how goes it?"

She moved past him into the hall beyond. The smell of dust met her, together with the dead odour of neglect. The Roman House, she realised with despair, was nothing more than a seedy, Northern relic, a pit-stop on the way to greater things. What had once been a land mark, a place of pilgrimage, had faded into a greasy no man's land. No one had swept the floor, no one had cleaned the windows. No one had checked the bathhouse and seen that the toilets – put in at such expense – were scrubbed. They smelt of urine, the tiles cracked, and from the storeroom came the unmistakable odour of mice.

It was not her mother's fault; Mary was getting older and her time was better spent with her father. She had tried to safeguard the place, but her loyalties had been divided, and much as she respected her husband's achievements, Mary wanted to spend whatever time was left with him, not at The Roman House. Dispirited, Misia walked around, putting out her foot and prodding an old punch bag which had been thrown to one side in a corner.

Then she moved back into the gym.

"Louis, come here."

The fighter walked over to her, embarrassed. What in God's name had happened to him? Misia wondered. The thin, long limbed boxer who used to jump over the ropes to get into the ring, then pause, his white head and white lashed eyes cast down in prayer before a match, his voice coming over strong, begging, pleading God to wreak havoc on his opponents. 'Louis Mills Kills' had been his slogan, the chant going up before every fight.

MILLS KILLS!

MILLS KILLS!

And now he was shambling in front of her. Shame-faced, white as a sugar mouse. Pitiful.

"You look pathetic," she said simply. "Why aren't you training?"

"I've been ill."

She turned to Nat: "Is that true?"

The American nodded.

"Okay, what about Dan? DAN!" she called out to him. "Come over her." He walked over, arrogant, his head high, his eyes sullen. "What's your story?"

"What d'you mean?"

"MRS. BENNING!" she snapped. "What do you mean, Mrs. Benning." She paused, then leaned out and touched his arm, "What are these?"

"Arms."

Louis Mills sniggered softly beside him.

"The tattoos, was what I meant," Misia said quietly.

She was stunned by their reaction to her presence. No welcome, no respect, no affectionate remembrance of her or her father. In her childhood she had always felt safe amongst the boxers – but not now, now she felt threatened. The were not evil men, merely idle, indulgent and weak willed, but they unnerved her and she was determined not to show for an instant that she was afraid.

"You didn't have tattoos before, Dan."

"I wasn't married before."

Misia nodded; she had heard that he had married a woman with two children; she was a dancer, so the story went, mixed-race, come over from America two years earlier. Misia had seen her once, standing smoking a cigarette in St. George's Square at around ten at night. A dancer? she thought not.

"You're out of condition," Misia said coldly. "You had a great future, Dan, what happened?"

He shrugged, then turned as Lenny Davis walked over. He was a cocky as he had ever been, and as rude as he dared. His dream of marrying Misia and inheriting The Roman House and everything that went with it had been scotched. Misia Razzio had never even noticed him. Instead she had married some barrister, some ugly bastard come up from the Smoke. All his visions of an easy future had disappeared, all his memories of a younger Misia had been usurped by this composed young woman the woman who now wanted to tell *him* what to do. Lenny had fantasised about them being partners, but she had come back as the boss – and he hated her for it.

"Things are looking bad," he said, with a note of triumph in his voice, "we can't seem to get the fights the way we used to."

Nat shot him a granite look. "It's true that things have been a little slow, but they'll pick up —-"

"They will, now that I'm back in charge." Misia stared into their faces, standing her ground in front of the four men. "I give you two weeks to get into shape, and if you're not ready, you can look for someone else to promote you."

"But –"

"– you had your chances!" she retorted violently. "You've shown me what you can do, now I'll show you what I can do." Her feet tapped across the wooden floor of the gym. "Nat, this place wants cleaning up – now. It's filthy." Quickly she moved towards the office, "and I want to see the books. Everything."

"Your mother –"

"– is not me!" she finished, cutting Lenny off in mid sentence. "You all took advantage of her. You knew she would be spending more time with my father then she would here. She didn't have time to check up on all of you, did she?" Misia smiled bleakly. "Well, I have."

"I thought you had a family," Lenny said viciously. "Or doesn't your old man want you home?"

She turned and walked back, standing in front of him; "Do you want a fight, Lenny? I can't give you a run for your money in the ring – and I can beat you hollow out of it." She turned, "And the same goes for the rest of you. If you want to stay with Guido Razzio – and by that, I mean me – you have to start working."

"For a woman?" Dan asked incredulously, a slow whistle escaping his lips.

Misia frowned. "Yes, for a woman," her tone was incredulous. "What happened to all of you? You worked for my mother for years and then you worked for both of us. You were pleased to have the name of Razzio behind you then, only too willing to take on the prestige and the protection it offered. Oh, you wanted us then all right," she paced between them. "When you were hungry and nothing more than a kid, Lenny, I can remember you begging my father to take you on." She spun round to Dan, "And you, when you had no roof over your head, it was my father who put you up, rent free, for over six months, until your first fight."

She went on.

"And what about you, Nat? You came over from America because the game was crooked there; you came to see Guido Razzio because he had a clean name. You respected him, and you respected yourself then."

"Listen," he drawled. "Just let me have another go at this, lady."

Misia turned away, she had already made up her mind and having Nathaniel Nayton as her head trainer didn't fit into her plans. She walked to the door of her father's gym hearing their voices muttering behind her, their animosity coming in noxious waves. Where did all the real fighters go? she wondered. And where did the kindness and the pride go? Had they been the last of their ilk? There was a brutish feel about the place which had never been present before. And it was on the streets too and in the newsreels; pictures of Adolph Hitler and of the Japanese bombers who had battered Shanghai. Misia had seen a newsreel of a burned child screaming for its mother and had turned away, surprised by her sudden squeamishness.

"Dear God, Portland," she had said, horrified. "what's happening to the world?"

"Europe's on a knife edge. We thought the Great War was the last, but many people think – myself included – that there's another one on the way." He had caught hold of his wife's hand in the dark cinema. "Mosley and his Fascists are bringing hate into this country. In fact England is surrounded by hate, and before long, some of that emotion will enter the hearts of its people. I see it in court, Misia: see it when it's justified, when men have lost their jobs and they're desperate to provide for their families – and I've seen it when it isn't justified: when something sullen, evil, creeps into an expression or a tone of voice. I used to feel so hopeful for the future, but now, now I'm not confident anymore."

Misia had been thinking of their sons, and of her husband if another war broke out; and remembering the boxers who had died in the last skirmish.

"What can we do?"

"We can hope." Portland had been holding her hand so tightly that her wedding ring bitten into her finger. "We can hope."

*We can hope.* Misia remembered the words as she left The Roman House and walked out into the dark street. The huge high windows of building flung light out onto the pavement in front of her, but she felt more alone that she had ever done, and the illumination did nothing to light her way.

# Twenty-Nine

"I'm in trouble."

"I heard," the man said flatly: "You need help."

"Yes, I do," Misia replied, moving over to a table in the Snug of the Bell and Monkey pub.

The landlord had died the previous summer, a new man was in place, leaning depressively on the bar when she had walked in that morning. A few men had looked up, then turned back to their pints, morose, unemployed, the fire gone out in the grate, a slow patter of rain on the windows outside.

Misia rubbed her hands together and looked round: "It's cold in here."

"So?" the landlord countered.

She sighed: "I'm meeting a man called Tom Abbot –"

Which was when he had materialised at her shoulder and steered her towards the Snug. The frosted windows prevented them from seeing out – and from anyone seeing in – but the rain kept pelting down against the glass unceasingly outside, the iron leg of the table cold against Misia's calf.

Sipping her sherry, she glanced furtively at her companion. Tom Abbot was over six feet in height and barrel chested, his neck blending from his chin into his shoulders without any apparent interruption. He had come in wearing a bowler, but when he took it off the top of his head was bald and a dusky pink, a rim of grey hair running like a coronet above his protruding ears. Abbot by name and Abbot by appearance, Misia thought dryly.

Apparently unaware of her scrutiny, he downed half the beer, wiping the froth off his mouth with the back of his hand, his eyes half closed. Misia had put out feelers the night before, ringing every contact she knew and every one that Mary could remember from the old days. Some had died, some did not return her calls, some had fallen out of the fight game, got old, got fat, got greedy, ruined their own chances: and some had disappeared, no one knowing where they were. Others surfaced; drunks down by the docks, t'ppy h'ppy barkers on the fairground, one old fighter selling shirts up on Harry Field's market.

It had seemed hopeless, but someone had got a message through to Tom Abbot and he had materialised like Gargantua in a bowler.

"I'm Misia," she said simply. "Guido Razzio's daughter."

He nodded. "I know. Everyone knows about Mr. Razzio around here."

"I need a trainer."

"You've got one. Nathaniel Nayton."

"I don't like him."

He grimaced, pulling on one large ear. "He's American," he said, as though that explained everything.

"You're supposed to be a good trainer."

He banged his head down on the table suddenly. In the other bar, a dog barked suddenly in fright. "I don't let my men get uppity."

Misia looked at the vast, liver spotted hand. "I need someone who can discipline the men, make them train, get The Roman House back into shape," she paused, "You had a place of your own, didn't you?"

"Lost a fortune," he replied. "But then I was no good as a business man. I'm a trainer and it pays to know where your talent lies. Horses for courses."

"Mr. Abbot –"

"Just Abbot, if you please, Mrs. Benning. I've always been called that. Abbot. I look like one and the men remember it."

"Abbot, I need help."

"You said that," he replied, gesturing to the landlord for another pint. "You want another?"

She shook her head, then looked at him hard. "Do you drink?"

"Have done since I was a baby," Abbot replied smoothly.

"I mean – are you a drunk?"

He laughed, his ears reddening. "Well now, Mrs. Benning, I think that you and I might get on well. I'm direct and you're not exactly shy." He gulped at his fresh pint. "No, I can't say I'm a drunk, though it's not thru' want of trying. I could hold my drink at ten and I've never changed. Drink and I are like man and wife; I'd be miserable without the company of a pint. What better way to keep you cheerful at night? My mother was the same, drank like a fish – like a shoal of fish – and flourished."

Misia studied him thoughtfully. "What happened to her?"

"Died. Only a few years ago, well into her nineties. The doctors at the old hospital in Bootle asked for her body, to look at – you know the kind of thing, see if the drink did anything to her." He finished his second glass. "I told them, the drink pickled her, kept her as fresh as a herring."

"Most herrings don't live into their nineties," Misia said evenly.

"How do we know that?" Abbot asked her, leaning forwards. "How do we know for sure that the sea's not full of little old fishes?"

She was beginning to wonder about his ability to hold his booze, when Abbot suddenly became serious.

"Your father built up a great stable of boxers, and I was proud of the way he went after Jack Dudley, the bastard." He glanced at Misia, "Sorry, I've been with men too long. I forget my manners."

She brushed aside the apology; "That's all the more reason why I don't want to see everything he's worked for destroyed –"

"It won't be."

"I want the clear out the fighters who are no good and find better ones –"

"No sooner said than done."

"I want The Roman House to be as it was – a place people respected."

He looked at her calmly for a moment. "Mrs. Benning, why are you doing this?"

"For my father."

He shook his head. "No, not really. Part of its for him, but part of its for you." He blew his nose loudly. "It's not a job for a woman, even one who grew up in it. You've got children of your own, why would you be wanting to spend time away from them?

125

Because you'll have to, you know, if you really want to get the business back to where it was. It won't be done overnight, it'll take work, and plenty of it." He finished off his pint. "It's not a woman's job. Any woman's."

"I have sons," Misia replied calmly. "In time they'll inherit what my father created. In the meantime, I intend to rebuild the Razzio empire and hold it in trust for them." She glanced up at the window and the driving rain drumming against the glass. "There's talk of a war coming. God knows what will happen if it does. We all have a part to play in life, Abbot, as you said – horses for courses. Well, I intend to rebuild and preserve what my father created. Then, if God's with us, I intend to pass it on to my children."

He nodded, moved by her words. "How many boys have you got?"

"Three," Misia said with pride. "Three sons."

He raised his glass in the cold noon light. "Well, here's to your boys," he said loudly. "Here's to the Benning Brothers."

# Book Three

# The Razzio Line

# Thirty

## Rome, Italy

If you move out from the city and into the countryside which borders Rome there are houses – estates really – which boast architecture and gardens cosseted for centuries. There is nothing new here; old trees, old bushes clambering over and beside ancient walls, well rooted shrubs laid out in marshalled rows between the soft lapping of water coming from ornamental fountains. There are a plethora of statues, a multitude of putti, cherubs grown blurry with age, the patina of moss and lichen marking their stone heads and smoothing down the antique curls.

There is a quiet here which hums with sound; unseen insects, the dry brush of a visiting breeze; and sights which tantalise the memory; a heat haze shimmering over a white road, the smell of fruit, of bread baked hot, and above it all, the moist sweet scent of water running. Money has been invested here, laid out in silver gridding to irrigate the gardens, the sun striking it and turning it violently platinum under the noon heat. Long, limpid shadows fall from high trees, and in the mossy, drowsy, musty cool, vegetation grows low and moist to the touch.

Where the house stands it is built high, raised over the gardens which surround it, a terrace rising like a stone moat to separate brick from earth. It requires a staff of ten to attend it inside, and three to work the grounds, one gardener always accompanied by dogs to deter strangers. Inside the house the chambers are shady, kept cool by shutters and by the building of high rooms. Frescoes, restored over the centuries, decorate the reception rooms, whilst tapestries, mellowed with sun, hang from the cornice and fall as a backdrop to the ranks of marble heads which stand to attention along the wall.

Pillars at the base of the stairs shine in the light, gold flecks speckling the smooth surface of grey marble, two bronze hunting dogs, their heads at knee level, standing watch, whilst a vast ormolu mirror hangs at the head of the stairs. Reflections capture and magnify what the viewer might have missed; the painted cupola above, the arrangements of Peace lilies on the first landing, the gilded torcheres held aloft by blackamoors. And in all this magnificence, in all this fabulous, chilling splendour, a child cries in a nursery above. There is a rush of feet, a quick noiseless closing of a door, and the crying stops. Silence thunders round the house again. This is Drago Razzio's home.

It is a showplace for a man who has infiltrated the highest reaches of Italian society; the acquaintance of royalty, politicians, and the leading members of the arts. From his beginnings in Liverpool Drago has used his skills as a surgeon to transform his life and himself. He is no longer boorish, outwardly cold; he is polite, courteous, even courtly. His manners are envied, his comments treasured and repeated all over Rome. He is the dark hero of the war, the surgeon who restored the features of some of the most badly burned victims of the fighting. He is respected, idolised, admired.

He has worked for this eminence. Worked harder than any man, honed his abilities until his hands to effect miracles. In the cool white hospital passages he is watched, whispered about: patients and their families standing in awe of him, watching him with reverence. He is loved, he is loved. He is deified, photographed: he is amongst the chosen, and has the skill of the newly bewitched.

Is there nothing of the old Drago about him? Yes, he demands the same degree of loyalty; is injured by the same slights; is wounded by anyone who seeks to undermine his position. He begins work at the hospital in the same way every day – except for Sundays when he attends Mass, his wife, daughter and son accompanying him – and begins by checking the instruments in the theatre, making sure that each is in its allotted place, turned to the same angle, the corners of the white cloth upon which they are laid ironed in the same exact pattern. His operating gowns are always prepared by the same nurse, tied in the same way, his gloves put on in the same manner – first the right hand then the left. He washes himself thoroughly before an operation and afterwards he bathes. Not simply a scrubbing down of the hands, a full body bath in his own private chambers. Then he wraps himself in a towelling robe and sits for a time, dictating notes to his male secretary, his feet bare footed, his hair damp.

At his home, it is the same. Food must be cooked precisely, and he knows to the last second if something is not served to his instructions. Curtains blown for an instant out of alignment are re-arranged, the fringe on the rugs smoothed out obsessively. Even the garden must be controlled; leaves are never to lie in changing abundance at the end of summer; they are hustled into sacks and burned, and even the fountains dare not sprinkle water further than their stone surrounds. His life is ordered down to the most minute of details, his staff controlled, his family overshadowed by the terrifying vastness of his success.

Having come from a moneyed background herself, Catherine Clark was no stranger to luxury, and she did, within days of meeting Drago Razzio, fall into that heady and uncontrollable infatuation of all consuming love. Her adoration however, was muted by her personality, her affection delicately expressed, her true feelings always suppressed under a soft coating of reserve. She loved Drago absolutely, compellingly, and yet knew that he would resent any vulgar show, any excessive affection. So she kept her love dampened. Alberto had been right when he told Misia that she might love Drago too much for happiness, she did. Her personality longed for a reciprocation of commitment, but it was never forthcoming.

Her husband was in love with his skill, not her; he slept dreaming of his rise and of the steady accumulation of his power. When he touched her it was with a cool and practical passion, love making was a function, no more. He might have become a spectacular lover, but for the ever present third party who was always in his bed and in his heart. Ambition corrals love.

*"Who is the third who walks always beside you?"* Alberto asked him one day as they walked in the grounds.

Drago turned his head, his heavy lidded eyes were unblinking, his full lipped mouth compressed.

"What?"

"It's a quote from T. S. Eliot – an American poet –"

"I don't read American poetry."

Alberto wasn't fazed and leaned against the stone wall of the terrace, his spectacles reflecting the sun as he lit a cigarette. "Catherine looks pale."

Drago's mind was wandering, his eyes had alighted on a slight unevenness in the edge of the grass and he signalled to the gardener. The man followed his gaze and began, methodically, to clip at the offending grass.

"She was tired by Courtney's birth."

Alberto glanced at his friend. Courtney was now six years old, it was a long time to suffer from exhaustion, even for someone as fragile as Catherine. He had seen her as he arrived, standing motionless in the window of the library, a book in her hand. She had seen him too and waved, beckoning him over. She came into focus slowly, as a ghost might, her narrow shouldered, narrow hipped body, dressed entirely in white giving her the wan appeal of a child, her face dominated by a pair of almond shaped eyes, the colour of malachite.

He reached her and took her hand, kissing it gallantly, hearing her laugh in that distant, disembodied way which was peculiar to her.

"How are you?"

She touched her cheek in a nervous, defensive gesture. "Drago says I look much better."

"That wasn't what I asked," Alberto chided her. "How do *you* feel?"

"The summer's been a long one," she replied, moving away. He noticed then that she was barefoot.

"The children are growing up," Alberto said, changing the subject and glancing down into the garden where a young girl tried, unsuccessfully, to fly a kit. There was no wind.

"Pila's nearly nine," Catherine said suddenly, as though the fact surprised her. "Almost grown up."

He kept his eyes on the girl: dark, like her father, but too thin, her high cheek boned face oval, inquisitive, alert.

"And what about your son?" Alberto asked, "how is he?"

Catherine winced; the movement was delicate, pained. "Courtney still has his moods," she said quietly. "I never knew children could be so … violent."

In the background, Alberto could hear Courtney's voice, the thin, reedy shout of the boy. If Pila was like her father in looks, Courtney had inherited something of Drago's obsessive, driving nature. He demanded attention, demanded toys, demanded constant stimulation. He needed to be the nucleus around which the house spun, and could be – when his father wasn't home. But when Drago was there and he was usurped from his pinnacle of power, he became sullen and withdrawn, a loose-limbed, idle boy, without charm.

"I think he's going to be very gifted," Catherine offered, as if in apology for his shortcomings. "They say that difficult children often are."

Alberto thought otherwise; he thought that Courtney, indulged and thoughtless, might grow up to be the typical vicious offspring of a distant father. It was doubtful if he would ever be able to match Drago in achievement, never be able to stand shoulder to shoulder with a behemoth of a man. So what else was there for someone of his temperament? Resentment, that was all.

"You should rest more," Alberto said, turning back to Catherine.

Her fingers toyed with the edge of the book she was holding. "I thought I thought I might visit my father. Drago doesn't need me here all the time."

That much was true; as Drago relied more and more on the adulation and admiration of his circle to exist, Catherine withdrew. At first she had been the one with the social contacts, and the dainty grace of someone well born. But as her husband's achievements had expanded, her role diminished. She had begun as his necessary consort; now she was merely a tired onlooker. As a tutor is outgrown and discarded by its pupil, so she had been used; sucked dry by Drago's ambition; her contacts stolen, her chief purpose fulfilled. She had provided him with two children and an heir – after that her pre-eminence had slipped. Her looks were too fine to stand up to the opulence of her surroundings, her cultured, civilised manner too frail against the hustle of a sophisticated Italian lifestyle – it was obvious to everyone that Catherine had not stood astride her position, but had, like the worn putti in the gardens, dwindled helplessly into her surroundings.

She knew it, and so did Alberto. In the thirteen years that she and Drago had been married she had lost her hold. Not that she had competition from other women. She never had a bodily rival with whom to compete. No, she was up against a far more subtle foe – her husband's status. The anxiety which had begun after the birth of Courtney had expanded gradually. At first she began to refuse invitations to social gatherings, pleading that her children needed her; but later she found herself avoiding any type of social function, and before long the invitations ceased altogether.

The house became a retreat, a place familiar and therefore safe. The clothes she had worn when they were first married were locked away in other rooms, the ridiculous assortment of shoes, bags, furs and hats secreted away. As though that Catherine had died, the second Catherine scoured away all trace of her, and in doing so, let go of her previous self.

She drifted, she read, she was a good mother and a confidante of her daughter, but as for her husband, she retired from active service. Drago and she might still, intermittently, sleep together, but in all other respects, they were estranged.

There was room for estrangement in the house; they never had to suffer the embarrassment of a bad marriage in the cramped confines of a flat; never had to endure the scalding recriminations over a few yards of territory; never have to ignore each other whilst dressing, backs turned away, the violent indignation of failure mopping the rooms. In the huge wilderness of an Italian palazzo, Catherine could avoid unnecessary confrontations. A footfall on the stairs could be heard long before Drago was seen, giving her ample time to avoid her husband. And so, when they did spend time together, it was courteous, chillingly formal, but not without a type of acid grace.

She would never give him up; never divorce him. Theirs was to be a marriage which endured, and was endured. Drago had no desire to woo another woman and Catherine was too frail, too emotionally tired, to want to attempt another love. Instead she relied for her affection on Alberto; the pock-marked, bespectacled friend who amused her, and who was safely, albeit eccentrically, married.

"You should get more rest," he said again.

She shrugged. The white material of her dress hardly moved. "I'm perfectly all right."

He touched her briefly on the cheek: "I have to go and talk to Drago – will you join us for lunch?"

A look of fleeting panic came into her eyes: "No … no, I don't think so. I have to attend to the children."

They both knew she was lying.

Drago was snipping at the moss on the stone balcony when Alberto approached him, his hair dark under the sun, without any lighting of red or gold. Black, ebonised.

"I've just seen Catherine."

He made an intelligible sound, the scissors making sharp clips in the stillness.

"The war's caused devastation. I was over in London last week and areas of the East End are completely destroyed," Alberto paused. "Liverpool's been punished too. But Misia said that Portland's almost recovered now. Quite a hero, in fact," his voice took on a lilting quality. "Your sister's organising a grand fight in October, some kind of tribute to the war dead. She really is astonishing, I never thought she'd manage to keep that business afloat."

Drago's expression was unreadable. If another man had mentioned his sister he would have been outraged, banished them from his home. But he tolerated Alberto, relied on his sly friend to bring him news of a family he had deserted, used him as his eyes and ears in England. In Italy there was no one other than Alberto who had any inkling of his past. To all intents and purposes, Drago had been educated in England and had undergone his medical training there, but nothing more. No mention of The Roman House or Liverpool ever contaminated his life, or was allowed into his speech.

But in his thoughts … That was another matter entirely. Over the years Drago had followed his sister's life, her marriage, her career, her indomitable determination to keep the boxing business going. He had no admiration for that, but as time passed and he heard of her children, a sleepy, half hearted envy began to take root. First one son, then another, and then another. Three sons, the Benning Brothers, as Alberto called them – as everyone seemed to call them – three heirs. He resented that; looked at Courtney, at the sickly, peevish caricature of himself, and wondered about Misia's sons. Studying the photographs that Alberto had given to him of the boys, Drago thought of Portland Benning – that hulking clever animal of a man – and knew instinctively that, coupled with his sister's athletic physique, their sons would be redoubtable.

Three boys, three healthy boys … His jealousy unsettled him, coming stealthily and then growing into a monster thought. He felt his envy crouch on his shoulders and found himself greedy for news, Alberto's nonchalant remarks dancing on his nerves.

"… there a great English boxer coming up – Freddie Mills," Alberto went on, the ash hanging off the end of his cigarette. "Misia wants to set up a match with him and one of her new fighters. She's got a man called Perry Fields whose a monster," he laughed, roundly amused.

Alberto had seen Fielding fight only the previous month, jerking out of his corner like a speeding train, his arms flailing. He thought in that moment that – confronted with this vision of two hundred pounds of muscle and a head jammed down into a pair of Neanderthal shoulders – he would have been over the ropes at a speed faster than the naked eye could follow. Fielding fought with a blank expression, taking punches with indifference, his ungainly style throwing the opposition. He was, quite simply, terrifying.

Only one person knew how to handle Fielding – and that was Abbot. He would watch the round and then, when the boxer had returned to his corner, he would slap him roundly across the face. The first time Alberto had seen it he had expected to find the trainer propelled to the back of the arena, but Fielding seemed unmoved, listening carefully to a stream of abuse coming from the bowler hatted Abbot as he squeezed a sponge of cold water over his head.

"… her youngest boy is incredible," Alberto continued, changing the subject back to Misia. "Vincent, he's called. You should see him, Drago, he has no fear at all. He's only nine, but he can't keep away from The Roman House, he knows all the fighters reaches and their results, he runs and fetches for them, and plays practical jokes on them," he laughed, thinking of Misia's youngest son. "You'll see, in time that boy will take over."

Behind them, suddenly and without sound, Courtney emerged. He stood in the shadow of the wall, his narrow head on one side, his eyes, so like Catherine's, alert and suspicious. At six, he was already sly, listening at doors, watching, forever watching the staff and his sister. He had been rebuked many times for repeating rumours and telling tales, had been punished for thoughtless cruelty to the dogs, but he was naturally spiteful and took such reprimands as proof that Pila was the favourite. Courtney believed himself unloved, no matter how much attention was focused upon him, and was constantly trying to ingratiate himself with his father.

"Papa?"

Drago turned. He was thinking of Misia's son, and when he saw his own child, hanging back, his bony figure casting a sickly shadow on the terrace, he was unreasonably annoyed.

"What is it? Can't you see we have a guest?"

Courtney came forwards slowly towards the two men. He walked without making a noise: but the quietness which was so attractive in Catherine, was somehow aggravating in him and Drago glanced away.

The child stopped, blinked slowly under the sunlight and then moved back, without a word, into the house.

"You shouldn't do that."

"What!" Drago snapped, turning back to his friend.

"You treat that boy badly," Alberto went on. "He knows you don't like him."

"He is my son –"

"Then you should treat him like your son."

Drago's expression closed: he was annoyed suddenly that his friend should presume to criticise him. After all, his comments about Vincent had been provoking, almost malicious. He glanced at Alberto – was he really only talking, chatting about his sister and her family? Guileless, as usual? Or was he baiting him? For a fleeting second, Drago mistrusted Alberto and then his friend turned to him and smiled.

The look was too easy to be guilty. No man smiled so readily, and with so much affection. Alberto was the only person who accepted him utterly, Drago realised; the only one who loved him without exception. And for that, he would continue to endure the provocation – whether intentional or not. He felt a foul emptiness open up inside him all at once; he had done well for his family, for his wife and children, and yet they didn't love him, just as his parents had never really loved him. For all his success and fame, he felt removed from everyone; separated from the world by his own loneliness.

Only Alberto offered affection constantly, not seeming to mind if it was reciprocated or not. Only he could continually amuse Drago and bring him records and books, and irritate him with his fatuous comments about plays he had seen and people he had met. He had the jester's protection; to be thought a fool. Alberto could say anything, sometimes even making precise and biting comments which would cause trouble for another man – but he was Alberto, so people laughed or dismissed what he said. All except Drago. He knew deep down that he was not the fool he pretended to be. Strongly religious, profoundly Italian, Alberto seemed to merely skim over life, whereas, at heart he was a politician, a pure Machiavelli.

It was no coincidence that he quote the writer often, But what did Alberto really want from life? Drago wondered. He was a reasonable surgeon, careful, but not gifted, a man who was a better assistant than a pioneer. In fact, Drago liked him to assist him at operations; Alberto knew almost telepathically what he wanted and was quiet, only offering a joke to relieve tension, his eyes guileless behind his horn-rimmed glasses. The nurses adored him: not as they idolised Drago: but with Alberto they felt no threat, they relaxed, made friends with him and gradually found that they relied on him.

Many of them fell into love affairs with Alberto. He was harmless, a relief from the turbulent relationships they had had, and he, the eternal friend, managed in this way to deftly secure an active sex life. A politician in life and in the bedroom, Drago thought, surprised that he was momentarily jealous of his friend. No, he assured himself hurriedly, Alberto was no threat. Not Alberto.

He turned to look at Drago in that instant. Were his eyes quite so innocent, quite so blameless?

"We should go to the opera, before they close it for some reason – probably out of deference to our lately departed King. Maybe some struggling composer will come up with a Requiem in memory of our sovereign's ill fated thirty days." Alberto's voice was easy, relaxed. "You know, I took your father some records last time I was in England – he loves Othello."

Drago winced, but said nothing.

"… I've often wondered – do stop me if you don't want me to talk about it – but I've often wondered where your father came from originally. Haven't you?"

Blank faced, Drago turned away, his movements, always slow, seemed to dissolve into the heat haze.

"No."

"I would want to know –"

"I don't."

Alberto lit up another cigarette.

"Why the hell do you do that?" Drago snapped. "You're a doctor, you know it's not healthy to smoke so much."

He was sublimely unconcerned. "I'd be so curious if it was my father. In fact, I doubt if I could let the matter rest. You know he came from Italy, it couldn't be that hard to find something out." He blew a languid smoke ring and then poked his index finger through it. "Guido Razzio's very well read, very cultured – he must have come from a moneyed home. He might be the son of a famous family." Alberto said artlessly. "D'you want me to look into it?"

Drago turned and with a quick gesture, knocked the cigarette out of Alberto's mouth.

He jumped back, startled. "What the hell!"

"I've told you," Drago said coldly. "you smoke too much."

## Thirty-One

Pila curtsied to the woman standing in front of her, Drago smiling distantly behind.

"This is Princess Gianna Ferenza," he said, offering her a seat.

Transfixed, Pila stared at the old lady, her face obliterated by a heavy veil, her right hand clasping an ornate silver rosary, her left lying clenched on her lizard skin bag. She was breathing heavily, the noise coming, disembodied, from under the veil. In and out, she breathed, in and out, the sound mesmerising in the consulting room.

"Princess Ferenza wanted to meet you," Drago explained to his daughter, who stood, wide eyed and unmoving.

"Come here," the old woman said in Italian. Her voice was calm, quiet.

"Pila, do as Princess Ferenza says."

She moved forwards slowly, her eyes fixed on the veiled seated figure in front of her. The smell of gardenia came to her suddenly, the sunlight glinting sharply on the clasp of the old woman's bag.

"You are quite lovely," Princess Ferenza said at last, then turned to Drago. Her veil shifted, but did not expose anything of her face, but down the side of her neck Pila could see a row of fresh stitch marks. "Your daughter is charming," she went on, "I would like her to visit me sometimes."

Drago bowed, extending his hand to his child. For an instant Pila didn't know how to respond, the gesture was so alien. Then gingerly she took Drago's hand and stood stiffly by his side. His palm scalded her skin, her head swimming with the unexpected show of affection.

"She would like that," Drago said, "wouldn't you?"

"Yes, Papa," Pila said at once.

"I like children," the old woman went on, her breathing making the veil rise and fall softly. "I never had children of my own, not in three marriages." She leaned towards Pila, "Would you like us to be friends?"

She wanted to go home, to run to her mother and tell her about the old lady in the veil who smelt of gardenias – but her father was holding tightly onto her hand so she nodded obediently instead.

"Then I'll send the car for you next Thursday," Princess Ferenza said. "At four."

\*

Courtney had bitten his fingernails down to the quick, even causing his thumb to bleed as he chewed at it, his eyes, puffy from crying, looking down into the garden below. Why should his sister go to the old lady's house? Why had she been picked and not him? His father had see to it; had put forward his favourite, chosen his daughter over his son again. Courtney was breathless with rage, his eyes narrowing as he watched the chauffeur driven-car come down the driveway to the house. A moment later Pila walked out, pausing momentarily before climbing into the back seat.

The car drove off slowly, leaving dusty tracks in the gravel. A long shaft of sunlight broke into the room like a thief; it made huge shadows out of the furniture, dust motes turning lazily in the heated light. Courtney slid off the window seat and moved towards the door, looking down the corridor to see if anyone was about. Satisfied that he would not be seen, he ran down to his sister's room and closed the door behind him. The walls were painted deep pink, Pila's collection of fans hung in rows, a large white feather fan, almost two feet across, secured over her bed. It was her prized possession, a gift from Drago for her last birthday. Courtney remembered how she had behaved when she unwrapped it, waltzing around the room, then hiding her face coquettishly behind the feathers as her father looked on.

Hurriedly Courtney clambered onto the bed and reached for the fan, tugging at it. Securely fixed, it remained on the wall. He tried again, freeing it suddenly with one tremendous wrench. It was surprisingly light in his hands, the feathers soft against his palms, the handle warmed from the sunlight which had come in from the window. Slowly, methodically, he began to pluck out the feathers – with all the composure of a housewife plucking a dead turkey – and before long the bed was covered with the broken white plumage. His heart rate accelerated quickly, his mouth expanding into a smile, the feathers dropping one by one until he was left holding only the gilded handle.

His triumph was complete; the fan, the treasured possession, was ruined. His sister had been punished, and by proxy, so had his father, the giver of the gift. Wait until they see this, he thought, sliding off the bed and creeping out of the room. Wait until they see how much they've hurt me, how they made me do this. Then they'll be sorry, he thought self pityingly, then my father will stop treating my sister better than me.

*

"In London," Princess Ferenza said, passing Pila a picture book, "they have ghosts. London ghosts." She sat down carefully, her veil caught in the afternoon breeze from the window. Slowly she lifted the gauze, her face exposed, her neckline and jaw gridded with scar lines, a fine crusting of dark blood black against the white skin. She touched them self consciously and then picked up a mirror, moving her head from side to side to study her profile. "Your father is a very clever man," she said approvingly. "Day by day I see an improvement. Soon there will be no scars left."

Horrified, Pila watched her. She could not see the ruin of an old beauty, only the scars. The terrible marking prevented her from noticing the fine bones, the narrow bridged nose, the long, unlined neck. Not understanding, she thought that the old lady had been hurt.

"Are you ill?"

The princess paused in her scrutiny. "Do I look ill?" she asked imperiously.

Pila faltered. "No … no, not at all."

The old lady face lost its look of irritation, understanding taking its place. "Oh, I see … your father, my dear, is a very gifted surgeon. He repairs ruins," she laughed at her

138

own joke. "I was a beauty, but I was old. Now he has restored me, lifted my battlements, shored up my foundations." A maid came in with a tray: she waited until the servant had gone before continuing. "You see, in a little while this will all fade and I will look wonderful again; and young."

Pila listened, but she could see nothing of the expected transformation. All she could see were the hideous scars cutting into the skin, the faint puckering around the holes where the stitches had been, and the smudging of bruising around the jaw line. Her father had done this. Her father had made this woman ugly … she glanced down at the floor, the pale Aubusson carpet making patterns round her feet. It was horrible, frightening − her father did this for a living − and the old lady was happy! He had cut her flesh and put stitches into her face and neck, and she was looking at herself as though she was the most beautiful woman on earth.

"You look alarmed," the old woman said, laying down the mirror. "You shouldn't be, one day, when you're old, you'll do this."

Never, Pila thought violently. Never, never!

"The young all think they are immortal. I did too, once," she continued, her voice wistful, one arm going behind her head giving her a grotesquely flirtatious air. "I've had three husbands, I wonder how many you will have."

Pila shuffled her feet, her eyes cast down. The room was too hot to be comfortable, the windows closed, the smell of gardenia leaking out from the many plants placed against the oyster coloured walls. The palazzo was no larger than her own home, and no more beautiful, it was merely strange, filled with objects of fascination. In the huge bay window hung a witch ball, its dark amethyst belly reflecting the room, and on the table underneath was a plaster head, marked out phrenologically

"You like unusual things?" the old woman asked, watching Pila carefully.

She nodded. "They're strange."

"Yes, strange but fascinating," Princess Ferenza agreed, getting to her feet and walking over to a heavily carved bookcase. The glass doors opened stiffly, her hand reaching in and withdrawing a book with a punched leather cover. Carefully she laid it down on the table and beckoned Pila over.

"Look at this, this is a book of magic." Her head was suddenly illumination by a splatter of sunlight, the red scars on her face glowing like worms. "My father gave me this, and his father gave it to him. See how the pages come to life?" she opened the book, her hand turning over the first sheet. It depicted an engraving of a woodland scene, three hunters returning from the kill, a dead stag suspended between wooden poles, a gun dog running behind, barking. The sky was heavy, clouds portentous, a stream running dark under the harrowing sky. From nowhere, a breeze began to blow. It seemed − in the heat of the room − that the engraving shuddered on the page, a dog's barking sounding somewhere in the distance.

Pila wanted to turn away, but was unable. Her eyes seemed riveted to the page, her palms moist. The hunters *were* moving, she thought incredulously, and she could hear them − a hoarse exchange of words, a broken laugh, and the steady deep rustle of trees before the outbreak of a summer storm. Her eyes blurred, cleared, then blurred again, and in that instant, from behind a copse of trees, a figure emerged, walking rigidly towards the hunting party. It was gliding, without gender, its head covered, but the sense of menace, of foreboding, was so intense that Pila took in her breath and stepped back.

In that instant there was a knock on the door, Princess Ferenza slamming the book closed. "Come in."

The maid materialised again. "Will there be two of you for lunch, Princess Ferenza?" she asked in Italian.

Already unsettled, Pila stared at the servant. She was surprised that she was Italian; they were few women so blonde in Rome. She also seemed curiously superior in the presence of the old lady; not like an employee at all, more like an equal.

Pila wanted to be gone suddenly. "I have to go home now."

Surprised, Princess Ferenza looked at her and then moved away, opening the windows and leaned against the wall, her face turned towards the breeze. The cool air came in hurriedly, soothing Pila and taking away the atmosphere of malice. The curtains began to shift gently, the trees ruffling, and on a table by the window two crystal lights tinkled, their glass droplets shivering against one another.

"Do you *really* have to go?" the old lady asked, suddenly pleading. "Your father said you could stay until evening."

Pila realised that she had no choice in the matter. The Princess wanted her to stay; was begging her to stay, and besides, her father had spoken for her. How could she go home having defied him? He wouldn't shout at her; he never did, he would withdraw instead, his silence effecting an injury far more severe than physical punishment. He would remain withdrawn too; possibly for a day, possibly for a week; all her attempts at getting his attention would be ignored – and her mother's intervention on her behalf would also be useless.

She would keep to her room, waiting, as she always did for a sign that she had been forgiven and accepted back into the fold. Sleep would be hard at this time, Pila would murmur in her dreams, waking without being refreshed, aware only of the dead sense of loss and rejection. The punishment was exquisite because she never knew how long her father would continue to overlook her. A day, or a week – she never knew, so when the forgiveness came – Catherine coming to her room and taking her hand to lead her down to see her father – the relief lead to a kind of sickness; her head drumming, her legs unsteady, and when he smiled at her, she felt a physical relief which was almost painful.

It was an experience Pila would do anything to avoid.

"I would like to stay, Princess Ferenza," she lied. "As long as you want me to."

# Thirty-Two

There had been no reason for the operation to fail; it had been minor, a simple adjustment of the woman's nose. As usual, Drago had taken a meticulous medical history, asking intensive questions, checking and re-checking his patient's story. He knew how many women wanted to have plastic surgery, knew how many believed that the problems of their lives could be repaired by a face lift or the acquisition of a new profile. He had heard many a chilling story of his colleagues being duped; of patients with a history of mental illness or depression, who had not admitted such facts during their consultations.

Only a year before Alberto had been working on a case with another surgeon. The woman had been middle aged, her looks dimming, her husband a notorious philanderer. She had been perfectly reasonable at the consultation, had explained to the surgeon that she realised an improvement in her appearance would not necessarily cure her husband's infidelity, but it might help their marriage. She was calm, rational, and only a week later, she underwent surgery.

Her patience was stoical; she never complained of pain, never was impatient to have the bandages removed; she sat submissively, waiting to heal. She read, (Alberto related to Drago later,) read constantly. European novels, some poetry; from morning to night. As she waited for her flesh to heal and her bruising to disappear, the patient drifted in and out of the fictitious lives of her only companions. For she had no visitors. Her husband sent flowers every other day, but no one came to the hospital and her children never called. The patient told the staff that she had kept the operation secret, that her embarrassment at such an obvious show of vanity had forced her to deceive her friends.

The explanation was a familiar one and no more questions were asked. She ran through Zola, Balzac and was well into Conrad when the day came for her bandages to be finally removed. She had already had the stitches out, so this time she would see her face almost as it would remain from then on – a little puffier, but no more. The surgeon removed the bandages and examined her, then stepped back, offering her a mirror.

Alberto continued the story, his voice hushed:

"… she looked and looked, she smiled. She was, I tell you, lovely again. Oh, not too young looking, not too pretty, but she had a kind of severe and longing attraction which was very powerful. Her age had gone; her weariness had gone; and she was, in that instant of first seeing herself, more than she ever had been before. Her husband would be mesmerised, I remember thinking … The surgeon was delighted, as you well may imagine. He knew that he had done a marvellous job, and more, he knew he would get considerable work as a result.

"The patient went home two days later, dressed in Valentino, her car coming to the hospital to collect her … We heard no more, until one night a couple of months later, when the surgeon was called to her home. Her husband was distracted, unintelligible; he could only take my colleague up to his wife's bathroom and then hurry away … She was lying on the floor, a razor blade still in her hand. She had, with terrible precision, cut her face open, following the faint lines where the scars had been – her features were savaged, skin hanging away from the bone, the bathroom an abattoir of blood.

"'I shall never forget it as long as I live,' the surgeon said, trying to stop the bleeding. 'I shall never forget'... She died a day later in hospital. She had, you see, hoped that her husband would stop his adultery. Far from it being a matter of little concern to her, it was her last wretched attempt to hold his love. She had thought that, being handsome, he would want her again, and that he would stay with her. But he didn't ... so she destroyed herself and in mutilating her face she also destroyed the dream, and the hope she had clung to ... The surgeon was shattered. He did operate again, but not with any confidence. I believe he retired soon after."

Drago remembered the story and flung down the patient's notes on his desk, sitting down, his breathing rapid. He *had* checked on everything, he knew that, and yet, somehow they had missed a heart defect, a condition lying hidden and dangerous. It was no comfort to him that the patient had not known before the operation and therefore could not report it; that was irrelevant. He *should* have known. It had been a minor operation, and now the woman was dead. A cardiac arrest on the operating table. A simple rhinoplasty indirectly causing her death.

He closed his eyes, seeing again the look on Alberto's face, his bespectacled eyes sympathetic and questioning, the anaesthetist shouting out the woman's dropping levels to Drago, and then the pounding, disbelieving silence afterwards ... It was not his fault; it was simply one of those unfortunate million to one chances, the kind of random horror medicine always has in store. If it hadn't been the operation, a shock might have killed her; a minor trauma having the same effect ... but Drago knew it *was* the operation which had ended her life. His operation, his theatre, his responsibility.

Opening his eyes, Drago looked around, panic threatening to overwhelm him, the footsteps passing outside tapping like the sound of a million birds on the glass skylight. Tapping, tapping ... he forced himself to breath regularly, then leaned forwards and straightened the desk-set in front of him. The action seemed to soothe him and he stood up, walking over to his shelves and meticulously rearranging his books, each spine aligned in the same way, ordered in height. He then walked back to his desk and took out some cleaning fluid, returning to the shelves and lifting the first of his collection of antique surgical instruments.

In silence, Drago Razzio worked. He had found, over the years, that his obsession with order, far from being unproductive, did, in fact, relax him when nothing else could. He realised that his attention to detail and cleanliness was phobic, but he also realised that it acted as a compensatory measure. His mind, so agile, could easily be thrown off balance. He knew, too well, that his talent was so finely tuned that it left small leeway for his emotions. Worry made him hysterical – he had discovered that as a boy in Liverpool – he over-reacted, became nervous, lost his sense of proportion. Only routine, repetition, calmed him.

So he cleaned the first item of his collection, and then laid it back on the shelf and picked up the next article, a seventeen century speculum.

"Dr. Razzio?"

He didn't answer, didn't move.

"Dr. Razzio?"

"Go away," he said simply.

The nurse closed the door without another word.

Ten minutes later the door opened again, Alberto walking in, smoking and gesturing to the surgical instrument in Drago's hand. "How much did you pay for that?"

"It was a good price."

"I can imagine," he replied dryly, glancing about him. The scene was not remarkable to him; he knew all of Drago's habits. "No one could have foreseen what happened –"

"Pass me that cloth, will you?"

Alberto shrugged, then passed him the clean, carefully hemmed rag. A hem on a cloth. Dear God! he thought, sitting down, whatever next?

"She had a bad heart –"

"I don't want to talk about it," Drago said heatedly. "I can't …"

"You should, bottling it up will do nothing to help," Alberto said easily. "Her family understand. They were upset, but they realise it was nobody's fault."

Drago continued to polish the metal, his hands working backwards and forwards rhythmically, the light glinting on the steel. The room was cool, shaded by blinds, the floor, with its black and while tiles, well polished. The walls were bare, only a clock ticked high up. Apart from that, and the display shelves, there were no ornaments. So many people had come to this room, some disfigured beyond belief, others wanting restoration of previous beauty, and all had been soothed by the man who now worked so obsessively the speculum turned repeatedly in his hands.

Drago felt a guilt which was both unexpected and unwelcome. The operation had proved his fallibility, his status was no longer godlike, Drago Razzio had erred, the fates had hobbled him, brought down his pride. He felt exposed, vulnerable, childlike, and a moment later, flung the instrument to the floor and walked out.

\*

"What did you do!" Catherine said sharply, looking at the destroyed fan on Pila's bed. "Courtney, why?"

The boy stood defiantly staring at her. "You all hate me. All of you!"

She reached out for him, but he ducked back, avoiding her touch: "That's not true," Catherine said gently. "I love you, we all do."

"My father hates me, that's why he let Pila go to see the Princess!"

"It wasn't your father's choice," she replied quickly. "Princess Ferenza asked for Pila. She wanted her to visit – it wasn't up to your father who went."

He refused to be mollified. "But why did she want my sister? Why not me?"

"You aren't a girl," Catherine replied, seeing her son begin to chew at his nails, the familiar timbre of hysteria rising in his voice. "She likes a have a little girl with her, to read to her, to talk to her."

"I could read, I could talk –"

"Then read to me, talk to me," Catherine said kindly, reaching out to her son again.

He came towards her sullenly. "You like me, don't you?" he asked, moving into his mother's arms.

"I *love* you, Courtney," she said honestly. "But you must never do anything like this again. Pila will be so upset."

He clung to her frantically; "Sorry … sorry …"

A little while later, Catherine left him, taking with her the damning evidence of his vandalism. When Pila came home she would have to explain, soothe her daughter, beg her not to tell Drago. But would she keep such an act secret? Pila was her confidante, her loved child, but would she forgive her brother and conceal what he had done? The fan had been a present from her father, and valued as one of the few displays of affection he had ever shown. Drago would not know it had been destroyed – he seldom went to his daughter's room – but in time, would one of them let some comment slip?

And if they did, and if Drago found out, how would he react? He demanded honesty from all of them; demanded total obedience. How would he feel, knowing that his wife and children had deceived him? And what would he do to Courtney if he found out what his son had done? … The last thought decided Catherine on her course of action. She loved her husband, but she loved her children more and was prepared to protect them in whatever way possible. Carefully she wrapped the broken fan in paper and then walked to the outhouses where the rubbish was collected, ramming the parcel down into the bottom of one of the metal bins.

She had just finished the task when she heard a car in the driveway and turned, surprised to see her husband drive up. Her face coloured with guilt. An instant earlier and he would have caught her … Slowly, smiling like a pliable child, Catherine moved over to him.

"Hello, Drago."

He got out of the car and took her hand. The gesture was unexpected and for an instant, she stiffened. "Come in," he said simply, walking her through the entrance hall and hurrying her up the marble stairs.

Their feet echoed in the stillness, their reflections thrown back at them as they rounded the bend in the stairs. He was moving so fast that Catherine was almost running, her heeled shoes almost losing their grip as he opened his bedroom door and hustled her in. The room was in semi-darkness, the bulky curtains drawn against the noon heat, his monogrammed slippers lying, perfectly positioned, by his chair.

Catherine seldom came to his room – he, in the rare occasions they made love, came to hers – and it seemed for an instant that she was in a stranger's home. The sensation was unsettling, and she found herself suddenly threatened. He was still gripping her hand as he pulled her towards the bed, lifting her skirt as he pushed her down, his body moving on top of hers. Catherine lay still, accepting his kisses, his tongue working frantically against hers. Then he stopped. His excitement had faded, he was no longer aroused, only angry and bewildered. Jerking her to her feet, he dragged her to the bathroom and once there, pulled off his clothes and turned on the bath taps.

"Wash me," he said hoarsely.

"What?" Catherine whispered.

He pressed the soap into her hand and stepped into the running water. "Wash me!" he repeated, lowering himself into the rapidly filling bath.

She knelt by his side and began, timidly, to lather his arms, his hands and then his chest.

"Lower," he said, his eyes closing. "Lower."

She paused and then began to move her hands under the water, his breathing accelerating rapidly, his head moving from side to side. His mouth opened suddenly and he moaned, climaxing, his rigid body relaxing back into the soapy bath as Catherine rose to her feet and walked out.

*

Pila finally left Princess Ferenza at seven thirty, driven back to her home and left on the doorstep like a late delivery. She rang the bell twice, the maid letting her in as Catherine came out of the library to greet her. She was about to say something when she noticed the expression on her daughter's face, an injured look which had not been there that morning.

"What it is, darling?"

She moved to her mother's side, sliding her arms around Catherine's waist. "I don't like it there."

"At Princess Ferenza?"

She nodded; "It's strange – odd things happen."

Catherine drew her daughter into the library and closed the doors. They both loved the room, the panelled walls shelved and weighty with books, a frieze of Carracci figures painted above, and two globes – one celestial and one terrestrial – flanking the doors which lead out onto the terrace and the closed garden beyond.

"What kind of *odd* things?"

"She has books …" Pila hesitated. She was home now with her mother, perhaps such things seemed foolish; perhaps she only imagined them.

"Go on," Catherine prompted her.

"Well, she has books with pictures," Pila paused, "that seem to move. You know, when you look at them, they seem to be alive. There was this picture of some men and a dead animal and then suddenly, there was someone else in the picture who hadn't been there before." She glanced at her mother. "Honestly, I promise, he – it – wasn't there before."

Catherine didn't doubt her. Courtney might be hysterical, capriciousness, sly, but her daughter was a calm child, reluctant to lie.

"I believe you. What else?"

"She has these huge coloured balls hanging up at the window and a head with things written on it," Pila shrugged, suddenly embarrassed. "I sound like a baby, don't I?"

Catherine shook her head. "No, you sound as if you didn't like Princess Ferenza's home, and that's perfectly all right, you don't have to like it there."

"So I won't have to go back?"

Catherine hesitated, Pila saw the pause and hung her head. "I know, I have to go back, don't I? Just because she's a friend of Father's."

"She's a patient too. The Princess has been very helpful to your father over the years.

She's sent many people to him and helped to build his reputation." Catherine glanced away. "Princess Ferenza believes your father to be a genius, a Merlin –"

"Who's Merlin?"

Catherine smiled distantly. "When I was a little girl, growing up in London, my mother used to read to me about Merlin. He was a magician in the court of King Arthur – you remember I told you about King Arthur? He was a king with his Knights of the Round Table." Pila nodded. "Well this king was very wise, and Merlin was his magician," Catherine hesitated; how long ago had it been since she had read that story? How long? She had dreamed of her own King, a man of honour coming into her life to rescue her … "Merlin was a very clever man, who could work magic. Well, Princess Ferenza thinks that your father can work magic when he makes people look young again – "

"But she looks *frightening*," Pila said hurriedly. "She has marks around her face."

"They fade," Catherine explained. "And when the scars, go, then she'll be lovely again."

"I don't think so," Pila said seriously. "I don't think she's good enough."

Surprised by the remark, Catherine looked at her daughter. Pila had always been a reliable child, a daughter who had grown up to be a great source of comfort to a lonely wife. She had never been fanciful, and it seemed suddenly that she might be lonely. Oh, Pila had friends at her school, but they seldom visited the house, and she seemed reluctant to mix with her own age group. As though she sensed that her mother needed her, she gravitated to Catherine more and more over the years, their bond intense.

They had shared so much; Courtney's tantrums, Drago's withdrawals; and they could, with a look, communicate with, and support, each other with a form of emotional symbiosis. Each felt for the other, each reacted for the other. They did not talk about their feelings, but they both understood each other telepathically – and it was apparent to both Courtney and Drago how strongly they had bonded.

It was a source of fury for Courtney, and of reserved irritation for Drago. He was too busy to care over much, but he did feel himself excluded at times, catching a glance exchanged between mother and daughter which he felt, by rights, should have belonged to him. His longing to control, was powerless in this relationship. He might cow Catherine or Pila when they were alone, but together they had a calm, impermeable, defence.

Pila's unease worried Catherine and for the second time in the day she found herself thinking of the Benning family in England. Alberto had told her all about Misia and her sons, making her laugh when he described the formidable Portland. He was a brutish fellow, Alberto had said; looking more like a boxer than the boxers themselves. But he sounded so good, Catherine thought longingly, so supportive, so warm. Her mind ran on. Misia had three sons. Surely if Courtney had other boys to grow up with, he would improve and settle down? He had been expelled from two schools already, even at the age of six, a series of tutors being brought in to educate him privately.

They had little effect. Whatever approach they took, her son viewed them with suspicion. Courtney was cruel, malicious, and had even told his father lies about one man which were patently untrue. Catherine knew that – but she couldn't prove it – and the teacher was dismissed. Why Drago took his son's side was a mystery for a while,

146

but now she realised that although her husband did not like Courtney, to admit it publicly would be a form of failure. His son was to be perfect, the heir who would one day take on his father's role.

She knew it was a fantasy, and so did Pila.

"Sweetheart," Catherine said gently. "I have to tell you something." Her daughter regarded her steadily. Courtney is very jealous that you went to the Princess's home, you know how upset he gets –"

"What's he done now?"

"He spoilt your fan," Catherine said simply. "The one over your bed. He ruined it."

Pila's eyes widened. "The one Father gave to me?"

Her mother nodded.

"Why?" Pila said sharply. "Why? I never spoil anything of his, why should he spoil my things? D'you know, the other day I found him going through my room, and when I told him off he just began screaming and said that if anyone came in he would tell them that I'd hit him." She closed her eyes for an instant. "He should be punished."

"But if your father finds out, he'll be furious," Catherine said quickly, "and you know who'll suffer. Oh yes, Courtney will at first, but we'll be the ones who have to take the brunt of it." She stroked the back of her daughter's hand. "It's not fair, I know that, Pila, but we have to stuck together. Your father is … upset today. I don't want him to be provoked. You have to help me. Will you?"

Pila sighed, she wanted to run after Courtney there and then, catch hold of him and give him the beating he deserved. He was a spoilt brat, a hideous, snooping, eavesdropping brat. But he was *safe*, saved by being his father's son. No one could touch Courtney whatever he did. He was not to be revealed as he was, but presented forever as the promise of the future. Pila knew it, and had grown to accept it. Besides, she did not want to be her father's favourite, she was afraid of him, and was more than happy to be her mother's beloved child.

So her response was obvious. Turning, she laid her head against her mother's shoulder: "Of course, I'll help you. Don't I always?"

Catherine rocked her daughter slowly. "I promise you this won't be forever. In time, things will be better. Trust me." Her voice dropped to a soothing lull, "I'll always help you –"

"– and I'll always help you," Pila answered.

"Forever?"

"Forever."

# Thirty-Three

He was uncontrollable, screaming, the vast house echoing with his cries. Unable to control him, Catherine had locked Courtney in his room, his feet drumming on the floor, his violent shouting coming like a threat down the marble staircase. The staff heard him too; the gardener looking up from the lawn to the window above, one of the dogs barking and straining at its lease. Courtney had been rebuked by his tutor, soundly admonished, and he reacted in the way he always did – with aggression.

Books had been hurled at the unfortunate Italian, pens following, and then the unholy crash of a desk being turned over had resounded loudly as the teacher left the room.

"I'm sorry, Signora," the man said to Catherine at the foot of the stairs. "Your son is unteachable."

She glanced up to the noise from the first floor, Drago materialising from his study, his steps measured, slow, as he crossed the hall. "What's all this noise?"

"Your son," the teacher said flatly, "is uncontrollable."

"You should be used to children –"

"I am," he replied hotly, "but your son doesn't want to learn and he will not take instruction."

Drago's expression was threatening. "I pay you well."

"Not well enough," the man retorted. "I'm sorry, but I have to hand in my resignation."

Drago blinked, the heavy lidded eyes deceptively sleepy. "As you wish – but don't ask me for a reference."

The man left without another word.

Avoiding Catherine's gaze, Drago moved away. He wanted to be gone, but for once he was reluctant to escape to the hospital. The previous day's death had unsettled him and the incident with his wife afterwards had done nothing to soothe him. He felt cut off, rejected from his family, his son's cries almost an expression of his own inner distress.

He had slept badly, rising at dawn, his head filled with drumming anxiety. He knew that later he had a long operating list to deal with, and was grateful that his assistant was Alberto; but he still lingered over coffee far longer than he should have done, and only a questioning call from the hospital forced him to move. The day was overcast, heavy with rain, the clouds banking the garden as he paused for a long moment on the terrace before finally turning and moving back through the house.

The frescoes, usually so clever and bright with life, seemed dulled, the painted figures artificial, dead. Even the marble statues and busts did not please him; they were all deceased replicas of life, without blood, without heart. He felt, for a grinding instant, his own mortality, and was unexpectedly intimidated by the grandeur of his home. It was his, he had earned it. But in time to come some other man would own it and walk its gardens and touch its walls. Drago might believe he was successful, might cling to his fabulous power, but after death he would be relegated, overtaken, his possessions lost to him.

The house was not his, not truly. Even his family would continue without him. He was a father, and fathers die. After all, he thought suddenly, it was just, a horrible retribution. He had rejected his own parents, what right had he to expect more from his own children? His guilt shouldered into him, knocking him off balance. Perhaps he should contact his home? Phone Misia? Try to repair the damage his cruelty had inflicted in the past.

But then again, why had she not contacted him? Why had the years passed and there been no word – apart from the snippets Alberto had passed on. He had been right to leave England, Drago assured himself, if he had stayed he would never have risen so far. He was settled in Italy, had secured his career and his contacts, had brought up a family here, had made it his home … *his home?* No, he thought, not his home. It has never been my home. Nowhere has ever been home to me.

He thought of Misia again and then resisted the idea of contacting her. She had three sons, all of whom could only underline the shortcomings of his own child. Drago could not face the humiliation or the envy her family and her happiness were sure to provoke; she was safe, she had the love of her own children and her parents. She had earned it, hung onto it, whilst he had given it away so lightly.

Unsettled, Drago drove to the hospital and scrubbed for surgery without speaking. Inside the theatre he looked at the patient's notes again and then nodded briefly to Alberto, before lifting a scalpel to make an incision around the man's cheek. The patient was badly mutilated after a car accident: weeks of preparation had gone into his case, X-Rays studied, the cheekbone area to be rebuilt, the eye realigned in the socket. A delicate operation which called for all of Drago's skill; an operation which he would usually relish.

But this time he hesitated before making the incision. The man's unconscious face was deformed; a grotesque lump of flesh without nobility or charm. Transfixed, Drago stared at it, hearing the patient's slow breaths under the anaesthetic, the skin paled, waiting. Admiring perfection, Drago could, for a moment, see only ugliness, a gross misalignment, a God forsaken wilderness of feature which repelled … Can you make me look normal? the man had asked, his wife beside him. Can you? … Princess Ferenza had said Drago was a miracle worker, a Merlin, a man who could restore the unreasonable. But to what end? The patient could be helped, could be made acceptable, but what of *him?* His mutilation was inside, a hidden destruction which no one saw. How could he be made perfect, normal?

Alberto saw his hesitation and glanced at the nursing sister beside him. He had seen how badly Drago had taken the death of the woman the previous day and presumed that his uncertainty related to that. Tactfully, he coughed behind his mask.

Nothing.

Again, he coughed.

Again, nothing.

"Are you ready?" he asked at last.

Drago blinked, his eyes bewildered for a fleeting second, and then they cleared, the scalpel coming down and slicing neatly into the waiting flesh.

# Thirty-Four

Pila was eating a piece of sweet pastry, her eyes fixed on Princess Ferenza's maid as she poured some milk. The young woman seemed impervious to her scrutiny, her lustrous blonde hair casting a tawny shadow over her cheek as she bent forward. Beside her, the old lady was gazing into the fireplace, her shoulders covered with two fringed shawls, the sudden, unexpected cold of the morning locking into her bones. On a table beside her, a cup of coffee lay untouched, steam rising in a milky vapour, the soft patter of rain gridding the windows.

"Dona, thank you," she said listlessly to the maid.

The young woman bobbed her head. "Anything else, Signora?"

Slowly she looked up, regarded the maid thoughtfully, and then glanced over to Pila. "My maid, Dona … " she said, shifting in her chair, her right hand fingering the same weighty silver rosary she had carried the first time Pila saw her. "… came from Sicily. Didn't you, Dona?" The young woman dipped her head again. "She was from a very poor family. You don't mind that I tell our young friend this, do you?"

"No, Signora."

"She was the seven child, seventh of seven daughters. Do you know what that means, Pila?"

She shook her head. "No, Signora."

"It means that she has second sight." Princess Ferenza's head tipped upwards, her eyes fixed on the maid. "That was why I hired her. I like to know about such things, and I think you do too," she said, glancing back to Pila. "Am I wrong?"

"Yes … no …" she said hurriedly. What was second sight? What did she mean?

"Dona can see into the future," Princess Ferenza said, as though answering Pila's thoughts. "She can read your future for you. Would you like that?"

Pila hesitated. She didn't want the woman to tell her future, and seemed to know instinctively that it would be wrong. Yet she dared not refuse.

Expectantly, the old lady watched her: "Well?"

"That would be nice," Pila said without conviction.

Princess Ferenza was suddenly galvanised into action, her body leaning forwards, her hand gesturing to the maid. "Move the table, yes, there," she ordered, a small stand being placed between her and Pila, the ornaments removed. "Now, give the child the cards," she demanded, Dona passing a pack to Pila. Curious, she looked at the painted figures of the Tarot and then, following orders, shuffled them. Her hands were small and she dropped several, the old lady clicking her tongue in impatience as Dona stooped impassively to pick them up.

"Now, chose ten," the maid said to Pila, drawing up a chair and sitting beside the child. The room was shaded, rain making the shadows lengthen, the soft patter of the water curiously hypnotic.

"Ten," she said again.

Slowly Pila counted them out, laying the cards, face down, on the table top.

Dona glanced over to her, turning the cards upright without looking at them, then, when she was finished, she looked down at the spread. Her face was composed, her eyes fringed with their straight lashes, tranquil. Several minutes passed, Pila not daring to look at the old lady, her eyes fixed on the maid instead. She breathed steadily, altering her position twice, and then looked at Pila.

"Your hand, please."

Pila extended her palm.

"I see," the maid said evenly. "You will marry –"

The old lady laughed delightedly.

"– and have two children, and you will go to England. It is very clear. You will live in another country." She read the cards slowly, methodically, turning them over onto their faces as she finished with them. "You will marry – but you should not."

"Why, what do you see?" the old lady said urgently, leaning forwards. "What is it?"

But the maid ignored her and let go of Pila's hand, her voice steady.

"Do not marry. Please."

"She *has* to marry! All women marry," Princess Ferenza snapped. "Even if she gets divorced it's better than being a spinster."

"She should not marry," Dona said hotly, rising to her feet and collecting the cards together.

"Nonsense!" the old woman snorted. "You talk like a peasant."

Ignoring her, Dona turned back to Pila and then, with a gentle gesture, she touched the girl's cheek. "Remember what I said. Don't marry, and you will have a happy life."

"But if I don't marry, I won't have children," Pila said, suddenly distressed.

"The choice is yours," Dona said. "Children. Or happiness."

"I don't understand!" Pila shouted, suddenly unsettled and upset: "I want to have children and I want to get married."

"Ssh. They're only cards," Dona said gently, tucking them into a nearby drawer. "Nothing to disturb you. Nothing important."

But it was too late, Pila was distraught. It was not so much what the maid had said, but what she had left *unsaid;* a warning, a sounding of disaster, an innuendo which was left unchecked and hanging in the dull air. The room was now abhorrent to her, the old woman with her marked face, suddenly wicked. Pila had only one thought and that was to leave, to go home, to return to the one person who was her whole security. Catherine would tell her the truth, only she could help her.

"I want to go home," Pila said, hurrying to her feet.

"Oh, my dear, don't be afraid," the old lady said, pointing to the window. "Wait until the rain stops, at least."

Pila could see the logic of the suggestion and stood, her head bowed, in the middle of the shady room. But no amount of coaxing could lift her spirits; no amount of food could draw her attention back. The dark image of the cards had impregnated her; had soiled her and taken away the last optimism of childhood. For many years Pila had shared an emotional harness with her mother, enduring it and dreaming of a future in which she was to be spared further pain. But it was not to be – in the years which were to come something waited for her in the shadows; something indefinable, unclear, and yet, in that instant Pila knew that when the moment came, she would recognise it, and

151

see it, face to face.

# Thirty-Five

Alberto woke up and turned over, getting out of bed gingerly to avoid waking the woman next to him. Quietly he closed the bedroom door and moved into the bathroom, pulling on his dressing gown and then picking up his glasses. Absentmindedly, he polished them, then put them on, checking his reflection in the mirror. His skin, badly marked from chicken pox as a child, looked pitted under the bad light and he sighed, clicking off the switch.

Coffee restored his good mood, as did the cheese he ate with two rolls of bread, his hand reaching out for his first cigarette as he studied the paper in front of him. He inhaled deeply, and then jumped, snatching up the phone hurriedly on the second ring.

"Si?"

"Alberto? It's Misia."

"Ciao, Misia," he replied smiling. "How are you?"

"I'm fine ..."

He wedged the phone against his shoulder as he moved towards the settee and sat down. "But there's trouble?"

"My father ..." she said, breaking off. It took her a long moment to continue. "My father's very ill, Alberto."

He had expected as much. The last time he had visited Guido in Liverpool he had been aged, turning into an old man within weeks. His progress had fooled all of them – except Alberto. He was the doctor, after all. The family had merely seen his tiny recovery, heard the small conversation and followed all the minute and precious movements – but to a medical eye Guido Razzio was never going to fully recover. He was using his will in a particular way, pulling himself back as far as he could, so that the time which remained to him would be rich. The effort such a partial recovery had demanded had, in the end, undermined his health, and he was, at seventy four, exhausted.

But he had had the satisfaction of time spent with Mary, and he had been able to talk to her. Not at great length, but the important things he wanted to say needed few words, and his wife was a ready interpreter. Alberto remembered the last time he had visited, Mary had been sitting with Guido by the window, looking out over the park. For a while she had not known Alberto was there, and he had, he was ashamed to admit it, not given his presence away immediately. He was aware that he was watching a great love; something infinitely tender.

"D'you remember how my mother used to long to live here?" Mary had asked him, taking Guido's hand. "She worked so hard and was so happy when we moved to this house."

Her voice had been different; Alberto had never seen the tender side of the redoubtable Mary Razzio and was touched by it.

"But you know, my love, I wouldn't have cared if we'd stayed in Cranberry Street."

Guido had made a noise, a subdued, almost clucking noise. It had taken Alberto several minutes to realise that he was laughing.

"… remember Morrie Gilling?" Mary had then asked, "well, you thought he was a hard man, but you should see Abbot with the boys. He slapped Perry Fields so hard the other day I thought he was going to pass out." Her head, its dark hair now an iron black, had rested against the back of her husband's chair.

"Love – you," Guido said had haltingly, the words hard to decipher, muffled.

But she had heard them and answered. "And I love you. I was lucky to find you, Guido, and luckier to love you."

Alberto had made a movement then, breaking into the intimacy of the moment, Mary rising to her feet. The soft look of her face had gone. She had been formidable again.

"Alberto, how good of you to come, Misia said you would." Mary turned back to Guido, "See, you have a visitor."

He had walked over, taking a seat beside the invalid, and fumbling for his cigarettes.

The clucking laugh came again; Guido loved the smell of tobacco, the memory of a smoke.

"I brought some more records," Alberto had said, lighting up and then placing the discs on Guido's lap. "You'll like the Rachmaninov."

"Thank – you."

"My pleasure." Alberto had been watching Guido carefully, gauging his decline. He had lost weight, his dark deep set eyes vast over the high cheekbones, his neck thin in the shawl which circled it. But the force remained, the indomitable spirit reaching out, Guido looking down slowly and smiling as he saw the records.

I wish I had known you earlier, Alberto had thought, I wish I had known you as a young man at your peak. He could imagine him with the fighters, piecing together all the legends and stories he had been told; could see him pacing The Roman House, darkly quiet, in control, a man admired; a stranger scratching out his own place. Alberto's curiosity had uncurled again. Where *had* Guido Razzio come from? Which home had he left and why did he never speak of it? Someone had to know, no man could carry a secret so long, and no one could carry it to his grave. Alberto knew he had never told Misia, and she, respecting his wishes, had never questioned her father. But surely he had told his wife? Alberto had thought, glancing over his shoulder to where Mary stood, making up some of Guido's medicine.

He knew he could have asked her – but he knew he would never dare. Like every man before him, Alberto was intimidated by her strength and by her reputation. So, in silence, he had continued to watch Mary as she had completed the tiny domestic chore, re-capped the bottle and then stirred the mixture into a glass. She had seemed benign, composed – and yet, many years earlier, this woman had killed.

They were two incredible people, a couple no other could match, and Alberto knew in that instant that when one died, the other would soon follow. Their life had been like two halves of a peach; perfect as a whole, useless and wasted in portions. Mary knew it too. He had realised that as he watched her. No one else would have seen it, but Alberto knew that Mary was a woman without any fear; when Guido died she would kill herself. Not by suicide; she would merely turn away from the world and join him. She may love Misia and Portland, and idolise her grandchildren, but they were not her life. Hers was not to be a long widowhood; Mary Razzio had no use of domestic trivia, the single life, the eternal sad odd number at table. She wanted to be with her husband, and was fully prepared to follow him to the grave. They had earned their rest. They had earned each other.

"… he's very ill," Misia went on, drawing Alberto's thoughts back to the present. "I think he's going to die."

He closed his eyes to the words. Misia adored her father. How could she cope not just with the loss of the man, but of an icon? And how would she manage the death of her mother which was sure to follow?

"Is he getting good care?"

Her voice was narrow, pinched with grief. "The best … Simeon spends a lot of time with him. He's very patient, sits with him for hours."

She spoke her son's name with gentleness. Simeon, the quiet boy of thirteen, the edgy son who suffered from recurrent headaches. He was not as strong as the stolid Harewood or as active as the lusty, noisy Vincent; he was only average height and finely built, with his grandfather's eyes and a sense of unidentifiable sadness about him. It was fitting that he would be the one to be present at the ending of Guido's life.

"How's he coping?"

"As though he's gone through it before," Misia answered.

It was incredible but true, Simeon was perfectly attuned to the dying of Guido, even more than his mother was. He knew the tone of voice to use and the way to handle his grandfather; knew when to move his cushions, and later, when Guido was confined to bed, he knew how to arrange his pillows to comfort him.

He read to him and played Alberto's records and talked and listened to the murmured responses, his deep soft laugh coming in reply. Sometimes Mary hovered outside and listened, an old jealousy rising in her, a resentment that anyone, even the beloved Simeon, could steal precious minutes from her. But she suppressed her feelings immediately; her grandson had a right to be there.

"I can't understand it," Misia said to her mother, "Simeon's most sensitive of the boys, I would have thought being with my father at this time would really upset him."

Mary looked at her steadily. "Simeon doesn't fear death – he fears life."

So he stayed, and Misia stayed too. Only one person was obviously absent – Drago.

"I should tell my brother," she said to Alberto. "But we haven't spoken for so long I don't know how he would take it coming from me."

"You want me to tell him?"

She nodded at the other end of the phone line. "Could you, Alberto? I think it might help my father to know he was coming."

"I'll tell him," Alberto replied, wondering how he would break the news. "I'll tell him this morning."

"If they could be reunited it would mean so much."

"For whom? Drago or your father?"

"For all of us," she replied honestly.

*

155

Drago listened patiently, but Alberto knew that it was professional attention, such as he used with his patients. There was no obvious emotion; he listened to the medical details and asked questions, but there was no show of anxiety. His father is already dead to him, Alberto thought chillingly.

"I know they want you to see him," he said, "It would mean so much, Drago."

"I have work here."

"Which could wait."

There was a flicker of irritation under the heavy lids. "I have patients who need me."

"You also have a father who needs you."

"He never needed me before," Drago said sourly. "In all these years, he's never been in touch."

"You turned your back on him! You rejected him, you were ashamed of him!" Alberto said incredulously. "How could you expect your father to reopen contact between you? You don't understand, do you, Drago? I thought for years that it was a game with you, this feud. I thought you were just being pig headed, but you simply don't understand."

Drago's expression was blank, he merely glanced down at the notes on his desk and said: "Is that all?"

Alberto's patience, so limitless, finally broke. "Don't be a bloody idiot!" he snapped. "You have the chance to make your peace with your family now, a way to put the past behind you. Your sister wants to see you. She has a family, a home, she's part of you. If you don't care for yourself, think of your own family. Pila and Courtney have cousins they could visit – they could only benefit from a reconciliation," he paused. "And Catherine's becoming more and more withdrawn, you know that. She feels like a foreigner in Italy. It would be wonderful it she could have someone to visit in England, someone who was a relative. Someone to talk to –"

"Thank you for the vivid assessment of my problems," Drago said frigidly. "I hadn't realised quite how much my wife confides in you."

Alberto coloured with outrage. "Don't try to make something innocent into something immoral," he said with disdain. "Catherine and I are friends – and friends she needs."

"And you think that my sister would make a good friend for her?"

"Why not? Misia's a strong woman, a woman with a completely different way of life –"

"That is precisely the point!" Drago hissed, getting to his feet and standing in front of Alberto. The consulting room was sullen under an overcast day, the clock ticking monotonously on the wall, the metal instruments winking coldly on the shelves. "I do not want my family involved with the Bennings," Drago went on, "with boxers! With all the crude hangers on, the trainers, the promoters, the women. I grew up surrounded by them, I was soiled with them, dirtied by them. What kind of life is that? The lowest, basest, there is," he said, answering his own question. "I couldn't wait to leave it behind, and now you think I should go back, and not only that, that I should take my family with me? To what end?" he asked, leaning down to where Alberto sat, unmoving, in his chair. "So that my children can learn about the rough side of life? You want them to talk to boxers when they could talk to artists? You want them to run around Liverpool when they could be in Rome? You want them to mix with the likes of Perry

Fields when they could mix with Princess Ferenza?" his voice was thick with disdain. "I worked to achieve my place in life. I worked to give my family a spectacular home with chances I never had. You have no idea how difficult it was for me. I had to hide everything I was, lie when I went to University, pretend I was someone I wasn't in order to be accepted. Every word I every said was considered, every thought was controlled, so that I would never give myself away. My well-bred peers would have despised me if they had ever found out where I came from. If they had known about my father and about my mother and Billy Poole." Drago was white, the old fear vivid again. "I've lived without confidantes. It took control, determination, ambition – but I did it. Any now *you,* Alberto, want me to go back, to jump back into that grubby little pit with its soiled, embarrassing memories – are you mad?"

There was a long moment of silence before Alberto finally spoke. His voice was flat, without feeling.

"I've known you for a long time, Drago, and I've admired you. I've watched you climb up to the top, watched you court the right people and attend the right functions, and I've seen you work all your frivolous miracles." He stood up and faced his friend, "I've also seen your wife turn from a loving young woman into a timid ghost, locked away in an exile without any hope for the future. Your glorious house is her daily reminder of your achievements – and how much they've cost her. As for your children – Pila has her mother's gentleness and some of her aunt's strength, she may well make a life for herself. But as for your son … Courtney is the child you deserve. Every mean thought, every callous action you ever undertook is reflected in him. Your rejection of your family, your heartlessness, your greed for success is in his blood. You've made a walking replica of your own shortcomings, Drago, and I pity you, because the future will judge you harshly. There is a barbarian within your midst, and in time, you'll be punished for the pain you've inflicted."

Alberto walked to the door, then turned. "I ask you once again. As a friend who loves you – will you go to your father?"

"No."

Nodding, Alberto walked out.

# Thirty-Six

It was six o'clock, the winter evening coming down, the park empty. No one idled there any longer on such cold nights, and only a few people still walked along the street, illuminated for a brief instant under the gas lamps before moving on. The fire in the bedroom warmed the walls, crept comforting over the bed and lit the side of Simeon's face as he sat by his grandfather. Neither spoke, and from a little way away a foghorn sounded eerily on the Mersey beyond.

Guido was dreaming. He was walking along Cranberry Street, the ship at the end of terrace huge and flecked with lights, the shouts of the seamen coming loud and raucous over the rocking tide. It was New Year, the first year of the Twentieth Century. He stopped at the door of No. 14 and opened it ...

"How is he?" Misia asked, coming into the room.

Her son turned; "Sleeping."

On the other side of the bed sat Mary, her dark red dress creased, the collar high around her neck, her black eyes fathomless, fixed on her husband.

"Can I get you anything?"

Her mother shook her head. "No. He's dreaming," her voice was controlled, without emotion, but her left hand held her husband's tightly. "You could go home, Misia. I'll phone you if there's any change."

"No, I want to stay," she said, then hurried downstairs at the sound of the door bell ringing.

Alberto was on the doorstep. He had made the trip to England without telling her, acting on a whim.

"Alberto – thank you for coming," Misia said warmly, automatically glancing over his shoulder.

"Drago's not with me," he said, moving inside. The hallway was cold, a mirror reflecting both of them. "I'm sorry, Misia, he won't be coming."

She seemed to expect it and said nothing.

"How's your father?"

"Dying," she said, her voice catching, her hand moving up to her forehead, "it can't be long."

"Can I do anything?"

"No, nothing," she said, taking him into the drawing room. "You were kind to come."

"I wanted to."

The room smelt old, unused, the walls shaded, the furniture having a lonely, neglected look. On the mantelpiece were a selection of photographs and the tiny painting Guido had done of Tita. The colours had faded, now all that was clear were the eyes, two bright highlights drawn out from the darkening background.

"Do you want to see him?"

Alberto hesitated. "Later perhaps."

She sat down, offering him a seat beside her. The Liverpool air was damp, the room sombre. Years before they had spoken at the French doors one night in mid summer, talking, Misia relaxed after the birth of her last child. The heat had made her hair damp against her neck, the scent of her flesh soporific.

"Simeon is with him."

Alberto nodded. "He's a remarkable boy."

"The other two come and go, they don't know what to say …" she paused, "neither would I, at their age. But Simeon stays …"

"Is he well?" Alberto asked.

Misia sighed. "He still gets the headaches. But he's not suffered an attack for weeks, not whilst he's been with my father."

The conversation halted. The room was no comfort.

"Would you like something to eat?"

Alberto shook his head. "I'm fine."

"A drink then?"

"No."

"How's Portland?"

She smiled. "Supportive – always at the end of the phone. He's looking after the children," she was talking in short, jerky sentences. "How long can you stay?"

"As long as you want me to."

*

Fitting Billy was there suddenly at the end of Cranberry Street, Ron lumbering behind him, his ponderous, heavily freckled face thoughtful under the Army cap … *Don't put 'im in a home, Mister Razzio, 'e'd be better off dead, 'e would, honestly … He never went in a home*, Guido said, answering him, *I kept my promise.* Ron disappeared then and Guido was suddenly in The Roman House, listening to Morrie Gilling talking.

*I thought you were dead, Morrie.*

*That's a hell of a thing to say to a bloody friend*, he replied, laughing and shaking his bald head. *We've got a fight tomorrow.*

*Good*, Guido replied eagerly, *I haven't been to a fight for a long time.*

Simeon stirred, putting some more coal on the fire and drawing the blanket up around his grandfather's chin before sitting down again. Guido's skin was thinning, veins showing up around his temples, his nose pinched at the bridge. The deep set eyes were closed, his eyelids smooth. Simeon glanced up, and catching Mary watching him, smiled. She responded slowly, her lips mouthing the single word.

Thank you.

In his sleep, Guido was moving on again, suddenly gone from The Roman House and now walking down to the tailor's. He stopped, hearing the church bells and setting his watch. The weight of it felt good in his hand: gold, something valuable, something earned. By his side he was suddenly aware of a shadow and looked down.

*Tita*, he said, smiling and picking up the dog. *Hello, little one.*

They moved on together and then, in an instant, they were transported to an old church site, a ruined patch of dirt where two men fought. Guido watched, recognising George Slater and Bryn Davis – no, he thought in his dream, that can't be right, I didn't know you then, Bryn.

Then his eyes were caught by the sight of a young woman standing by the only remaining stone wall of the church, a tall young woman, whose black eyes were fixed on his. His heart warmed, lifted, all the anxiety of loneliness gone within an instant. Oh God, Mary … he thought … Oh God.

"He moved," Simeon said gently, glancing at the clock. An hour had passed. "He might wake."

Mary stared at her husband's face. "No," she said simply. "He won't wake."

Go on, my love, she willed him. Go on, wherever you are, go on. I'm not afraid, I won't ask you to stay. You've done all you can, no man could have done more. There's nothing left to prove, and nothing left to do. Take your rest, my love.

They could hear Alberto and Misia's voices below, their murmurs coming in time to the clock ticking and the slow steady burning of the fire in the grate.

"Do you think we should call the doctor?" Simeon asked.

Mary stared into his eyes. He met her gaze, one of the few who could. He knows, she thought, he knows that the end is very close now. Her eyes held his, her black gaze looking into his dark eyes; she talked to him without uttering a syllable, asked him for his allegiance and then, when he answered her, she looked back to her husband.

Let go, she urged him, I'll follow you, wherever you go, you know I'll follow you. It's just a little step, Guido, and we've gone so far together. Just a little step on. You can't be afraid, you were never afraid of anything. And I'm not afraid. Let go …

Morning coming over gardens, coming in warm waves of dawn. Italian scents of orchid and mimosa, the sweet long curl of water coming down from upper gardens, down to shimmering glades of light. A horse whinnying, a gate opening … Guido paused in his dream, the gate widening, turning from the worn old warp of wood to something opening without effort. Through this gate I left my home so long ago. Through this gate I walked into a damp morning, and left my family … he paused, glanced back. But there was no woman standing, as his mother had stood so many times before, her disquieting ghost dogging his footsteps down the years. She was no longer there, in his heart or head. Her power had gone and left no shadow.

Guido walked towards the gate, this time without any fear. There was to be no leaving, after all, only a sense of finally, blessedly, coming home. He paused at the entrance and looked ahead …

"Grandma?"

"Ssh …" Mary said, leaning towards her husband, her lips against his ear. "Go on, my love, go on …"

I will not look back, Guido thought in his dream, seeing Mary for an instant and knowing then that he *could* go on. I will simply follow the sound of the boat's horn and the shouts of the boxers, and all the men I knew and all the men I loved. And the woman, the woman calling.

Then Guido Razzio stopped breathing.

Bereft, Simeon laid his head down on the sheet beside his grandfather, Mary straightening up and walking to the door without looking back.

# Thirty-Seven

Drago was dressing, his evening jacket brushed, ready to put on, his grand form reflected in the cheval glass. His hair was thick, black under the overhead light from the chandelier, his feet planted firmly on the silk carpet. There was a reception at the Ambassador's home that night, which all the top echelons of Italian society would attend, together with a few prominent foreigners. It was hinted that Terence Rattigan – fresh from his triumph 'The Wilmslow Boy' – would come, together with the notorious Jean Cocteau. Drago studied his reflection – was it true that Diaghilev on being confronted by Cocteau issued the order 'Astound me'? Drago smiled distantly; it was a part of his life he had neglected until now, perhaps he should meet more artists, develop himself creatively.

Perhaps he should begin to collect paintings or books. Before he had been too busy before, but now he was forty one, and had enough money to buy well. After all, what was the point in buying obscure works? If you wanted to add to your status you had to be seen buying respected artists, not the work of fumbling tyros. Drago pulled on his dinner jacket: a few carefully bought paintings could make an impression in the first floor lounge, could take away the dull monotony of the watered silk walls.

He tugged at his sleeve, suddenly irritated. It wasn't pressed exactly to his liking. Catherine should have seen to it, not left him to discover the negligence just as he was about to go out. Of course, such things did not matter to her; she had no desire to be seen and judged; she preferred to skulk away like someone with something to hide, not like the wife of a prominent surgeon.

Alberto's words came back to him and Drago paused, his hand still clasped around the cuff of his jacket. He had called her a recluse, had hinted that her condition was due to her husband's behaviour, and he had gone on, criticising his children … He would never speak to him again, that was final; how could he, when his closest friend had turned on him? His closest friend – his only friend.

Drago felt a sudden vulnerability agitating him and making him sweat. His shirt felt moist under the arms, his back clammy, and he scrambled for a seat, sitting down and trying, unsuccessfully, to loosen his bow tie. His father was ill, dying. He wanted to see his son … Drago rubbed his forehead with the tips of his fingers. Maybe he *should* have gone back, maybe he should have phoned Misia at least. But his father was a strong man, the chances were that he would recover and that any reunion would have turned out to be an embarrassment.

He was right, Drago consoled himself, it was unnecessary to go running back to Liverpool. His father would recover and in time they would be reunited. No point panicking and forcing the issue. Drago felt calmed and stood up, adjusting his dinner suit and walking out onto the landing. Ahead of him, Catherine walked like a flimsy spirit, her silk trousers and loose top accentuating the paleness of her hair and skin.

"Drago?" she said, turning.

He was unexpectedly affected by her appearance.

"I'm going to the Ambassador's cocktail party," he said, adding hastily. "Why don't you come?"

She shook her head; her hair, bobbed to her shoulders, seemed weightless. "You know I don't care for things like that –"

"It would be a change," he hurried on, suddenly not wanting to go alone. He wanted company, any company, and his wife was gentle, quiet. "Please."

"No, Drago," she said, turning away.

He caught hold of her arm, jerking her round to face him: "Why don't you want to go with me? Why aren't you proud of me?"

She was unconcerned, removed. "You're a very clever man, Drago, and a very gifted one. Go to your party –"

*"You hate me!"* he shouted suddenly.

She raised her finger to her lips to quieten him: "Ssh!" she said, looking round. "You sound like Courtney, saying such things."

"Perhaps my son and I have a lot in common."

Her eyes were unforgiving. "You saw to that from the moment he was born."

*"What the hell does that mean?"* he shouted.

A maid scurried past at the top of the stairs.

"You know actually what I mean, Drago," she answered. "Your son is like he is because of the way you treat him. You've never shown any real affection to either of the children, but with Pila it hasn't been so destructive because she's close to me. With Courtney it's been disastrous."

"You're being ridiculous –"

She was suddenly striking out; looking at her husband in all his finery, knowing that he would attend the party and talk, and impress everyone; people would admire him, place him again on that eternal medical Parnassus, whilst she sat at home with his children and wondered how to repair the damage.

"Drago, you have never treated your son right. I've wondered about it for years, but now I realise that you can't change. You're pushing Courtney away from you day by day. In the end he will leave because you've forced him to; he will have no other choice. Don't you realise how history's repeating itself? You left your home and he will, in time, leave his. You won't hold onto your son through your achievements. He'll leave because he's not happy here – just as you weren't happy in Liverpool."

"Have you finished?"

"No," she said flatly. "You made the greatest mistake of your life rejecting your background. You cut yourself off from your beginnings and you'll never be rooted again." She turned, suddenly exhausted, "I want something better for my children."

"OUR CHILDREN!" he bellowed.

"They don't feel like your children!" she countered. "You don't spend time with them, you don't listen to them –"

"I'm working."

"The eternal cry of the poor father!" Catherine snapped, her pale skin colouring. "Every man who ever neglected his family uses that as an excuse – 'I did it for you. It's all your fault really.'"

He struck her once with the flat of his hand.

Catherine rocked on her feet. Silent, she then studied her husband for a long instant. "Your tie is crooked," she said finally. "Straighten it before you leave."

Having dismissed the chauffeur, Drago drove impatiently, turning the Daimler into the Ambassador's residence, the tyres scuffing on the gravel drive. Lights shimmered into the night, the cries of peacocks coming eerily from the dark grounds, the assortments of limousines lined up in rows outside the palazzo. He got out of the car reluctantly and was immediately assaulted by the noise – the voices and the music coming louder than was usual, the white banking of steps to the front doors uninviting and curiously ominous.

Ponderously, he mounted the stairs and then bowed when the Ambassador came over to him, his arm held as he was steered towards a muddle of chattering Italians. A glass of champagne seemed to come into his hand without him realising it, and for once he drank quickly, without savouring the vintage. The alcohol seemed to go to his head in an instant, a peculiar mistiness affecting his ears, a dryness starting at the base of his throat. The voices were disembodied, shrill, the bass notes of the orchestra pounding into his chest.

His body was suddenly assaulted by the sensation and he grabbed at a passing tray, downing another drink and then another, his brain, usually so controlled, lapsing into garble of thoughts, his speech unsteady. As a big man, his sudden unexpected behaviour was not unnoticed, a young woman in a black crepe dress moving quickly to his side.

"Come and get some air," she said simply, leading him out onto the balcony.

He followed meekly and then looked at her. She hovered in and out of focus, her silk tawny, her eyes dark rimmed, her voice slowing and speeding up alternately.

Stumbling, she caught him and he found himself kissing her, the sweet taste of lipstick clinging to his lips, her hands pressed warmly against his chest.

"I'll get come coffee," she said kindly and moved away.

But he didn't wait for her to return, instead Drago stumbled back into the reception rooms and drank several more glasses of champagne, the nausea hitting him suddenly. Panicking, he lumbered out into the hall and up the stairs, throwing up on the floor of the nearest toilet, the acrid vomit bubbling round his lips. Shivering, he slumped to the floor and grabbed at a towel, soaking it with cold water and then wrapping it around it shoulders, the damp seeping into his dinner jacket.

His shame was complete, yet when the nausea subsided he stood up and threw the towel into the bath, opening the door and stepping out into the corridor. Several people passed, the young woman appearing again and standing at the top of the steps. She said something Drago couldn't catch and then gave him three tablets, passing him another drink with her other hand. He had never been a part of the drug taking clique, never wanted to be out of control; but the day had been full of old memories and his guilt begged to be obliterated, so swallowed the tablets, the taste bitter on his tongue, and then followed the girl downstairs.

With terrifying rapidity the room speeded up; the walls yawning then closing in on him; the windows turning to water, the whole shimmering bank of guests vaporising into a mirage. Drago blundered forwards through the crowd, the girl following; his immaculate suit wet along the shoulders and mottled with vomit, his dark hair damp with sweat. He was immortal suddenly; a god amongst all the peasants who surrounded him. With loathing he looked into their faces. He had created many of them; repaired their features, soothed their egos, made little graven images of them so that lesser mortals might look at them in awe.

He could do anything; he could recreate the world and all of God's creatures. Swaying, Drago looked at his hands and began to laugh, waving his palms in front of the startled faces, his fingers wriggling – look, look, look at what I can do. Look at the hands which can work magic. The nausea came again, and he tripped, lurching down the front steps and falling head first into the gravel. He laughed to himself softly, his palms pressed downwards, his right cheek grazed.

A group of guests had followed his departure and stood at the top of the steps watching him – Drago Razzio, the gifted, brilliant surgeon, the man who was always diplomatic, guarded, cautious; Drago Razzio lying drunk under the blind stars.

Awkwardly, Drago rolled over, making a superhuman effort, his hands stretching upwards towards the silver planets in the black vacuum sky. The ground no longer felt hard, it felt instead like marshmallow – he had fallen into marshmallow! Drago thought disbelievingly, laughter rising to his lips, Why was everyone staring? Didn't they realise how good it felt to fall into marshmallow? …

The young woman ran down the steps and knelt beside him, her knees bare, the knee cap defined. Drago stared at her kneecap, saw under the skin at the bone below and touched it gently.

"Lovely …" he burbled.

"Get up," she said, trying to pull him to his feet.

He remained stubbornly supine.

"Help me, somebody," she called.

A man ran down the steps towards them.

His feet sounded metallic. *He was a robot!* Drago thought blindly. A robot from the stars, come down to kidnap him and take away all his secrets.

Finally Drago moved, sitting up and then getting unsteadily to his feet. The gravel rasped under his feet, the faces at the window blobs of white fat, the orchestra grinding on, on out of tune instruments. He pushed the couple away and moved to his car.

"You can't drive –"

Drago easily overpowered the man; it seemed to him that he fell as slight as a piece of paint chipped from an upstairs windows. He *was* a robot, after all, Drago realised, sliding into the driver's seat and starting up the engine. Wanting to say something, Drago wound down the window and then remembered an old line from a Marx Brothers film;

"I've had a wonderful time," he bellowed. "but this wasn't it."

Laughing, he pulled away, his headlights pointing him home.

Time passed, the second spiralling into hours. Time elongated, the clock on the dashboard making faces at him suddenly, the sound of the engine and smell of the leather seats bringing back his nausea. Parking, Drago closed his eyes and then, after gagging ineffectually, fell uneasily to sleep.

He woke at just after three in the morning, his limbs cramped, wincing in pain as he moved his head. The memory came back in hideous pieces. Had he really shamed himself? The acrid smell of old vomit was on his jacket and he grimaced, ripping it off and throwing it out of the car window. He felt chilled, sick, waves of nausea making him unsteady on his feet. He wanted, above everything, to get warm and sleep, but how could he, when he kept remembering what he'd done?

Helplessly, he clenched his fists and pressed them to his eyelids. *Why* had he done it? Why had he destroyed his reputation? After so long cultivating his status, why had he ruined it so recklessly? He remembered the young woman and the tablets. Jesus, what had he done, what could he have been thinking of? Drugs – if anyone found out he could be disciplined, even struck off. He wanted to drive away, but he couldn't, the headache and nausea prevented him – so instead he was forced to sit and wait for it to pass.

The darkness was absolute. Even the silver stars which had seemed so amusing had gone out. Drago was in an deserted area, without houses, without street lamps, without noise. A closed land, full of darkness and emptiness. It was Alberto's fault, Drago thought suddenly, and Catherine's. Everyone had pushed to madness; blaming him for this, blaming him for that. His fault, always his fault, never a word about what he had done for them, only what he had *failed* to do for them. And what was that? I have failed to make them happy, he thought bitterly. Well, so what? They didn't make me happy either.

And then he remembered his father and Alberto asking him to go home … Was it only that morning? Only hours ago? How could so much happen in one day? How could so much work and success be threatened in one day? How could his life, his family, his beliefs, all be tried and judged in one small, bitter day? His eyes closed, his head lolling back against the seat, his mouth open. He shivered, turning on the engine and feeling the heat coming in on his feet … What could he do now? How could he repair the damage? … He burped, bile filling his mouth, his eyes dry, itchy. Dear God, Drago thought despairingly, what more can happen?

The night went on: no moon, no stars, only darkness, the car a little metal animal left out in the cold. Lonely, like the man inside it. His guilt was complete, overwhelming; and in those sobering, shivering, sickened hours Drago saw for the first time the callousness of his actions. He had been ashamed of his home, of his parents, of his father's work. He had never seen that Guido had had to struggle as much as he had done; he had simply been repelled by his father's choice of business and that repulsion had coloured everything, had taken away rightful respect and admiration from a man who had done so much.

Injured by his own family's coldness, Drago saw then how much his attentions had wounded his parents. He had patronised his father and despised his mother. Afraid that someone would discover the details of Billy Poole's death. But why? She was worthy of respect, awe, genuine admiration. Which woman would do as much for him? Drago wondered. By his own cruelty he had forfeited the chance of redemption: by his own refusal to love he had made himself unlovable. It was no one's fault, except his own, that he was surrounded by a family who went in fear of him. Alberto's words came back to him in that instant. He was right, Courtney *was* the barbarian within their midst, and he had been created in his father's own image.

For a man who made people beautiful, it was a grotesque punishment. Had he been a kinder man, he could have created a loving family but instead he had ground any peck of love and was left with resentment, fear, and a terrible vacuum. Who would care for him when he was old? Who would sit with him, mourn for him? Who would love him? … His stomach lurched, then settled again, sweat skimming his top lip. I can still make amends, Drago thought, if I start now, I can still make amends … He shivered again, his skin sticky but cold. If I go home now I can be reunited with my parents, see my father, be reconciled with Misia. He turned off the heater and sunk further down into the leather seat. When the morning comes, I'll cancel my operations and fly over to England. He was determined, desperate to relieve the emptiness inside him.

A memory of Guido's face came to him then; the strong face of his childhood. His father had taught him Italian, the language Drago now thought of as his mother tongue. He remembered sitting with Guido and repeating the words carefully, patiently … How much time had he spent with *his* son? Drago asked himself, guilt driving a steel pin into his guts. There was only one solution, one chance of forgiveness. He would go home and ask his father to forgive him. He would make amends, and hope to be taken in by the family he had dismissed so ruthlessly.

Another hour passed. Drago dozed, woke, tormented with guilt, sick with fatigue and alcohol, his mouth dry, his lips sticky. He moved, but slumped back into his seat again, and again, dozed. The night turned over above him, it slid towards dawn, the first markings of light coming on the horizons when Drago woke for the third time and turned on the engine.

He felt violently ill, but he could no longer stay out in the cold and was desperate to get home, to begin preparations for his trip to England. The car came to life under him, the engine seeming for a moment too aggressive, too huge to control, before Drago eased off the hand brake and moving out into the road. He drove slowly, turning on the window screen wipers to clear a sudden shower, his eyes fixed unwaveringly on the road ahead.

At five thirty six he turned into his driveway and parked, resting his head for a moment on the steering wheel before finally getting out of the car. The immense house was black against the lifting sky, the gardens marked out in living chess squares, ebony poplars flanking the horizons. Chilled, Drago walked through the front doors. No one had waited up for him. Ponderously he climbed the marble stairs, his feet making unearthly footsteps, the noise rising through the silent house and vibrating in the cupola above. He looked up, his head swimming for an instant; the painted angels gazed down compassionately, their faces offering comfort.

It would be all right, Drago consoled himself, it was not too late. His shirt was sticking to his back, his skin clammy, his hand leaving a damp mark on the gilded banister rail as he paused again before moving on. The children would be asleep, he realised, but he would take them out at the weekend, when he returned from England. He would buy them toys, and talk to Courtney. Yes, talk. He would have to, to point out what was going wrong, to get his son back on track. Drago nodded to himself, his breaths coming in uneven gasps as he rounded the bend in the stairs. He would have to explain what could happen if his son carried on the way he was. He would have to discipline him – no, Drago thought suddenly, no discipline, he would love him instead. He would love them all. Courtney, Pila and Catherine – he would love them and they would love him in return. As his father had loved him; as his father had given him a home, a name, a place to belong.

Drago moved towards his bedroom door and then leaned heavily against it, finally turning the handle and walking in. His bed was turned down, inviting him to rest, but he moved to the bathroom instead and hung over the basin for a long minute, his head bowed.

"Drago?"

He turned at the sound of his wife's voice. Catherine stood motionless in the doorway, her hair lose, her eyes still dark from sleep. "Are you ill?"

"Catherine …" he said simply, reaching out to her.

She stepped back, quick and silent.

"Catherine," he repeated.

She could smell the vomit on him and the odour of sweat coming cold from his skin. Her look of disgust was scorching and he floundered.

"Catherine, I … I …"

"You have to operate in the morning," she said, her tone flat. "You should wash and get some sleep."

He shook his head. "No, I'm going to England," he said, straightening up and facing her. "I'm going to see my father." Her expression flickered. "I have to go. Come with me, Catherine," he begged. "Come with me, you'll meet my family."

She stood without speaking, without moving.

"Everything will be better from now on, I promise," he continued. "I just have to make my peace with my father –"

"Drago –"

"When I've seen him everything will be all right," he interrupted her. "I just have to see my father, that's all."

"You can't" she said softly, "he's dead."

There was a sudden noise of shouting from far away; a piercing howl which was remote, unexpected at that hour of the morning. Startled, Drago turning in the direction of the sound and then caught his own reflection in the mirror – his mouth wide open, the noise issuing like the whine of an ungodly whistle blown fiercely and wickedly into the dark.

Book Four

The Outsiders

# Thirty-Eight

## 1959
## London

Imagine this – a man of Polish origins, around thirty, having inherited a silver shop on Carlos Place from an uncle; a man standing nearly six feet, unshod, a little more in the best Oxford brogues; well muscled, with a compact head, brown hair crisp and short. This man, (blue eyed, long nosed,) has a pale lipped mouth and a beard. Not the kind of beard that children draw at Christmas, more a soft velvety coating to the bottom half of his face; well trimmed, tailored to the line of his jaw. His beard, unlike his hair, is prematurely greying; it picks up the blue colouring of his eyes and echoes it flatteringly.

He dresses as people do when they have inherited style. Clothes sit well on him; they fit. He knows instinctively which articles compliment him, his wardrobe playing host to his personality. The word handsome is not accurate, he transcended good looks; he is urbane, cultivated, witty, good humoured, an easy host and a magical guest. Invited to many weakened house parties, he bring not a bottle of wine or a box of chocolates, but something which appeals directly to the host. A brace of kippers he has presented; at another time he gave a pair of theatre tickets – he gives thought to his gifts, and people respond to his attentiveness. When he departs at the end of the weekend he leaves his room immaculate and, if their are no staff, he assists his hostess by stripping his bed and folding the sheets ready for laundry.

He is called Caryl de Solt, this man. Caryl de Solt. 'Never at Fault' is his sobriquet; he has never been known to give offence, be aggressive or demanding. His talent is limited; he is no businessman, but has the money to employ sound accountants and managers to look after his affairs. He glides through London society like a happy child, with no thought of yesterday or tomorrow.

That is his particular skill; his refusal to consider anything beyond the five minutes he immediately inhabits. Past promises, arrangements and beliefs are always superseded by the promises, arrangements and beliefs of the present. He has no sense of past or future; the here and now, the moment, is his only stalking ground. Because of his luminous, benign charm he escapes censor, people are compelled to forgive him, to forget the promised appointment, the cancelled arrangement. It is not his fault, they argue, it is simply the way he is.

If you look to him for amusement and distraction, he is the perfect guest. He can quote Homer, and tell you everything about the restoration of the Farnese murals. His brain is a receptacle for information, but he has no opinions, nothing to upset anyone seated at the dinner table. He acts as a well behaved child; listens to his companions and reforms his opinions to suit the company. He can see good in the devil, and, if pressed, evil in God. He sways, this man, and walks within the immediate present without being touched by the past or intimidated by the future.

Had he met a woman of a similar nature – someone with the attention span of a boiled egg – he might have settled down. He might have bought a house and brought up children who would also remain mentally grounded. But he did not. Instead he fell in love with a woman six years older than himself and spent five years getting a divorce from her. Portland represented him; his towering bulk looming over the seated figure of Caryl de Solt like an admonishing parent. The judge was soon on the claimant's side; the wife was patently unreasonable, demanding, shrewish. How could there be anyone more amenable than this man? Caryl de Solt – Never at Fault.

Portland was amused by him, even invited him to dinner, Misia sitting at the table and watching the Pole thoughtfully. She was forty nine years old, ageing slightly, her eyes shrewd under the dated fringe. Looking down the table towards her, at first Portland saw the girl he had met that first day at the railway station, for once blanking out the truth, but then he blinked and saw her in reality. She was, he teased her, his pet armadillo, bound to become a tough old lady, his resident harpy. He liked the idea of that, liked to think of her thin and whippet-quick, dressed in trousers, giving him hell – just like she gave the boxers; just like she gave everyone. No one could fool her, she was a walking Geiger counter for deceit, and could uncover a poseur quicker than a pig could scent truffles.

So Portland watched with interest as she listened to Caryl de Solt; Misia smiled now and then, as though amused; and she swapped stories with the Pole, but her eyes had the look of someone regarding a unfamiliar species, one which did not immediately impress.

"Well, what do you make of him?" Portland asked when Caryl de Solt had left.

She blew out the dinner candles one by one before answering. "I suppose we should be grateful that he isn't one of twins."

Portland laughed. "You don't like him! You're in a minority, everyone else thinks the world of him."

"I seem to recall," she said tartly, "that they said the same about Hitler once."

"Oh, come on! He's not that bad."

"I worry about anyone who's idea of conversation is to parrot back anything his hostess says," she snorted. "If I wanted that kind of attention, I'd buy a macaw."

Oh, poor Mr. de Solt. Had he heard what Misia had said he would have been distraught, uncomprehending. After all, hadn't he been charming? Hadn't he eaten an almost inedible roast and declared it wonderful? Hadn't he heard all about the fight arranged in the Albert Hall for the next month and kept his face impassive when Misia told him about one of her boxers having a ruptured spleen? Hadn't he sat by the window and never said anything about the draught coming down on his back? Who would have thought that the houses were so chilly in Holland Park?

He would have mortified to be so ill thought of, even though he had had certain reservations beforehand. Not that he hadn't wanted to visit the Bennings; they were too well known not to admire; Misia's quizzical face cropping up endlessly on the Sports pages. Who could resist an invitation to see how such a mismatched couple lived? A barrister and a boxing promoter, swapping verbal punches and sparring like professionals at table … But if he had known what Misia thought of him he would have been wounded, especially as it was unjust. Caryl de Solt – Never at Fault.

"Don't invite him again, Portland," Misia said, turning at the top of the stairs.

"That bad, hey?"

She nodded. "'A honey tongue, a heart of gall' – that's an Italian proverb my father used to quote."

"I don't think Caryl de Solt has the personality to be dangerous," Portland replied evenly.

"You may be right," Misia said, walking up the stairs ahead of him.

"But you don't think so?"

She turned. "I wouldn't trust him, that's all," she put her head on one side: "Has he paid your fee yet?"

Portland laughed: "Point taken."

# Thirty-Nine

## Italy

Catherine's condition was deteriorating, Pila could see it, could measure it daily. Her mother was not well. She hadn't been fit for a long time; but having always been listless no one had attributed her lethargy to a medical condition. She said nothing about it herself, seemed unconcerned, unwilling to talk.

Only Alberto confronted her about it: and only Alberto could illicit some response. "I feel tired," she admitted, "that's all. Don't worry anyone."

Was she thinking about her husband? Alberto wondered incredulously. Was she still caring about what he thought?

Against all the odds Drago had regained his status after the debacle at the Ambassador's party. When people discovered that his father had died that night they were instantly sympathetic, attributing his behaviour to grief. Despite death and estrangement, Guido had provided the perfect alibi, and his son never suggested that there was any other cause for his temporary lack of control.

But Drago never risked his reputation again: and his fleeting guilt on that chilling night turned into pathological mistrust. He had been cheated out of his chance of redemption and was embittered; the only safety was in work. Not in family; only the hospital offered sanctuary and to her cold white arms he turned, working endlessly, honing and perfecting his skills until he was inundated with patients. But as the years passed he found that cosmetic surgery did not fully satisfy him; people's vanity had a limited appeal and he was rich enough to avoid the label of society doctor.

Reconstructive surgery became his new cause: he lectured and travelled, and undertook the hopeless cases no other surgeon would risk. One particular case became famous. An Arab had come to Drago suffering from infectious tuberculosis, his lower jaw and nose eaten away. Mystified, Drago asked why the medication had not stopped the progress of the disease and was told, through the interpreter, that the man had sold the drugs for money. So over the months which followed the tuberculosis had spread, and now he had come to Drago with only half a face.

Before surgery, Drago had taken the patient to an important medical convention, the Arab wheeled in, his face covered whilst Drago outlined the history of his case. His voice was strongly confident, his movements deceptively lazy, the birthmark on his forehead darkening to a dun brown. When he knew he had his audience captivated, Drago took the covering from the patient's face. Almost as one, they moved forwards, looking curiously at the havoc of the man's features. As the doctors moved, the patient leaned back automatically, his eyes rheumy above the black expanse where his nose and mouth should have been.

"Gentleman, we have a very interesting case here," Drago said, "but not a hopeless one ..."

He talked on, outlining the way he would reconstruct the features; a new jawbone constructed from a small rib.

"… the vocal chords have not been affected yet. Thankfully we managed to start medication again and halt any further advance of the tuberculosis …"

The patient turned his head; his eyes fixed on Drago. He didn't understand what he was saying, he saw only a man in his fifties obviously at ease, a man who was much respected – judging from the way the other doctors listened to him. The patient swallowed, feeling hideously exposed, aware of the hundred eyes on him.

"… we will never be able to create proper lips, or sensitivity in that area, but a reasonable facsimile of a mouth, and later a nose, is possible …"

The patient sat still in his white gown, his legs bare. He swallowed again, aware of the odd clucking sound such an action made.

"… from the side view," Drago said, turning the man's head. "… you will see that there is no profile …"

The full extent of the damage was suddenly more obvious, the face caving away at the bridge of the nose, a space were the bottom half of the face should have been, the muscle and tissue exposed.

"… he will never be a Adonis," Drago said, smiling dimly as the audience laughed, ".. but I can make a reasonable face for him. I can certainly make eating more comfortable, and I am fairly certain that I can make talking possible again …"

The patient closed his eyes, humiliated by the multitude of stares, and bowed his head. Drago saw the movement and responded, re-covering the lower portion of the Arab's face with white gauze, and then touching him for an instant on the shoulder. The action had been so slight that anyone else might have missed it, but the patient felt it and took comfort from it – his eyes following Drago gratefully as he moved away again.

Alberto had also noticed the action, the unexpected tenderness offered, and he sighed. If only Drago had learned to express such kindness to his family. But they were forever off limits: time distancing them, Pila now twenty two, Courtney nineteen. They had grown up in an emotional wilderness and never escaped from the barrenness of their childhood. Catherine had loved both, but her influence had never been sufficient to compensate for their father's relentless neglect. She had partially succeeded with her daughter, but her son had not turned to her for comfort and as he grew older Alberto's prediction came true. Courtney was indeed the barbarian within their midst.

He had no interest in work, certainly no interest in medicine; he had no interest in anything other than his own closeted world. His friends were few, hangers on, boys of his own age who liked him for his wealth only. Courtney knew it, and he used the fact, putting the boys through a series of mental hoops, degrading them, bullying them, then making recompense, rewarding them for allowing him to humiliate them. Physically he was smaller than his father, and had remained thin, narrowed shouldered, his hands bony, big-wristed. He had no look of his parents, with his eyes protruding slightly over the gaunt cheeks, a cleft in his angular chin, and his fingernails bitten to the quick.

Alberto had seen him grow up, turning from the tantrum throwing child, to the lost boy on the balcony, and then into a young man with a peculiarly bleak and yearning look. Courtney Razzio was hungry, voracious for something, Alberto thought, but what? Money, no, he had that. Status, no, he had no apparent ambition, then what? … He had visited he house only the previous day; before he and Drago flew out to the Madrid conference; and had spent several moments watching Courtney unobserved. He was sitting on the side of the fountain eating sweets, idly flinging the wrappers into the clear water, where they bobbed under the overhanging putti … Alberto wondered what would happen if Drago saw what his son was doing, and then realised that Drago never saw anything that Courtney did. He had blocked off his son; had already judged him and considered him odious.

Courtney turned suddenly, his eyes fixing on the window where Alberto stood. Automatically he dipped back, then felt horribly foolish and surprised by his reaction. What on earth had spooked him? Courtney was only a young man, he had no power, no reason to intimidate him. And yet the look on his face had been gloating. He had known Alberto had been watching him and had wanted to catch him out – had wanted to embarrass and discomfort him.

"Alberto?"

He turned at the sound of Pila's voice.

She stood at the doorway, lean, tall, her eyes as dark as coal, her hair full and curling about her face. Walking towards him she smiled, some goofy dentistry leaving her teeth slightly crooked at the front. It added a sudden and welcome reality to her face.

"Pila, ciao," Alberto said, kissing her on both cheeks.

Her skin was warm and smelled strangely of tomatoes. "Ciao," she replied, smiling again.

"Is your father ready?"

She nodded, "Papa will be down soon." Then she gazed towards Courtney. "I wanted to ask you something, Alberto. My mother's not well, and I wanted to talk."

"You can talk to me."

She smiled kindly, but distantly. "No, I need to talk to a woman – and there's no one here I can confide in." Her voice was muted, as though she was afraid of being overheard.

"What about your friends?"

"No one has friends here," she admonished him, "you know that, Alberto." He said nothing, so she continued: "I've been thinking about my aunt."

It was the last thing he had expected her to say and threw up his hands in surprise. "Pila, why now?"

"Why not?" she countered. "I can't stay here always, Alberto, not if anything happens to my mother. I know she's not going to die …" Pila continued, frowning, lines appearing across her forehead. "… but we've talked about the future, and we think that it might be a good idea for me to make contact with the rest of my family." She leaned towards the window, staring out at her brother. "I couldn't stay here alone with Courtney."

"He's never hurt you, has he?"

She laughed, the sound was unexpected "No, Alberto – but he might, in time. He might when my mother's gone and my father's away. He follows me now, watches me … he always has, but not like he has done lately. Now he looks as though he's waiting," she paused, her palm slid down the glass, her hand falling to her side. "I'm sorry, my imagination gets the better of me sometimes."

"You know you can call on me anytime, don't you? You have my home number."

Pila smiled again, then pulled back her hair, her neck exposed for a long instant before she let the curls fall again. Alberto was aware – as he had been for some years – of Pila's sensuality. She didn't try to gain attention, she merely moved in a way which was naturally sexual. The thought worried him as he glanced out to the figure by the fountain.

"I think you and Catherine are right. I think you should get in touch with the Bennings."

Pila seemed relieved, no longer so earnest. "Then I will. I'll write, or should I phone?" she frowned, "But what happens if they don't want to see me?"

Alberto looked at her incredulously: "Misia's your aunt, she's always wanted the family to be reunited. She'll welcome you."

"What's she like?"

He laughed. "Thin, formidable, a tongue like a steel trap – a good person to have on your side, and a terrible enemy. She wears trousers a lot," he placed his index finger across his forehead. "… and she has this ridiculous fringe which she's had since she was about twenty."

Pila laughed. "What about her husband?"

"Well, Portland's a man you don't forget. He was always big, but now he has a 'bay window'."

Pila frowned. "A what?"

Alberto made an expansive arm movement. "A belly." He shook his head indulgently. "He's like a big old dog, good natured but tough, very tough. He won a murder case the other week, got a woman off by his sheer size – I'm convinced of it. He put all his physical and moral weight behind her and he won. It was incredible, nobody expected her to be acquitted."

Avidly, Pila listened. "And they have sons, don't they?"

"Three," Alberto agreed, "Simeon, who's twenty six, Harewood's who's twenty four and Vincent's who's twenty two. They're all totally different: have virtually nothing in common but their name – the Benning Brothers. They were well known as babies because of the boxing, and it's never changed, it seems that England likes to know everything about its famous trio."

"They're famous?" Pila said, stunned

He nodded. "In a limited way. Remember, Misia's mother ran a string of boxers in the 1920's when such things were unheard of. She was very fierce – she had to be, no one gave her an easy time. Then later, after the war, Misia helped her mother to rebuild the business and now, well now, it's a industry in its own right. 'The Benning Boxers' and 'The Benning Brothers' are indistinguishable in the public's eye."

Pila considered the information thoughtfully: "And they help their mother to run the business?"

Alberto rubbed his nose with his forefinger, his eyebrows raised: "That was the way it was *supposed* to be, but unfortunately Simeon turned out to have no interest in the fights, and Harewood's followed his father into the law." He smiled wickedly.

"Harewood's a bit of a snob actually, Pila. He's not unlike your father for that – thinks *boxing's* below him, tries to distance himself by living in the London house with his father and Simeon, whilst Vincent and Misia spend most of their time in Liverpool."

"But if my aunt and uncle are married why do they live apart?"

"Because they always have," Alberto replied evenly, "They were never conventional – that's probably why the marriage works so well. They love from a distance."

Pila turned and looked down the garden again, frowning. Courtney had vanished.

"I want to get to know them, Alberto," she said quietly, "I think I would be safe with them."

*

*My dear aunt Misia,*

*This is very difficult to write, because I don't know what to say. I'm your niece, Drago's daughter – well, of course you know that. I've heard all about you and your family from Alberto – he's kept my mother and I in touch with news for many years. He tells us about the boxing and about you.*

*I don't know how to say this, so I better just write it down. I would like to know you. There, that's said at last. Catherine, my mother, sends her regards – (believe me, she means it, she's kind and always honest) She hasn't been well, nothing serious, just a lack of energy. I think, I hope …*

*Alberto tells me that he has spoken of us – so we can't really be strangers, can we? I hope not. Well, whatever you decide to do, I send my kindest thoughts to all of you.*

*Pila*

"Get off it!" Misia snapped, knocking Vincent's hand away from the letter. "I want to read it again."

"You've read it four times," he replied, "You could recite it word for word."

She ignored him and stared at the paper, cream coloured, topped with an ornamental crest. "So Drago's delusions of grandeur increase, do they?" her fingers ran over the design. "Embossed – how elegant."

"What are you going to do?" Vincent asked.

Misia turned and looked at her son thoughtfully. Pila, such a foreign name, and yet such an easy way with her, at least in her writing. Good English too. She stared at Vincent, curly brown hair, eyes the colour of God's Knows what, strong teeth, his nose broken across the bridge from a fight when he was thirteen. Some boy broke my nose, Mum, he'd said … Well, what did you do to him? she'd replied … Vincent had grinned. Knocked him out cold, he's said, knocked him out cold.

"She sounds all right."

Misia raised her eyebrows. "There isn't a woman born who doesn't sound alright to you."

He leaned back in his seat, big, like his father. At ease. "I just meant –"

"She's your cousin, remember?" Misia interrupted deftly. "I would like to think that

178

you could restrain yourself for once."

"So you're going to invite her over?"

Misia tapped the letter with her fingernail. "That is for me to know, Vincent, and for you to guess."

Portland was firmly in favour. He had watched the feud continue year after year, bitter and unending – or so he had thought. The death of Guido had been the coup de grace, the final provocation which made Misia swear revenge on her brother. She had terrified Portland that night; her voice low, her eyes narrowed as she walked out into the garden of the Liverpool house, her arms wrapped round herself. It was too cold to be out, but she had stood under the Northern moon and couldn't, and *wouldn't*, cry.

Her father wasn't dead to her; the one person she had idolised all her life wasn't gone … In those harrowing minutes after Guido's death, Portland looked at his wife and tried to comfort her. But she was beyond it, and it was unnecessary, after all, Guido was still alive … He tried to reason with her, but she wouldn't listen, and then she turned and saw Alberto standing at the French windows – and remembered her brother.

Although she would never admit it, Drago saved her sanity that night. In hating him, Misia found a way to scream out her agony to the gods who had taken away her beloved father. In cursing her brother she exhausted herself. In damning him, she absolved a pain which was, quite literally, too much to endure. She stood under the moon and barked her curses into the darkness, screaming into the night, repeating her brother's name over and over again until she was hoarse.

Distressed, Portland walked over to her, but she moved away from him, returning to the house and scribbling something on a piece of paper. It was a ritual he was familiar with: undertaken at every New Year to ensure that a wish would come true in the twelve months to come. You were supposed to write what you wanted onto the paper and fold it, then burn it, the wish carried up to Heaven on the smoke … Misia scratched a few words on the paper and then folded it, laid it in an ashtray and put a match to it. It caught alight immediately, Misia's face distorted in the sudden flashing of light. Then, when the flames went out, she turned to her husband.

Portland took hold of her arm. "What did you wish for?"

"I wished," she said evenly, "that my brother would die."

He remembered her curse and felt the force of it for a long time afterwards. Although not a superstitious man, for months Portland expected to receive news from Italy – daily anticipating Drago's death. But the year passed and he lived on, and Misia never mentioned the incident again. Until now, Portland thought. Now she was bound to think of it. Drago's daughter had written to her; opening the lines of communication which had been closed for so long. The wall was being breached at last.

But would Misia relent? Would she want to end the feud, would she allow her brother's child into her home? Would she, could she, trust Pila? Could she ever forget that she was Drago's daughter? The sins of the fathers go back a long way, Portland thought soberly.

"So what *are* you going to do?" he asked her that weekend.

Misia shrugged. She was pulling on her gloves, her hair hidden under an old trilby. "I'm going to the gym, where else?"

"Don't be obtuse," he said, walking over to her and pulling her collar up round her neck. "It's cold out."

She wrinkled her nose. "Why don't you come with me?"

"I can't. Leamington managed to find me another divorce case. I have a lot of reading to do."

Misia looked up at her husband: "How are his daughters?"

"Still unmarried. But still fascinating. To their father, at least."

"You know," Misia said, tapping his stomach. "You're getting a bit portly, old love."

"And you're a stringy old boiler."

She chuckled softly. "Wait up for me?"

He nodded. "You know I will … but what about Pila?"

Misia moved away, suddenly distant. "What about her?"

"What are you going to do?"

"I've done it," she said, walking to the door and pausing on the step. "She's coming over to see us next month."

# Forty

"I don't know how to tell him," Pila said, sitting by her mother's side in the library. Catherine had bought a selection of American thrillers: rubbish, Drago called them, pot boilers. But they amused her, kept her mind occupied, so she kept buying them – and saw that they were delivered when her husband was away.

"What d'you think he'll say when I tell him I'm going to England?"

Catherine looked up. Her face was translucent, her figure as insubstantial as smoke. "I want you to go, Pila. I don't care what your father says, and neither should you. They're welcoming you into their home. You have to go now. Make a success of it, sweetheart, they're family, after all. I don't want you ending up like me. You've got cousins, an aunt, an uncle, they'll have a different way of living. We've been shut away here for so long we think there IS nothing else out there."

"Do you think they'll like me?"

Catherine looked into her daughter's face. "Don't be afraid – that's always been my problem, I don't want you to be like me."

Pila thought of the vast house, of Courtney sidling round, of the servants walking silently down the corridors, and of the mordant, crushing quiet.

"Will you be alright without me?"

Catherine smiled. "What have I got to be afraid of here? This is my sanctuary," she replied, taking her daughter's hand, "Go to Liverpool, Pila, go out into the world. Do it to please me. Do it for me."

There was a knock on the door, interrupting them, Courtney walking in and leaning against the side of his mother's desk. His expression was hostile, his actions jerky. "I want to go too."

Catherine turned away, biting her lip.

"Go where?" Pila asked her brother.

"To England," Courtney replied, "I know all about it."

"You never could resist listening at doors, could you?" his sister replied, getting to her feet and facing him: "So what do you want?"

"I've told you, I want to go to England –"

"You can't."

"Why not?" he replied, grinning; "Does father know about this trip? I mean, I'm sure he'd like to."

"Implying that if I don't let you go with me, you'll tell him?"

He nodded. "Something like that."

Catherine's was flushed: "Courtney don't –"

Pila turned to her mother. "It's okay, let me handle this," she said simply, glancing back to her brother. "You think you can blackmail me, do you? Well, I'm sorry to disappoint you, but I'm just going to tell my father about the trip. D'you want to come?"

"You're not!" Courtney replied hotly. "You wouldn't dare."

She moved to the door and then paused. "Are you coming or not?"

He hesitated, looked first at his mother and then at his sister, his eyes suspicious. "I don't believe you," he said at last.

"So follow me," Pila said coldly, as she opened the door and walked out.

Her footsteps echoed on the marble stairs, Courtney following her hurriedly, moving close to the wall, his eyes fixed on his sister. He was curious, but afraid, torn between wanting to see Pila confront their father and yet scared that he might be exposed as the reason for her confession. She kept walking confidently, her dark head erect, her back stiff – and he kept following, turning at the foot of the stairs.

"You won't *really* tell him."

Her tone was sour with contempt. "You're the coward, Courtney, not me."

"But if you do," he said, running over to her and putting his head on one side, "you'll ruin our chances."

"What chances are those?"

He frowned, surprised. "Our going to England –"

"You're *not* going," she snapped, moving away.

He crouched over the banister, dropping his voice to a malevolent undertone. "He'll hate you if you tell him. He'll hate you!" Courtney hissed.

"Like he hates you?"

Too stung to reply, Courtney watched his sister walking across the hall, passing the marble busts and the tapestries: her figure a moving, living creature amongst all the dead. Mesmerised, he continued to watch and then slid off the last step and continued to follow her from a distance, seeing Pila turn at the end of the corridor leading to her father's study.

She had been too angry to feel any fear until then, but now that the door was in front of her Pila hesitated and found herself gulping for breath. Just go in and face him, she willed herself, just tell him … But she still couldn't move, the window at the end of the corridor looking out on the soft Italian morning, the water sparking light of its surface. Go on, move …

"I knew you wouldn't dare," Courtney said softly. Pila turned. He was standing a couple of yards away from her, his back pressed against the wall. In a sudden flash of sunlight his eyes were transformed, without colour. "I knew you wouldn't dare."

Her hand went towards the door. He watched her; she hesitated; he laughed softly and in that moment of indignation and fury, Pila knocked.

Courtney disappeared; gone in an instant.

"Come in."

The door opened slowly, a heavy walnut door which creaked as she closed it behind her. Drago was sitting at his desk, the walk from the door stretching into infinity.

He looked up. "Pila … what is it?"

She began to take steps towards him, keeping her eyes ahead, trying not to turn and walk out. She struggled to steady herself. She was not a child, she was twenty two years old and he was her father – what could he do to her? What would he want to do to her? She was merely going to England, that was all; going to visit family. Family – the family which had never been mentioned – the Bennings – about which never a word had been exchanged. In twenty two years her father had never mentioned them to her; to all intents and purposes they were dead. And now she was going to visit them.

Going into the enemy camp.

Her courage nearly failed her, but the thought of Courtney's sneering forced her on. The desk was opulently grand, stretched out before her father like an operating table, his hands resting on the black marble top. He said nothing, his expression a void.

"Papa. Have you got a moment?"

He nodded. "Of course. What is it?"

"I want to take a trip –"

"Princess Ferenza again?" he asked hopefully.

Pila shook her head. No, it wasn't another of the old woman's trips to France or Vienna, Pila acting as bait to lure male interest.

"I'm going to England."

"England," he echoed.

"I don't want to lie to you …" she went on. "… I don't want to do anything behind your back."

"Go on," his voice was chilled, suspended in ice.

"I'm going to see my aunt."

He rose to his feet so quickly that she jumped back, bumping into a small table behind her. The ornament which had been on it fell to the floor, making a piercing crash.

"Sorry," she muttered, righting the table. "sorry …"

"My *sister*," Drago said flatly, leaning over the desk, his palms flat on its surface. "WHY?"

Pila met his eyes: "We thought –"

"*We?*"

"I," she corrected herself quickly. "I thought it would be a good idea to see something of the rest of the family."

"Oh, get out," Drago said wearily, slumping into his seat.

Pila had expected anything other than this. Anger, yes; recriminations, attempts at convincing her that she should not go. But resignation? No, she had not anticipated that.

"Listen, Papa."

"Get out," he repeated, picking up a file and opening it.

She stood in front of him and strained to find something else to say, but nothing came. As he had done so many times before, Drago had closed off. His daughter was a disappointment to him: she had betrayed him and she was going to be punished by a withdrawal of his love. All her life Pila had been subject to this process. She knew then that if she gave in and said she would not go to England her father would reward her, give back the poison of his affection. But she didn't care any longer: the house, her brother, her father, were not enough to make her stay; and her mother was enough of a reason to make her go.

Go for my sake, Catherine had said to her. Go for me.

So Pila turned without speaking and walked out – just in time to see the guilty, scurrying figure of Courtney crossing the hall.

# Forty-One

**London**

Pila walked towards the car which was waiting for her. She could make out two figures inside. An angular woman wearing a trilby and a stocky man reading a newspaper. Her legs felt suddenly weak, her mouth dry. Was this Misia and Portland? Were these the people she had defied her father for? Would they like her? Would she like them?

Her courage failed her, suitcase in one hand, shivering in the cold. And then Misia looked up and saw her. Hurrying out of the car, she ran towards the waiting girl, Portland following. Then as she reached Pila, Misia stopped, scrutinising her niece. Slowly she regarded her, taking in the exotic looks, the expensive clothes, and the shivering figure of the girl.

"So," she said simply, "you're my niece, are you?"

Pila nodded, glancing over to Portland who had taken hold of her case. "I don't want to be a nuisance. I just came for a short visit –"

"Nonsense!" Misia barked. "You're here to stay."

# Forty-Two

"What are you doing?" Pila asked, walking into the dining room where Simeon was sitting at the table, reading. The rest of the family were out; Portland at the Old Bailey; Misia and Vincent visiting the gym over the 'Thomas a Becket' pub on the Old Kent Road; Harewood out on the circuit with his property case. Only she and Simeon were left in the house, and it had taken her several minutes to find him.

"Well, what are you doing?"

He motioned for her to sit down: "Do you believe in the occult?"

She frowned, then pulled the sleeves of her jumper over her hands to warm them. "What d'you mean by occult?"

"The paranormal."

Pila shook her head. "I don't like it," she answered sharply, thinking of the time Dona had read her cards. *Don't marry. If you want to be happy, I warn you, never marry.* "I don't like anything to do with it."

Simeon pushed the book he was reading over to her. "Go on, look. It won't hurt you."

Immediately Pila leaned back in her seat, putting distance between her and the volume. "No, really, Simeon, I don't want to know."

"That's okay," he said, pulling the book back towards him. "You don't have to."

"I think it's wrong – bad for people."

"Maybe," he conceded.

"So why are you interested?"

He studied her for a long moment. The morning was another cold one, the windows frosted, outside bare under-nourished trees standing guard in the London garden.

"I'm curious," Simeon answered. "I want to understand what no one can understand." He smiled, almost embarrassed. "There's a story about London ghosts –"

"I've heard it," Pila interrupted. "My father has a hideous friend – some branch of the Italian nobility, Princess Feranza. I used to have to visit her; in fact, I still do. I was supposed to go on holiday with her instead of coming to England."

"How did your father take that?"

"Badly," she replied, looking beyond him into the garden. A woman passed by the gate, pushing a pram. "He's disgusted with me for coming here."

"But you still came?"

"For my mother's sake as well as my own," Pila confessed. "She wanted me to come here so much, she *really* wanted it, and she asks so little. It seemed as though I'd be letting her down to refuse." Idly, Pila traced the edge of the table with her index finger. "Catherine believes that if there had never been this feud in the family everything would have been so different – perhaps not so much for me, but for my brother." She glanced warily at Simeon. "Do you believe in evil?"

He nodded. It seemed as though the question was almost expected.

"There's something wrong with Courtney. I thought he'd grow out of it, but he seems to have got worse as he's got older. My father doesn't notice, or if he does, he never says anything. We're both disappointments to him." She stopped, uneasy that she had confided so much.

"Go on."

"There's not much else to say, Simeon. You were talking about the occult and I thought of my brother."

"Why?"

"I don't know really. My father has a nickname – the Magician – because of his work. People think his talent is godly, although I've heard some joke that he made a pact with the Devil." She was uncomfortable with the idea and shifted in her seat, tucking her legs under her. "I don't think he's a bad man, just … oh, I don't know."

"Has he still got the birthmark on his forehead?" Simeon asked.

She nodded.

"Did he tell you how he got it?"

"No."

Simeon leaned towards her and then told her about the night her father was born. She listened, mesmerised, imagining the fire in the marquee and Mary Razzio giving birth, Morrie Gilling holding up the lamp in the darkness. Then Simeon told her about the mark on Guido's head, the same mark which appeared on the head of his new born son.

"My father never said anything about it," Pila said when he'd finished. "And my mother doesn't know, or she would have mentioned it."

"So now do you believe in the supernatural?"

"I never said I didn't believe in it. I said that I thought it was dangerous." She changed the subject. "Is your grandmother still alive?"

Simeon shook his head.

"No, she died soon after my grandfather did. Or maybe I shouldn't say she *died,* she simply picked her side. She had family, but the one person she loved the most had gone. And she wanted to follow him."

He thought back to the evening he had last seen his grandmother. Dressed sombrely, sitting in a chair in the drawing room, her eyes alert – but not looking at him. Instead she had the appearance of someone waiting for a train that was overdue. Instinctively Simeon had known what was happening. The Mary Razzio he had loved; the redoubtable grandmother who had played such a part in all their lives hadn't been in that Liverpool house. It was true that she had still been sitting amongst the furniture and photographs, but in reality she had gone. Her breathing heart hadn't belonged there, she had already left and all that remained had been the slow winding down of her body.

Simeon hadn't seen a vision of his grandfather that night – but he had known he was there. That Guido had come back, one last time, to claim his bride.

At three in the morning Mary Razzio had died.

"That's sad."

"No," Simeon replied, "It was what she wanted."

Shrugging, Pila looked at the book which lay on the table between them. "What are you reading?"

"It's about the Ancients and about their prophecies."

"Did all the prophecies come true?"

"The ones they recorded, yes," he answered smiling. "I suppose there were millions of others which never did."

"I was wondering …"

He prompted her. "Go on, ask me."

"I was wondering what do you did for a living …"

Simeon's laugh was deep, hardly audible. "I'm the family thinker," he answered, his eyes dark, unreadable. "I was ill as a child, sickly, the runt of the litter. I had terrible headaches which used to last for days. Now they've discovered that I actually suffer from migraine – although giving it a name doesn't lessen the pain any," he smiled; again the unutterable sadness. "I've been on medication for years; in and out of school, tutored at home mostly. I passed my exams, but there was nothing I was particularly good at, and in the end I concentrated on the other thing I was interested in – the paranormal. So I decided to do some research on the occult. I could work at home; it would be a solitary, quiet, something I could do at my own speed. Then, out of the blue, I was asked to do some research for a parapsychologist."

"A what?" Pila asked.

"Someone investigating the occult. It was incredible. The more I read, the more I wanted to know. Well, I finished the research for the author six months ago, but I keep on reading and I haven't stopped yet. That's it, really," he shrugged. "Maybe I'll write a book too someday."

"What does your father think about it?"

Simeon smiled. It was an out-of-the-way smile, distant. "He's just concerned that we all do what we want with our lives. That's all. He's never come the heavy hand, never pushed us. He accepts people for what they are. That's his gift, that's why people confide in him and that's why they trust him." He paused. "Don't let him fool you into thinking he's a simple soul, my father does very well in his profession."

"And Harewood – what about him?"

Simeon raised his eyebrows: "He'll do well too – but in a different way. He's got the tenacity and the eye for detail. He hasn't got our father's charisma, but then, who has? Apart from Vincent, I mean."

Pila frowned, putting her elbows on the table and cupping her chin in her hands. "He's very cocky,"

"– or very easy with people," Simeon countered.

"Too easy?"

He smiled again, they were of like mind, and both of them felt in that instant. "Don't be hard on him. He's just Vincent. The boxers love him because he's no fear. I suppose, in a way, our grandfather loved him for that too."

Pila's voice was low: "But you were his favourite."

"Who told you that?"

"Alberto – and he knows most things."

Simeon glanced away. "He came when my grandfather was dying, did you know that?" She nodded. "Came all the way from Italy, just to pay his respects."

"And my father refused to come."

187

Simeon nodded. "I'd just like to know his reasons," he said, rubbing his narrow forehead with his fingertips. "I would just like to understand why. And then it wouldn't matter so much. D'you know why he didn't come?"

"No. I only know that he fell out with his parents –"

"He didn't want anyone to know about the boxers or about his past. He hated Liverpool and wanted to get away, and he didn't care what it cost anyone to escape. He hurt my grandparents very much."

"How?" Pila asked, her voice cool.

"Because he told them he was ashamed of them. He went to the Liverpool house and had an argument with his mother, talking in front of my grandfather as though he was already dead, some kind of unhearing, unseeing, useless lump in the bed. Guido had done everything for him!" Simeon said hotly. "And he despised him, he was ashamed of his own father. The same man other people looked up to – he loathed."

"I can't believe –"

"I'm not saying it to hurt you," Simeon interrupted her, "but you should know what started this feud. When my mother went to see him and ask him to apologise, he refused. She swore then that she'd never contact him again. But she did, when Guido was dying. Your father refused to come. They asked him, begged him – but he refused to come."

Pila stood up and walked to the window. The wind had gathered strength and in the driveway a swirl of leaves twisted in a sudden bluster.

"I didn't know anything about this."

"No, I thought you didn't."

She turned, her face strained. "I don't think I should have come –"

Simeon rose to his feet hurriedly and joined her at the window. "But that's the point, you *had* to come. All this bad feeling has to stop. We're all part of the same family, we should be friends."

"I don't think my father will ever see it that way."

"He might."

Pila shook her head: "No, I know him better than you do. He never changes his mind."

"So where does that leave you?" Simeon asked anxiously. "You defied him to come here – what's he going to say when you go back to Italy?"

"He'll ignore me," Pila replied, her eyes turning back to the blowing leaves outside. "I'll return and go to my room and now and again we'll pass in the corridors and he may, or he may not, speak. He'll see this visit as a betrayal. But now I don't care as much as I did. Now I know that he betrayed his own family, I don't see why I should feel honour bound to obey him." She shivered: cold by the window. "I'm tired of my life in Italy, Simeon. You've no idea how much. I'm tired of watching my mother fading in front of my eyes, and wondering about my brother. Trying to work out just what it is I'm afraid of … I'm glad I came here because I was beginning to see my whole life in terms of that house, and the friends chosen for me. Friends my father approved of – the Princess Ferenza's of the world." She paused, tired by her confession, and turned to Simeon. "I lied to you before, I don't know the story of the London ghosts. The old woman started to tell me once, but she never finished."

Simeon leaned against the window seat, his head framed by the cool daylight behind.

"There's a belief that London's populated by ghosts, and that they walk amongst the living. They say that every fifth person you pass is a spirit. Walking down the street, on a bus, on the underground – that fifth person who crosses your path is always a ghost. They never die, never leave, they are tied to the city, and continue to walk the London streets forever." He stopped, then stared at her, suddenly anxious. "Are you all right?"

Pila had slumped against the window seat next to him, her hand grasping his arm. Her face was waxy, her hair unnaturally black against her skin.

"I had the most horrible feeling …" she stammered, "… I saw …" her eyes turned on him blindly. "I saw myself then, Simeon. When you talked of the London ghosts walking amongst the living, I saw myself."

*

Portland was listening, the opposing counsel putting forward a neat argument about the forensic evidence. He glanced down at his hands and then scratched his left ear. Anyone watching him would have thought he was day dreaming, uninterested in the events taking place. But they would have been wrong, Portland was merely soaking up the facts as he always did, conserving his energy for the time he would pulverise the witness.

There was a tap on his shoulder and he turned. Leamington's spoon shaped face was inches away from his own.

"Note for you, sir," he said simply, smiling in his overshot way. "Bonny girl, that niece of yours."

Quickly Portland read the page and then glanced up. In the public gallery sat Misia and Pila.

"… I managed to get them seats at the front, seeing as how it was the first time Miss Razzio's been to court."

"There was a queue round the block this morning, Leamington, how did you manage it?"

He smiled knowingly. "I just called in a little favour here, little favour there," he said, backing away.

Portland watched him go and then smiled briefly at Misia and Pila before his attention returned to the doctor in the witness box. He had the look of many successful medics, butter-fat, grey haired, luminous with his own importance. He had droned on for several minutes without pause, holding a medical lecture in the Old Bailey, the judge making copious notes. Oh God, what a windbag, Portland thought.

"… it is my considered opinion …"

His client, Forrester, was innocent, Portland assured himself. He smelt innocent.

"… there are several determining factors which indicate …"

It was just the entry of the wound which seemed suspect. If he could nail the witness on that.

"… In my experience …"

There was a shift of movement in the court, the judge peering out from the bench, a low rumble of voices beginning, the dying down again.

"Order. Order!" he called, then turned back to the witness. "Please continue."

The doctor, miffed that his speech had been interrupted, continued readily, his tone raised.

"… in conclusion, I confirm that this is my opinion."

The opposing counsel glanced triumphantly over to Portland: "Your witness."

He smiled winningly and rose to his feet. "I am most grateful to the learned witness for his enlightening evidence. At one time I myself considered going into the medical field, but now it only goes for me to say that I am sure that I chose the right profession."

Portland's tone had been so bland that it took a while for the implication to sink in and then there were several sniggers in the court, the doctor looking suddenly uncomfortable.

"You said that the defendant was seen on the …" he went on, his tone easy, deceptively friendly.

Up in the gallery, Misia watched him, then glanced over to Pila. "Some kind of a man, hey?"

Her niece nodded eagerly. "Everyone's watching him."

"Oh, they always do. Everywhere Portland goes, people watch him – they just can't help it. I keep telling him it not his bloody looks!"

Below them, Portland was warming up: "… but you said, doctor – do let me check my notes – that you 'had never seen anything like this before'."

"Correct."

"So how can you say it's not possible?"

"Because I've never seen it before."

Portland scratched his ear again. "So on your premise, anything which you have not seen, is not possible."

The doctor looked uncertain. "Yes."

"Are you a Christian?"

"I beg your pardon?"

"I asked if you were a Christian?"

The doctor nodded. "Yes, I believe in God."

"And you believe that Christ was resurrected from the dead?"

"Yes."

"But how could you? You didn't see Him resurrected – or did you?"

There was a rush of laughter in court, the judge glancing down at his notes.

"It's not the same thing!" the doctor snapped, reddening.

"But you said in your evidence that a wound could not be caused in this manner by another person *because you had never seen anything like this before*. Now, did you, or did you not, say that?"

"He's dead in the water," Misia whispered upstairs. "Look at the jury, they don't believe a word that doctor says now."

The man was deflating before their eyes: "But …"

"So it might be possible that someone else *did* cause the injury?"

"Not in my opinion."

190

"Oh, but I think we've dealt with your opinion, doctor," Portland said, turning away. "No further questions."

They went for lunch soon after, Portland taking them to a eighteenth century pub off Fleet Street. It was already filled with a mixture of counsel, office workers and a few idlers leaning heavily against the bar. He nodded at the landlord and they were shown into a small bar where a fire blazed, an Alsatian dozing by a pair of brass fire irons. They ordered and then Portland leaned back in his seat, his face warming from the fire's heat as he rubbed his hands together.

"God, it's freezing." He turned to Pila, "Have you got enough warm clothes?"

She nodded. "Aunt Misia –"

"Just call me Misia," she replied, sipping at her gin and tonic. "I can't stand the 'aunt' bit."

"Misia," Pila went on, smiling, "leant me some of her things."

"Not that bloody trilby, I hope?" Portland said, winking at his wife.

"Portland," a voice said suddenly, a figure pausing by their table. "How are you?"

They all looked up. Caryl de Solt was pulling off his gloves, his dark overcoat and suit perfectly pressed, his beard trimmed, his eyes transfixing blue.

"Caryl," Portland said, smiling. "Good to see you."

He returned the smile and then turned to Misia: "How are you?"

"Love the suit," she replied evenly. "Does it light up later?"

He held the smile and turned to Pila, his eyes fixing on her. "I'm Caryl de Solt."

"I'm Pila Razzio," she replied. "I'm Portland and Misia's niece."

He seemed intrigued. "How charming," he said, "Are you visiting them for a while?"

"A couple of weeks."

"During which time she's fully occupied," Misia cut in, downing her drink. "We're going up to Liverpool soon – to show her The Roman House."

"Do you follow boxing?" Caryl asked.

Pila shrugged, flattered by the attention from such a glamorous man. "I don't know that much about it – but I want to learn."

"It's always good to learn new things."

Misia coughed loudly, throwing a fierce glance in her husband's direction.

"Well, Caryl," Portland said, "it's been good to see you again."

He took the hint deftly. "And it's been good to see you all again," he replied, turning back to Pila. "If you need a guide whilst you're in London, I'd love to show you around."

"Oh good, food," Misia said hurriedly as the barmaid moved towards them. "Bye, Caryl."

They watched him go, weaving his well tailored way through the pushing throng of people, a cold blast coming from the door as he opened it. Hungrily, Misia cut into her cheese and then scooped it onto her bread, taking a bite. Her hands, decorated with only her wedding ring, were hard, white, like bone.

"Who was that?" Pila asked her uncle.

"I did his divorce for him," Portland replied, taking a long sip of his beer. "He's a man about town type, a real charmer."

"He seemed nice," Pila said quietly.

Misia looked up: "Do you have a boyfriend back home?"

She shook her head. "No one special. I go out with some men occasionally, the ones my father approves of. He vets them for me."

"I can imagine," Misia said dryly.

"I liked one boy a year ago, but nothing came of it," her attention wandered; she was musing about Caryl de Solt, wondering about him.

Misia knew what she was thinking and continued to eat, then paused, her tone nonchalant. "I think we should go up to Liverpool the day after tomorrow. If you'd like that?"

Pila's thoughts returned to the present. "Oh … yes, fine."

"You could see The Roman House, and meet the boxers," she went on. "And you'll like the place we have up there. The house by the park. It was my parent's."

"Guido's?"

Misia nodded, touched by her interest. "Yes, Guido's. Your grandfather." She paused, suddenly softening. "I've got photographs of him up there, and some of his things. And some of my mother's too. It was very much their house – we haven't really changed it at all." She wiped her mouth with her paper serviette and then crumpled it. "I'm afraid it's a bit rough and ready up there though. I mean, there's a housekeeper, but only Vincent and I spend any real time in Liverpool," she said, nudging Portland. "This reprobate never stays away from London too long."

"The plumbing's even worse than it is at Holland Park," Portland warned Pila: "but the food's good. Take plenty of clothes and a few books. The TV broke down months ago and we never got it fixed."

Pila smiled, looking from one to the other, but her thoughts weren't on Liverpool, they were on the man who she had seen for only a minute, Caryl de Solt. Never at Fault.

*

Vincent was brooding, his hand on the telephone, a dog standing beside him. He had heard about Caryl de Solt from his father, had followed the case and even met him once – all aftershave and charm – coming down South Molton Street. But he didn't like him, and he didn't like the idea that he had just phoned, asking for Pila. Unused to feeling jealous, Vincent was nettled, turning when he heard the dining room door open.

Misia walked in, then stopped short, her index finger pointing at the white greyhound by her son's side.

"WHAT IS THAT?"

"A dog."

"I can see that, Vincent," she said chillingly. "What is it doing here?"

"It was going to be put down, so I rescued it," he said easily, smiling. "I knew you wouldn't mind."

"We have three dogs already, Vincent," she replied. "And that's three too many. Get it out of here."

"I told you, he was going to be put down –"

"By me, if you don't move it."

The greyhound was cowed, but Vincent was impervious. He had gone through this particular conversation with his mother three times before; in fact, every time he brought home another stray. There was always the same excuse – it was going to be put down – and then an argument, and then the dog was allowed to stay for a couple of days until they found it a permanent home. Then Misia forget about it, and the dog became a fixture. All Vincent had to do know was to appeal to her better nature.

"He's blind."

"A blind dog!" she snapped. "You know, Vincent, most people get a dog to help *them* around, you've managed to get a dog *you'll* have to help around."

"He was a Champion once."

She eyed the greyhound thoughtfully; "Was that before or after he lost his sight?"

"Aw, come on, Mum –"

Suddenly Misia's eyes fixed on the message pad. "What's this – *Caryl de Solt*," she turned to her son. "What did he want?"

"Pila."

"I bet!" she retorted, tapping her foot and thinking. If she didn't tell Pila she was acting as Drago did; censoring her, running her life for her. But if she did tell her, and Pila became involved with the likes of Caryl de Solt … "Oh hell!" Misia said, turning and nearly tripping over the dog.

It yelped pathetically and ran behind Vincent's legs.

"Move that animal!" Misia howled at her son. "I don't want to set eyes on it again."

Caryl de Solt took Pila out for dinner in a fashionable restaurant in Chelsea, the head waiter coming over to him as he walked in the door.

"Mr. de Solt, wonderful to see you again," he enthused. "Would you like to go to your table straight away?"

Caryl nodded, taking Pila's arm and steering her towards a discreet table at the corner of the room. Candlelight flickered on old mirrors, a collection of ornamental china acting as a frieze around the room. It was delicately furnished, almost Continental, the type of restaurant a foreign man might chose; the type a foreign girl might feel at home in.

Pila was excited, flattered and nervous. She had brought one suitable dress over from Italy, and had put it on that night, the dark green silk covered with a heavy, embroidered shawl, her hair lifted away from her face. When she came downstairs before leaving, Misia had stared at her, Portland kissing her loudly on the cheek.

"You look amazing," he said.

Vincent whistled approvingly, the greyhound's ears pricking. "Quite a revelation," he said, grabbing hold of the dog's collar before it bumped into Pila. "Yes, quite a revelation."

She blushed, her hair glossy, abundant. Dear God, she looks like Drago, Misia thought.

"Have a good time," Portland said.

Misia edged him out of the way. "Now remember, if de Solt starts anything, you just get up and phone us. We'll come and get you."

"Ignore her," Portland said. "Just have a lovely evening."

And she was having a lovely evening: she was being made to feel special, and more than that, she was being made to feel desirable. Having only the examples of her father and her brother to follow, Caryl de Solt had no competition. His charm soon captivated; his words easily believed; his flattery taken as truth. If Pila had grown up with a father who had been loving, her needs would already have been partially met; but her childhood had been dogged by the rejection of her father and the peevish jealousy of her brother. She did not know she had been looking for a man to offer kindness; did not realise she needed affection, male attention; did not understand that the warm sensation flooding over her was sexual attraction.

Misia was right; Pila *was* young for her years. She had grown up over-protected and under-loved, a deadly combination. Her life had been constructed for her, and Catherine's adult problems she had taken on as her own. Anxiety had left no space for the recklessness of youth, no chance to behave as her peers did. She had been a worried child, born into an unsettled home, and without seeing affection between her parents, Pila had never expected it for herself – until she met Caryl de Solt.

Her face, in the sensual candlelight, was soft, a dark-silk shadow under her chin, her eyes listening, accepting. He thought her desirable and told her so, and Pila wanted him never to stop talking, wanted the words to go on and on, because he made her mind blur and her body dissolve.

"I should take you home now," Caryl said at last.

She was immediately afraid. "Why? Can't we stay a little longer?"

He took her hand; her face was achingly young, he thought, untouched. "Can I see you again?"

It was what she wanted to hear and nodded eagerly. "When?"

"Tomorrow?"

"Yes … oh, no, I can't," she hesitated, alarmed. If she couldn't see him tomorrow, would he ask her again? "We're going up to Liverpool for a few days."

"Then I'll call you when you get back," Caryl said simply. "I promise."

The added the last words as an after thought, knowing that she would cling to them and believe them.

"I had a lovely evening," Pila said shyly.

"The first of many," Caryl replied. "Remember that."

When they parted that night Pila went to her room, Misia nudging Portland in bed. "She's back."

"Of course she's back."

"And that's the phone," Misia went on, exasperated. "It'll be bloody de Solt, you mark my words."

And it was, Pila answering and whispering down the line. "I was thinking of you."

"I was hoping you were," he replied.

"Did you think of me?"

"Only every moment," Caryl said laughing.

194

He was flattered by her obvious interest and sure that she would soon be falling in love with him. Used to sophisticated women, Pila Razzio was a very enchanting novelty. Well read and well bred too, he thought, smiling to himself. His friends would like her, she was just the kind of girl who could mix amongst society easily – fancy her being the niece of old Portland Benning. And Misia. Caryl wasn't a malicious man, he hadn't the energy or the memory for grudges, but he resented the way that Misia obviously disliked him, and for a moment saw a way of provoking her. It was harmless, after all, to show affection to someone as sweet as Pila. He was just being kind. There was no danger in it.

"I'll phone you when you get back."

"Good," Pila said eagerly.

"And it's good to hear your lovely voice," Caryl answered. "Bye for now."

In his flat, Caryl put the phone down and smiled, then he saw the Apollo magazine and began to flick through the pages, becoming quickly absorbed in an article about Marcel Duchamp; his attention sliding effortlessly from Pila to the printed page.

*

Simeon woke some time after eleven. A bell was ringing a long way away and he thought for a moment that it was inside his head, the noise waking him urgently. He sat up, relieved that the migraine had at lasted subsided. Slowly, he walked to the door and out into the corridor, looking down to the man standing below. Teller, the odd-ball that Misia had hired years earlier. A butler unlike any other butler. An ex boxer, in fact.

"Who?" Teller asked in the hall below. "I'm sorry, the line's bad, I can't hear you." There was a long pause. "Okay, hang on a minute ..."

Teller's crooked face peered up the stairwell to Simeon. "I thought I heard you moving about. It's a call from Italy – someone asking for Miss Pila."

Simeon hurried downstairs and took the phone.

A fine, slightly whining voice came over the line. "Is my sister there?"

"Who's this?"

"Courtney Razzio – who's that?"

"Simeon Benning. Your sister's in Liverpool, I'm afraid – but I can give you the number up there."

"Hurry up then, this is long distance."

Simeon frowned, surprised by the arrogant tone, then recited the digits and paused, waiting for thanks. There were none, the line simply went dead.

"Would you believe that?" he asked Teller. "That was Pila's brother."

"What did he want?"

"He didn't say, and he didn't give me time to ask." Simeon rubbed his forehead. "Could I have some coffee, Teller? I'm parched."

The man looked at him sympathetically; "Headache gone?"

"Yes, for now."

"I don't know how you cope with those things. I used to get headaches – but only after some bastard had knocked seven bells out me."

Smiling, Simeon walked into the conservatory, flicking on the electric fire and glancing out of the window. It was a clear night, promising frost, the moon high and full. A witch's night, he thought suddenly, his mind turning back to the phone call. Preoccupied, he sat down, Teller leaving the coffee beside him. Steam rose from the spout of the pot; milk, heated as it liked it, smelling softly in the dim light.

Slowly, Courtney poured himself a cup of coffee and sipped it, allowing his mind to wander, his eyes blurring. Nothingness came to him unbidden; complete emptiness of thought, a non-existence. He drifted, his head leaning back against the chair, his lips slightly parted. There was a garden, then a gate … Simeon moved in his chair, shivered and then relaxed, breathing through his nose … yes, a gate and a house with a terrace … he sighed, slid down into the thought … sickness, there was sickness … he felt it and knew it. His skin was sticky with sweat in an instant, his teeth chattering uncontrollably, his hands clenching the wicker seat.

Sickness and a woman lying on a bed … she was blonde, and it was *her* sickness he felt … Simeon shivered again, his breathing altering, his breaths coming fast and painful … she was ill and something else … afraid. Oh God, he thought, this woman is afraid … he wanted to go on, but he was blocked suddenly, pushed out of the house mentally, his last image being of a young man listening at a closed door.

Simeon snapped awake. His shirt was soaked through, his hands imprinted with the marks of the wicker seat. He grabbed for the coffee and drank it, his mind clearing. It was about Pila, he knew that; just as he knew that the woman he had seen was her mother. Unsettled, Simeon staggered to his feet and went into the hall, dialling the Liverpool number, his hands trembling.

*

"You have to come home," Courtney said meanly, phoning his sister in Liverpool. "Mother's ill and Father's away."

Pila was terrified over the long distance line. "Have you called the doctor?"

"I thought I'd wait until I spoke to you."

"CALL HIM NOW!" Pila shouted, Misia running down the stairs to see what was happening. "You call him, Courtney, just as soon as I put the phone down. I'll be home as soon as I can."

"But –"

"I want to talk her," Pila said, her tone high with panic. "I want to talk to my mother."

"She's sleeping."

"Then wake her up!" Pila snapped. "No, no, don't do that – just tell her I'm coming home. You will tell her, Courtney, won't you?"

"Of course," he said wearily, "after all, I asked you to come back, didn't I?"

Cautiously, Misia moved over to her niece, watching as she put down the phone. "Is it serious?"

"I don't know, my brother hasn't called a doctor," she replied. "You never know with Courtney, he might just be doing it to make me go home."

"Why?"

"Because he's like that," Pila said flatly, moving upstairs. She had lost her youth in an instant, her movements listless, fatigued, and when she turned at the top of the stairs Misia could see her as she would be older.

The phone rang again, Misia snatching it up: "Hello?"

"Mum, it's Simeon. Did Pila's brother call?"

"Yes, he did. Her mother's ill, she has to go home," she said. "He rang you first then?"

"Just a minute ago," Simeon replied. "Listen, something's wrong with all of this –"

Misia listened carefully; she had never scoffed at her father's intuition and realised early on that her first son had inherited Guido's gift. But with Simeon it was more advanced; he did not simply feel things, he saw them and heard them as well. Many times during his childhood he had been unable to sleep, too afraid of the nightmares which dogged him to even close his eyes. She had spent long nights with him, sitting by the bed and talking to keep the ghouls away.

At first Misia had hoped that her son might grow out of it, that the clairvoyance might fade as he moved into puberty: but it increased, not decreased, and the only way Simeon could cope was by learning to accept. So he allowed himself to hear and see whatever came to him, and he kept notes and managed to keep himself reasonable stable, monitoring his own moods, although the headaches accelerated. Portland talked to him and Misia sat with him, but no one fully understood Simeon, and he could never make friends with boys his own age. He was an outcast who had lost his place in the world through no fault of his own and wandered, adrift.

"Why does it happen to me, Mum?" he asked her once.

She had looked him full in the face: "Because that's just the way it goes."

He had smiled, grateful that she hadn't lied to him. "Will it go on forever?"

"I don't know," she said honestly.

Then one night Simeon had seen Billy Poole – Fitting Billy Poole, standing by the French windows in the Liverpool house. He had been drawn downstairs on some irrestible impulse and had walked into the drawing room. A moon was making patterns on the wall, throwing shadows, black tree shapes – and then another shape, of a man hunched over. In his head Simeon had heard the beating of Billy Poole's gloved hands on his thighs and the endless repeated question.

*Is it time? Is it time?*

He had never gone back to the Liverpool house, and after that night, no one ever asked him to. For Misia, her son's sanity was too important to risk, and Holland Park became Simeon's home. He had never even phoned them in Liverpool – until then.

"Pila's mother is really ill," Simeon said, "she *has* to go home."

"She's going, Simeon, don't worry," Misia said, "I'll find out the time of the first available plane –"

"Something's wrong, really wrong," Simeon said urgently. "Tell her to stay there until she's sure her mother's well again. You will tell her, won't you?"

"I tell her, Simeon."

He nodded. "And tell her to phone me when she gets home."

"I'll tell her," Misia assured him. "Now you go to bed, you sound tired. Are you all right?"

"I'm fine, honestly."

"Get Teller to make you something to eat."

"Don't fuss," he said gently.

"I'm a mother, I supposed to fuss," she chided him, then her voice changed, infinitely gentle. "Go and have a talk with Portland, love. Tell the old man what you saw."

Simeon rested his head against the banister rail and nodded. It was the ritual they had perfected over the years: after one of Simeon's clairvoyant episodes he always went and told his father what had happened, talking, laying the terror to rest.

"Yes, I'll go now."

"Good," Misia said, her tone brisk again, "and tell the old bugger I love him whilst you're at it."

*Dear Misia,*

*I can't believe how suddenly everything has changed. Catherine is better, but not well, I spoke to my father last night but he seems unable to recognise that she is sick. Perhaps he doesn't want to; perhaps (and I shouldn't say this) perhaps he doesn't care. He's travelling again now, off to a medical convention in the United States – taking some of his patients. The Freak Show, Courtney calls it.*

*Alberto called to see Catherine again this morning; he's keeping an eye on her, but she won't have tests, she says it just tiredness. I wish I was as sure as she is. She looks very frail, but she's happy in herself, glad I'm home and we can have our old talks. I've told her all about you and your family – she presses me for details. Which reminds me, could you send me some photographs to show her?*

*Write and tell me about what you're doing. I love to hear about everyone, and I'm only sorry that I never saw any boxing – or The Roman House. Perhaps another time?*

*With much love,*
*Pila*

*Dear Pila,*

*Thanks for your welcome letter. The photos you asked for are enclosed.*

*All here send their love. Simeon is writing separately, and Vincent has enclosed a photo of that crazy dog of his.*

*I'm glad to hear that Catherine's better, but keep an eye on her, she's not a complainer, and she needs looking after – which of course she will be, now that you're home. We all miss you; your visit wasn't long enough and I am under instructions to demand a replay!*

*The boxing goes well; I've just signed up a middle weight called Larry Blunt – he's as mean as hell, thank God. Abbot (the trainer) says that he could be a champion one day, but who knows? At the moment we just have to keep him off the booze and in regular training, which isn't as easy as it sounds. Vincent, as ever cocky, sparred with him the other day and got flattened – I warned him, but he never listens, so now his profile has been rearranged once again. Even your father would have his work cut out for him. Vincent insists that he likes his nose this way – says it makes him looks like Charlton Heston, although I can't see the likeness myself. He's got cotton wadding stuffed up each nostril and eats with his mouth open – now tell me you're missing us!*

*Keep writing, and keep your spirits up,*

*Love,*
*Misia*

### December 10th
### Rome

*Dear Misia,*

*It is nearly Christmas again, and I've just put the tree up. In the garden we've got two enormous firs decorated with lights and the fountain's illuminated too. Why? Because we're having a party for my father's important friends; politicians, actors, artists and royalty like Princess Ferenza; it's in honour of his being decorated by the Government for his contribution to medicine. They're giving him a ribbon, or something. He seems very proud, very friendly all of a sudden. That could be due to the fact that he wants his family to put on a good show – does that sound hard?*

*I'm sorry, I didn't mean to moan by letter, but I don't think my mother's up to it. My father says that she won't have to do anything; that he's got it all organised; but she WILL have to be the hostess – and she's dreading it.*

*I have one surprising piece of news – Courtney has suddenly developed an interest in design. Some friend of my father's suggested that he had talent and he's been working on some drawings – clothes, hats etc. I have to say that he's quite good; the drawings aren't brilliant, but the designs are original – maybe he's found his feet at last? I hope so, anything that keeps him occupied and away from us is a bonus.*

*Tell Vincent that I saw his photograph and that he DOES look a little like Charlton Heston! And give my love to Portland and Harewood. I'll reply to Simeon's letter separately.*

*I will come and see you again – I want to very much.*

*All my love,*
*Pila*

### London
### December 14th 1959

*Dearest Pila,*
*Thank you for your last letter, I treasure it. I miss you, darling, very much, and think of you all the time. How is everything with you? How is your mother? Your brother? Your life? And when, WHEN, are you coming back to London? Letters are not enough, Pila, I want to see you. I want to hold you and tell you what I feel.*

*You are my whole heart, be sure of that. If there is anything I can do for you, tell me, and it's done.*
*With devotion,*
*Caryl*

## Rome
### January 4th, 1960

*Dear Simeon,*

*How like you to understand. I can't tell anyone else how I feel, dead inside. The house is a tomb, chillingly bleak with the cold snap; marble echoes, and the garden looks unfriendly. I should go out more, but with whom? I don't have any close friends, just social contacts, people my father approves of. I should make friends for myself, I know that, but somehow I don't feel easy away from my mother.*

*I think she's ill, Simeon, really ill, and it frightens me. Her weight is dropping and she seems oddly calm. Am I imagining something? I don't know, I just know for certain that there is an awful emptiness about all of us here. I wait. What for? I can't tell you. I just wait.*

*Caryl writes almost daily now; I need his support – perhaps I rely too much on it. I don't know. He talks about loving me – is that true? Do people fall in love so easily? I know I did when I was in London - I was dizzy thinking about him, but now I'm afraid to believe that what he says is true, just in case he changes his mind. I couldn't bear to be disappointed. And yet he's being so loving, so caring. I feel I know him more from his letters than face to face. People think he's superficial, I don't find him so.*

*He talks of coming to Rome – surely that means he's serious? What do you think, Simeon? Tell me, I trust you more than anyone.*

*With much love,*
*Pila*

## London, Holland Park
### 9th January 1960

*Dear Pila,*

*What do I think? What do you want me to say? I can't see into Caryl's mind and tell you if he's genuine, only you can hope to know that. Loneliness is a terrible burden to carry, Pila, I know how it frightens you, but being with someone doesn't necessarily mean you've not alone. Caryl is supportive at the moment, and you need him – but if you weren't so afraid, would you rely on him so much?*

*I remembered a line from a poem – 'If we could find our happiness entirely, in someone else's arms' – well, if we could, it would be so simple, but in truth, happiness is learned, not loaned. Try to find the strength in yourself, Pila – it's the only guarantee against despair.*

*But having said that – if you love him, take what happiness is on offer. And hold onto it.*

*Your loving cousin and friend,*
*Simeon*

**London**
**January 10th, 1960**

*Dear Pila,*

*I love you – that's all I can say. I'm coming to Rome and I want to talk to your father. I want to marry you. That's all there IS to say. Yours, for ever,*

*Caryl*

**Rome**
**January 20th 1960**

*Dearest Misia,*

*I couldn't talk on the telephone, words failed me. They still do, but maybe I can communicate by letter.*

*My mother died last night in my arms. She simply let go, without warning. She had been very cheerful during the afternoon, very light hearted, talking about the days before she married my father, and then about him. She loved him to the end, I didn't realise how much, but I think she wanted to die whilst he was away, didn't want to risk … what? His neglect? A final example of his lack of love? I phoned him in Vienna – he's coming back. He sounded rigid, shocked, although he should have known how ill she was. He's a doctor, after all. He should have known, he should have been with her.*

*The funeral's on Friday; the newspapers have been ringing all morning, journalists at the gate. I can't believe I'll never see her again, or talk to her again, I can't believe the best thing in my life has gone …*

*It is very cold here. Tonight I'm going to sort out her clothes and then … what? What IS there? I don't know. I don't know.*

*Please write,*
*Pila*

**London**
**January 24th 1960**

*Dearest girl,*

*I told you over the phone that we're here for you, whenever you need us, we're here. I don't know how to comfort you – I never knew your mother but I knew how much she meant to you, and there's nothing I can say which will lessen her loss. They say time heals: well, time passes at least, and every day the grief lifts a little, until one day you'll think of your mother and remember her easily, without wanting her back, or feeling that no one will ever take her place. You'll marry, Pila, and have your own children, and you'll live with them and through them. I lost my parents too, and only*

202

*my family compensated me for their deaths.*

*You never have to feel that you're alone. You have a family here, ready made. Borrow the Bennings until you have your own – it's the best offer I can make.*

*Loving you, and feeling for you,*
*Portland and Misia*

## Rome
## February 1960

*Dearest Misia,*

*Caryl and I are to be married. My father approves – he seemed all too willing to agree. He's in shock for my mother's death, I don't think he imagined for one moment that she was so ill. Perhaps at the root of his grief is the fact that he hadn't taken more notice. He sits alone a great deal of the time now when he's not working. Alberto comes to see him, but Courtney is hardly here.*

*Our family, such as it was, has dissolved. I don't know how my father will cope with so much empty space; he looks older now, Misia, changed. But he says little – at least to me. I couldn't have stayed here. Not without my mother. I realise now that I wanted to escape for a long time, only she kept me tied to this house. Not that I wanted to leave her. She was beautiful, you know, not just to look at, but to be with. Gentle, always kind, always sweet. At night sometimes I think of her and imagine her voice. They say you forget, but you don't. I will carry my mother's voice to my own grave.*

*We are to be married in Rome – no family, just a quiet affair, without guests. So forgive me for not sending an invitation – it is too soon after Catherine's death to celebrate. I am coming to live in London with Caryl afterwards.*

*I look forward to seeing you very soon,*
*My love to you all,*
*Pila*

# Liverpool
## The Roman House
### 1968

Vincent was leaning against the ropes, eating an apple, his curly hair damp against his forehead, his shirt sticking to his back. Below him, Abbot was haranguing a young boy, prodding him with his forefinger, his bowler hat tipped back on his head. The trainer had put on weight over the years, so that now his bulk was vast, his ears seeming to grow with his girth, standing away from his head, an impressive, violent pink.

"You don't get in that ring until I say so!" he hollered. "I'm the boss here, got it?"

The boy cringed, then nodded.

*"And don't you forget it!"* Abbot shouted after him as he walked away.

Vincent threw the apple across the gym, smiling as it fell into the bin four yards away. He had had a wearing morning, a fight he had wanted to lay on for September in London had been cancelled and the television people were playing hell. It wasn't his fault, the American promoter had called in his boxer at the last minute, but the producer was deaf to reason and it took a sodden lunch at Claridges to soothe him.

Suddenly Vincent straightened up and jumped out of the ring. "We need some new blood," he said to Abbot, "someone flashy, someone the media will like."

"Cassius Clay already has a manager," Abbot replied sourly.

Vincent was unmoved: "They're others," he said thoughtfully. "We want someone with style, charisma. Someone the press will take to."

"We want a champion," Abbot retorted. "Someone who can beat the shit out of his opponent."

"I heard about some Irish guy," Vincent went on. "I might go down to London and have a look at him."

"Well, whilst you're at it, have a look at that gym down the World's End, someone said it was going for a song – a give away 'cos it needed so much repairing."

"I'm not sure we need a gym down South –"

"We do!" Abbot said emphatically, lighting a cigar and nodding. "We bloody do."

But Vincent had other matters on his mind when he talked to his parents later. Misia was at Holland Park and Vincent was regaling them with a story.

"So I saw de Solt and decided what to do."

"Which was?" Misia asked suspiciously"

"What anybody would," Vincent said easily. "I walked over, smiled at the woman and then asked Caryl how his wife and kids were."

"Good move," Portland said appreciatively. "What happened then?"

He paused, still stroking the monkey. "Then I did the only thing anyone could do in the circumstances. I slipped the doorman a fiver to do me a favour –"

"Oh God," Misia said, covering her eyes.

"– and when the interval came, Caryl got a message – supposedly from the police – to say that the silver shop had been broken into and that he had to go there immediately."

"Oh, I like this," Portland said admiringly.

"And so, regrettably, they had to leave," Vincent sighed. "Of course, it didn't break up the relationship, but I like to think that it made Caryl de Solt look a right jerk in front of his girlfriend."

Misia walked over to her son and tapped him on the head affectionately. "Well done, lad. A real chip off the old block … you always liked Pila, didn't you?"

He nodded, looking up at his mother. "I had a thing about her, you know."

"Yes, I know."

"And I don't like to see any decent woman treated badly, not by a shit like Caryl de Solt." Carefully, he placed the little monkey on his knee. "He can dance, you know, and jump through hoops."

Misia studied the animal thoughtfully; "I bet Pila knows exactly how that feels."

*

Two ruff necked doves had settled in the garden, taking a rest on the cedar tree by the fountain, a table laid for one placed under the shadow of a parasol. On the marble top lay a lobster salad and a glass of Chablis, a linen napkin lying beside it and small book resting on top. The noon heat was pleasant, agreeable without being too warm, the flush of summer insects dying back, the first settings of an Italian summer coming down from the high ground.

Under the shade, Drago sipped his wine. He was little changed, still carrying a full head of hair although it had whitened in flashes at the crown and at the parting on the left hand side. It gave him peculiarly striking look, especially with the birthmark darkening over the years and marking his forehead like a brand. He was very still, his movements, as ever, languid, and when he ate he cut everything into exact portions, working his way through his meal as though through a mathematical calculation. Carefully he stirred the salad dressing in the silver jug next to him and then poured a little onto the side of his plate, grimacing when a drop slid onto the table top.

He seemed calm: in fact, an onlooker watching him would think him a lucky man to have so much: but his mind was fretful, his thoughts incessant and tormenting. Arthritis had been diagnosed a while ago, the consultant breaking the news with all the compassion possible; but it still came with whip-like sharpness, and its sting lodged bitterly inside Drago from that moment onwards. *Arthritis* – the most debilitating disease, the most crippling, and it had started in his hands. His hands … Drago paused, laid down his knife and fork, his appetite gone.

No one had known how quickly the illness would develop; could be months or years, or decades – well, not decades, though maybe, if he was one of the lucky ones – years. But Drago Razzio had been one of the lucky ones too long; his good fortune had now run its course and he was suddenly confronted with a future which was threatened – and with that future, the whole reason for his existence.

He had been a poor father and a neglectful husband; he had been, above all, a callous son. His sins, which he had avoided for so long, were turning on him, coming into rest like so many lost ships coming home to port. His wife was dead, his daughter was distant in London, and his son was a stranger to him. The last had been expected;

Courtney had only ever caused unease, disappointment, malice. Drago had longed to see his son leave his property, had wanted to be free of Courtney's eavesdropping and his bilious remarks; had wanted to avoid the constant reminder of the barbarian within his own house. But his son didn't want to go – or wouldn't.

Bisexual and malicious, Courtney had brought trouble to the house and to the Razzio name. He had mixed constantly with social misfits and deviants; he had wallowed in the mire and revelled in the humiliation his behaviour brought on his father. Spiteful, vicious, envious and cruel, Courtney inherited the worst of his father's traits and embellished them with his own shortcomings. He drank to excess and used drugs; he was caught in possession of cocaine and held overnight in a Roman jail and only the intervention of a friend of Drago's managed to secure his release. There were no thanks, and a week later Courtney was caught smashing the window of a prostitute's house; she owed him money, he insisted, she hadn't done what he asked, she was a stealing, thieving whore.

But he was at home amongst the clubs and the whores and always having money, he was indulged. Nothing he did was punished; he had to account for nothing, to apologise for nothing, to work for nothing. He had been given everything by a father who neither loved nor even liked him. Courtney was fed and housed and satiated because he was his son; no other reason … Drago could not understand his behaviour, could not even have a conversation with him; they were two bitter people occupying a magnificent home; two ill-matched tenants locked into their own independent misery.

For a while Drago believed that his son might turn out to be a criminal; once, not long after the death of Catherine, he caught him opening his safe and challenged him.

Courtney was startled, but not cowed. "Well, what do you expect – I need money."

"You could ask."

He was wearing black trousers and a white silk shirt; his light brown hair long against his hollow cheeks, his tongue flicking over his dry lips. He was smaller than expected, Drago thought, he hadn't remembered how small his son actually was.

"This is my house, you should come to me –"

"You're never here!" Courtney countered. "How can I ask a ghost for money?"

"I give you enough,"

"I need more," Courtney persisted, snatching a wad of money out of the safe and walking over to his father.

Disbelieving, Drago looked into the hungry face: "What do you need it for?"

"Pleasure," Courtney replied curtly, walking past him into the hallway.

His shoes made no sound on the floor; Courtney always wore rubber soled loafers so no one could hear him coming, or know that he was listening at a door. It was a thief's trick, Drago thought: only a thief would want to go about silently. He has all the makings of a criminal, he realised, following his son and watching as he moved towards the stairs. Did he always walk so close to the walls? Always move so quickly, as if ready to run? Why? Run from *what*? Did I ever hit him? Did I ever hurt him? What in God's name made him like this? Drago thought helplessly. He's a misfit, a stranger, who takes everything and offers nothing in return.

Just as I did, he thought suddenly, understanding coming quick. *Courtney is the child you deserve*, Alberto had once said. *Every mean thought, every callous action you ever took is reflected in him. You have made a walking replica of your own shortcomings, and the future will judge you harshly.* The prophecy had been hideously accurate and in those moments Courtney seemed not flesh and blood, only a creeping polluting shadow of his father's sins.

Hurriedly, Drago moved to the stairs. Courtney heard him and turned, crouching slightly, willing his father on, inviting violence. He was terrifying in his ferocity; in the fearless hostility with which he seemed to welcome the threatened punishment. But as Drago looked at his son he could only step back, unnerved, his own courage failing him … For weeks afterwards he had anticipated injury; he would lie awake listening for the hint of a footstep in the corridor outside; or wait, tensed, crazily expectant that from behind some screen or door, his son would jump out, knife him, maim him. Even kill him.

But he never did. Courtney's power was in the uncertainty of his actions, the suggestion of menace – not in the act itself. I am afraid of my own son, Drago realised, and then also realised that the situations had been finally, and fittingly, reversed. His punishment was worthy of a Greek tragedy; as he had terrorised, so he was to be terrorised. He knew it; and his son knew it too.

So as Drago sat under the shade of the parasol, he was not seeing the opulence of the garden in front of him or musing on what he had achieved, he was waiting for the enviable, unavoidable punishment which was sure to come. Either slowly, a creeping disease disabling him; or quickly, some final act of malice from the source he feared above all.

"Drago." He turned, relieved to see Alberto. "Do you want company?"

He nodded, then motioned for the servant to get another chair, Alberto then settling himself and lighting a cigarette. The smoke limped upwards into the cedars.

"How are you?"

Drago sighed. "My thumbs are the worst, they ache, and now and again I'm clumsy."

"But you said you were on some new medication," Alberto replied consolingly. "Give it time – it takes time to work."

"I can't stop operating!" Drago said suddenly. "I would have no life without my work."

"You could lecture," Alberto suggested, leaning towards his friend urgently; "Face reality, Drago, you might *have* to stop operating before long. You don't want to start making mistakes. If it has to end, then it's better that it ends when you're still at your peak. No surgeon, no matter how gifted, goes on forever –"

"It's my life!" Drago said sharply, "it's all I have. I made a god out of my career, I worshipped it, put it above everything and for what?" He paused, threw down his napkin. "I have no family left – and before you say it, I don't deserve one."

Gently, Alberto touched his friend's arm. "Listen to me, you did what you thought was right."

"I DID WHAT I WANTED TO!" Drago shouted, the doves startled and scattering frantically into the sky. "I satisfied myself without thinking of anyone else, and now I'm getting what I deserve." He paused, his eyes were heavily shadowed, resigned. "I'm not pitying myself – I deserve my torment, just as I deserve my son, I just feel …" he struggled to put his loss into words. "… I just feel bereft at losing my skill."

"Then pass it on," Alberto said simply.

"I can't."

"Jesus!" Alberto hissed softly. "You *are* a stubborn bastard. You could lecture – that's how you could pass on what you know, Drago. Doctors need your experience, your talent – you could teach them. Someone has to take over from you."

"My son isn't capable –"

"I'm not talking about Courtney, and you know it!" Alberto snapped. "But there are others who could; many doctors starting out just like you did. Young, clever, eager to learn. Hospitals all over the world would welcome your skills and the chance to learn your techniques."

Drago listened, his thoughts running on. So it might not be over, there might still be some way of avoiding the inevitable decline and the grim overhang of the future.

"I could hold lectures, I suppose."

"You're sixty three, Drago, you could go on for another twenty years."

"And you?" he asked, turning to his friend. "What about you, Alberto?"

"I shall retire very soon and then travel the world," he answered.

"Will you marry again?"

"No … will you?"

"I wouldn't know how to talk to a woman now," Drago admitted. "Not intimately. I forgot how to love a long time ago." He looked down the garden, by a stone wall a shadow moved. It seemed for a moment like the outline of a woman walking. "I should have loved Catherine more."

"Yes," Alberto said simply.

"I should have known she was so ill."

"Yes."

"Do you think," Drago asked quietly, "that I will ever be rid of the guilt?"

Alberto ground out the cigarette in the grass and then turned to his friend.

"No."

Drago nodded.

"I think," Alberto continued, "that it will be, from now on, your mother, your father, your wife and your children. Your guilt is your life and your family."

"Then it's too much to bear," Drago said, bowing his head and staring at his hands.

"You could relieve it," Alberto said quietly. "You could contact your sister and stop this feud. You could wipe out the past by simply calling a truce, by ending any more ill feeling." His voice was rapid with certainty. "Drago, you lost a family, but you have another one. I know Misia, I know her children, they would accept you, believe me – there's no reason to carry on a grudge. It's just pride, stupidity."

"I can't do it."

"Why not?"

Drago turned in his seat, glancing away. "I can't go to her now and beg for acceptance. I can't go back now, not when I'm getting older and getting sick. I won't let her see me this way!" he said fiercely. "I can't let her see what I've lost. I couldn't bear to see her gloat over me. I can't do it. I can't -"

"Misia wouldn't see it that way –"

"*I would!*" Drago shouted. "If there was ever a time to go back it should have been when my father died. But I was too late, and now there'll never be another chance."

"Your pride's all that holds you back," Alberto said harshly. "And how you hold onto it! Have you ever realised actually what it's cost you – and what it still costs you? Would you honestly rather die alone then ask your sister to forgive you?" he shook his head disbelievingly. "You're such a fool."

Drago's voice was fixed, unmovable; "I just can't do it."

"Then you're going to be a very lonely man."

Drago stared ahead blindly, struggling to find something to hold onto, a hope, a belief: some little way to escape terror. "I'm afraid."

Alberto nodded. "We're all afraid. For some of us, life is only ever twenty minutes away from despair."

The words chilled the warm garden; the shadow by the wall moving and passing on.

"If I did lecture …" Drago said suddenly. "… I might find someone to pass everything on to. An heir, someone to inherit my role."

"You have an heir," Alberto said, looking at his friend, his tone warning: "Don't try to find a replacement for Courtney, don't look for a surrogate son. It would be a dangerous act, with all kinds of repercussions. You have a family in England – go to them."

"It's too late. There must be another way."

"Forget it," Alberto retorted. "You have a son – because you've failed with him, don't go looking for someone else to take his place."

"Why not?"

"*Why not?*" Alberto repeated. "Because it could only lead to tragedy, that's why."

# Forty-Three

Vincent was smiling, leaning against the ropes, his arms folded, a series of camera flashes clicking off, a journalist looking at him, asking questions. He was amenable, affable, courteous; he gave time to everyone and was amusing and easy going. Not a walkover though; everyone agreed on that; he might seem to be a curly headed uncomplicated lad but his record said differently.

They had just finished filming a documentary called *'The Long Walk to the Ring'* in which Vincent told the story of his grandfather coming to Liverpool in 1900 and setting up a string of boxers. A born tale teller, Vincent created a myth out of a man who was already well known and revered; Guido Razzio seemed real to the crew after a while, his famous ROMAN HOUSE pitted with memories, old stalwarts like Abbot adding detail to the stories which had been handed down for decades. Their research was extensive, but Vincent was the one who found the photographs of Jack Dudley and his 'boys', and the old Championship poster for Potter Doyle. They might guess at how it had been, but Vincent knew first hand, through his grandmother and then his mother.

Refusing to take a major role in the documentary, Misia did, however, appear in a stunning and unforgettable cameo. Sitting in the drawing room of the Liverpool house, she talked about the war and about the birth of her brother during the night the marquee went up in flames. The interviewer was entranced and pressed for more details about Mary Razzio; Misia, blunt as ever, told her that there was no more to be said on the matter.

Then, unexpectedly, during a break in filming, the director asked Misia where her father had originally come from. Italy, she said. Where in Italy? No one ever knew.

"But someone must," he persisted. "Aren't you curious?"

"My father never spoke about where he came from, so I presumed he didn't want to talk about it," Misia replied evenly, but she was unsettled. She didn't want any outsider to start overturning the past. Neither of her parents had ever referred to Guido's origins and Misia had been content to leave it that way. Until now; now some nosey little media type was starting to pry.

"It would be very interesting for the viewers to know where the story of Guido Razzio began. I could make some enquiries and see what we turn up."

She kept her voice calm. Show any anxiety and they sense a story.

"Well, I know it was near Naples, or was it Pisa?" Misia said, frowning as though she was trying to remember, "but I think someone said that the village – I can't remember its name – was destroyed in the Great War." She dropped her voice conspiratorially, "I think there was just my grandfather and his mother – or was it his sister?" she paused again, "We heard so many stories."

"Well, maybe it doesn't matter that much," the director said, foreseeing a hideous confusion of fact and counter fact. "There's more than enough to create atmosphere for the film. We don't have to fill in all the details, do we?"

"And you do have the casino to cover as well," Misia said evenly.

"Yes, we're going to show how The Razzio Fighters became The Benning Boxers and then how the business has expanded into other fields," he said enthusiastically. "I saw the casino this morning, it's quite a place."

It was, Misia thought, oh, yes, it was quite a place. After all the wrangling and the persuading, Vincent had managed to get his licence and open his casino, choosing a site in Knightsbridge where there had been an old gaming house. It had been for the vastly wealthy in the 1930's, an upper class, select hiding place for the aristocracy and visiting Hollywood stars. Fortunes had been frittered away, many a debt repaid by an indulgent father or studio head. When Vincent discovered it, it was decorated in the heyday of the Art Deco era, with clean uncluttered lines, walnut furniture, white walls and carpets, and numerous Lalique images adorning mirrors and screens.

On the first morning he saw it, the place had been closed for a long time and was overrun by mice, the smell pungent as Vincent opened the door and walked in. It was damp, musty, the blinds mottled as he pulled back a pair of rotting curtains to let in some daylight. Its sadness swung down from the flaking ceiling and slid against the broken screens, a woman's hairpin winking on the dusty floor. Vincent bent down and picked it up, turning it over in his hand and wondering what she had looked like – the woman who had once come here and played here.

Surprised by the effect the house was having on him, Vincent left soon after and for the next twenty months he fought to take possession of No. 100, Blenington Row. He never gave it a name, only called it No. 100, and after a while everyone else referred to it in that way. No 100 was this; No 100 needed that; if we got the licence for No 100; if we could just organise the fire regulations for No 100   No 100, No 100, No 100 …

It became Vincent's obsession. He showed everyone the place and took his girlfriends there, walking them round and seeing how they reacted, if they felt the same kind of thrill that he did. They didn't, of course, it was Vincent's love affair, not theirs, and so they fell by the wayside and other girls came in their place to be tried and tested. There were always others; because with Vincent there were always girls; drawn by his charm, his fame, his sense of fun. His animals helped too; for years old blind Milton, the greyhound, had captivated many a girl's sympathy, and as for Abernathy, the monkey.

"He's the best aphrodisiac known to man," Vincent said happily to Simeon. "You should borrow him, then walk down the King's Road and see what I mean."

Simeon smiled wryly. "I don't think I could carry it off – I don't have your aplomb."

"You're too reserved," Vincent replied, "You should get out more, talk to some girls, relax a bit."

"I'm busy –"

"I'm busy too," Vincent answered, "but I still find time for a sex life." He looked at his brother carefully, "You wouldn't have all those headaches if you got out and about."

Simeon knew it was useless to argue; Vincent was well meaning but, in some ways, emotionally superficial. He didn't understand his brother because he couldn't; he saw life simply on one level – you loved, you worked, you lived – that was his charm, his energy coming from his marvellous uncomplicated openness of character. Vincent understood money, ambition, fame and family – he understood how to treat women and they responded. But he didn't *understand* – or want to *know* – about the dark side of humanity. He might have a soul, he argued, but what purpose did it serve talking about things you could never prove?

"You worry about my soul, Simeon," he said, "and I'll worry about you getting a girlfriend."

In the end even Harewood was impressed by what Vincent had achieved. He didn't approve of the boxing or the gambling, but he admired the single-mindedness which had brought the No 100 Club about, even though he was constantly harangued about his brother's success.

"Look at him," his wife, Leda, said, "Vincent must be worth a bomb and we're still struggling –"

"You should spend less," Harewood said softly.

She was lying on the settee in the lounge, several chocolate wrappers on the floor around her, Lalo asleep by her side. The boys were in bed, only Deandra was still alert. He studied her seven year old profile, the dark hair cut to her shoulders like a Japanese doll's, her eyebrows dark, her nose short and straight.

"Deandra?"

She turned and the transfixing eyes fixed on his. The shock of her beauty always mesmerised Harewood; where had this incredible child come from? he wondered. She was unlike Leda and himself, unlike any of the other children – she was a cross-over, more a member of the Razzio line than the Bennings. Fascinated, he continued to stare, seeing something of Pila in her: but it was only a fleeting resemblance. This child was an original, a marvellous changeling.

"What is it, Daddy?"

"Come here," he said, lifting her onto his lap and stroking the jet hair. "Have you been good?"

"I'm always good."

He laughed, glancing across to Leda. She had fallen asleep, bored, her lips parted.

"D'you want to go for a walk?" Harewood asked his daughter.

"Just us?"

"Yes," he replied, "just us."

He loved her company, she soothed him, made him forget about Leda and his money worries; made him forget that however hard he worked there were always bills to pay. Car bills, heating bills, clothes bills. Harewood had a good salary; his career was progressing well, and yet there was no peace, no sense of achievement. His home and family demanded everything, took everything. He didn't mind the children taking from him; that was accepted, but that his wife should keep admonishing him for his slowness, his lack of success – it was unfair, unreasonable. Unkind.

He held onto Deandra's hand as they walked up St. John's Wood Road, smiling when he saw people look at her. She was his prize; no one would have expected dull old Harewood to sire a daughter like this.

"Uoy evol I."

She giggled, one gloved hand over her mouth. "Again, Daddy, do it again!"

"Uoy evol I," he repeated. (I love you.)

"Say – 'I like cats' backwards." she asked happily.

"Stac ekil I."

She laughed again, clapping her hands together. "No one else's father can do that. I asked at school and no one else's father was as smart as you."

Harewood's eyes misted behind his gold rimmed glasses. "That's good," he said softly.

"I told them all how clever you were," she continued, pulling off her gloves and pushing back her hair with her hands. "Are we going on holiday?"

Harewood frowned. "When?"

"Mummy said we were all going on holiday soon."

"I don't think we can."

"I thought not," Deandra said, interrupting him and then glancing away. Her face looked older than her years and gave a hint of the woman she would become. "Mummy gets mixed up sometimes."

Harewood glanced at his daughter in surprise. Then, as though she knew he was looking at her, she glanced up at him, smiling the sweet and secret smile of understanding, and took his hand, walking along, chatting as though she was the parent and he was the child. Gratefully he followed her, listened to her, and felt the muscles in his neck loosen, the dull ache of panic and unhappiness lifting. This glorious child is supporting me, Harewood thought wonderingly, she is helping me ... Together they continued to walk, until the light began to fade and a chill came in with the impending dark.

Deandra was beginning to tire, her voice fading, but she kept making her father laugh as she talked to him, the two of them throwing shadows on the pavements, long black shapes moving ahead of them.

"What's a shadow?" she asked suddenly, stopping to stare at their silhouettes.

Harewood hesitated, preparing an explanation. "It's a dark figure, projected by the body, which intercepts the light's rays.'"

"Oh," Deandra said simply, looking up at her father. "You know everything, don't you?"

Her adoration was complete; he was her idol. In her eyes, Harewood was invincible. Not balding, not pedantic, not a stuffed shirt – to his daughter, he was a god. And he loved her, not only for her beauty and her sweetness, but for her blind devotion. In time, Harewood knew, she would change. Another man would take his place and he would grow older and been found wanting – it was life, the natural order of things, the way a father stood aside for a husband. It was normal ... but for as long as he could, Harewood was going to hold onto his daughter, because only she offered that gentle balm of approval and the unquestioning acceptance of love.

*

"It was the only thing I could do, in the end," Pila said, her voice emotionless. "Caryl wants to marry some woman called Emma Legg – I couldn't keep him. Not when he wanted to go." She paused, glancing around for Norton's satchel and pushing her son's school books into it. "I can't say I'm even surprised – I was warned years ago that my marriage would never work out."

Simeon frowned, pushing aside the coffee she had made him. "You never said anything about that before. What happened?"

"That vile Princess Ferenza had a maid called Dona," Pila explained, "she read my Tarot cards for me once and told that if I wanted to be happy I shouldn't marry."

"But you did."

Her eyes were sharp with irritation. "Are you telling me that I should have believed what she said? That I shouldn't have married because of what someone saw in a pack of cards? Oh, for God's Sake, Simeon!"

"But she was right."

*"I don't want to talk about it!"* she snapped. "I don't believe in the occult, you know that."

"I know that you say you don't believe, but that's because you're frightened of it," Simeon replied evenly. "Did this woman say anything else?"

"Only that I'd have two children. She was right there." Pila's patience evaporated. "What the hell does it matter anyway? Caryl's left me. That's the only thing that matters." Her head dropped forwards and she sat down, taking Simeon's hand. "I thought we'd go on forever, you know. I thought somehow – oh, I don't know how – but I thought he'd keep having his women, and I'd keep ignoring what was going on, and that in the end, he'd get too old to bother and stay home with me … stupid, wasn't I?"

He stroked the back of her hand gently. "You love him."

"Misia said I was grateful to him, and that was why I kept forgiving him," she stopped suddenly, bit her lip. "I can't let him go, Simeon. I just can't. I can't let that woman have him; I'm his *wife*. I had his children." She stopped, her energy evaporating. Under her eyes, fine lines flecked the skin; lines of tiredness, of sleep-cheated nights.

"You have to let go," Simeon said quietly. "You can't hold onto someone who wants to go."

"Tell me, did he ever love me?" she asked, looking at him, pleading with him.

Did he? Simeon wondered. In a way, maybe. In his five minute attention span maybe Pila had – for a brief interlude – captured Caryl's emotions. But love? No, Simeon doubted it. There was nothing in the man which could feel deep love. Charm was not love; good company was not love; affection was not love – and this was all Caryl de Solt could offer. He skimmed across life, putting his needs put before anyone else's. It was his character, not his fault.

"Perhaps if I talked to him," Pila said hopelessly.

They both knew there was nothing to talk about. If she did plead with Caryl he would listen, and be kind, and say what she wanted to hear in that instant – and the moment she left he would renege on his promises, even his thoughts. Better to lie than face a scene.

"He might listen to someone else."

Simeon shook his head. "Much as I care about you, Pila, I won't talk to Caryl. It would be a waste of time, and you know it. He's not worth fighting for."

"He's my husband."

"Not in his head or in his heart," Simeon said, his voice low. "You have to marry someone you wants you, Pila, someone who values you. Caryl values no one but himself. If you hold onto him, you'll only suffer for it. Let go now and you'll find someone else."

"I don't want someone else," she said blindly.

"He's gone," Simeon said, "you can't force him back. You know that."

She looked up, her eyes meeting his. He was reminded of the first time he had seen her in the Holland Park house, sitting in the conservatory, a pale dark plant amongst all the abundant greenery. Young, temporarily running away from her father's neglect and her mother's neediness. Escaping for such a little time … Oh God, Pila, he thought desperately, what happened? Why, of all the men you could have met, why did it have to be him?

"I suppose divorce is the best way," she said, her voice empty. "… I'll have to tell the children."

Simeon thought of Ahlia, eleven years old, with the face of a early Madonna, bland, secretive, a child who never expressed what she was feeling – and then he thought of Norton, only nine, a round-faced, unremarkable boy, always overlooked. Neither of the children were like their father, none had his voluminous charm – or his superficiality.

"You'll bring them up better on your own," Simeon said honestly, "and if you need anything –"

"I still have money," Pila replied, "even though Caryl tried to relieve me of most of that," she sighed jaggedly. "Their education's provided for. My father arranged all of that. And as for this house, it's in my name."

"You'll recover," Simeon said quietly. "You think you won't, but you will … and I'll come and visit you."

"Often?"

He nodded. "Often. I promise."

"I don't want to be alone," Pila confessed, her voice dipping. "I'm afraid of being alone … I think that's why I stayed with Caryl for so long/ Anything was better than loneliness."

Simeon took hold of both her hands; "You're not alone. If you want me, call. Anytime, day or night, call, and I'll come straight away." He sighed, turning her hands over and staring into the palms. "Try not to fear the future. I do – all the time – and it's no way to live."

She looked at him for a long moment: "Simeon, if there is anything I can ever do to help you, you will ask me, won't you?"

His expression was past hope, past self delusion. "If I knew what help I needed, Pila, I would."

"But if the time came –"

"I would come to you, yes," he promised. "Oh yes, Pila, I would come to you."

# Forty-Four

**Italy**

Drago waited for son all night. He sat in the library with the door open and the light on in the hall. When Courtney came back he would confront him; he wasn't going to endure any more scandal; he wasn't going to be laughed at by his own son. If he wanted to foul himself, then he could, but not his father, not Drago Razzio, not after so much work and so much anguish.

He couldn't eat, wouldn't eat, and sent the servants to bed. The clock ticked on the minutes, swinging round the hours and jumping midnight. Twelve chimes, Sunday – no sign of his son, no sound of a motor bike, no key in the lock, nothing except the silent house. And time to think. Time to sit and stare and think. Time to remember Catherine in the same room, hiding her detective books, blonde haired, bare footed, a ghost before death. The logs shifted in the grate, the fire spurting back into life. Strange how silence is so threatening, Drago thought, strange how a guilty conscience made the shadows leap.

Courtney had gone too far this time. He was his son, but nothing could excuse this. Drago knew that Courtney was deliberately provoking him, setting out to force a response, however dreadful, however violent. He was, like his father, beyond caring what happened; if there was to be a tragedy it would be no surprise to either of them. There was a terrible inevitability about their destruction. Some peck of malice had been implanted many years before; its effects were impossible to avoid or resist.

Drago's head shot up. The sound of a motor bike ground over the gravel drive, the engine violently loud before it was suddenly turned off and the night ploughed into silence again. Absolute silence; stillness chock-full of menace. Drago stiffened in his seat. The footsteps came up the front steps, a key turned in the lock, then silence again, the rubber soled feet noiseless on the marble floor.

"Courtney?"

A pause. Not heard; imagined.

"Courtney?"

He materialised in the doorway; magicked himself into his father's line of sight.

"What is it?"

He was a sullen silhouette, leaning against the door jamb, his right hand to his mouth. Chewing his nails, Drago thought, gnawing away.

"I heard about –"

"Heard about what exactly?" Courtney interrupted, walking into the room and standing by the fire. The light did not flatter him; it emphasised his hollow cheeked, avaricious look and the deep indentation in his chin.

"About you and Thomasco Denvento."

Courtney turned towards the fire and stretched out his hands as though to warm himself. But the action looked false; Courtney was not in need of warmth. He was thinking instead, watching the fire phantoms.

"So?"

Drago struggled to keep his voice even. "Do you realise what you've done?"

Courtney turned: "D'you mean sleeping with a man?" he replied, his tone mocking: "I've been doing that for years."

Drago glanced away from his son. He didn't want to know any more; didn't want to hear the details or be forced to accept the inevitable. The dreaded scandal had finally broken. Everyone in Rome was talking about Thomasco, son of the influential Denvento family, being found with his wrists slashed, a suicide note left by the side of his body. He had done it for love of Courtney Razzio, the note read dramatically; he had been used and abandoned and couldn't face the world any longer.

He didn't die, instead Thomasco was admitted to the Italian Hospital outside Rome where the paparazzi flocked to the gates and photographed everyone who visited. Like Courtney, walking past them wearing sun glasses and a biker's jacket, looking feral and thin and soul-cold. His personality came over in the newspaper pictures; the wide bleakness of him palpable on the page. They had expected him to show remorse; but there was none. Courtney visited his lover as a man might visit his wronged mistress; he made no apologies and gave no explanations.

Let them think what they liked, his expression said. Let them burn with envy and hatred; he felt neither shame or fear. Drago glanced at him warily – Courtney *was* the barbarian within their midst, but the time had finally come for him to be controlled.

"I want you to get married."

Courtney laughed. It was humourless, a dry bone of a noise. "It's illegal to marry a man."

"I want you to marry a woman!" Drago snapped. "I want you to get married. I won't have any more scandal."

"Why should I?" his son countered. "Everyone knows I'm gay –"

"I've have arranged everything. I want you to marry Nancy Gilchrist," Drago said, interrupting his son. "She's American, in the design world, so you have something in common."

"What *are* you talking about?" Courtney asked in astonishment. He had some animation now, some peevish interest. "I'm not marrying anyone."

"If you don't, I'll cut you out of my will," Drago said simply, chillingly. "No money, no house, nothing. Your allowance will cease. From here on in, you'll be penniless, Courtney, and frankly, it's what you deserve." Drago leaned forwards in his seat, watching his son. "Unless you marry this woman, you'll lose everything."

Courtney regarded his father thoughtfully, then moved towards him. Instinctively Drago leaned back, but his son merely passed his chair and walked to the window. Slowly he looked out into the garden, raising one finger and tracing the round orb of the moon on the glass.

"Why would this woman want to marry me?"

"I've paid her to."

Courtney laughed again. "How typical of you, father, to organise everything so neatly. How like you to want to control peoples lives." He tapped the glass with the tip of his forefinger. It made a dull thudding on the window. "I suppose she's ugly."

"No," Drago answered frigidly. "She's attractive."

"So why would she agree to this scheme?"

"Money."

"Money," Courtney echoed. The room was cool with spite; it hung with resentment, old fear and coming troubles. Too many ghosts walked there, too many peoples' histories of misery. The moonlight shone through the high windows, picking out the murals and the stacked books, the globes, the torcheres; it made silver statues of the Apollo and the Brutus busts and here and there it washed over a piece of furniture like a freak snowstorm.

"She needs money?" Courtney asked his father.

"She does," Drago replied, his tone distant. He had organised everything. Nancy Gilchrist was a talented designer without funds; she had been struggling for years in Rome without ever breaking into the top echelons, either socially or professionally – until she met Drago at a party. He had been pre-occupied, intensely withdrawn, and unwilling to talk; but she had chatted on easily and in her optimistic, cheerful way, she had talked of her big breakthrough.

"So you have something in the pipeline?" Drago had asked.

"Well, no …" Nancy admitted, shaking back her straight dark red hair, her oblique turquoise eyes guileless. "I just think that everyday might be the lucky one. And one day I'll be right."

Drago almost dismissed her then, thinking her fatuous, but there was a freshness about her he hadn't seen for a long time and he stayed to talk. They ended up having lunch the following day; there was no attraction on Drago's part, more an instinctive hunch that this redhead would be of some importance to him. She talked about her designs and about the Italian designer houses and he offered to put her in touch with some contacts of his.

Her eyes had narrowed. "Are you hitting on me?"

He blinked. "Pardon?"

"Is this a line before you ask me to go to bed with you?" she asked, without embarrassment. "Because if it is, I'm not interested."

Drago sipped his wine, mortally discomforted. "Miss Gilchirst … I meant no such thing … I never …"

"That's fine then," she said easily, "I just wanted to make sure that we both knew where we stood. You see, for the record, I'm thirty one years old, I've never been married, but I've had a few affairs. I've no children, but I'd like some; I've got loads of talent but I've not succeeded – either in New York or here in Rome." She held his gaze with her unflinching turquoise stare. "I want to make something of my life. I want success and money, and I want a family. That's it in a nutshell."

He looked at her for a long moment without replying, then said: "I could help you."

She shook her head. "No, no one does something for nothing. I don't want you to help me for no reason. Offer me help when I can do something for you," she said, shaking back the fall of hair. "When I can *do* something for you, then I'll accept something *from* you."

The conversation had occurred two years previously and in that time Drago had stayed in touch with Nancy Gilchrist. He didn't know why, he just knew that he should, and then, suddenly the reason was apparent. Yes, she said when he phoned, she had seen the unfortunate news about his son … would she have lunch? All right, she answered, if you like … So they met the following day and she told Drago that she was still struggling to make a living and that her design business was due for closure.

"Do you want to keep it?"

She narrowed her eyes. "Hey, why would I want to keep it? There's only ten years of my bloody life invested in it. Why would anyone hang onto that?"

He was impervious to sarcasm. "I can help you – and you can help me now."

Nancy stopped eating, her fork poised in her hand. "How?"

"I can give you contacts and enough money to ensure that you could save your business and make a breakthrough."

Nancy studied the man sitting opposite her. He had a patrician look, his hair starting to grey, his heavy lidded eyes watchful under the dark birthmark.

"What would I have to do for you?"

"Marry my son."

She dropped her fork. It landed heavily on the plate, several diners turning to stare at her. Drago was unmoved, and waved aside the waiter who hurried over to them. "Well, what do you say?"

"Your son's homosexual -"

"Bisexual," Drago corrected her.

"Is that supposed to make me feel better?" Nancy asked, her eyes alternating between amusement and outrage. "Is this a serious proposal?"

"I have never been more serious in my life," Drago responded. "I won't have any more scandal – my son is a worthless profligate, demanding and malicious. He has, almost single-handedly, tried to bring down the name and reputation I have worked so hard to attain." Drago looked at the woman opposite him. "There's nothing that can be said in his favour; you couldn't like him, and I don't suppose anyone has ever loved him. He's not handsome or good, but he *is* the answer to your problems. If you marry Courtney you can realise your dreams."

"I've never even met him," Nancy said incredulously. "How could think of marrying someone I've never even met?"

"Because it would be a marriage of convenience – a business proposal, if you like. You would have security and I would have protected my name."

"And your son?" Nancy asked coldly, "what makes you think he would agree to this?"

"Money," Drago replied. "Courtney will do anything for money. Anything at all. When I tell him to marry you, he will – when he realises that the alternative is to be disinherited."

Nancy glanced away. She was tired of struggling; she had no family, no means of support either financial or emotional. For years she had struggled for a breakthrough, dreamed of it, longed for it, planned for it. But time had passed and it had not materialised; she wanted children, wanted a home, wanted a husband, a place in the world. But it hadn't come her way. It was always some other woman, some other wedding, some other baptism. Luck had missed her, passed by, dodged her, avoided her perhaps – but never dropped in on her, and she was, if she admitted it, tired.

But was she tired enough to marry Courtney Razzio? And if she did, what would that mean? *Was* it a stroke of good luck, or a ticket to some doomed outer wilderness? An arranged marriage, neatly organised by a father who would do anything to avoid further scandal. A man determined to get what he wanted, whatever the cost … But what of her? Nancy had seen Courtney's photograph in the papers; that angular yearning look had greeted her many times over her breakfast. She knew of Drago Razzio's fame and of the early death of Catherine Razzio. She had heard about the tragedy, and had also heard of the daughter who lived in London.

It was a wretched, miserable family, the story went, with vast problems, and little to hope for. Father and daughter were almost estranged and Courtney was … well, Courtney was a blight on the family name. Drago Razzio, Nancy realised, must be looking at the future and despairing.

"Listen, I don't think I can do this."

"Please," Drago said simply, leaning towards her.

"But why *me*?" she asked incredulously. "I'm American, you must know some eligible Italian girls you could ask."

"None of which would have Courtney," Drago replied. "You see how frank I am being with you? Nancy, listen to me. You need what I can give you."

"I want children –"

"Courtney could give you children."

She hung her head. "Without love."

"There's a price for everything in life."

She glanced up, her expression fierce; "No, not always!"

"Really?" he queried. "Since when has anything come easily to you, Nancy? Your work, your love life?"

"I could get lucky tomorrow," she replied, artificially cheerful. "I could meet the man of my dreams –"

"You won't," Drago replied, "and we both know it."

She shuddered and got to her feet. "You can't buy me, or frighten me into agreement," she said angrily. "I can get by on my own, I always have."

Drago waited for two days and then, one burning hot morning, he drove out of the gates and found Nancy Gilchrist waiting for him. Signalling for the chauffeur to stop, he climbed out of the car and began to walk with her. She was wearing a cream linen suit, a panama hat covering her dark red hair, her oblique eyes shielded by sunglasses.

"I've been thinking," she said slowly, "I'd like to accept your offer."

"Are you sure?"

She stopped walking. "Hey, you were the one who was pressing me before!"

"Yes, but now I want you to be sure. I don't want this marriage to fail, Nancy. I don't ask that you fall in love with my son, but I do ask that in return for a very opulent lifestyle, you stay with him. No separations, no divorce."

The road was white with dust, a heat haze skimming the dry grass.

"I have to meet him first."

"No," Drago said firmly, "the decision will be presented to my son as a fait accompli. What you agree to now I'll make you stand by."

She laughed, suddenly threatened under the opening sun, the heat making her thirsty, her mouth dry.

"You want me to sign my life away?" Nancy asked, her cheerful tone forced. "Like Dr. Faustus?"

"I'm not the devil. But I do want you to accept … I like you, Nancy, and I'd like to have you as my daughter-in-law. I believe you've a goodness about you which I've lost, and which my son never had." Drago paused, the car's engine hummed on the road behind them. "Give it a chance, Nancy, please. Marry Courtney, make something of him, give him children, make it work. Please, please, do this," he begged her. "You see, the past is … the past …" his eyes were blank. "… only you can make it stop."

Nancy could feel the pressure of his hand on her arm and winced: "Make *what* stop?" she asked, looking up into his face. "What?"

He was about to continue, but then turned, walking away hurriedly.

In that one shimmering instant, Drago Razzio had had a look of something damaged and dammed – and it had moved her. Disturbed, Nancy ran after him and caught hold of his jacket sleeve.

"Look, I'll make it all right," she assured him, as a mother would assure a child. "Don't worry, it'll be all right."

"I can't –"

She covered his mouth with her hand. A quick, maternal gesture accompanied by a fulsome smile. "Hey, trust me, okay?"

Blindly, Drago nodded.

"That's right, you trust Nancy," she ordered him. "Nancy will make it okay again."

# Forty-Five

Harewood was standing in the bedroom in St. John's Wood, Simeon sitting on the window seat, both of them staring at the packages Harewood had found. He had been searching for an old case in the attic and had suddenly discovered a pile of carrier bags. At first merely surprised, he had opened them, and then, growing more and more alarmed, he had taken them downstairs. All thirty four of them, of differing sizes and weight, but all full.

Of clothes. Dresses, evening and day, suits, shoes, hats, underwear, tights, make up, etc, etc. Harewood had emptied them onto the bed and then onto the floor, tipping out the contents in waves, his eyes baffled behind his glasses, his thinning hair dishevelled. Leda was out with the au pair and the children; she had left a note stuck to the fridge, written in red felt tip and signed simply – L. She hadn't said where they were going, or when they would be back.

"Why did she buy all this stuff?" Harewood asked his brother blindly. "I keep telling her we don't have the money for this kind of spending."

Simeon looked at the mess of clothes. Many too small for Leda, some the size she used to be when she was at her peak. A size ten, long legged, making the men gape.

"You have to talk to her," Simeon said simply, "she has to be made to see sense."

"There's nothing for the children!" Harewood said suddenly as though the thought had just occurred to him. "She bought all this stuff for herself, and nothing for the children. Can you believe that?"

"I don't think any of it's rational, Harewood, she's not buying all this for any *logical* reason." He glanced over to his brother. "She's not happy –"

"I'M NOT HAPPY EITHER!" Harewood snapped, suddenly furious. "I can't make Leda happy, Simeon, it's not possible. I try to, I always have, but she's not interested in me any more. I even wondered if there was another man, she was acting so oddly, but no," he stopped talking, jabbing at the clothes with his foot, "no, nothing so simple as an affair. When my wife gets depressed she has to go out and buy half of Harvey Nichols instead. Jesus!" he said bitterly. "What in God's name am I going to do with her?"

"Find out why she does it –"

"She'll say the same as she always does." Harewood snapped. "When I ask her about money Leda always says that she 'spends money to make herself feel better'."

"Why does she need to feel better?"

"Apparently the children aren't fulfilling," Harewood explained bitterly. "She says that they demand all her time and that she can't go out with her girlfriends as she used to." He was snappy with irritation, "She *has* no friends left, Simeon. She dropped them when she had Lalo. She said she didn't want anyone seeing her when she'd put on so much weight. After she'd lost it and got back to normal, then she'd contact them again – but she never did. Instead she had Deandra, Tom and then Fraser; stopped talking about going out with her old friends and went out to spend money instead." He paused, exhausted, and leaned against the wardrobe door. An old photograph of Leda, aged twenty five, had pride of place on the bedside table. "I know she's lost her looks, but it doesn't matter to me. I still think she's lovely. I still love her."

Simeon looked at the photograph. No trace of this Leda in the blowsy woman he now knew.

"Have you told her how you feel?"

"Why? It doesn't matter to her," Harewood said with crushing honesty. "She wants what I can't give her – she wants her youth and her beauty back. I think in a way she's even beginning to punish the children for what she thinks they've done to her."

Simeon looked up at his brother. "What d'you mean?"

"She gives Lalo and Deandra too many sweet things," Harewood said, his voice low as though he was ashamed of what he was saying. "It's almost as if she wants them to be like her. She doesn't want them to grow up pretty, she wants them fat – they wouldn't be rivals then."

"Maybe Leda should see a doctor."

Harewood shook his head. "You mean a psychiatrist … I suggested that, but she went crazy, refused point blank. Leda thinks her behaviour is perfectly rational. She just likes to spend money, she says, and what woman doesn't?"

"Most women don't hide what they've bought in the attic," Simeon countered.

"I should talk to her again."

Simeon nodded. "Yes."

"Try to make her see sense."

"*Make* her see sense,'" Simeon repeated softly. "I wonder why anyone ever uses that expression? How can you 'see sense'?" he smiled that sad, long distance smile. "I wonder what sense would look like if we could see it. I've a hunch that 'sense' would be a little dwarf of a man, with a notebook and a deep voice." He shrugged, "Or maybe not, maybe 'sense' is a tall thin woman with hard hands. 'I'll make you see sense' would take on a whole new meaning then."

Harewood sighed. "I never know what you're talking about half the time …" he admitted, sitting on the edge of the bed. "How are the headaches?"

"I don't get them as much as I used to," Simeon replied. "They always came before something happened – you know what it was like. I'd get a migraine and then see or hear something." He paused. "But lately there's been nothing. I've just worked on the book, glad of the hiatus. No headaches, no worries."

"D'you think it's over?"

"No," Simeon said honestly. "I think it's just lying low. I don't want it back, Harewood, but I know it *will* come back. It's part of me, you see, just like Deandra's black hair or your short sight. It's part of me."

Harewood looked around him; "Like Leda's shopping?"

"No, her shopping is a symptom of unhappiness."

"But I don't have the money to support her whims!" Harewood said desperately. "I can't worry about work, worry about money, *and* worry about her."

"Ssh!" Simeon said suddenly, standing up.

There was a sound of feet on the stairs, Leda walking into the bedroom and jumping when she saw them.

"Jesus!" she shrieked. "You frightened me." Her eyes took in the mess of clothes which were scattered around. "So you found them, did you, Harewood? Well, so what if I bought myself a few treats? You're never home – I have to do something to cheer myself up."

Lalo had sidled into the room behind her and clung to her mother's skirts. Her cheeks were red from the cold wind, her plump knees chapped.

Harewood looked at his wife pleadingly: "Listen, darling –"

"And what is *he* doing here?" Leda asked, turning to Simeon. "I want to know what he's doing in my bedroom."

"I asked my brother to come over," Harewood said, walking over to Leda and taking her arm.

She shrugged him off, her face hard with fury. "I don't want him here, picking over my clothes. It's not natural."

Harewood was outraged. *"Leda!"*

"I'm going," Simeon said calmly, walking to the door. As he passed he could see that Leda's make up was stale and guessed that she had slept in it overnight. Her clothes too had the first look of neglect, and Lalo's wool jumper was stained.

"Bye, Harewood –"

*"Oh, just get out,"* Leda snapped, Lalo moving towards her father hurriedly. "Get out of here, Simeon, we don't want you noseying around."

Harewood immediately rose to his brother's defence: "I asked him to come –"

"Well, I didn't!" Leda retorted, slamming the bedroom door closed as Simeon walked out.

He moved down the stairs in silence, crossing Deandra on the third step. She was still wearing her coat and had her right arm around her little brother, Fraser, who was deeply asleep. Hearing his footsteps, she turned and smiled at her uncle, her fantastic beauty tranquil. Returning the smile, Simeon sat down next to her and gazed at Fraser. His face was spotted with chocolate, his hands grimy, dirt under the nails, his nose running.

"Fraser's fast asleep. You must have had a busy day."

Deandra nodded. "He's tired," she said simply, with utter composure.

"Did you have a nice time?"

She turned her spectacular eyes on her uncle: "We went to the laundry."

"The laundry?"

"Yes, we went and watched everyone's clothes going round."

Simeon frowned, certain he had misheard. "A laundry, Deandra? Are you sure?"

"Oh yes, Mummy said that we were going to see a film – and that's where we always go to see a film." She dropped her voice, "It's not like a real film, not like on the telly."

Simeon struggled to keep his voice steady: "You, Lalo, and your brother went with your mother to the laundry?"

"Yes," she answered, "Tom went for a walk with Sue."

"The au pair?"

She nodded, clutching Fraser tightly. "It was nice there. Very warm."

"In the laundry?"

Nodding again, she changed the subject. "Are Mummy and Daddy arguing?"

Simeon frowned. "Do they argue a lot?"

"Oh yes," she replied easily. "Well, Mummy shouts at Daddy a lot."

"And how does that make you feel?"

She gave him a questioning look: "Are you staying for tea?"

Simeon realised at once that she wasn't going to answer the question, and rose to his feet. "No, sweetheart, I'm going home."

"To Grandma's?"

He shook his head. "No, to my home. Do you want to come?"

Deandra glanced upwards, listening. There was silence: apparently the argument had finished. Slowly she looked back to Simeon, smiling at her uncle as though to reassure him; "No, thank you. We're fine here."

Touching her lightly on the head, Simeon walked out, only pausing when his name was called from an upstairs window.

"Simeon Benning!"

He looked up.

Leda was leaning out of the window. "Clear off!" she shouted. "Go on, get lost! And don't come back!"

He could hear the mumble of his brother's voice and then suddenly Leda ducked out of sight, Harewood taking her place at the window.

"Sorry ... sorry, Simeon."

The night was cooling, darkness coming down to earth.

"Forget it."

"We talked it out," Harewood continued desperately, "and we're going to make things better. Things will improve. Honestly, they will. They will, Simeon, I can feel it. You'll see, things will be better from now on – No won morf retteb eb lliw sgnihT – things will be better from now on." His voice was fading as Simeon walked away. "… you'll see, everything will be fine in the end."

225

# Forty-Six

"Vincent's monkey did that," Misia said, pointing to the wallpaper which had been pulled off in uneven strips. "The vet said that animals can't tell colours – but Abernathy can – and he doesn't like green."

Pila looked at the ruined wall. Apparently the monkey had jumped onto the sideboard and ripped off all the wallpaper within reach. The devastation was patchy, but effective.

"I told Vincent that he could pay for the damage by having the room redecorated," she winked at Pila. "Actually that bloody monkey did me a good turn, I've been wanting to redecorate for years, but never got around to it," she laughed and then turned to the door.

A young girl stood there, her face pale, serene, her hair mid-coloured, her eyes also between shades. She was like a vapid Crivelli Madonna come to life; her appearance shifting in changing lights and changing environments. Misia regarded Ahlia thoughtfully; she had nothing of Caryl's obvious charm, and certainly nothing of Pila's sensual dark looks; she was too shy to shine, and yet there was some strength about her; some hint of a personality under the expressionless exterior.

"You're getting tall," Misia said simply.

Ahlia smiled; always eager to please, and yet always reserved, shy, secret.

"Your favourite man's coming home soon," Misia went on easily. "Your 'Darling Portland'." She guided the twelve year old into the kitchen, "Have some cake, sweetheart, it's good, I haven't poisoned anyone for weeks."

Ahlia hesitated, Pila following them into the kitchen and reassuring her. "Go on, have some."

Gingerly she took the cake. "Thank you."

"My pleasure," Misia replied, slapping several pieces of cheese on the plate and passing it to the girl.

Ahlia regarded it suspiciously.

"It's the way you eat fruit cake up North," Misia explained. "It's a tradition. Cheese and cake – oh, do stop staring at it Ahlia, it won't bite!"

"She's just not used to it," Pila said sliding into one of the kitchen chairs and gesturing for her daughter to sit down next to her.

She had been glad to visit Misia, glad of the invitation and of the chance to get a break from her house in Clapham. Her house? No, not really, because even though Caryl had been gone for over nine months, many of his possessions remained. At first Pila had wanted him to take everything; lock, stock and barrel; move each minute particle of himself out of her life. He had chosen another woman, the rejection was hurtful and absolute, and Pila wanted no reminders of him.

Which was impossible, of course. There were reminders on every wall, every piece of furniture, every silly ornament they had bought on a whim. Caryl de Solt leapt out from the kitchen cupboards in the shape of mugs; fell out of the hall closet in the shape of a gardening jacket; and crept up on Pila unexpectedly every time she opened the bathroom cabinet and found his antacid tablets. She threw the first packet away, but when she found the second, she kept it. No logic to the action – but then there was no logic to their behaviour.

Caryl might live with his mistress, Emma Legg, and he and Pila might have hurried through a speedy divorce, but their separation had never really been enforced. Caryl visited Clapham often. At first, only once a month, then a couple of times a month and then once or twice a week.

Pila had been curt, dismissive. "I don't want you around," she said hotly. "It was your idea to leave, you chose to go, so now stay away."

"I like to see you –"

"Caryl, stop trying to make everything pleasant for yourself," Pila said bitterly. "You want me to stop hating you, just so you can stop worrying about what you did. You want me to tell you that you have nothing to feel guilty about," her dark eyes were heavy with outrage. "Well, you have plenty to feel guilty about. Your children miss you. They miss their father, and you weren't the one who had to explain why you had upped and left. 'Doesn't Daddy love us anymore'? – that was what I heard day and night, and you were never around to say – 'No, darlings, Daddy still loves you, Daddy has just fallen out of love with me, that's all, sometimes these things happen to grown ups.'"

He had reached out for her hand, Pila drew back, then let him take it. His eyes were still startlingly blue, full of remorse.

"Pila, I still love you –"

"No, you love Emma Legg now," she said coldly.

"She's more my type."

Angrily Pila shook off his hand. "*Your type!* Jesus, Caryl, why did I ever think there was anything about you? Why did I expect you to behave like a normal man? You got bored with me, and so you left. In time, you'll get bored with Emma, and you'll leave her." She smiled bitterly. "Your five minute mentality, Caryl, that's what rules your life. Whatever happens in the next five minutes is all that matters – before and afterwards, nothing important – just the present moment. You'll never change," she said, her tone resigned, "but I'd like you to do something for me, I want you to keep away, Caryl. See the children by all means, but keep away from me. I don't want you around and I don't want you stopping me from making a new life."

"With a new man?"

She stared at him in disbelief. "You're jealous! You can up and leave me, but if you even think that I might be looking for someone to replace you – you can't take it." Her voice was dismissive, "Well, we're divorced now, so my life's my own."

Or it should have been. But Caryl kept coming to Clapham and he kept visiting his children, and before long, he was calling in around at dinner time.

"D'you mind if I kibbutz?"

Pila stood on the doorway, her arms folded. "Meaning?"

"A person who kibbutz's is someone who sits on the sidelines, you know, chats whilst others eat."

"Why don't you eat with Emma?"

"She's busy."

"So am I," Pila retorted, closing the door in his face.

She felt good about it; glad that for once she had been strong enough to resist Caryl. Because she couldn't stop loving him; even after the divorce papers came through, and the solicitors bills had been paid, even then, her breathing still accelerated when she heard his voice on the phone, and her hand still shook slightly when he called round. I was married to him, she thought furiously, we divorced, it's finished, why can he still have this effect on me? It's over.

But it wasn't, not for her, or for Caryl. He put on weight whilst living with Emma and grumbled about ageing. Pila listened and found herself comforting him, then drawing back, pulled between emotions. She had to protect himself from Caryl; had to appreciate that he was a user, a man who needed constant forgiveness and acceptance, a man who wanted to be approved of – even when he had behaved abominably.

"Listen, Caryl, you'd made your choice, now stick to it."

"I might have been wrong."

The telephone shook in her hand. "It's too late. You wanted the divorce, you hurried it through, you were the one who wanted to marry Emma – 'the love of your life' you called her. Don't tell me you're bored already."

"You're the only one who really understood me," he said plaintively.

"Yes," Pila replied, "that's why I'm not having you back."

But back he came; and soon he was round at the Clapham house twice a week, eating dinner with Pila and the children, Norton reserved, Ahlia, as ever, disguising her true feelings. Then one night when the children had gone to bed, Pila was washing up and Caryl came into the kitchen to talk to her. She was wearing a clinging jumper and slacks, her figure outlined, her hair thick and heavy. He approached her, smelt the same dark scent she always wore and slid his hands over her breasts.

She froze, her hands in the washing up water, her head falling forwards, her face obliterated under her hair. He pulled her backwards, pressing his body against hers, his hands moving under her jumper, his mouth against her neck. She turned, moving in slow motion, her wet hands pressed against his back, her mouth finding his. They made love urgently on the floor, Caryl weighty on top of her, Pila moving in rhythm with him, the table kicked to one side. Every sound intensified – their breathing; their noises; their simultaneous excitement and orgasm coming hot and forbidden – and then, when it was over, Pila struggled to her feet, pulling up her trousers, her face flushed.

"Go, Caryl. Please, get out," her voice was drowsy, almost welcoming.

He stood up and tried to take hold of her.

"NO," she snapped, "Go home."

He left without another word.

She couldn't sleep, couldn't rid herself of the scent of his skin and the feel of him. Throughout the night she dreamed, then woke, and felt a longing for him which scorched her. She was burning inside a fire: every thought, every moment committed to him; her breathing painful, her body aching, and when the morning came she looked into the mirror and saw what she was most afraid of.

Misia saw it too. "Are you in love?"

Pila glanced over to the window, Ahlia had gone into the garden with her beloved

Portland, Norton trailing behind them and kicking a football half-heartedly. Misia was peeling potatoes, her face turned towards Pila, her expression questioning.

"Well – *are you?*"

"I … in a way," Pila admitted, her colour warming, the sensual swing in her voice betraying her.

"Who is he?" Misia asked, sitting down and pushing away her fringe impatiently. It flirted back into place, dated, greying, endearing.

"He's …"

"Oh shit!" Misia said suddenly, leaning back in her seat and crossing her legs. "Not Caryl?"

"It was an accident –"

"What was?" she asked, aghast, then paused. "You're sleeping together, aren't you?"

"He's my husband."

*"You bloody idiot!"* Misia said simply, turning to glance at the door as Portland walked in.

He smiled broadly and moved over to the sink, rinsing his hands. "The kids are still outside," he said, "I'm knackered."

"Pila is sleeping with Caryl," Misia said flatly.

"Ah …" he said, wiping his hands on the tea towel and walking over the table. "Is that wise?"

"IS THAT WISE!" Misia exploded. "What kind of a fool question is that? After the way that sod treated her –"

Pila put up her hands: "Listen, it won't happen again," she said, then glanced quickly at Portland. "And anyway, why should I have to defend myself? It's my life."

"Pila," Misia said calmly, "I'm the nearest you've got to a mother now. Your bloody father might be totally uninterested, but Portland and I think of you as a daughter – and we care."

She paused, her mind going back to the time Pila had first come to England; quiet, nervous away from home; and then she thought of Caryl de Solt walking into her niece's life when she was at her most vulnerable. The knight in shining armour, the answer to a prayer. She knew that was the way Pila still saw him; as the man who had listened, who had saved her. She had had no other male figures in her life to contradict her devotion, no other men by which she could assess him – only her father and her brother, neither of whom had given her the affection and support she needed. Pila had had no Portland, no Vincent, Simeon or Harewood – she had seen the worst of men and had judged all others by what she knew.

In her eyes, Caryl had been kind, and that was the way she would always judge him. He might have been unfaithful, callous; he might have left her and divorced her in order to marry his mistress; but now he was back – surely that meant he still cared for her? … Oh, yes, Misia could see the way Pila was thinking; and could recognise the desperate desire to hold onto a belief, a hope.

"Don't let him back into your life," Misia said warningly. "He'll only hurt you again."

"He said he might have made a mistake."

Portland and Misia exchanged a glance.

"Sweetheart," Portland said, sitting on the edge of the kitchen table, "the man's a loser. He's not right for you. Let it go and then you can look for someone else."

Pila stared at him, then nodded slowly. "You're right … I know you are. I don't want him back really, I would never have contacted him, but he just started to visit and then the visits became more and more frequent and suddenly he was there most of the time … it doesn't help that the kids want him back."

"They want what's familiar," Portland replied kindly. "Children need security, and he's their father. But if you let him back into your life – and theirs – when he goes off again – and he will – think how difficult that'll be to explain." He took her hand, "Look, I'm not saying it's easy, I'm just saying that it's dangerous – and it's not good for you *or* your children."

"I know …" Pila said quietly.

"Don't think I don't understand," Portland continued, "I was lucky meeting Misia, I thank God for that daily. I couldn't have lived without her. It's harder for you, you're on your own, with kids – but don't turn to Caryl, Pila. I never interfere in your life, you know that, but I tell you this, if you take him back it will be the worst mistake you've ever made."

"He won't listen –"

"Make him!" Portland said heatedly. "You owe him nothing. No love, no loyalty. He forfeited the right to that when he left you. Move on. Someone else *will* come for you – but not if he's still hanging around."

He paused and studied Pila's face; she was luminous, the look, the expression of a woman who was in love. Oh God, Portland thought, why her? Why couldn't a woman so lovely and so loving, find a happiness which was long overdue?

"Tell him to bugger off."

She nodded, taking Portland's hand. Immediately, he pulled her to her feet and hugged her protectively, looking over her shoulder to his wife, his expression for once cold.

# Forty-Seven

Nancy Gilchrist was standing on the terrace of Drago's house in Rome. She was staring ahead of her, looking down the long stretch of gardens, her gaze finally settling on the fountain. The putti were mottled with water, their stone limbs fixed, their amorous expressions flirtatious under the hot sun. She had been summoned at last, the call coming that morning as she worked on her designs, Drago's voice expressionless.

"Come to lunch," he said simply. "Courtney's waiting to meet you."

Immediately a flutter of excitement and apprehension had welled up in her. For an instant she had wanted to refuse, to pack her bags and leave Rome; to escape the madness which was coming. But she hadn't, instead she had written down the time she was expected and then rung off.

Yet as the morning continued her nerves accelerated; she didn't know what to wear, what image to project, and washed her hair twice, finally letting it dry lose on her shoulders. Her flat was cluttered, as all places are where space is limited. Designs hung from makeshift hooks on the plastered walls, a battered portfolio propped against the bed, her jewellery hanging haphazardly over the mirror. What was she about to do? Nancy asked herself repeatedly, knowing that there was no one she could turn to for advice, and no one who would stop her from taking the inevitable step. She had committed herself to a match with Courtney Razzio; a marriage without love or honour; a bonding between two people which would cement the respectability of a famous name, no more.

If she chose to run, to back out at the last minute, what would she do then? Work on, as she had always done, chasing the mirage of success, getting older without status, without family. Distressed, Nancy laid her hands on her stomach. She had always wanted children; having lost a baby through miscarriage years earlier, she had never stopped grieving for that little truncated life. The child would have been ten now, she thought, a boy; and she would have been a mother, a woman with someone of her own. A family of her own, not a woman walking from disappointment to disappointment, forcing herself to believe that one day some miracle would happen.

Miracles were for other people, she realised, looking into the mirror. Or maybe not; maybe this was *her* miracle; maybe this frightening, chilling arrangement might turn out to be her salvation after all. Nancy forced herself to smile, she had to believe in something, and believing in herself wasn't enough anymore. Courtney Razzio can give me children, she thought desperately; in return for the respectability I can give him, he can give me a family.

It didn't seen so terrifying then; although her hands were clammy as she picked up her bag and her eyes for a moment filled when she looked into the mirror. This is it, kid, she said, jollying herself along. This is the best chance you'll ever get ... But when she walked to the door Nancy paused, turning for a moment to look at the meagre little flat – I gave it my best, she thought, I did all I could, but I couldn't hack it – then she walked out without looking back.

"Nancy?"

Drago's voice cut into her thoughts and she stiffened, unable to turn.

"Nancy?"

Slowly she moved, her shadow moving with her. Drago was coming towards her on the terrace, a man walking alongside him. A thin man wearing sunglasses. Nancy stared, Courtney coming into view second by painful second. He walked close to the wall, his face hollow, the deft cleft in his chin as dark as a ink mark. But she couldn't see his eyes behind the sunglasses and hesitated when he stopped in front of her.

"Courtney," Drago said simply, "this is Nancy."

Take off your glasses, she thought frantically, let me see your eyes.

Courtney folded his arms, refusing contact. "So, you're Nancy. Why don't you take off your glasses, so I can see you?"

She fumbled with them awkwardly, dropping them onto the terrace and then bending down to pick them up. But when she looked at him, her oblique turquoise eyes were steady, challenging.

"Very nice, father," Courtney said approvingly, "she's good looking."

"Well, now you've had a chance to view the merchandise," Nancy said, forcing a cheerful tone into her voice. "Why don't you let me have a look at you?"

Courtney paused, then took of his own glasses. His eyes were green, unexpected, the expression wary. But not cruel, Nancy thought with intense relief. Not cruel.

"So, what's the verdict?" he asked her.

"You're cute."

"Jesus!" he said fiercely.

"It's a compliment," Nancy replied, trying to fight her nervousness; "Americans always say that when they find someone attractive."

He gave her a slow look. "Don't fuck me about –"

Drago turned on his son violently. "Stop it!" he snapped. "I won't have language like that in my house – and I won't have you talking to Nancy that way."

"Listen, Father," Courtney said, his tone amused, "why don't *you* marry her? You seem to like her well enough."

Drago's face was hard, "I'm warning you, Courtney."

"Yes, I know," he replied, stepping forwards and unexpectedly taking Nancy's arm. "Come on, we can work out our damnation on our own."

Surprised, she walked with him. He took her down the lawns, passing the fountain and into the maze laid out by the enclosed herb garden. The hedges were lofty, casting long shadows, clouds scuffing the high sun. Unsure of herself, Nancy didn't know what to say and Courtney was content to be silent, until, finally, he sat down on a white bench and lit a Marlboro. He offered her one.

"No, thanks."

"You don't smoke?"

Nancy shook her head. "No."

"Not even pot?"

"No."

"Take any drugs?"

"No."

"Drink?"

She sat down next to him. "Just wine, sometimes."

"What about sex?"

"What about it?"

"You straight?"

"Yeah," she said, staring at him, "and I don't have to ask about you – the papers gave me plenty to go on."

He laughed, unexpectedly amused, "I deny nothing."

"I didn't expect you to."

"What *did* you expect?" he asked, turning to her.

"Someone more … vicious." She paused, "Oh, no, that's the wrong word. Someone cruel."

"I can be cruel."

"Yeah …"

"That doesn't worry you?"

She shook her head. "Oh, it worries me. But others things worry me more."

"You're blunt, I'll give you that," Courtney said. "What do you want from me?"

"You know the deal."

"I know my father's terms – but I want to know what you want," Courtney said, inhaling deeply. "Is it the money you're after?"

"Not just that."

"So what else?" he asked, genuinely interested. Nancy Gilchrist wasn't what he expected; he had anticipated some hard faced Yank, or some down trodden no hoper; not an attractive woman who was obviously intelligent.

"I want …"

"Go on," he prompted her. "What *do* you want from me?"

She turned. Her oblique eyes were open, without guile, an unnerving honesty in them. "I want children from you."

The words had the force of years of disappointment and heartache behind them. They were not said glibly, or to impress; they were frank words, inviting ridicule. As he looked at her, Courtney realised what a chance she was taking in exposing herself completely, emotionally laying out her needs. This is what I want, she said, answering him without lies, without deceit. He felt a instant and unsettling respect for her.

"Children?"

She nodded. "Yeah."

"How many?"

Nancy turned, screwing up her eyes against the sun. "To use your earlier words – don't fuck me about."

He laughed, and kept laughing. She thought at first that he was laughing at her and then realised that he was genuinely amused.

"How many?" he asked at last.

"Two would be okay."

"Boys?"

"One of each, if possible."

"No trouble," he replied, still smiling, then sobered up immediately. The relaxed look had gone, he was suddenly suspicious again. "You should get out of here – it can't work. We both know that."

She was wrong-footed and blustered. "I didn't realise how much you wanted to be poor."

He winced, knowing he had met his match: "I didn't realise how much you wanted to be rich."

"Ouch," she said simply, watching as he ground out his cigarette in the gravel. "Listen, Courtney, we could try to make a go of it. Neither of us has anything to lose – and neither of us has any real choice."

"You can't blame me if you end up miserable," he said. "Remember, none of this was my idea."

She nodded:

"No, it wasn't – and you can't blame me if you end up miserable either." Nancy paused. "Then again, you can't blame me if you end up happy."

He made a quick sound of disgust. "Happy – what the hell is that?"

"Something that comes when you've given up on it," Nancy replied evenly.

"In that case, I should have been delirious for the last decade."

She smiled: "Poor little rich boy?"

Courtney ignored her and carried on with his own train of thought: "If we go through with this, I won't be faithful. I'll still want other people – men and women." He glanced over to her, her expression was unreadable, "I'm not going to lie to you, I want to be fair from the start. Despite what you might have heard, I'm not a complete shit. We might look like a respectable married couple from the outside, but I'm not going to change to way I live my life."

Nancy nodded. "Unless you want to?"

"Yes," he agreed, "unless I want to."

# Forty-Eight

Simeon was asleep in his flat, dozing uneasily and then waking with a start. Jerking upright in bed he pulled back the curtains and looked out. The Kensington street looked back, the early morning damp with dew. No one was about, apart from a workman stopping to light a cigarette on the corner. He paused, inhaled, then threw the match into the gutter and moved off, whistling.

The low ache was starting again, Simeon tensing immediately. Oh God, he thought, not now … Gingerly he got out of bed and padded to the bathroom. His reflection was ominous, the grey white skin skimmed with sweat, the light burning into his eyes. Feeling suddenly nauseous, he leaned over the wash hand basin and then wiped his mouth with a flannel. His hands felt unnaturally cold against the oily heat of his face, his neck tightening with tension.

Carefully he shook two painkillers out of the bottle and swallowed them, turning off the light and moving back to bed. Maybe it would pass; maybe it was only a headache … But he knew otherwise. This was something more, and soon, without warning, the images started to flicker against his closed lids. He began to shiver then, pulling the sheet around his body, his legs drawn up against his stomach, the noises overlapping each other and drumming against his ears.

People whispered to him, and then others, unknown, came into his thoughts … The morning shifted past the curtains, the first London buses breaking on the bend of Kensington Church Street. Rigid, Simeon lay fighting sickness and the dark red pain in his head. It had been months since his last attack; he had hoped, against hope, that he might never have another, even though, every morning, he had waited for the signals which heralded another migraine. And now, finally, it had come.

The images were jumbled; the British Museum, the library, a woman he had once known walking in the rain. And then Misia, Portland turning as he skipped over a chasm … oh no, not my father, Simeon thought, not him … the image disappeared and another took its place. A beautiful girl with her hair cut like a Japanese doll's – Deandra – but not Deandra now, Deandra older. Spectacular, more lovely than anyone he had ever seen … She was dancing under a street lamp with a man in a dinner jacket … What now? Simeon wondered, a house cropping up, a palatial house in a foreign country, where a fountain played. Where was it? he wondered, turning over and gagging, the pain in his head making his eyes burn. Jesus, stop it … stop it …

Then suddenly there was another picture – of Ahlia, the beguiling, secret Madonna. Pila's daughter, the little twelve year old, the secret shy girl. Was what it? Simeon asked … what? She was running away, running away … where? where?.. and then there was Caryl, crying, his head in his hands, his nose running, his grey trimmed beard almost as white as his face, and his eyes blue crystal … Ahlia … but where? where was she going?

Simeon tried to sit up and then vomited, falling backwards, dark patches of sweat pooling under his arms, his back stiffening. His eyes rolled upwards, the pain intensifying in his brain, the bus outside seeming for an instant to smash into his room, crashing through the walls and pinning him under the wheels … But Ahlia was still running, screaming, Ahlia … where? where?

Out into the street, into the street in Clapham, running away … from what? Simeon begged, jerking on the bed, his teeth clenched. Show me, tell me … show me … A running Madonna. Silent now, a girl with an expressionless face without speech. She was dumb. DUMB? … Show me! show me! Simeon begged, turning on the bed, his mouth opening as the last scene presented itself … Caryl de Solt turning at the end of a long shadowed corridor, walking with others, and Ahlia, running, running away …

*

He had been watching the house in Clapham for over two hours. Standing on the corner like a thief. Caryl felt into his pocket and took out a bottle, swallowing what was left of the gin and then chewing a couple of mints, the taste pungent on his tongue. He was bored with Emma – bored rigid – he had made a mistake and wanted to come home, his eyes fixing blearily ahead. The house looked inviting and he was suddenly swamped with self pity. He wanted to be inside, to be sitting in his old chair, watching television or reading, comfortable, at peace. Pila would be making something good to eat, she was a clever cook, anything she prepared, however simple, was always appetising.

Emma couldn't cook, Caryl thought petulantly; she didn't like making things, or even keeping the flat tidy. Pila had always kept everything clean, his clothes laundered and ironed, his children well mannered. She was a good wife, and he had been a fool to leave her … but she wanted him back, whatever she said, she wanted him back. He knew it, he knew enough about women to tell that she was still in love with him. After all, hadn't they made love again? He had called round to see her, catching her fresh from a shower, her dark hair clinging to her damp shoulders.

She told him to get out, but he'd insisted. The children were at school, he had said, what was the harm? She had been angry, pushing him away, strong for her size, brittle with anger, but he had stayed, making coffee and taking her a cup upstairs. She was standing in her underwear and turned when she heard him, surprised, thinking that he had already left. He had dropped the cup and pulled her onto the bed; she had stopped struggling almost at once, letting him enter her, her lips moving over his face. They had clung to each other greedily, turning over, Pila suddenly on top of him, her hair falling dark around the shaded eyes, her tongue running down his chest.

"No!" she had said suddenly, getting off him and pulling on her clothes. "No. Get out, Caryl."

Baffled, he had reached for her again, but she had ducked back, running down the stairs as he followed her.

"PILA!"

She had stopped by the front door, opening it onto the street. Her eyes had been full of tears. "Please … let go!" she had begged him. "It can't work. It's over."

"No, it's not. It's *not* over," he replied, catching hold of her arm.

She had shaken him off. "Just go," she had said. "I can't live like this – I WON'T!"

He had known that she had meant it and had left. But hours later Caryl had begun to long for her again and he also began to plot. If he went back he could convince her, could make her want him again. It was simple really; they were supposed to be together; he might have acted like a fool in the past, but he had finally come to his senses. All he had to do was to convince her – and he was always convincing. So he had decided to come back that night and wait until he saw the lights go out in the children's rooms; then, when he knew Pila would be alone, he would let himself in with his key. The one she didn't know about, the one he had always kept.

The idea had seemed plausible, but as the day progressed Caryl's courage began to waver and at lunchtime he had several drinks to calm his nerves. She would resist, he knew that, but in the end she would give in. They might even make love, quietly, not to waken the children … Hurriedly Caryl downed his third gin, thinking of his ex-wife naked, and wanting her, mesmerised by the memory of her voice in the dark and the slow languor of her lovemaking.

The afternoon had gone past in a stuffy blur of alcohol, and then finally, when dusk came, Caryl had made his way over to the house in Clapham. Avidly, he watched the windows. At nine they were still blazing, and then Ahlia's went out. But not her brother's. Apparently Norton was still up. God, Caryl thought impatiently, didn't that boy ever sleep?

He finished the half bottle of gin and half an hour later his son's light finally went out. Only one light still burned, the drawing room light. He watched; a shadow moved across the blind – Pila – then the light went out and seconds later another came on upstairs. She had gone to bed early, he thought, she was getting undressed, ready for him ,,, He was suddenly hot with excitement, his confidence heady as he walked up to the door and silently unlocked it.

The house was tomb quiet, not a noise. Slowly he felt his way round, touching familiar objects and making his way to the stairs. There was no moon, no illumination other than the half inch of light coming from under Pila's door. He paused, listening for any sounds issuing from his children's rooms, but there was none, and so he moved on, turning the handle of the bedroom door and walking in.

She was reading in bed and turned, frightened. "God Almighty!" she snapped. "What the hell are you doing here?"

He weaved on his feet, tipsy, unsteady, as Pila got up and faced up. "You've been drinking."

"I came to see you …" Caryl said, touching her face.

She knocked his hand away irritably. "I'll get a cab to take you home."

"I'm not going home," he said, grabbing for her and catching hold of her nightdress.

"Caryl, stop it!" she snapped warningly. "I want you out of here – and I want my bloody key back."

He was tugging her towards the bed, his eyes damp. "Listen, darling, I'm sorry. I want to come home –"

"Caryl, I'm not talking to you like this. You're drunk and I don't want the children to find you here."

"They're my kids too!" he snapped pathetically. "They might like to see their father –"

"Not in this state!" she hissed, trying to tug the nightdress out of his hand. "Let go!"

"Come to bed …" he said blearily, "please …"

"Let go of me!" Pila shouted, pushing him away.

He fell heavily onto his side, then rolled onto his knees, clutching onto the bed for support as he struggled to his feet again.

"God," she said, furious. "Look at you! You think you can creep in here and I'll take you back. 'Welcome home, Caryl!'" her voice was thick with disgust. "You're crazy – and I want you out of here, NOW."

He hadn't expected her anger and was slow to respond, his thoughts refusing to clear, a slow burn of humiliation spreading through him. Women wanted him, all women wanted him, he'd never been rejected – who the hell was she to reject him? Caryl thought furiously, buoyed up by the gin. He had come back to her, and now the cow was trying to throw him out.

"Pila, come here!" he said, hurrying after her as she moved to the door.

She turned at the head of the stairs. "I'm calling for a cab," she said, cold with repulsion. "Keep your voice down, I don't want the children wakened."

He saw her turn, saw the beloved head glance away, saw her olive skinned hand on the banister rail. How dare she! he thought, after all he had done for her. He had saved her, taken her away from Rome after her mother died, looked after her. Bloody witch, bloody cow … He was Caryl de Solt, the man who could have had any woman in London – he had chosen her, and now she was rejecting him.

His hand gripped her shoulder fiercely and she winced.

"GET OFF!" she spat. "Get off me, or I'll call the police."

He blinked, suddenly threatened by the words. Police, he thought, Jesus, not police.

"Pila, no …" he begged, trying to pull her to him, his other hand reaching out for her. "Calm down –"

But she was too angry to listen and jerked herself free, her face a hate-filled oval in the dim light.

"I want you out of my life forever," she said, "I want you away from me, and away from this house. I never want to see you again," her voice was maddened, but without fright.

He moved onto the step above her, his arm suddenly sliding round her neck, his lips pressed to her ear. His head was buzzing, the veins in his neck pulsing, a sudden consuming rage making him violent.

"You can't tell me what to do!"

She began to struggle then, fighting to release his grip around her throat, her bare feet scrambling for purchase on the step.

"You *can't* get rid of me," Caryl said hoarsely, "You bloody ungrateful bitch! YOU BLOODY WHORE!" he shouted, increasing the pressure around her throat.

Frantically, Pila's hands reached up, trying to release his grip, her breath leaving her, her right foot sliding off the edge of the step. She jerked forwards suddenly, Caryl feeling her weight against his arm and realising that his grip was all that prevented her from falling down the stairs. His mind seemed to jam, to expand and contract, his thoughts blurring under the alcohol, his anger all consuming – then he suddenly jerked his arm free and stepped back, grabbing the banister to stop himself lurching forwards.

238

She fell into the darkness, her body striking first the wall and then the floor when she landed heavily at the foot of the stairs. Transfixed, Caryl waited. The silence was huge, swallowing. Five minutes passed. Pila didn't move. Another minute passed and then slowly, timidly, he moved downstairs. The house was silent. Listening. No lights. He stopped, bent down, laid his hand against Pila's neck. No pulse. He was sober instaneously, and began frantically to try and lift her, feeling the dead weight in his arms, a scream of panic starting in his chest.

Then he noticed a movement out of the corner of his eye and spun round. At the top of the stairs stood Ahlia. She was wearing a white nightdress, her eyes fixed on her father, her mouth open.

"Ahlia," he said, beginning to mount the stairs. "Ahlia, it was an accident …"

She stood, paralysed by shock.

"… I didn't mean for it to happen," Caryl babbled, Oh, God, he thought, how much did she see? How much did she know? If she'd been there all the time she would have realised that he let her mother fall.

"Ahlia …"

She never moved. She was stiff, unblinking, her hands locked by her sides, her eyes staring.

And Caryl kept moving towards her; up the dim stairs, one by one, foot by foot towards her. She saw his shadow on the wall, moving with him, and her mother's body at the foot of the stairs. But she couldn't move.

"Ahlia, darling," Caryl said, within feet of her then, his right hand extending towards her.

She screamed only once, the sound startling her father so much that he fell back against the wall, his daughter running past him so quickly that he had no chance to stop her. And she *kept* screaming, avoiding her mother's body, wrenching open the front door and running out into the street, the unearthly wail echoing long after her.

Caryl didn't follow her. He simply sat down, his head in hands, his eyes fixed on the open front door in front of him. Lights went on outside, urgent voices calling out, the sounds of approaching feet coming loud down the dark street. But he never moved. A light came into the hallway suddenly, illuminating Pila's body – then slowly the beam moved upwards, settling blindingly and accusingly on the hunched figure of Caryl de Solt.

# Forty-Nine

"I don't know what to say to him," Misia admitted, her voice low. "Dear God, Pila was his child. How would I feel if Drago phoned me to tell me one of my children was dead?" she stopped short. "Dead … Pila is dead," her voice plummeted and she stood up, pulling her jumper down over her narrow hips, her movements quick, agitated. "She was only thirty four … I warned her about that bastard de Solt, we all did."

Portland moved over to his wife and put his arm around her. They had been talking for over an hour, the news coming fast, a policeman on the doorstep only minutes after Pila's death. They had all been laughing in the Holland Park house, Vincent telling some far fetched tale about Abernathy, the monkey punctuating the story with its own impromptu performance. They had all been laughing, as Portland had answered the door and hearing the news first.

He stood, blank-faced, uncomprehending: "What did you say?"

"Your niece, Mrs. de Solt, has been killed –"

He could hear Misia laughing in the study, Vincent bellowing for Teller to bring some drinks.

"Killed?" Portland had echoed, for once unable to believe what he was hearing. Not Pila, she was too young, he had seen her only the other day. "How … how was she killed?"

"An accident we think, sir," the policeman had continued. "But they've taken Mr. de Solt in for questioning. He's been a bit hysterical, I'm afraid. Difficult to get a clear story from him. He'd been drinking."

Another belt of laughter from behind, Portland ushering the policeman in.

"Come in, come in, forgive me, I didn't think …" he had glanced towards the front door. "Where are the children?"

"In the police car outside, sir," the officer had answered. "We didn't know where else to take them."

"They should be here. You did right … where's their mother? Where's Pila?"

"At the hospital – St. Georges. I'm so sorry, sir."

"How …" Portland's voice had jammed on the words. "… how did she die?"

"Broken neck."

Broken neck.

Portland had lifted his hand to his mouth, pressing it hard against his lips. He remembered Pila at the kitchen table, laughing, her arm slung over the back of her chair, her full dark looks luminous under the lamp light. Another thought occurred to him; Pila as the young girl come from Italy. Oh, Jesus, Portland had thought suddenly – Drago.

"Who is it?" Misia asked, walking out into the hall and flinching as she saw the policeman. "Has something happened to one of the children?"

Portland had turned to her, his expression blank. "It's Pila."

"Is she hurt?"

"She's dead."

"Dead?" Misia had repeated stupidly, turning to the policeman in disbelief. "There must be a mistake, I spoke to her only a couple of hours ago."

"I'm afraid there's no mistake, madam," he replied, looking at her and thinking of all the articles he had read about Misia Benning and the Benning Boxers. She was just as she looked in her photographs, same odd clothes, same direct, no nonsense expression.

"There must be!" she had snapped, turning to Portland. "You find out about it, you know about these things," her voice had the sharp edge of fear in it. "Portland, find out what's really happening –"

"There was an accident," he said, taking her hand.

She had snatched it away. "Accident? How?"

"Pila fell, she broke her neck."

Misia's eyes had been blank with disbelief. "*How* did she fall?"

There was no reply from Portland. Impatiently she had then turned to the policeman. "How did my niece fall?"

"Apparently there seems to have been an accident – or so her husband says."

"Her husband?" Misia's voice had uncoiled, lashed out. "Was Caryl de Solt responsible for her death?"

Portland held up his hands: "They don't know that –"

"Well, I *do*!" she had snapped. "I warned her, we all warned her about him."

Portland caught hold of her arm: "Misia, stop it. The children are outside in the car. You have to see to them," he said firmly. "I'll go to the police station and find out what I can."

Misia had nodded, her head seemed rigid, her eyes fixed. "The children," she said simply, walking to the door. "Please bring in the children, officer, if you would." She had turned back to Portland as the man walked down the drive, "Find out what happened, and if that bastard's responsible, I want to know –"

"I'll sort it out," Portland said calmly. "You just look after the children."

She had nodded, watching him walk to the door just as Norton was ushered in by the policeman. He had been wrapped in a blanket, his round face white from sleep, his expression bland. Behind him had come Ahlia, her eyes fixed ahead of her, obviously in shock.

"Sweethearts," Misia had said, walking over to them and taking Norton's hand. Ahlia hung back, following a pace behind them as they had moved into the study. The room had been warm, comforting, Vincent turning with a smile on his face.

"Well, well, well, who have we here?"

"Get the doctor," Misia said, settling both children on the settee and banking up the fire. "Go on, Vincent, call him out. I want him here NOW."

Quickly he had moved into the hall, Misia following, then closing the door behind her. "Pila's been killed."

He had blinked, confused. "What?"

"I think it's something to do with Caryl de Solt," Misia said bitterly. "Get Teller to make up the beds upstairs and get the bloody doctor round." She had dropped her voice, "Norton looks okay, but Ahlia … she's in shock."

Misia hurried away, Vincent moving to the phone and calling for the doctor then walking back into the study. The room was as haphazardly untidy as it always was, books scattered, the papers left open on the table, a bowl of half eaten pasta left on the window ledge. Norton had fallen asleep, his head on the arm of the settee – but Ahlia was still staring straight ahead.

"Hey," Vincent said, kneeling down beside her. "Are you okay?"

She kept staring, without speaking, Misia walking in with two mugs of cocoa.

"Drink this, love," she said, passing one to Ahlia and laying the other on the floor by the sleeping Norton.

Ahlia didn't move, didn't reach out for the cup, didn't react at all. "Ahlia?"

Nothing.

"Ahlia?" Misia repeated, then glanced at Vincent. "Where the *hell* is the doctor!"

"He said he'd be round immediately."

"So where is he!" she snapped, taking Ahlia's head. Still no response. "It's okay, sweetheart, it's okay … it will all be fine."

The doctor came soon after, examined both children and then sedated Ahlia. She said nothing: she was pliable, allowing herself to be touched and then carried up to bed. But she didn't sleep, didn't even close her eyes. She lay looking at the ceiling, unblinking, unseeing. Alarmed, Misia stood by the bedroom door, then turned when she heard someone come in downstairs.

She tensed, Simeon hurrying into view. "What's happened?"

"Pila's dead."

He rocked, his hair was uncombed, his face waxy. Misia knew then what had happened; he had seen something; known something.

Her voice dropped. "Norton's okay, I think, but Ahlia's not saying anything."

He had seen it, Ahlia running down the street in Clapham. Dumb. Running.

Quietly he moved over to the bed and touched Ahlia's forehead. She never moved. Then slowly he sat on the edge of the bed and picked her up, holding her to him, his eyes filling: Misia turning away. Simeon had loved Pila, loved her as much as he had ever loved a woman; had found an easy companion in her, a meeting of minds. Distressed, Misia moved away and closed the door behind her. She listened on the corridor outside; but there was no sound of crying, no indication that Ahlia had broken her silence, or that her son had found a way to voice his grief. Dear God, she thought brokenly, the children, the children.

Portland phoned shortly afterwards from the police station. Apparently Caryl had Pila had an argument and she had fallen down the stairs. That was Caryl de Solt's story, and it was the version of events he stuck to, although he asked repeatedly if his daughter was all right, admitting that she had probably seen everything. The police were suspicious, Portland said, and were holding Caryl in custody. He had been drinking, and there was a damning bruise on the side of his face … Misia listened rigidly, and then put down the phone, Vincent standing beside her.

"I have to let my brother know," she said at last. "Drago *must* know." Her voice was toneless, her actions stiff as she dialled the number in Rome. A few agonising seconds later she was told by a servant that the doctor was abroad. Wearily Misia re-dialled, a familiar, welcome voice coming over the line.

"Si?"

"Alberto?"

"Misia!" he said happily. "How are you?"

"There's been an accident," she said simply. "Pila is dead."

Another long pause. How many pauses, she wondered, how much time spent trying to accept the unacceptable?

"Pila?"

She nodded dumbly. "She fell – we think that Caryl de Solt's responsible, but no one's sure yet. I can't get hold of my brother, apparently he's abroad somewhere."

"Venice," Alberto said distantly. He could hardly believe what he was hearing, could only see Pila as the young girl he had known, walking with her mother in the house in Rome. Tall, headily sensual Pila – no, she couldn't be dead, she was young, it was time for the older generation to die. Him, or Drago, or even Misia, but not Pila, not at that age.

"I don't know how to tell my brother," Misia went on, "we haven't spoken for years, I don't know if he'll want to hear it from me."

Alberto hesitated, trying to gather his thoughts. He had seen Drago only days before, his old friend for once almost content. Courtney had married Nancy Gilchrist, and Drago had believed, stupidly, blindly, that he had finally controlled the barbarian, finally brought order to his damned house. He had even spoken of their marriage as bringing some overdue good fortune into their lives, talking with the desperation of a person running from certain ill luck. But after the euphoria, there was this to follow; the death of his daughter; the evidence that, in the end, nothing would never be well.

"Do you want me to tell him?"

Misia hesitated. "I don't know. I feel I should, but I think he would take it better from you."

Only months earlier Drago had been so afraid of Misia's contempt, so certain that she would gloat over his misfortunes. How could Alberto recommend that she tell him of his daughter's death?

"I'll phone him," Alberto said simply. "I'll tell him."

"I'm so sorry," Misia replied, "tell him how sorry I am … tell him … tell him that I'll do anything to help. You will tell him that, won't you?"

\*

Drago heard the news over the telephone, told Alberto to inform Misia that he wanted his daughter's body flown home, and then replaced the receiver without another word. He then caught the next flight back to Rome and arrived at the house when night was falling, parking the car and walking in to his study, locking the door behind him. He ordered no food and took no messages, he simply opened his desk drawer and took out a selection of cloths and some cleaning fluid. Carefully, meticulously, he began to polish his collection of silver instruments, his hands working methodically.

He thought there were ghosts in the room with him, turned round often, expecting to see Catherine or Pila, standing by the window, or sitting in the chair opposite him.

Shadows held their spirits, noises their voices. I will go mad, he thought – working, cleaning – I will go mad … There was no escape from what was to come, he realised. He might hope: he might, at times, almost believe that he could deflect his fate, but he was wrong. He could find no one to comfort him, and no one to explain – but he could find someone to *blame.*

If Pila had never gone to England, she would still be alive. It had been her idea to go, her determination to seek out the missing part of her family. If she had never gone, she would never have met Caryl de Solt and never have died. It was not his fault, not this time; this time, it was Misia's fault. His hatred shuddered inside him, coupled with his grief and guilt, and it made him malicious. He had nothing, and Misia had everything; a husband, a family, a contented home, success – she had everything. She had stolen his parcel of good fortune, had hogged his happiness, had usurped his position, had been granted wish upon wish whilst he had lost his wife, been hated by his son, and finally cowed by the death of his daughter.

Drago stopped polishing and looked up. A shadow moved against the wall and he called out to it. But there was no response, just a shadow moving on a dark night. He spoke his daughter's name, using tenderness, trying out the two simple syllables on his tongue. Pila, Pila … but she didn't answer. She was, like Catherine before her, deaf and blind to him. Drago moved around the desk and went to the door, dropping the silver instrument in his hand, the noise echoing on the marble. Pila? he asked again, walking into the hall. The coolness slid over his skin, suffocated him, tomb cold. Pila?

Her picture seemed to be everywhere. Photographs on tables, pictures around corners, the dark watch of her eyes following him as he moved upstairs and into her room. The old collection of fans were still there on the walls, the shadows of the trees outside making marks against the silk bedspread. He had never talked to her here, never sat on the bed and listened to her … She had always been once removed, talking in whispers to her mother, turning at the head of the stair, her shadow on the terrace following her as she left. He struggled to hear her voice, but another voice came instead, Catherine's, soft with compassion. Panicked, Drago hurried out of the room and ran down the stairs again, hurrying towards the garden.

But they followed; they teased him from behind hedges, called from the fountain, ran ahead of him, or behind him – but never with him. Their spirits were everywhere, dead and deadly, two ghostly companions. He knew then that he would never be free of them; they were closer to him now than they had ever been, and they would remain with him as long as he lived. That was their punishment – their souls coming out to play with him, their spirits skimming through the majesty and hollowness of everything he had ever created.

He knew he was to live amongst the dead from then on: amongst dead hopes, dead dreams, dead women – Drago stopped walking, his breathing intensifying, panic taking hold. He had worked so hard, but for what? His skills were fading, illness limiting him, his mantle left discarded, without an heir to take it on for him. His position was threatened, outsiders taking over, age belittling him.

There was nothing to fill his life. No family, no grandchildren – Misia had those too, he thought bitterly. He should have insisted on seeing them, should have made Pila visit with her children. Why hadn't he? Why hadn't he *loved* more? *Thought* more?

*Lived* more? … The house stood behind him, towering and cool, empty, except for the ghosts who waited for him. At the windows, at the doors, walking with him. You never wanted us alive, they seemed to say, and now that we are dead you can never have us. They would never leave, Drago knew that, they would cling to him, and in a blasted, empty way, they would love him, blocking anyone living from taking their place.

He was sweating with fear. His sister had everything; and he had nothing. Nothing! Whilst she gloated, surrounded by her family, he walked, damned, in a dead house … the realisation of his future winded him, Drago moving down the steps of the terrace towards the fountain. There, he glanced into the still water, his face looking back at him.

For a long moment he stared at himself without recognition, and only moved on when it seemed, for an instant, that two other faces appeared next to his own.

# *Fifty*

Ahlia could remember nothing. No details. The night of her mother's death was wiped from her memory as surely as the tide obliterated footsteps on the sand. Simeon sat with her and for days she said nothing, her shock so intense she could neither sleep or eat. Gradually she began to listen to him, to follow the words of the story he read to her, her eyes focusing at last, her lips moving, speech coming back.

He never forced her to talk, but she would only have Simeon with her. No one else. Pila's love for him seemed to be passed into her daughter and Ahlia turned to the quietest of the Benning Brothers for comfort. Which Simeon gave unconditionally. Nearly a week after her mother's death she began to eat and on the rare occasions that he left her, Ahlia followed him, standing mute on the stairs or waiting at the front house of the house in Holland Park.

The papers trumpeted the tragedy, took photographs, pressed for interviews, Caryl de Solt taken to trial during that winter of 1971. Ahlia could be of no help to her father, she remembered nothing and could neither defend, or damn him. The case caused unprecedented coverage: the Bennings were well known, and a murder charge seemed to go hand in hand with the demi-monde aspects of the boxing and casino worlds. Unusually uncommunicative, Vincent kept out of the limelight and refused interviews, Portland fronting the family, photographs of Pila's darkly sensual face staring out from the newsstands daily.

At the Old Bailey, people queued for seats, wanting to catch a glimpse of the glamorous Caryl de Solt, wanting to know every detail of his life and that of his wife. Pila's glamour persisting after death; her looks, her Italian background, her famous father in Rome. Scores of column inches were given over to their lives, friends phoned, photographs snatched, the children pestered. Rumours abounded; Caryl de Solt's mistress giving interviews to the tabloids; the manager of his silver shop talking on the radio. Was he a violent man? Oh no, they said, never. He was a charmer. Caryl de Solt; Never at Fault.

He faded in prison, lost his preening, childlike air; but performed in court with his usual five minute mentality; Pila's death had been a mistake, a horrible accident, no more. He had loved his wife, they had been talking of a reconciliation. And in the meantime, Norton walked in the park with his grandmother, reserved, dispassionate; and Ahlia turned to Simeon. Always Simeon, always him, no one else. And he clung to her as well, berating himself constantly for not acting sooner, for not saving Pila. Reason had no effect: even Portland couldn't make his son see that there was no more he could have done.

"I had a premonition. I should have warned her."

"You had a snatch of something, no more," Portland insisted, sitting with his son in the Holland Park house. Simeon was losing weight fast, his face sharp with anxiety, the dark eyes shadowed underneath.

"I should have done more," Simeon insisted, "I should have done *something* to help her."

Against everyone's advice, Misia went to the court daily; she wanted Caryl de Solt to see her and know that she was there. She went in place of her niece, stood in for Pila, watched her murderer and waited, and prayed, and longed for him to be found guilty.

"You don't know he killed her deliberately," Portland said one night.

"I KNOW!" Misia snapped, touching her chest. "I feel it, I know it as certainly as if I had seen it happen. Caryl de Solt murdered my niece and I want him punished for it."

Portland looked down at his hands. "Have you heard from your brother?"

"No," she snapped, walking towards the fire and picking up a photograph of Mary Razzio. "No, I've not heard a word – except from Alberto and he says that Drago's given up, gone into himself." She took down the picture and stared at her mother. "I can't believe it, not Drago. He was always so sure of everything, always so willing to fight … I wonder what my mother would say now?" She stared into the fierce black eyes and then returned the photograph to the mantelpiece. "We've been so lucky, Portland."

"Why do you say that?"

"Because we've been happy, you and I." She moved over to him and touched his cheek, "We've always had each other, always known we had each other's support, love. Always taken it for granted, I suppose." She paused for an instant. "We have three sons, three boys who love us and who we love – and we've done well, always known that the boxing would carry on after I went, and that Harewood would fly the flag for you after you went …" she stopped, suddenly distressed, bending down and robbing her head against her husband's cheek. "Don't ever leave me, will you?" she asked, "Don't go and die on me – I couldn't bear it."

Portland leaned his head against his wife, smiling. "Where the hell am I going?"

"But if you died before me –"

"And what if you died before me?" he countered. "What would I do then?"

She smiled bleakly. "Probably marry some blonde with big boobs."

"No," Portland replied, "A redhead, maybe. A blonde, never."

Misia laughed, her head still against his; then her voice fell. "Do you think that people run out of luck?" she asked quietly. "You know – if they've been lucky for a long time?"

"Like us?"

"Yes."

He leaned back in his seat and looked up into his wife's face, flicking the fringe away from her eyes.

"When Napoleon was hiring new generals he used to wave aside their qualifications and say: 'Just tell me – are they lucky?'"

"What the hell does that mean?" Misia retorted. "He ended up in exile on Elba!"

Portland laughed. "If I end up in exile with you" he said gently, "I will count myself the luckiest man on earth."

*

At Drago's request, Pila's body was flown back to Rome, Alberto accompanying it.

Letters from Misia to her brother went unopened and unanswered, callers turned away from the house, Courtney and Nancy staying at their own apartment in Rome. Drago wanted to see no one; neither did he want revenge on Caryl de Solt – his only thoughts were on his sister and the bitterness he felt towards her. That, and the shadows which dogged his footsteps.

His rituals intensified, his mental state precarious. He bathed frequently, changed his clothes often, and had his food returned to the kitchen unless the temperature was exactly to his specifications. Any wrinkle in the curtains, any disorder of the carpet fringes sent him into a cold rage, hurling abuse at the servants, then storming off to the hospital to escape their sullen resentment. There he went through his old cases, thinking of the innovations he had brought to surgical procedures, digging out his glory days and wondering, always wondering, at what point everything had begun to sour.

Lecturing did not satisfy him; Drago wanted to be operating, not instructing. He was used to demonstrating his skills, used to thinking and reacting instantly, more skilfully and more quickly than his colleagues. The operating theatre had been his womb; an enclosed safe space where he was closeted, indulged. It had never worried Drago that he was dealing with peoples lives; he seldom lost a patient and his skills had transformed many a misfit. He had even welcomed the hideous results of car accidents or burns; welcomed the demands such cases made on his talent. His confidence had always been vast: matching his brilliance. He had never hesitated, never been uncertain. And the returns for his skill had been magnificent … Drago had thought it could go on forever, that for as long as he lived he would be courted and honoured, the confidant of society's upper strata – and then a disease had stopped him. Not age, not ineptitude, but arthritis.

It would have been amusing, had it not been so humiliating; but now the reign was over and the king was ousted to the sidelines. Where else was there for him to go? he had no successor. Drago glanced at the case notes in front of him; he remembered the man vividly and the operation, and remembered later cruising on the patient's yacht. They had all been *so* grateful – and now there would be other patients, operated on by other surgeons, to whom they would be grateful in their turn.

The phone rang beside him suddenly and he picked it up.

"Drago. It's Alberto. How are you?"

"Fine," the chill in the voice; the dead sound on the word.

"Shall I come round to the house tonight?" he asked, knowing that his friend would refuse, as he always did now. Drago would sit alone instead, listening for the voices, waiting for the dead to come and keep him company.

He will die if he carries on like this, Alberto thought. "Well, what do you say? Shall I come round?"

"No … I want to work."

"On what?"

"Work!" Drago snapped, "why do you have to know everything? Why are you spying on me?"

Alberto took in a deep breath: "I'm *not* spying on you, I'm just concerned."

"I'm all right, I've told you," Drago replied, his tone softening. "Have you been to

Pila's grave?"

"Yes, I went this morning, he said, then added, "The trial's still on in London."

"I don't want to know. It will do no good now."

Alberto carried on regardless. "They think that Caryl de Solt will be acquitted; there isn't enough evidence to find him guilty of murder."

"My daughter's dead, what difference does it make?"

"A lot, I would have thought," Alberto replied evenly. "It would be better to think it was an accident, rather than a murder."

"Death is death, however it comes," Drago said, changing the subject. "How are the children?"

"Living with Misia in London. She's given up the boxing business in Liverpool, so she won't have to travel all the time, and she's running the World's End gym now. Vincent's in charge of The Roman House and the casino." He paused. "Ahlia's getting better –"

"I couldn't have them here, you know," Drago said hurriedly: "This is no place for children."

"You don't have to worry, Misia's looking after them well –"

"I know!" he snapped bitterly. "You already said that."

Immediately Alberto rose to her defence: "You can't blame your sister for what happened."

"But I always will," Drago replied, his tone damning. "If Pila had never gone to England she would still be alive."

"That's rubbish, and you know it!" Alberto retorted heatedly. "It never occurs to you to thank Misia for what she's doing. You're so obsessed with this bloody feud that you can't think straight anymore. Even when she takes care of your grandchildren, you never think you owe her anything."

Drago's voice was hoarse with bitterness, "My daughter is dead because of her!"

"Dear God, you *can't* believe that."

"I believe it," he said coldly, "and I will never forgive my sister for it."

*

The verdict was hurled across every newspaper – CARYL DE SOLT FOUND INNOCENT – the case discussed and dismissed with the verdict. Misia had been in court with the decision came through, her eyes fixed on Caryl, her face set, her nails digging into her palms as the foreman of the jury spoke the words 'Not Guilty'. She heard them and blinked, then controlled herself, forcing herself not to call out, to hurl curses down on Caryl de Solt's head as he turned and shook his counsel's hand, smiling. Her heart seemed to swell inside her ribcage, forcing her breaths out uneven and ragged. Not Guilty, Not Guilty … She felt beaten for the first time in her life. She had known Caryl de Solt was guilty, and now she had to watch him walk away, free to continue his life. He was *free*, whilst Pila was dead and buried. Whilst their children were traumatised, he was *free*. There was no justice, Misia thought bitterly, none at all – and how would Ahlia and Norton grow up without a mother. And with a father who had been charged with her murder?

But not found Not Guilty. Acquitted. In the eyes of the law Caryl de Solt was innocent. Misia felt herself drained, exhausted by defeat – and she also felt that she had failed her niece. What would she do now? Bring up the children, yes, but how would she explain and avoid the gossip and the whispers which would inevitably follow them? You won't, a voice seemed suddenly to say to her. You won't avoid it, just as I never did. Misia nodded, as though she could hear her mother talking to her. Yes, that would have been what Mary Razzio would have said, she thought. A fight is a fight, is a fight. But there was no beginning, no middle, and no end to this bout; it was to be on going, and only the toughest would survive.

Misia waited until the court was cleared and then rose to her feet, her face emotionless. At the exit she could see a crowd of photographers and hesitated, unwilling to face them. Then she thought of her mother again and straightened up, walking out into the daylight, jamming her trilby on her head and hailing a taxi. The press followed her, jostled her, but she kept moving, her daunting composure caught on camera and reproduced later on the front page of The Evening Standard. The caption underneath read: MISIA BELLING – AUNT OF PILA DE SOLT – LEAVING COURT AFTER THE VERDICT.

It took nearly half an hour for her to return to Holland Park and when Misia finally stepped out of the taxi she found herself unexpectedly light headed and grabbed the door for support.

"Are you okay?" the cabbie asked.

"Fine," she replied, "I've just had a shock, that's all."

He knew who she was; everyone in London knew that; and he felt for her. She was ashen and seemed to be holding on to herself by sheer will power, nothing more.

"I'm sorry 'bout what happened," he said simply.

Misia nodded. "Me too."

"You won't be giving up though, will you?"

She stared at him, uncomprehending. "Give up? Give up *what?*"

"The boxing," he said, "The Benning Boxers. I've followed your lot for years. Bloody good fighters, all of them."

Misia nodded, buoyed up by the words. Yes, they *were* bloody good fighters, all of them. The Benning Boxers, the Benning Brothers, the Benning family – all fighters, like the ones who had gone before her and the ones who would follow afterwards, all ready to stand their corner and protect what was theirs against all comers.

It was in their nature; it was in their blood.

# Fifty-One

**Nine years later**
**1980 – Rome**

Cy Greyling was scrubbing up, soaping his forearms and then rinsing them under the tap. The air conditioning hummed overhead, the operating theatre cool as he walked in. Outside the Rome heat sizzled under a white sky, but in the Italian Hospital there was no evidence of heat; just white walls and steel, cold to the touch. Concentrating, he studied the skull X-rays and then looked at the dental records. The child had a cleft palate and hair lip; only eighteen months old, the deformed structure of the mouth arch obvious on the plates. He had examined the boy several times, reassured the parents, and was now aware that the operation was going to be watched by his peers in the viewing gallery overhead.

He was the outsider; the dark horse, they joked, making reference to his colour. Cy Greyling was used to being the butt of jokes, there were no other Moroccan doctors working in the field of plastic surgery. Not in Rome, at least. Originally from Tangiers, he had qualified in New York, then served his apprenticeship there before going onto operate in several other American cities – Chicago, Houston and New Orleans. He had disliked the latter, and moved on – it was his nature to move on. Cy was always restless, always in search of a place to settle but he had never found it, until he came to Rome. In the Italian Hospital Cy had been greeted with a mixture of curiosity and antagonism, fellow surgeons wanted to know why he had been invited to work there; why he had been allowed to display his prodigious talents on Italian turf.

The answer was obvious; he was more gifted than his peers and had been brought over to demonstrate his skills. So now they waited to see what he could do, craning to see from the viewing gallery above, all eyes fixed on the upright gowned figure. He was darker than they expected, his skin black without redness, his shadows around his chin and under his eyes, blue tinged. His face was half obliterated by the operating mask, only his eyes clearly visible, the brows drawn together.

The child was sedated, his hair covered with a cotton cap, the anaesthetist monitoring the blood pressure and breathing rate. Quickly, Cy began to work, the watchers startled by the speed at which he made the first incision, his hands working deftly, confidentially, as he drew back the skin of the upper lip and began working on the reconstruction of the upper palate. He said nothing, only intermittently asking for instruments, his attention fixed, his absorption total.

Unlike many of the other surgeons, Cy liked to operate in silence, no music for him, no jokes to relieve the tension. Instead there was only the steady sound of the ventilator breathing its careful rhythm, interrupted at intervals by the methodical reports from the anaesthetist. Blood pressure, heart rate. Holding … Cy continued to work on the upper palate then turned to examine the X-Rays again. He paused, by now forgetting the curious onlookers, and considered the structure of the child's face before turning back to the patient. The operation was over within an hour, the baby's upper lip stitched and bandaged, Cy stepping back from the table and turning his face upwards to the assembled audience. His eyes held theirs for an instant and then he walked out.

The operation had been successful, but there were few congratulations, rather a hushed resentment for the outsider. They might respect his work, but not one of the doctors was prepared to admit it, and, unaccompanied, Cy went back to the rest room to change.

He thought he was alone, until a voice suddenly said.

"Bravo."

Cy turned, pausing as he pulled off his operating gown.

From behind the lockers, Alberto emerged, smiling. "A wonderful job, you have my congratulations," he said in English, holding out his hand. "I'm Alberto de Brio, I was watching you operate."

Cy took his hand and smiled, his mask now removed, the long fine line of his nose and the high cheekbones betraying his Moroccan ancestors.

"Thank you, I think you'll be the first – and last – to congratulate me."

Alberto smiled. "Italians are suspicious, we don't like to welcome foreigners into our midst too eagerly. You mustn't let it worry you."

"It doesn't," Cy admitted calmly. "besides, I only came here because I was invited to operate."

"No other reason?"

"No, should there be?"

Alberto was relaxed, casual. "I wondered if the reputation of Drago Razzio hadn't been the siren call to lure you away from America."

Cy paused: "I've heard of him, of course. Anyone specialising in plastic surgery knows about him. He was an innovator."

His tone had genuine admiration in it, Alberto noticed with pleasure. He had been looking for a long time, nearly nine years, in fact. Nine tiresome years in which he had retired from operating and concentrated on his travels, returning to Rome every few months to visit his old friend. Each return was dreaded; each visit emotionally draining. Drago had aged, looking much older than his seventy five years, his steps faltering, his hair almost white, his eyes heavy lidded and weary under the marked brow.

Whilst Alberto revelled in his retirement, Drago had willed himself to die, but had failed, his crawl to the grave slow. After the death of Pila, he had turned away from his work, lecturing only occasionally in the spasmodic hope that one day he would find someone to take his place. For it had become a wearying burden. His skills, unused, hung heavily on him. He wanted to be rid of them, but had found no man ready to accept the gift, and no man worthy of it either.

So Drago tripped into depression, into compulsive behaviour patterns, into phobias and bitterness, and the only thing which drew any fire from him was the mention of the Bennings. The feud, Alberto realised, was the one thing which kept him alive. The bitterness motivated Drago in the same way that love motivated others; it was his reason to breath. He might wish to be dead, but his resentment kept him tied to the earth.

Alberto had hoped that Nancy might affect some change in Drago, but she had come too late into his life. Not that he wasn't fond of her; he had watched gratefully as the first two years of her marriage to Courtney seemed, beyond reason, to partially settle his son. Her good humour, her steady nature, held back his demons and there was, at times, a flicker of fondness between them, enough to curtail Courtney's worst excesses, at least. His cruelty was contained, his malice directed outwardly. He had even begun to work on his designs again, Nancy encouraging him, using her own experience and Drago's money to elicit interest. They worked together, her enthusiasm making him believe in his neglected talent, her drive awakening his own ambition. No one would have believed that Courtney Razzio could have created anything beautiful, but, away from his father's awesome shadow, he began to find some satisfaction in his own work and some unexpected pride in himself. Not that he could control his temperament; he bored easily, and threw tantrums when he was criticised, but with Nancy's encouragement he began, tentatively, to believe in his own worth and looked to her as his bolt hole.

Courtney's own death wish was in abeyance. He no longer drank to excess and his drug taking was limited, although criticism could provoke sudden and terrifying relapses. And all the time, Nancy remained good humoured, the one never-changing aspect of his life. She had made a bargain, and by God, she was going to keep it. Two summers passed, two Christmases, two winters coming into two springs, and then the twins were born. They were christened David and Lomond, Courtney warily pleased, Drago greeting the news with desperate hopefulness. Only hours after their birth, he went the visit the children at the hospital and sat with Nancy in her room.

There was no sign of his son; only a vast bouquet of flowers signed – *Courtney*.

"I've seen the twins," Drago said, smiling. "They're beautiful."

She smiled, the straight red hair hanging around her face, her oblique, turquoise gaze steady. "Thank you."

"For what?" he asked, surprised.

"For giving me the children I wanted," she said, "Hey, it wasn't such a bad deal, was it? We did well, you and I."

He looked at her steadily: "How does my son treat you?"

"Better than I thought he would," she admitted, smiling. "He's pleased with the kids – said he's coming over later."

"He should have been here when they were born."

"Are you kidding? This was one show I wanted no one to attend," she laughed, soft with relief.

Nancy had what she wanted, children. It was worth marrying Courtney to achieve her dream; worth the intermittent humiliations. She had learnt not to question his occasional disappearances or to grumble about his spasmodic drinking bouts. Experience had taught to avoid confrontations and warning signs – dilated pupils, little twists of foil in his pockets. Besides, his moods were settling, he was, at times, even kind. It had been difficult, but she had known what she was getting into when she agreed to marry him. She had accepted the conditions, and now she had her rewards – her children.

"Why don't you come back to the house to live?" Drago asked. "Your flat's too small for a family."

She tapped the back of his hand. "You really want your home overrun with screaming kids?"

"Better than ghosts."

Nancy hesitated. She had visited the house often since her marriage, talking to Drago, trying to compensate in some minor way for the emptiness of his life. She was the only female in his world, a breezy American with nothing in common with him. But she brought a gaiety to him; snatches of an optimism which was momentarily intoxicating. But only momentarily.

And now Drago looked at her and thought of the children and wanted them in his house. "Please, think about it, Nancy," he pleaded. "You would be so comfortable there."

But if Nancy was tempted, Courtney had other ideas, and dismissed his father's suggestion immediately. He didn't want Drago having any control over his children; didn't want to offer him any comfort, any release from his depression. His resentment of his father was total and all consuming; he had been ignored and despised as a boy and later he had been bullied into marriage; he had been controlled and manipulated – and now, finally, he had the chance to take his revenge.

"If he's lonely, let him get married again," Courtney said coldly. "After all, he seems very keen on the idea for everyone else."

Nancy looked at her husband, keeping her tone even, "Oh, Courtney, don't be too hard on him. He's lonely."

"He deserves to be."

So they never went to live with Drago; they bought a larger flat in the city instead and Nancy visited her father in law every week. The twins were almost six months old when she came one day, bringing them into the garden and put them on the lawn at Drago's feet. He had been reading William Golding's *Rites of Passage* and had paused, smiling as he looked at the children. Then suddenly he leaned forwards and picked Lomond up. Nancy glanced over, smiling, and then frowned as Drago began to feel the little girl's calves, his liver-spotted hands working over her skin.

"What is it?" Nancy asked, struggling to keep the panic out of her voice.

"Is she crawling yet?"

"What?"

Drago repeated the question, his tone professional. "Is she crawling yet?"

"No … she's slower than David," Nancy said hurriedly. "Hey, but that's not unusual, is it? I mean, some children crawl quicker than others." She moved over to Drago, her eyes fixed urgently on his hands, "What is it?"

"I think this baby has a problem," he said simply, his tone calm. The doctor talking. "I think we should get a specialist to look at her."

Nancy snatched the baby out of his hands. "She's fine!" she snapped. "What the hell do you know about it? You're a plastic surgeon, you know nothing about children. You're just trying to scare me, that's all."

Drago looked at her calmly: "I'm a doctor, Nancy. I don't pretend to be a paediatrician, but I know that your daughter has something wrong with her legs." He paused, then unexpectedly put his arm around Nancy. "She needs help … I'm sorry, but your baby needs help."

He was right, just as Nancy knew he would be. Within twenty-four hours they discovered that Lomond was suffering from a rare nervous disorder, her legs developing at a slower rate than the rest of her body, the prognosis bleak. She would be crippled, the paediatrician told her parents, in a wheelchair by the time she was five. For life? Nancy asked. Yes, he said, for life.

The brief twilight hiatus of calm dissolved in that single instant. All the pretence of normality collapsed, Courtney running out of the consulting room and leaving Nancy at the hospital alone. He had been a fool to think that there would ever be a chance for any of them, he thought bitterly. Happiness was not for the Razzios. They were damned, just as Catherine had been, and Pila, and now his daughter. There was no reason to pretend, or to hope; there was nothing ahead except despair. He lurched across the city streets, coming to rest at a bar and ordering a bottle of wine. For the next hour Courtney drank steadily and gradually, maddeningly, he became more and more sober.

Why them? he asked himself repeatedly. Why the Razzio line? Misia had been born of the same parents, but she had had nothing but good fortune, only his side of the family were unlucky, only his father's bloodline was condemned. Courtney drank on. He had believed for a while that he might be happy; he had grown almost fond of Nancy and the children had made him feel – he was embarrassed to admit it – as though he belonged somewhere. But he had been wrong. He had no real home, no real chance for happiness. He was his father's child, and damned because of it.

*

Alberto's thoughts returned to the present as he looked at Cy Greyling. Could it be possible after so long? Could this man be the one to recover the dream? He watched as Cy pulled on his jacket; he was thirty four years old, with enough experience to know the world, and enough youth to remain hopeful.

"Would you like to meet him?"

Cy turned. "Who?"

"Drago Razzio."

The black eyes were cautious. "Of course – but why?"

"He needs you," Alberto said bluntly.

"Needs me?" Cy echoed. "He doesn't even know me."

"Well, he does in a way," Alberto said, walking to the door with Cy. "You could say that he's been waiting for you for a long time." They moved out into the hot air. Rome was heavy with car fumes, the buildings pooling their shadows as they walked along. "He's dying."

Cy turned to look at the man next to him. "I didn't know."

"Oh, don't misunderstand me, Drago Razzio has no incurable disease. Arthritis, yes – that stopped him operating – but he's not clinically ill. There's nothing physically wrong with him."

"I don't understand," Cy said simply, pausing on the pavement and watching as Alberto lit a cigarette. The first fingers of his right hand were nicotine stained, his pox marked skin pitted under the sunlight.

"He's willing himself to die," Alberto said, putting his head one side. "Does that surprise you?"

"Yes," Cy admitted. "I'd have thought he could have retired and enjoyed his success, basked in his glory."

Alberto nodded. "But you can't enjoy something unless you have someone to enjoy it with."

"Meaning?"

"Drago has no family to speak of," Alberto explained, "no heir –"

"Except Courtney Razzio."

"You've heard of him?"

"Hasn't everyone?"

Alberto paused, inhaling deeply, choosing his next words with care: "Drago needs someone to whom he can pass on his skills."

"Someone he can live through?" Cy asked brusquely. "I'm sorry, I go my own way. I'm not prepared to become anyone's surrogate son."

"He could teach you a lot –"

"He could ask a lot too," he replied. "Listen, I've never taken anything from anyone, or asked anyone for a favour. I do things my own way."

Alberto was unmoved. "Well, you're as stubborn as he is, I'll give you that."

"Forget it," Cy said, moving away. "I'm not the man you're looking for."

Unperturbed, Alberto stood on the pavement and watched him go. He was a quick walker, his cropped head standing out amongst the crowd, his exotic bone structure making him an oddity amongst the soft Italian faces. Prickly, brash, gifted, opinionated and arrogant – Alberto smiled, oh yes, he had found his man. He had found his man at last.

# Fifty-Two

Ahlia was bathing, the windows open, her body taking on the soft air. She knew there was no chance that she was overlooked, they had no neighbours, the only visitors were stray cats and the foxes barking in the fields at night. Breathing in, she lifted her hair and pinned it on top of her head, the serene Madonna face turning away from the window as she lowered herself into the white enamel bath. The water was cool, pooling over her limbs as she relaxed, stretching out her left hand for the radio. Immediately a French station came onto the air, playing a John Lennon song.

The tune reminded Ahlia of London and of the time she had lived with Misia and Portland after her mother's death. The details were sketchy, she had sleep walked through those years without thought, without a plan for her life. Attending school she had never shone and had left at the age of sixteen, going to work for a friend of Portland's who owed a book shop. She liked it in St. Christopher's Place, it was quiet and no one bothered her, the customers usually as reserved as she was. Their conversation was never personal, never intrusive, they might inquire about a particular volume, but nothing they ever said made her anxious. Their attention was detached, remote – just as she was.

She liked to read, liked to absorb herself in other peoples stories, imagining herself living these other lives. It was her way of ducking out of reality, of negating her own past. Then, at the age of seventeen she changed her name, asking Misia if she could adopt the surname Razzio instead of the hated de Solt. No one objected, and so Ahlia Razzio came into being, and with her, a final rejection of her previous life.

After the trial Caryl de Solt had asked to see his children, Misia obstructive until he took her to court and won visitation rights. But, as ever, his interest was fleeting and within eighteen months, Caryl's visits to his children had petered out. He had other things to occupy his mind; another wife, Emma Legg, and then another child, Lukas de Solt. Caryl moved on, as he had always done, relieved that he no longer had to endure Ahlia's patent hostility.

Caryl never knew if she had seen him murder her mother; no one ever knew that, and she never admitted anything. She kept her father in suspense instead, inflicting her own chilling torture over the years, knowing that he wondered and would keep wondering, keep looking over his shoulder at that impassively still Madonna face. How much she had seen, only she knew. And Ahlia was never forthcoming.

Misia and Portland had brought up the children in the same way they had brought up their own. There was no lack of affection or attention; but whereas Norton needed the security of a family life, Ahlia was distant, and as time passed, she withdrew further into herself. She was close to no one, and allowed no one to get close to her – except

Simeon. Perhaps because of the love there had been between him and Pila, the two of them became close, their needs met by each other, and no one else.

Simeon was thirty four when Pila died, Ahlia only twelve and yet they were perfectly in tune. He was the first person to whom she spoke when she finally broke her silence; and he was the only person with whom she could relax. Having finally completed his book, Simeon was researching his next, travelling all over England to interview clairvoyants and mediums. Because of his own genuine talents he could easily spot a charlatan, and was fierce in his denouncements, exposing palmists and spiritualists for the cranks they were.

Worried about his son's absorption in his work, Portland wondered aloud if it could be healthy.

"I have to do it," Simeon answered, his tone resigned.

"Why? What's the point?"

"I want to understand …" Simeon said simply. "I *have* to understand."

That was the only argument he could offer, the only reason for his continued involvement. Tarot, crystal balls, runes, tea leaves, séances – he investigated them all, and found more often than not that they were simply palliatives. People were afraid of the future, afraid of death, and all to ready to believe that love, money or success were waiting for them.

Simeon knew otherwise; knew that his clairvoyance consisted of pain and trauma. He had never been privy to the delights of the future, only the terrors – and those terrors went with him everywhere. In time he had learned to accept them, to walk the streets with them … Simeon paused, thinking of the London ghosts he had told Pila about so many years before. He felt guilty suddenly, remembering how she had reacted:

*"… Oh God, Simeon, when you said that, I saw myself amongst them … for a minute, I saw myself."*

He had even expected to see her one day, one more London ghost amongst that lost battalion; had longed to catch a glimpse of her walking down an alleyway, or crossing a square. Come back and be a ghost here, he willed her, come back, come back.

"I worry for Simeon," Misia said shortly. "I don't like him getting so introspective. He's not interested in normal things."

"It's his way," Portland replied. "Simeon was always the family mystic."

"But is it healthy?"

"I don't know," Portland replied, "but it's him." He put down the letter he had been reading and looked at his wife. "He's not like us, you know that, he never was. He feels everything more deeply, see things we don't see, looks over a wall we don't even know exists. He can't change the way he is, no more than you could change the way you are. If he could, he would have done years ago and saved himself a lot of pain."

"But what's the point of it all?" Misia queried impatiently. "He wants the answers that no one has. It's a fruitless task."

"I know worse ways to spend a life."

"Well, I know better!" Misia snapped hotly.

Then Ahlia began to ask if she could help Simeon with his research. He was hesitant at first, unwilling to let her become involved, but soon he let her find books for him and then make notes. Never about Satanism or the black side of the occult, nothing dangerous, only the mundane, the dates, places and names. Always placid, she did the work carefully, happy to spend time with Simeon, relieved to be with the only person who understood her.

So whilst the short and stolid Norton attended school and then won a place at University to study Physics, Ahlia drowsed through her teens, and entered her twenties. From a distance Drago kept in touch with his grandchildren, providing for their education and setting up trust funds for them, just as he did for Courtney's offspring. Once he even suggested that they visit him, the invitation coming via Alberto, as always.

"I don't know him," Ahlia said simply.

"He's your grandfather," Alberto replied. "He would like to see you."

She was panicked by the suggestion and refused, although Norton went over to Rome for two weeks during the summer. He was easy-going, a little, round-faced, unemotional young man, who would never let an free trip pass him by. When he returned he was grilled for news by Misia, although Norton's lack of imagination was a drawback.

"What did he look like?"

Norton shrugged. "An Italian."

"Could you be just a little more specific?" Misia asked dryly.

"Big, white hair. Italian."

Exasperated, she sighed. "Did you take any photographs?"

Norton smiled. "Oh yes, many. I got some terrific ones of Michelangelo's David – "

"– who was also big with white hair," Portland said, laughing.

Then suddenly, in 1979, Simeon decided to move abroad. He was weary of London, he said, tired of the noise. He couldn't think, couldn't write … Misia listened, knowing that his migraines were more frequent, Simeon sleeping intermittently, his episodes of clairvoyance coming often. He couldn't stop it, couldn't control it, could only ride it, as he had done in his childhood.

"I want to live abroad …" he said at last. "I have to get away for a while, go somewhere quiet."

"But I'll worry about you," Misia said abruptly. "In London I can get to you, make sure you're all right. God, Simeon, how can you talk about going off into the wilds on your own?"

But he wasn't going on his own. He was going with his niece, Ahlia.

"AHLIA!" Misia eyebrows shot up. "What are you thinking of?"

"She wants to come."

"She's a young woman of twenty one, Simeon!" Misia snapped. "You might want to become a recluse, but she's too young to cut herself off from the world."

"It's not my choice, it's hers."

Misia did her best to make Ahlia change her mind, but she was greeted, as she always was, by the same still, expressionless face. What *is* she thinking? Misia wondered, ashamed that of all the children she loved this girl the least. She had tried to draw her out after Pila's death, had made allowances for Ahlia's grief, but she had always been greeted with the same reserve. Unreachable, untouchable, unlovable.

"Think about it –"

"I have," Ahlia replied evenly. "It's what I want to do."

"But you should be going out and meeting people, having boyfriends."

Ahlia's expression was closed off, remote. What did Caryl de Solt do to you? Misia wondered. What did you see that night?

"Ahlia, don't run away."

"I'm not, I'm doing what I should do," she said with equanimity. "I'll be safe there."

Safe, Misia thought, what was that? Pila had never been safe, not with her family or with her husband. But Ahlia was going with Simeon, she told herself, and with Simeon she *would* be secure. An unexpected jealousy crept over her – the girl with whom she shared nothing was going to live with her beloved son. Her favourite child. Oh, Misia loved Harewood, admired his devotion to the depressive and vulgar Leda; and she adored Vincent, because Vincent was put on earth to be idolised; but Simeon – *Simeon* – was her blessed misfit, and the closest to her heart.

So she let them go, and within days Misia received the first of many letters from St. Joryde de Chalais, Simeon covering several pages, Ahlia adding a measured postscript. She was keeping house for him, Simeon explained, tidying the small converted barn they had rented about a mile from the nearest town. It was warm and smelt of dust, he wrote, and at night the crickets chattered in the dry hedges and the pipistrels beat their wings against the moon.

He had fallen in love at last, Misia realised. Not with a woman, but a place. He wrote of the country as though he had never been happy before – and maybe he hadn't – and he wrote of Ahlia with a kind of spiritual awe.

*Dear Mum,*

    *We went for a walk this afternoon, trying to plot exactly how far we were from the nearest civilisation. Not far at all, if we clamoured over three fields and followed a dirt track to a cheap tin spire which juts up over the hill! Ahlia walks fast, without talking, her hair hanging over her shoulders, her eyes shaded by her hand. She was telling me about Freud later – all practicality – whilst I argued that he was a scientist and therefore had a limited view of the spiritual life.*

    *She is very secret about her thoughts, but then who ever saw a Madonna weep or show emotion? Maybe she is not real at all; maybe she is another phantom amongst all the rest. But a benign one. She intrigues – and she is the perfect companion, without demands and without temper.*

    *I will write again soon.*

*Your loving son,*
*Simeon*

*P.S. My love to you all – Simeon is working well on his book and I am about to paint the outhouse. Unfortunately, that is the limited of my creative skills.*

*Goodbye for now,*
*Ahlia*

Misia read the letter and tossed it over to Portland. "What do you make of that?"

He read it and smiled. "It means that Simeon isn't having headaches, and that he has the ideal companion."

"Is she ideal?" Misia asked, glancing over her shoulder.

"She is otherwordly, so I would have thought she was perfect." He looked at his wife, suddenly puzzled. "You and I both know that Simeon's gay. You're not worried about him and Ahlia, are you? Because if you are, you're wasting your time."

"If she becomes his muse it could be dangerous."

Portland sighed, stretching his legs out in front of the fire. "Mystics don't sleep with their muses, *or* their nieces," he said flatly. "In time, she'll leave, or Simeon will meet someone —"

"Some man?" Misia queried.

"All right!" he retorted, unusually sharp. "So what would you rather have? Falling in love with his niece or with a man?"

Outraged, Misia jumped to her feet. "You know I didn't mean that!"

"Then stop being stupid!" he snapped back. "You know our son, he'd never do anything to shame us, or himself. He's happy, Misia, so just let him be. If Ahlia needs a man, she'll find one. But any love Simeon feels for her is in his head, nowhere else."

# Fifty-Three

Lalo was sitting on the edge of her sister's bed, looking at Deandra in the mirror. She felt uncomfortable, her own features glaringly deficient in comparison to the perfection before her. Awkwardly she tucked her red-blonde hair behind her ears, her blue eyes, with their fair lashes, turning away from her own reflection and settling on her sister's again. Deandra wasn't beautiful, she was spellbinding, a perfectly oval face surrounded with the fall of dark hair, still cut like a Japanese doll's, her eyes long, her mouth darkly coloured without lipstick. There were no bad angles and no bad lighting for Deandra; the face was pristine, terrifyingly perfect at every turn. She carried it well too, seemed not to notice the galvanising effect it had on people, the dumb-struck awe which descended whenever she entered a room. Deandra Benning, at seventeen already in the papers, already photographed. After the Benning Boxers and the Benning Brothers now came the Benning Beauty.

Which left Lalo where? At nineteen, she was at art school, a second choice after she failed to get into University. She wasn't gifted, merely adequate, nothing special to look at, nothing special in her talent. Mediocre. Not that she didn't try, she had lost the puppy fat and – if you hadn't seen Deandra – she was a pretty girl. But Lalo would never believe that, and her mother did nothing to help her confidence.

It was always Deandra, Deandra, Leda seeing some of her own lost beauty resurrected in her daughter. Deandra this, Deandra that – Lalo always cast as Dr. Watson to her sister's Sherlock Holmes. The also ran, the girl who played eternal second fiddle. She had reason to be bitter, but that wasn't her nature. She wanted love, not revenge. So Lalo became eager to please, wanting to be liked, begging for attention. As a child she had sought refuge in food, but now she was comforted by sex. She was promiscuous not by nature, but by need. The attention her sister could so effortlessly command was hers only if she offered herself. Lalo didn't fully understand what she was doing, she only knew that sex was the only way she felt needed. She had been on the pill since she was sixteen, and had had various partners; but she wasn't proud of the fact and wondered constantly what would happen if her father found out.

Her mother, Lalo reasoned, would not be concerned, she was too absorbed by Deandra or her own depression. But her father would hate it if he knew, and that worried her … She had always loved him, been grateful for his affection and eager to keep in his good graces. Harewood had never been angry, never spiteful like her mother, instead he had been loving and encouraging – in his way. But he preferred Deandra. He couldn't help it. She was agreeable and beautiful – hard *not* to love. But hard to compete with.

Lalo turned over on the bed, her head hanging over the side. If she could just find herself a man who loved her; someone who wasn't besotted by her sister. But where? Everyone knew whose sister she was; every boy she met wanted to meet Deandra – she didn't have a chance unless she got away. Found someone on her own terms. Someone who had never seen Deandra … but who hadn't? Her sister's face was already in Tatler, already in the Evening Standard, Lalo fawn-like and pale beside her.

She closed her eyes and concentrated – she had read somewhere that you could visualise things to make them happen. You just imagined it enough and it came true. Childishly confident, Lalo kept her eyes tightly closed; conjuring up a picture of a boy who would adore her: some one who would never look at Deandra. Someone special, someone good, someone of *hers*.

# Fifty-Four

## Rome

Alberto had dozed off, his head falling forwards onto his chest, his cigarette dropping from his fingers onto the grass. The summer was limping into autumn, the heat going out of the sun, the nights beginning to shorten. Against the fading light, the cypress trees stood ebonised, the maze at the end of the garden only a hump of vegetation. A sulky breeze ruffled Alberto's thin hair, the dying sun glinting on his glasses as he slept on, his breathing sonorous.

Only yards away Drago was sitting on the terrace, Cy Greyling beside him, his dark skinned face caught by the lights from the house, his voice a low undertone to the sound of running water from the fountain. Above them, pipistrels flew overhead, the scent of honeysuckle and jasmine torpid on the moving air. Drago laughed suddenly, Alberto jerking in his sleep, Cy stretching his arms.

They had eaten well, the meal as well prepared as the previous dinners; the cook pressed into service after long neglect. There was a visitor, she was told ... A visitor, after so long? No, it wasn't just Alberto de Brio, there was someone new ... The house was courted back into life, rooms reopened, the study discarded in favour of the drawing room. The master had a visitor, the staff said, and not before time ... But what a visitor ... They expected a diplomat, a politician, a visiting writer, any of the long list of acquaintances Drago had once so assiduously courted. Maybe a member of the aristocracy, or even a woman.

The one person for whom they were *not* prepared was the exotic Cy Greyling. He had arrived that evening in a casual white shirt and navy trousers, walking alongside Alberto. Waiting on the terrace Drago had turned to greet them. He moved languidly, as he had always done, taking his time, his heavy lidded eyes watchful.

"Welcome – Alberto has told me a great deal about you."

Cy had shaken his hand. "He's told me a lot about you too."

"So we are hardly strangers," Drago said graciously, showing him to a seat.

But even though Drago employed all of his courtly manners, Cy Greyling was a difficult guest; on his guard, argumentative, dismissive of some of the most traditional and well used surgical procedures.

"... but *why* hold on it? I say that doing the procedure this way would shorten the time the patient has to be under anaesthetic –"

"There's no need to hurry."

Cy's voice's rose: "There is *always* a need to hurry. No surgeon wants to keep his patient under longer than he needs to. Anaesthetic always carries a risk."

"Anaesthetics are lighter now. Look at the ones adopted in London, they were written up in the Lancet years ago and researched thoroughly before they were used just to prove how safe they were."

"You saw those papers?"

Drago eyes glinted with indignation. "I keep up to date. I am not a senile old fool, I *can* still read." He leaned towards his guest, his temper curdling. "I can't use *these* any more," he snapped, waving his hands in front of Cy's face, "but I can use *this*," he tapped his forehead quickly. "You don't know everything, Mr Greyling, even though you think you do." His voice calmed, and he leaned back in his seat, studying his guest. "I was like you once. In a hurry, wanting to show off my talent –"

"– just a minute."

"No," Drago said, putting up his hands to avoid any further interruption. "You are in my house and so you must indulge me. It's only manners. Something you seem perilously short of."

Cy stood up, his black eyes keen, indignant. "I should go."

"Maybe you should," Drago said evenly, avoiding Alberto's anxious glance. He had heard the raised voices and wakened, walking onto the terrace, his hands deep in his pockets. "I have no stomach for this anymore. I don't want to have to mollify you, or anyone else. I'm getting old and bad tempered." He sipped at his wine, wetting his lips only. "I wanted to meet you, I hoped that we might be friends, that I might be able to help you in your career." His eyes held his visitor's for several seconds, "I wouldn't help you for nothing, of course. No one does anything for nothing. I think you and I would agree on that, Mr. Greyling. I was prepared to help you, using my influence and my contacts to propel you to the top of the dazzling medical mire." He dipped his finger into his wine and then smoothed it across his bottom lip. "I wanted, in return, for you to be seen as my successor; in that way I'd remain involved in surgery whilst I guided my heir towards genius and misery."

Alberto flinched, turning on his friend, "Drago, what are you saying?"

He smiled without warmth. "The truth." He glanced up at the man in front of him, studying the Moroccan features, an outcast in a Roman garden. As he had been an exile once, coming to Italy all those years earlier. "I won't lie, Mr. Greyling. I could give you everything I have – but I can't promise you that power and fame will bring you even a moment of peace. I'm offering you an opportunity, which may well turn out to be a curse." He shrugged slowly. "That's for you to decide. I can give it all to you – in return for my involvement in your career. That's all. I've nothing else to occupy me – my son and I are virtually estranged, I have no daughter, no wife, and this house …" he pointed over his shoulder, but did not turn round. "… this house is choked with ghosts."

Thoughtfully, Cy Greyling walked over to the low wall of the terrace and leaned against it, his arms folded; "What makes you think that the medical world in Rome would accept a stranger? A black one at that."

"They won't, at first," Drago admitted, "but power makes people acceptable, Mr. Greyling – and success makes everyone the same colour in the end."

Cy frowned: "You're a cynic."

"No. I see life as it is, that's all. I'm a pragmatist. I've learnt to see everything clearly now that I'm getting old. I rely on facts." He paused. "You would do well to do the same."

"I've got a pretty good grasp on reality."

Drago nodded. "Ah, but *what* reality is that? The reality of the here and now, or of what is to come?"

"We can't judge the future until it becomes the past."

Drago lifted his head slowly and glanced at Alberto. *"Time present and time past are both present in time future, and time future is present in time past.' –* T. S. Eliot, Alberto," he said smiling, "You remember how much you admired him?"

"I remember," he replied, watching at Drago as he turned back to his guest.

"I know how talented you are. I saw you operate last week at the Italian Hospital –"

"I never saw you."

Drago raised his eyebrows: "I've told you, influence can achieve anything. I didn't want you to know I was there – so you didn't." He paused before continuing, "I was impressed. But I need to know more, Mr. Greyling. Much more."

No one watching Cy Greyling would have suspected nerves. No one would have believed that he was cold with anxiety. "What do you want to know?"

"Tell me about your life."

"I was born in Tangiers, thirty four years ago, the only son of a shop owner. My mother's dead and my father has remarried – I don't see him anymore." He paused, taking in a slow breath. His prominent cheekbones were highlighted by the lamps, his skin the colour of jet. "I'm not married and I've no children. I've a small apartment in New Orleans, the city where I was last operating before I was invited to Rome … That's all there is to know."

Drago turned to Alberto: "Was I as arrogant when I was his age?"

Alberto smiled. "No – you were worse."

Drago grimaced, then turned back to Cy. "Well, thank you for the meat, but now I would like some vegetables to go with it. And a little desert wouldn't go amiss either."

"What's that supposed to mean?"

"It means – talk to me. It means – tell me what you want from life, tell me what you dream of, what you long for. Tell me what stimulates you, worries you, frightens you." He sighed, picking up his glass, "Do you like this wine?"

Cy nodded.

Immediately Drago threw it at his feet. It puddled on the stone tiles. "Do you *still* like it?"

His face was hard, threatening. "What the hell are you playing it?"

"But it's still the same wine!" Drago replied heatedly. "What makes it different? Has its taste changed? Its bouquet? Its colour?" He stood up, although stooped he was still tall and looked the Moroccan in the face. "What *changed* it? By lying on the floor and not being in a crystal glass? … Be careful, Mr. Greyling, it's a mistake to always judge the worth of something by where you find it. A man living in a palace isn't necessarily a king."

Cy turned away, Drago catching hold of his arm fiercely; "You take offence too easily. You're arrogant. As I was – as I have been all my life. Assurance can make a brilliant surgeon – but a lonely man."

"I'm not lonely."

"Not yet," Drago said coldly, releasing Cy's arm and sitting down again. "Do you want a wife and children?"

"In time."

266

"Why?"

Cy breathed out, exasperated. "Because I don't want to be alone all my life."

"And when do you suppose that it will be convenient for you to marry?" Drago asked, "When your career is well established? Or before? Will you want to marry later, to someone who will help you with her social contacts? Or to someone you meet and fall in love with?"

"I'm not a clairvoyant," Cy said, struggling to keep his patience. "I don't know what'll happen –"

"– but you're a very striking looking man," Drago persisted, "women must like you."

"I HAVE NO TIME FOR THEM!"

"Ah," Drago said simply, gesturing to the servant for a new bottle of wine before settling into his seat and crossing his legs. He seemed at ease suddenly, in full command, whilst Cy stood awkwardly by the wall, his expression hostile.

"What happened?"

Cy ignored the question, Drago glancing over to Alberto. Understanding immediately, he stood up and left the terrace, whistling as he entered the house.

"What happened?" Drago repeated.

"I met a woman – she left me."

"Did you love her very much?"

Cy nodded, then sat down in the seat Alberto had vacated. "I never thought I could love anyone the way I loved her," he admitted, "I thought she felt the same. We even talked about marriage and children. She seemed to want them. But …"

"Where did you meet her?"

"New Orleans." He glanced over to Drago, "And before you ask. She came from the French Quarter."

He closed his eyes to the memory, but he could still smell the scent of gardenia and see a woman in a red dress leaning over a rusty balcony and waving, her arm casting a shadow on the stucco behind. It had been hot, steaming, the nights drowsy. I'll give you the world … I know, she'd said, I know … there'll never be anyone else: never … she had turned in her sleep, her hand hot against the damp arc of his back, her hair sticking to the curve of her shoulder, her mouth open, smelling of wine … One long summer of indigo nights, lizards moving slow on the porch, netting at the windows, and the blues coming lazy over the radio …

"She left you?"

Cy nodded, all arrogance gone. "Yes, she left me."

"Why?"

"I was the wrong colour!" he snapped.

"*Was* that the reason?"

Cy paused. "No, I was the wrong man."

"A brave admission."

Cu shrugged. "It's the truth, that's all."

"The truth is always painful."

The evening was turning into night, the sweet wet smell of rain coming down sliding over the garden and making the terrace cool. The lamplight pooled, aureoles of colour haloing the yellow illumination.

"I want to help you," Drago said quietly. "I don't think you want to keep roaming the world, going from place to place, never settling, never finding a home in which you can rest."

Cy looked over to him; the first spot of rain fell on the back of his hand, cooling, the breeze pushing at the cypress trees.

"You're right, I've wanted to settle somewhere for a long time." His voice was low, the faint American accent hardly discernable. He was quiet, almost gentle, his dark hands round his glass of wine. All his energy and aggression had left him: he seemed older.

"Take what I offer," Drago said, "please – you would be helping yourself and helping me."

Cy tipped back his head, several drops of rain landing on his forehead and rolling down his cheeks like tears.

"Yes," he said simply, "yes."

They became inseparable quickly. Cy Greyling needed a father and Drago needed a son. They fitted into each other's lives so effortlessly that it seemed, within weeks, that they had always been together. Arguments were frequent, reconciliations quick, an affection building between them which neither had expected. Cy continued to live in his small flat in the city centre, but he visited the palazzo daily, reporting on his operations, asking advice, bringing notes.

The old study was busy again, the X-Ray viewing machine turned on late at night, its blue white light coming under the door as the maid came in with repeated cups of coffee and sandwiches.

"... I *still* say that the incision should be under the jaw –"

"– no!" Cy countered adamantly, "along the jaw line and behind the ear."

Drago looked back to the X-Ray. "You would be making work for yourself."

"Let me decide that, hey?" Cy snapped, then lowered his tone. "I want to do it my way."

He was right at times, and wrong at others. But knowing that he had Drago's backing, his confidence soared. He no longer felt like the resented outsider, although he knew that there was much jealousy over his good fortune. Not least with Courtney.

He might have no love for his father, but when he saw his position being usurped by a foreigner, he was enraged. Photographs in the newspaper and gossip columns fuelled his animosity, his felt himself scorned and laughed at behind his back. Always ready to feel slighted, Courtney retaliated in his own way; not by trying to inveigle his way back into his father's affections, but by embarrassing him.

Nancy was patient, she could afford to be. In the years since the birth of the twins she had managed through hard work and considerable charm to turn Drago's contacts into a fruitful business. She had talent and she used it; her designs were soon being incorporated into magazines, and later, in the summer of 1978, she had her own small show in Rome. Another woman might have be embittered by her daughter's condition, but not Nancy. She accepted that Lomond was handicapped and would remain handicapped for life; Why worry? she said to her friends. Lomond was a clever girl, and people could achieve a lot without the use of their legs … Her optimism was genuine; and besides she had a perfectly healthy son in David.

Cheerfully, Nancy managed to cope with her daughter's problems and her husband's erratic behaviour. Without ever considering the difficulties, she took her children to work with her in the school holidays, hauling Lomond's wheelchair through the busy streets whilst chattering endlessly to her son. No one could faze her, or depress her – Nancy had what she wanted, children, and even more than that, she had a burgeoning career.

And when Courtney worked with her, she was encouraging, enthusiastic about his designs, which were, against all the odds, innovative. Then, when he disappeared, staying away from home for days on end, she never admonished him, never reproached him, never by a word or look criticised him. It was her way of safe-guarding her own feelings and her children … You knew what to expect when you married him, Nancy told herself. So enjoy the good times and ride the rest.

There was plenty of the rest when Cy Greyling came to Rome. Sensing trouble, Drago told Nancy about the situation before she heard about it from anyone else. She was visiting him alone, the children in school, and had walked down the garden, waving and calling his name. He turned when he saw her and she paused, transfixed by the change in him. The stoop had gone, as had the fixed and guilty look which had been there since Pila's death. Even the house seemed less threatening, its size majestic, not imposing.

"Hey," she said approvingly, "you look great."

He smiled; she had never seen that smile before; that genuine open look. "I feel as though I'd been given a new lease of life," he explained. "How are the children?"

"Lomond's okay, doing her exercises, but complaining," Nancy replied, grimacing, "still, what can you expect? She's only eight. The special school's better for her though, she feels less out of place there." Dropping into step with Drago, Nancy walked with him to the maze. "David's doing well at school."

"I'm pleased."

She nodded, her turquoise eyes curious; "So how are things with you?"

"Better than they have been for a long time."

Her eyebrows rose, "How come?"

"I've found a wonderful surgeon, someone I can teach, help – someone who needs me."

Nancy kept walking, her voice steady. "Who?"

"Cy Greyling," Drago answered. "He's an American, a very gifted surgeon."

"As good as you?"

"As good as I was – at my peak," Drago said, sitting down on a bench.

Nancy sat beside him. It was the same bench on which she and Courtney had sat so many years before; talking about their marriage, their future … Idly, she laid her arms along the back of the bench, her face turned up to the pale autumn sun.

"I'm glad you're happy," she said genuinely. "You needed some happiness in your life. It was long overdue."

Drago stared at her profile. "I wanted to love Courtney," he confessed. "… but I was a poor father to him when he was young, and later the damage was done. We have nothing in common now."

"But you and Cy Greyling do?"

He nodded, glad of her frankness: "You were always direct."

"I find it's the best way to be," Nancy replied, turning her head and smiling.

"Courtney may well resent Cy …" Drago said carefully. "… and that worries me. I don't want you to suffer for my actions."

"I won't. Courtney will be furious, will think himself rejected, will believe that you have set out to undermine him by taking on a prodigy – I know how he'll react – we both do – but I can cope with it."

"I can get on with Cy," Drago said, his tone wondering, as though he had never expected to feel happy again. "… we have a lot in common. The surgery, the ambition," he smiled, his mouth relaxed, without the hard lines of bitterness. "I feel a part of the medical world again, not some old forgotten horse put out to graze. I can help him, introduce him to influential contacts, the usual … And Cy helps me. People respect me again, I'm still a player in the game."

"So you're not lonely anymore. I'm glad," she smiled her luminous, happy go lucky smile. "Drago, don't worry, and don't feel guilty. You've got a second chance at fatherhood – don't blow it."

He didn't, he did everything instead to smooth the way for Cy, and in his turn, Cy did everything to repay his mentor. They were soon attending every important medical convention together, Cy giving lectures, or demonstrating operational procedures, Drago at the back of the lecture halls or theatres, making notes, keeping records that later he would pass on. You should have said this … have you thought about doing that? … His fabulous reputation went before him, and, after years of being a semi-recluse, Drago Razzio had the satisfaction of being feted and courted all over again.

Once, in Berlin, he was even given a standing ovation when he was spotted in the audience. He rose to his feet, his heavy-lidded eyes betraying nothing as he bowed and smiled in his old languid way. Life was kind again, his diary full of events, social invitations extended once more. The lion was not dead, he had been in resting, that was all … Drago seemed, through that autumn, to be renewed, cheating his age; his hope restored, and with it, his life energy. But he was clever enough not to stifle his prodigy and realised that Cy was not a man to be controlled. He might guide him, but not manipulate him. As two people similar in temperament, Cy knew how much he could say and how much to leave unsaid; and Drago understood that in order to keep his surrogate son he had to give him a long leash.

So now and then he would draw back, decline a trip, letting Cy go alone. Knowing that he would return full of news: eager, willing to share.

"You should have come to Stockholm," Cy said, sitting down, his legs stretched out in front of him. "Everyone asked about you – they all thought you were going to be there."

Drago looked over the rim of his glass. "You should be seen to be your own man. You don't always want me there."

"You were called 'The Magician'," Cy said, grinning, "that's a hell of a sobriquet."

"I was one of the first to go into plastic surgery – we were thought of as miracle workers then." Drago paused, glanced over to the fire. "It's Christmas soon. I wondered if you wanted to spend it here with me? … I mean, if you have other plans," he was rigid with unease, dreading rejection. "Naturally, it's up to you."

Silent, Cy turned away. Christmas, dear God, how he hated Christmas. All those holidays spent at parties he never wanted to attend; with people he didn't care for; eating and drinking mechanically, and later falling asleep in front of the television, waking in the early hours to and empty screen and the lonely sound of static. Christmas – shops full of families shopping, cards, fathers carrying trees home, and children … he thought of New Orleans suddenly, and of her … when we are married, we'll have loads of kids and big family Christmases … when we are married.

"Cy?"

He turned. His eyes, Drago saw with surprise, were moist. "I'd like to spend Christmas here," he said at last. "Thank you."

The same invitation was extended to Nancy and Courtney, but Courtney refused and in the end he left Rome for the season without telling anyone where he was going. Cheerfully hiding her humiliation, Nancy packed up the children and moved into the palazzo, organising the tree and the meals and generally behaving as though she had not a trouble in the world.

"God, I don't know how she copes with him," Cy said to Drago one night.

"She made a deal – and she stuck to it," he replied, hearing Nancy's screech of laughter from upstairs. "I admire her enormously. She has no illusions, and can make the best of everything. Very few people have her courage."

"But your son treats her so badly."

Drago nodded. "True, but you forget something – he gave Nancy what she wanted – children. She's prepared to put up with anything in return for that."

Cy shook his head. "I couldn't live that way."

"That's because you're a romantic," Drago teased him. "You believe in love, a pure love that conquers all," he laughed kindly. "Well, I hope you find it. I never did. That's a lie, it was offered to me once and I didn't accept it – until it had gone." He changed the subject hurriedly, "Nancy! Come in here!"

She materialised within seconds, pushing Lomond, David running behind her. For an instant she paused in the doorway, breathless, laughing, her face flushed, her eyes bright as a cat's, the full impact of her spirit and affection swamping the room.

Fascinated, Drago stared. She stood like a red headed angel, the vast decorated tree shimmering behind her.

He was suddenly and unexpectedly moved. "Happy Christmas …" he said gently, walking over to her and kissing her on both cheeks, then bending to kiss his granddaughter. "Happy Christmas – and thank God for it."

# Fifty-Five

"No, not London," Drago said firmly. "I don't go to England."

"Why not?" Cy countered, glancing over to Alberto, puzzled. He shook his head, gesturing for Cy to calm down.

"I don't like the place, that's all," Drago replied coldly. "Let's leave it at that, shall we? If you want to go, then go. In fact, I think you should – Frank Collings is a wonderful surgeon, you could learn something."

Cy nodded. "All right then, I go alone."

Drago turned, his tone softening. "Please forgive me – but I have my reasons."

Outside, Alberto paused in the driveway and lit a cigarette, then shivered and climbed into his car. At once Cy ran over and leaned down at the open window. "What was all that about?"

"A feud," he said simply, his breath vaporised in the cold air. "Hasn't he told you about it?"

"No, he never said a word."

Alberto rubbed his hands together, the cigarette dangling jauntily from his lips. "Jump in, I'll give you a lift."

"But what about my car?"

"Get a taxi back later," Alberto said. "D'you want to hear the story or not?"

Driving quickly, Alberto turned away from the city centre and into the surrounding country. He was whistling under his breath, the car hot and full of smoke, Cy staring ahead at the white road. They drove for nearly twenty minutes, Alberto finally parking by the road side and turning off the engine. The winter silence was immense.

"So, what do you want to know?"

"You said they was a feud? What happened?"

"Drago rejected his parents and his sister." Alberto explained. "He was ashamed of them –"

"What?"

"His father was Guido Razzio, and he ran a string of boxers. Drago thought he was better than they were, so he left to make his own way in the world. Unfortunately," Alberto paused to light another cigarette, "his fame brought him only misery. He feels guilty, you see, especially for the way he treated his family – and his sister."

"What about his sister?"

Alberto pushed his glasses up the bridge of his nose: "Misia lives in England, sometimes in Liverpool, sometimes in London. She runs the boxers with her youngest son." He inhaled slowly. "Funny thing is, that now Drago's jealous of *her*. After despising everything she stood for, he's jealous of her now. He thinks she was the lucky one, the one with the good marriage, the happy family life. Every loss of his he sees as something she would gloat over. After being so proud, so arrogant, he's now hounded by envy ... Strange how life works out."

"Are they never in contact?"

"No. Drago hates his sister and besides, he holds her responsible for his daughter's death."

Cy breathed out slowly. "I heard about that. She was killed in London, wasn't she?" he stopped short. "*London*. Oh, I see, that's why Drago won't go there."

"That's one reason – and the other is that Misia lives there part of the time. He connects London with the Bennings, and all the things he resents and coverts." Alberto glanced over to him. "*Now* do you understand why I wanted you to meet him last year? Why I hoped you'd get on? You know him now, Cy, but you never saw him before. He'd given up, getting old, scared, jumping at ghosts, waiting for death. He needed you – and you don't know how glad I am that it's worked out."

Cy chose his words carefully, "Does he talk to you about the Bennings?"

"No," Alberto said smiling slyly, "but I talk to him about them, I always have. I keep both sides of the family in touch with one another – that's one of my functions in life," he chuckled, wickedly amused. "You see, I love them both, Drago and Misia. I've known them for decades, known their partners, their children, watched how their lives have developed, even been there when some of them died ..." he thought of the night Guido Razzio passed on, he and Misia standing by the French windows, waiting. "They are family to me – after my wife died, I had no commitments – so now I flit from one to the other, from England to Italy and back again, carrying news like an old carrier pigeon." He coughed suddenly, a hacking sound from deep in his chest.

Concerned, Cy glanced over to him. "You smoke too much."

"Uh, no, not you too!" Alberto replied, laughing loudly as he restarted the engine and turned back to Rome.

*

Misia was watching one of Vincent's latest enthusiasms, a Mancunian called Terry Gibbs, who was at that moment sparring with a youngster who had come in for a try out at The Roman House. Gibbs was quick on his feet, his hair gelled back, with an earring in his left lobe and his right eyebrow missing.

"This had better be worth coming all the way from London," Misia said, folding her arms and nodding to Abbot.

"He's a natural –"

"– if I had a tenner for every time I had heard that, I'd be able to retire to Monte Carlo."

Vincent pulled a seat up next to his mother's, the two of them facing the ring, his latest greyhound by his side. "Listen, Terry Gibbs could be big, *really* big. I've already got him lined up for a fight at Wembley."

Misia watched the bout hotting up, assessing Gibbs professionally, cool-headedly. "He's brilliant –"

She turned to her son: "Are you up for Salesman of the Year Award?" she asked

273

dryly. "I've got the point, Vincent – you like him. Now shut up, and let me make up my own mind."

Gibbs was a jerky fighter, and he dropped his hands too much, leaving his chin exposed; but he had good variety of punches, and he was quick, following through when he knew had rocked his opponent.

Vincent couldn't contain his excitement, "LOOK AT THAT!"

Misia shot him a warning look and turned back to the ring. She was glad to be back in Liverpool and on her own turf, happy to be mixing with the boxers again and old Abbot. The years spent bringing up Norton and Ahlia had not been hard, but she missed her work and the freedom of travelling between cities. Besides, now that Portland was retired he was easily bored and irritated by domestic routine, trying a score of hobbies before finally lapsing into a passion for chess.

An old colleague of his had started the obsession, a man of similar years who wanted to keep his mind active. Soon Portland was playing once a week and then several times a week, asking Misia repeatedly if she minded. She assured him that she didn't, privately thanking God. Never had a square of wood been put to better use, she thought, listening patiently to the re-runs of games and the moves and counter moves. Her ageing husband was happy again – and now she was free to see if she might not put her own talent back to use.

But tact had never been Misia's strong suit, and Vincent was immune to subtlety, so after various abortive hints, she had asked him outright:

"Well, can I do something in the business or not?"

He had stopped chewing the toast he was eating and looked at her. At forty four he was still unmarried, and although he had his own flat, he still spent much of his time at the Holland Park house.

"What?"

"Can I help?"

"You're too old to be a croupier."

"Not in the casinos." Patiently Misia had poured herself some coffee. "But I know more about boxing than you'll ever learn."

"Why d'you want to go back in the fight game?"

She was grey now, her frame wiry, her voice clipped, "Why not?"

Vincent had bitten into his toast and chewed it before replying. "What d'you want to do?"

"I want you to take me on as a sparring partner!" she had snapped. "Use your head, Vincent, I want to do what I did before."

She had thought he was going to refuse, to make an excuse, to protect his territory from any outside influence – even his mother's. Misia wouldn't have blamed him; after all, she had left him to look after the boxing and the casino almost single handededly after Pila's death. But she had missed it, and longed for it, and although she would never beg him, she had willed him to agree.

Vincent finished his toast and rose to his feet, checking his reflection in the hall mirror as Misia had followed him. He had been casually dressed and although his hair was sharply cut, he had too little vanity to have his broken nose corrected. Carefully he had arranged the collar of his open necked shirt.

"Liverpool. Tomorrow. All right?"

Misia had blinked. "Are you talking in semaphore, or is that an invitation?"

He walked to the door and grinned wolfishly. "I bet you won't last a week."

Misia had liked to think of how she would make him eat his words as she chatted on the way to Liverpool, her legs cramped up in the front of his sports car.

"Aren't you a little old for this?" she had asked. "I mean, most men give up sports cars when they're thirty."

Vincent weaved into the outer lane. "This little beauty has pulled many a girl," he replied happily. "Not that I need her for that anymore."

Misia turned to look at her son's brutish profile. "No!" she said simply. "I don't believe it! You've found someone."

"Annabel," he had said simply, turning on the radio.

Immediately Misia leaned forward and turned it off. "What's she like?"

"Little, blonde, a bit … well, she can be a bit tactless at times."

Misia's face had been rigid. If Vincent had noticed that someone was tactless, they were seriously outspoken. "How old is she?"

"Twenty eight."

She had closed her eyes; her ears throbbed with the news. "That's quite an age gap – does she know how old you are?"

Vincent winced. It was his one vanity – he lied about his age. In every newspaper article it was quoted differently, Vincent having adjusted the years since continually he was thirty. "Well … she thinks I'm mature."

"Which means she thinks you're about thirty nine."

"Hey, Mum –"

"I know you, Vincent," she had replied, trying to keep the amusement out of her voice. "Thirty nine sounds young – forty four doesn't."

"It's harmless."

"That's what you think. What if she was hiding something from you?"

"She is," he had replied, "she lies about her age too." He winked at her mother good naturedly. "She's thirty four – and I reckon we're perfectly suited."

Which was more than the boxers were. Vincent assessment of Terry Gibbs had been sound; he was a very able boxer and, with coaching, might having the making of a first class draw, but he was sloppy in his footwork and tediously over confident. After the bout he walked over to the side of the ring, his Mancunian accent thick, guttural; "So, what d'you think, Mr. Benning?"

"You're not bad."

"Hey, do us a favour," he snapped, wiping his nose on the back of his glove. "I were a killer in there."

Misia glanced up at him. "You drop your hands too much."

Terry Gibbs's face was a study: "Do you always take yer mother with ya? Or is she on a day pass from the home?"

He didn't have time to see Abbot's hand descend, he just felt the stinging pain in his left ear and yelped. "Bloody hell, mate! What's that fer?"

"Cheek," the old trainer said simply, his breathing laboured. "Now, go and get yourself changed." He watched the boy go and then turned to Misia. "They're all the flaming same these days, no discipline." He looked at Vincent questioningly, "Well, what d'you think?"

"Give him a try."

Abbot nodded then turned to Misia. "And what d'you think?" he asked wheezily, his bowler resting on his prominent ears. "I imagine you're going to be having a say in things again, or you wouldn't be here." He stuck his hand through the bars and clasped hers. "Welcome back, Mrs. Benning. We missed you."

# Fifty-Six

Portland was on fourth chess move when the phone rang. Reluctantly he rose to his feet, keeping his eyes fixed on his partner as he picked up the receiver.

"Yes?"

"Ciao, Portland. It's Alberto."

All thought of the chess game was abandoned. "Alberto, it's so good to hear you! We were only talking about you at the weekend and saying we hadn't seen you for a while. Where are you?"

"I'm coming to London next week for a medical lecture – same old same, nothing changes." He paused. "To be honest, I'm glad of the trip, I thought I'd love retirement – but how much enjoyment can a man take?" he laughed loudly. "So how are things?"

"Quiet. I still pop into chambers, but nothing's the same as I was and I can't bear going near court anymore. Leamington died the other week …" Portland thought of the three daughters standing by the graveside. The Hapsburg Harpies, someone had once called them, but they were kind to him, invited him back to the pink semi and plied him with pink-iced cake.

"Misia's back at work."

"Do you mind?"

"Mind! Hell no," Portland said hurriedly. "I was dying for her to get an interest, she was under my feet all day." He glanced over to his companion, "I took up chess again."

"I'll give you a game when I come over."

"You're on," Portland said happily. "Listen, why don't stay with us whilst you're in London?"

"I would, but I'm not alone."

"God, it's not a woman at your age, is it?"

"No, it's Drago's prodigy."

"That should be a hellish companion," Portland said wryly. "I'm amazed anyone would go near that bugger – present company excepted, of course."

"Drago's changed."

"There was room for improvement," Portland said sharply. "He's never been in touch with us, you know. After all that happened, you think he's have written at least. I can't believe anyone could keep up a feud this long."

Alberto tensed on the other end of the line. He was not prepared to tell Portland how Drago felt, or that he still held Misia responsible for Pila's death.

"So I'll phone you when I get to London?"

"Oh, come on, Alberto, you can stay here – even with Drago's little running mate."

"You'll like him."

"I doubt that."

Alberto laughed. "He's very talented, very much the up- and-coming man."

"Listen, if you like him that's enough for me," Portland said generously. "Just warn him to keep off the subject of Drago when he's around Misia, that's all – otherwise I can't vouch for his health."

It was the second of February when Alberto arrived in London, Cy following from Washington where Ronald Reagan had been newly inaugurated as President. Moving swiftly amongst the crowds at Heathrow's Arrival Lounge, Cy spotted Alberto and waved vigorously as he hurried over to him.

"God, it's cold," Cy said with feeling. "I thought Washington was bad enough."

"You wait until you use the plumbing at Holland Park," Alberto answered. "The hot water never gets above tepid."

Cy paused, "Listen … I've been having second thoughts about staying with the Bennings."

"Why? It's no problem," Alberto answered evenly.

"If Drago found out he would think I was going behind his back – you know he would."

"You can't live your life to suit him."

"No, but I owe him a great deal, and I don't want to cause trouble."

"If that's the way you want it –"

"It is," Cy replied firmly. "I'm not getting involved in any family feud – and I'm not taking sides."

"But you'll come and meet the Bennings?"

He nodded, all agreement, "Oh yes, I'll meet them. There's no harm in that."

But Cy didn't meet Misia the following day, even though he had lunch with Portland and Alberto. His wife was still up in Liverpool, Portland explained: apparently Vincent was having some trouble with the Council, The Roman House's fire regulations inadequate, the building considered a death trap. So she and Vincent had decided to stay on and settle the matter before returning to London:

"There's trouble brewing up in Liverpool," Portland went on, "street fights. Some people are worried that there might even be riots."

"In England?" Cy asked disbelievingly.

"Yes, in England. Seems incredible, doesn't it? It's the kind of thing you'd expect in America, but not here." He changed the subject quickly, "Misia asked how long you were staying."

"I have to go the convention," Cy replied, "but after that, my time's my own."

"And my time's been my own for years," Alberto replied, lighting up. "What's she got in store for us?"

Portland grinned. "I think she wants to show you the World's End gym, and the casino –"

"I thought she didn't approve of gambling," Alberto said, his look teasing.

"She's didn't – until No 100 Blenington Row started to make a fortune," Portland replied, smiling: "then she suddenly overcame her reluctance."

"Vincent leads a charmed life," Alberto said admiringly. "He's made a fortune out of that place, and got some good boxers in tow. His grandfather would have been proud of him." He rose to his feet and walked over to the mantelpiece, passing a photograph to Cy. "Look at that," he said, "Guido Razzio – you'll never find a man to match him." Thoughtfully he studied Cy, the downcast head, the fine bones, the dark refinement of his face. "If you followed his example you'd do well."

"Rather than follow Drago's?" Cy countered.

Portland and Alberto exchanged a glance.

"I didn't mean that …" Alberto said carefully. "I just meant that Guido Razzio was extraordinary."

"His son is too," Cy retorted.

Portland was watching him curiously. He hadn't know what to expect; had suspected a milk-sop underling, a pawn in Drago's master plan. The one person he hadn't anticipated was this formidable man, with his brittle, suspicious personality.

"No one's attacking you," Portland said with equanimity. "You should defend Drago Razzio. You owe him a great deal and we should always repay our debts."

The implication was obvious, and hung uncomfortably on the air. Cy might admire Drago as his mentor, but his loyalty was not matched by Drago's own behaviour.

Unsettled, Cy glanced away. "I'm sorry … I didn't mean to offend you."

"You didn't," Portland said easily, getting to his feet, "you're not responsible for the past. Drago's actions are his own responsibly, not yours."

Cy left soon afterwards, explaining that he had some work to complete before the talk tomorrow. He was giving the introduction, he said, and waited it to go well; it was vital that he make the right impression. Standing on the doorstep of Holland Park, Alberto watched him leave and then turned back to Portland.

"Don't judge him too harshly –"

"D'you want a game?" Portland asked, interrupting him immediately. Alberto nodded, watching Portland set out the chess pieces. "I don't dislike him, you know – but he's very prickly."

"He's had disappointments in the past. Personal and professional. People resent brilliance."

Portland glanced up, holding the King figure in his hand. "He should learn to live with it, and adapt." He laid the piece on the board, his expression thoughtful. "I can't think that someone like Drago is the best company for him, or the right example to follow – they're too much alike."

"You're wrong," Alberto replied. "Cy Greyling's a kind man, much kinder than Drago." He touched the top of one of his pawns. "You and I have had many conversations here, haven't we?" Portland nodded. "… talking about the people we've known in the past, about good times and bad ones. But I'll tell you this, Portland, Cy Greyling is very vulnerable. He covers it well – he's had to – and you mustn't mind him defending Drago. You see, he never expected anything from anyone and when Drago helped him, his gratitude was inexpressible. He's tied to him now, and his loyalty is his only means of showing his thanks."

Cautiously Portland made his first move on the board and then paused. "You put up a very plausible defence for him, Alberto, and you may well be right. But if Cy Greyling is the man you think he is – a good and honourable man – then I worry for him."

Alberto's eyes fixed on his friend. "Why?"

"*Put not your trust in princes*', as the saying goes," Portland went on, "Drago Razzio gives only to receive – and that young man might find more asked of himself that he can possibly hope to give."

# *Fifty-Seven*

"I've only just got back from Liverpool, give me a chance!" Misia said, dropping the shopping onto the kitchen table and turning to Lalo. "*Why* d'you want to sleep here? And why are you always arguing with your mother?"

Lalo started to put away the shopping, her voice gentle. "We don't get on, that's all," she said simply. "Oh, Nana, can't I stay here tonight? Please ..."

"What about your father?" Misia countered, throwing a sliced loaf into the bottom of the fridge. "Harewood might have something to say about all of this."

"He doesn't mind, he said so," Lalo replied hurriedly. "I phoned him at Chambers to check it was all right."

"But we've got guests," Misia replied, fighting to undo the plastic wrapping on some cheese. "Jesus! Which pervert invented this stuff?"

Lalo took it from her grandmother's hand and slowly unwrapped it. "Please, can I stay? I won't be any trouble – I'll stay out of the way, I promise."

"You're not a baby, Lalo, you're twenty years old, you don't have to go to bed early." Misia stopped, shamed by the hurt look on her granddaughter's face. "Oh, all right – but just for tonight. Tomorrow you go home and can sort it out with your mother. Meantime, you help me make dinner."

Lalo kissed her on the cheek quickly. "Who's coming?"

"Alberto de Brio. You know Alberto?" Lalo nodded. "And some doctor, who according to Portland looks like the Moor of Venice and has a very iffy temperament," she snorted. "I just love guests who are hard work."

"Oh, then maybe I should –"

"Oh *no!*" Misia said, looking at her granddaughter. "It was your idea to stay here, so now you can suffer like the rest of us."

Alberto arrived first, walking into the house and begging for a brandy, then coughing loudly before lighting up a cigarette.

"Your chest must be like the bottom of the Mersey," Misia said, shaking her head. "I just hope you've made a will."

"I'm leaving my body to science."

"I bet there won't be a rush for the brain," Misia replied deftly.

Portland was sitting on the old settee, Vincent's dog beside him, its head on his lap as it dribbled onto his trousers. "Where's Cy?"

"Coming soon."

"Lucky us," Misia said, checking the table and lighting some candles. "I hear that he's heavy going."

"He's fine, really," Alberto said, his tone soothing. "He's just takes a while to settle down."

At nine Cy finally arrived, apologising profusely, his embarrassment obvious. He had been taken to the wrong address and had had to run the remainder of the way, stopping for directions several times. His mortification was genuine, and he avoided

Misia's gaze, keeping his eyes on the place-setting before him. Irritated, Misia served him, slamming down his plate, her own resentment of her brother's prodigy, vicious and undisguised.

"It's spoilt, I'm afraid, Mr. Greyling," she said coldly. "I was never a good cook at the best of times, especially now that Teller's on holiday, but if you'd come at the right time it might well have been palatable."

"Misia, let it rest," Portland said, glancing round the table.

On his left, Alberto was eating hurriedly as though all the demons of hell were after him, and Lalo was silent, pushing her food around her plate, her head bent down, her hair falling across her face.

"So how was your talk?" Misia asked, her eyes boring into her guest's profile. "I believe we have a celebrity in our midst."

Cy hesitated, fighting back a desire to strike out. He felt cornered, threatened. Why in God's name had he come? It was obvious that the woman disliked him, and why shouldn't she? He was Drago's prodigy, the successor to her hated brother. Cy swallowed, he should never have come, should never have been such a fool.

"I imagine he did well –"

Misia turned her gaze on Alberto to silence him. "I wasn't talking to *you!* I was talking to our guest."

At the far end of the table, Portland sat rigid, too stunned to react. He had never seen Misia so angry; so bitter. Something about Cy Greyling had triggered an animosity in her which unnerved him. Hurriedly he glanced at their guest, and saw, to his consternation, a dull flush of colour under the black skin.

"Misia –"

"*What,* Portland?" she snapped, her eyes electric with rage. "I should forgive him for being late? For being thoughtless? Or should I simply treat him like a friend? Say a nice big welcome my brother's little ally." She stood up, throwing down her napkin. "You can eat with him, but not me."

Before she could say another word, Cy stood up and faced her.

"I'm sorry," he said simply, walking out.

Startled, Lalo looked around the table. Portland was staring at Misia in disbelief, Alberto leaning back in his seat, his head bowed.

On impulse Lalo jumped up and ran after Cy, catching up with him as he reached the end of the drive.

"I don't know what came over my grandmother," she said, shivering in the cold.

"Go in," Cy said, "you'll get a chill."

But Lalo was determined to explain. "She must be tired, that's all. She's very kind usually – oh, I know she can be sharp, but she's never cruel." Lalo looked up at him, pleading her case. "Please come back, I know how much Misia will be regretting what she said."

He hesitated in the drive way, torn. Lalo was shaking with cold, Cy realised, taking off his coat and putting it gently round her shoulders. Her face was pale, fragile.

"Please, come back …" Lalo urged him. "Please, for my sake."

*For my sake …* he stared at her, shivering in his overcoat.

"Please," she repeated. She was unaccountably panicked and didn't want this man to leave; didn't want him to walk out of the driveway and never come back. She felt a familiarity with him; a sudden and intense feeling of ease. I know him, she thought blindly. I know this man. Her eyes studied him, took in the dark brows, the long aquiline nose, the defined mouth. It was an unusual face, timeless, out of step with any other she had ever seen.

"Come back," Lalo said again, taking his arm.

He moved reluctantly, allowing her to lead him towards the house, letting her draw him towards the light. "I can't –"

"You can," she assured him, "you can."

"I'm not welcome here."

Lalo paused, her face a white oval above the hot redness of her dress. "Please, trust me."

Together they walked back into the dining room. Portland was standing moodily by the fire, Alberto staring into the candle flames, Misia sitting on the settee with her arms folded.

She looked up as they walked in, her expression hostile, then relieved. "I knew my cooking was bad, but I've never had a guest run away to avoid the desert," she said, moving back into the kitchen.

Portland turned from the mantelpiece, taking Cy's arm and leading his back to the table. "I'm glad you came back," he said, smiling at Lalo. "Please try to understand, Cy, it's not you. It's just that there's been a lot of bad blood between Drago and Misia for years and you caught out for it." He refilled Cy's glass. "My wife overreacted; she saw you as an enemy, a spy for Drago. It sounds ridiculous, I know, but this feud goes back a long way."

"I don't want to cause trouble," Cy said simply.

"You won't. In fact by coming back you've proved yourself." Portland looked at Lalo. "Well done, sweetheart."

She smiled shyly, sliding out of Cy's coat and laying it on the settee. Timidly she touched it, letting her fingers rest on the wool for an instant as though holding onto the man himself. The gesture was not lost on Alberto; he had regained his own poise and was casually cleaning his glasses, his eyes fixed on Lalo. Something had been set in motion, he realised, something powerful … Slowly his glance moved to Cy and then turned back to Lalo who had regained her seat at table.

Her face was altered somehow. Alberto put his glasses back on, studying Lalo. She was watching Cy thoughtfully, almost memorising his face, pulling in every detail of his features and every inflection in his voice. She was absorbing him, Alberto realised – and in that instant Cy turned to look at her. His eyes fixed on Lalo's face, and then, slowly, tentatively, he underwent the same process. He studied *her*, committed *her* to memory. A feeling built up between them; so strong it was almost palpable; criss-crossing the candle flames. Lalo watched Cy. She held his gaze, her eyes expectant; and he returned the look with the desperation of a man who had found something he thought forever beyond reach.

"Desert," Misia said simply, serving Cy a portion and then placing it in front of him. "I'm a ghastly old harpy," she explained, touching his shoulder. "Forgive me and put it down to my age."

Cy hardly heard her. He was moving in slow motion; drowning under the effect of Lalo's gaze. The candlelight seemed to have taken the air out of the room and his lungs were empty, void of life. He was unbreathing, unthinking, an embryo rocked in the safe and airless protection of the womb.

"It doesn't matter," he said at last, looking at Misia. "… but I'm glad I came back."

He looked over to Lalo, almost nodded to her, confirming what she felt. Yes, he thought, yes, it's real, she feels it too.

And across the table Alberto watched them and felt old, seeing in them the promise of something that would never again come for him.

\*

The following day Misia took Cy, Alberto and Lalo to a boxing match, the four of them sitting in the front row seats, taking their places quarter of an hour before the fight was due to start. The noise in the hall was immense, all seats taken, lights trained on the ring which loomed up in front of them. Abbot was standing outside the boxer's corner, chewing on the end of an unlit cigar, his bowler perched on his ears, the white ring of his hair fluffy as a dandelion. Seeing Misia he nodded, then glanced over to the aisle. Vincent was trotting towards the ring, only pausing to seat a tiny blonde in a black trouser suit, before running over to Misia.

"Is that Annabel?" she asked curiously.

"Yes," he replied, glancing over to Cy and shaking his hand. "I suppose you're our guest. You like boxing?"

"I never got around to seeing much," Cy admitted.

There was a roar from the crowd, the first bars of a pop song coming over the speakers, the referee climbing into the ring. Quickly Vincent straightened up and moved towards Abbot, watching the entrance for his fighter to appear.

He came in smiling, looking round, savouring his moments of glory, his name – JOHNNY DUNCAN – blared out over the speakers, a group of girls bearing placards walking either side of him. The lights were on him, the music loud, stimulating, his monogrammed robe over his shoulders, his gloved hands punching the air. He had worked hard for this moment, planned for it, and he intended to enjoy it – but his mouth was dry and his smile was fixed, his eyes flicking towards the ring nervously.

I can beat the bugger, he thought to himself, beat the shit out of him … They had faced each other at the weigh in, psyching each other out, glaring, staring, playing the game for the press and the punters. But the real test was in the ring and the ring was only feet away now. The chanting had begun 'JOHN-NY; JOHN-NY; JOHN-NY'; the foot stamping coming over the speakers, the contestant walking into the ring and being booed, his supporters trying to make themselves heard over the clamour.

He was nearly there, Johnny thought, his eyes fixed on the ring, seeing in his peripheral vision, Vincent winking and Abbot holding open the ropes to let him climb in. 'JOHN-NY; JOHN-NY; JOHN-NY'; came the cry, louder, hypnotic, then fading as the master of ceremonies introduced the boxers and then passed the fight over the referee. Beside the ring, Lalo turned, seeing her sister approach. Deandra's face was animated, her beauty mesmerising as she smiled at her sister and then leaned forwards in her seat towards Cy.

"Hello," she said simply. "I'm Deandra."

Lalo held her breath, waiting. She saw Cy turn and stopped breathing, seeing his momentarily astonishment at the perfection before him. He hesitated, then nodded.

"Hello," he said simply, then turned his gaze away from the astonishing Deandra and looked at Lalo instead. I prefer you, he said wordlessly. I prefer you.

She breathed out, her eyes seeing nothing, her ears hearing nothing as she stared ahead at the ring. He didn't want Deandra! she thought disbelievingly, he didn't prefer her; wasn't attracted to her. He wants me instead.

'JOHN-NY; JOHN-NY; JOHN-NY'; went the cry as the first punches landed, Deandra calling out her support, Misia watching, frowning, Vincent at the ringside next to Abbot. Lalo was suspended; removed. Her mind was wiped, all thoughts obliterated except one. He chose me. He saw Deandra, but he chose me.

Later Misia, Lalo, Cy and Alberto left, Vincent following with Annabel and Deandra, all of them meeting up at the casino. The doors of No 100 Belington Place were smoked glass, the handles brass, Misia walking in and leaving her trilby in the cloakroom before leading the way to the restaurant above. She was deep in conversation with Alberto, wildly berating Johnny Duncan's knockout in the eleven round.

"… bloody idiot, he should has seen it coming."

Alberto ordered and then shrugged. "He did well, he was unlucky, that's all."

"Unlucky, my eye!" Misia replied, tearing into her bread roll. "He should have been more alert. The sod was dozing up there." She paused, gesturing to the waiter for some mineral water, her conversation rattling on.

She hasn't noticed yet, Alberto thought, keeping his eyes on Misia although he was well aware of the couple facing him. She hasn't realised what's going on. You're getting old, Misia, like the rest of us, he thought smiling to himself, time was when you would have known immediately. Lalo was sitting by the glass wall of the restaurant, looking down into the casino below. Her hair was falling forwards, her shoulders round and smooth under the velvet jacket, her eyes luminous.

"Do you ever gamble?" Cy asked her.

She turned, looked at him. I want you, she thought, I want you so much.

Their attraction was mutual, Cy short on conversation, idiotically euphoric. Hold on, calm down, he willed himself, this is just a feeling that will pass … But he knew it wouldn't; knew wherever he went and whoever he looked at, Lalo's face would be in front of him. She was shy, kind, open, without malice – and he was besotted, unable to turn away from her as she kept looking at him, at the expression in his eyes and the movements of his hands as he tried to eat.

"What's the matter?" Misia asked him. "The food here *has* to be better than mine."

"It's wonderful," he said clumsily. "Really good."

She glanced over to Lalo's plate and raised her eyebrows. "So why isn't anyone eating?"

Fighting a crazed desire to laugh, Alberto cut into his steak and nodded to Vincent as he arrived, with Annabel and Deandra in tow.

"Fought like a bloody elf!" Vincent said, settling the two women at the next table and then leaning over the back of his own chair to talk to his mother. "Can you believe it? What a showing up." He glanced at Cy. "Sorry about that – I was hoping we could put on a good fight for you."

Cy's right hand had dropped below the table and was lying over Lalo's. He smiled, murmured something about enjoying himself – but he was fighting light-headedness, and a joyous, screaming sensation of delight.

"This is Annabel," Vincent said, introducing the blonde to Misia.

"Glad to meet you," Annabel said in a high pitched, girlish tone.

"I like your suit," Misia replied, studying the well cut trousers and jacket.

"Oh, thanks," she said happily, "but Vincent always says that women in trousers look like lesbians."

Misia's face set like putty as she crossed her trousered legs. "Oh, really?" she said, turning to her son who was wincing. "I see what you mean about Annabel – she wouldn't win the Diplomat of the Year Award would she?"

Lalo watched them, heard them, but sat stock still, feeling the pressure of Cy's hand on hers. They were all talking, laughing, a bevy of faces moving independently in some other sphere, whist they sat in their own secluded nucleus. If everything ended now, she thought, if the world stopped I wouldn't care.

"How long are you staying in London?" Vincent asked Cy.

"I go back to Rome on Tuesday ..." his hand pressed down on Lalo's, the message obvious.

"But you'll come back?" Vincent queried. "Everyone comes back. Look at Alberto – he can't keep away from us."

"I'd like to return," Cy replied, feeling a sudden and agonising ache in his chest. The voices around him were threatening all at once, his happiness due for termination in forty eight hours. No, he thought, I can't leave her, I can't.

Lalo felt the same sensation, her face turning away, her eyes fixing on the players in the casino below. He can't go. Not now I've found him. He can't go.

"Still, I suppose you're eager to get home," Vincent went on, unaware of the cruelty he was inflicting.

"Not really," Cy blundered.

"You must be! I love getting home after being away."

Cy glanced at the back of Lalo. Her expression was bewildered – forty eight hours left for them, she seemed to say, only forty eight hours? His hand fixed around hers, his despair apparent in that one tingling, suspended moment of time.

And in that moment Misia looked up. She paused, stared, and then, breathing in deeply, turned away.

# Fifty-Eight

"They can't be in love!" Misia thundered. "It can't happen that fast!"

"Oh no?" Portland queried, giving her a quizzical look.

She glanced at him in surprise: "Is that how it was for you? I mean, how did you feel what you met me?"

"Like I'd been mugged," he answered, grinning, "and I'm still suffering from the after-effects."

"Well, I thought you were the ugliest, most magnificent creature I had ever seen," Misia admitted, sitting on the edge of her husband's chair.

"It's no good trying to sweet talk me," he replied, running his forefinger down her spine. "I thought you were adorable. Too thin, of course, and that fringe was a real turn off –"

"It's amazing how you've disguised your revulsion over the years."

He nodded soberly. "I just learned to close my eyes."

Feigning outrage, Misia punched him in the chest. "*If* they are in love – *if* – it could turn out to be a problem."

"Why? Because of Cy's colour?"

"I don't care if he's black or covered in flock wallpaper, but I can't see Leda liking it. And what about Drago?"

"*What* about him?" Portland queried. "He doesn't want to marry Cy, does he?"

"You know what I mean!" Misia retorted. "He think we planned it. That we fixed it so his prodigy would fall in love with our granddaughter."

Portland burst out laughing. "Oh come on, even Drago couldn't be that paranoid."

"D'you want a bet?" she answered, then brightened up and got to her feet. "Still, why worry, it'll probably blow over – just turn out to be one of those instant attractions which fizzle out in time."

"You mean, like it did with us?" Portland asked wryly.

*

Lalo had gone back to her parents house in St. John's Wood, letting herself in and making her way upstairs before anyone saw her. She wanted to think, and she didn't want to have to talk to anyone – least of all her mother. Silently she hurried into her room and closed the door, sitting on her bed and pulling her knees up under her chin. There was a full moon, the curtains open, the light skimming the pale carpet.

"Lalo, are you in there?"

She flinched at the sound of her mother's voice, Leda walking in and snapping on the light switch. Wearing a quilted dressing gown and a pair of faded gold mules, she stood facing her daughter, her face bloated, her make up smudged.

"I *thought* it was you. What the hell d'you mean creeping in without saying a word?"

"I thought you were asleep."

"Like hell!" Leda snapped. "You could hear the television going. I want to talk to you."

"Mum, can't we leave it until tomorrow? I'm tired."

"I'M TIRED TOO!" Leda bellowed. "Although no one ever considers my feelings. I'm just expected to look after all of you and get badly thought of for my trouble." She flopped onto the bed next to her daughter. "Deandra never talks to me, she's always so thick with her father – and as for the boys, I never see them since they went away to school."

Her voice was thin with self pity, Lalo reaching out and putting her arm around her mother. "Come on, you know you can talk to me."

"I just get so depressed, so hopeless," she whined. "What's the point of it all?"

"You were better on those new tablets," Lalo coaxed her. "Go and see the doctor again."

"He can't help!" Leda said, pulling away. "No one how I feel – no one *cares* either."

"We all care about you, you know that."

Leda's eyes were shifty suddenly: "I bet your grandmother had something to say about me! She's never liked me."

"Nana never said a word," Lalo soothed her. "Come on, let's not fight."

Leda sighed, her head down, her voice pleading. "You won't leave me, will you? I couldn't bear you to leave …" her voice hardened. "Deandra's always out, and your father's always working."

"He has to, Mum. You know how much this house costs to keep up."

"My life didn't turn out the way I expected," Leda replied, self pity swamping her "I thought I'd have a great life, lots of parties, lots of fun – it turned out to be the opposite. A boring husband and a pack of kids."

Lalo flinched; the moan was an old one, repeated constantly. "Mum, go to bed, get some sleep," she urged her. "Things will look better tomorrow."

Slowly Leda rose to her feet, her hands fiddling with her bleached hair. "I'll go to the hairdresser – get a re-style, cheer myself up."

"Yes, do that. And take your medicine, Mum. You know it keeps your spirits up."

Leda nodded, already thinking of the shopping trip on the morrow, her slippers making scuffing sounds on the carpet as she left.

The night wore on, past eleven, past midnight, the moon high and clear, Lalo sitting still, her thoughts running over and over repeatedly. The front door opened then closed, Deandra's feet moving up the stairs, the click of the lock sounding on her bedroom door; then silence. Another half an hour passed, then came the sound of other feet, and a slow, heavy knock on her door.

"Come in."

Harewood walked into the room, smiling, his thinning hair combed back from his face, his expression weary.

"How's things?"

Lalo smiled, gesturing for her father to sit down on the side of the bed. "Fine."

"Really?" he asked. "Everything all right with your mother now?"

"Well, we're talking again."

He nodded. "Good, good."

"Daddy …"

Harewood turned, he was getting thinner, worrying and working too much. "What is it?"

"I've got something to tell you."

"Yes?"

"I've met someone … someone I really care about." Lalo paused, steadying her voice. "I met him at Misia's – he's a friend of Alberto's and Drago's."

"A doctor?"

She nodded. "A surgeon – he's brilliant, Daddy, really clever. And he's going to do well, everyone says so. Alberto said that he's going to the top." She paused.

"What's he called?" Harewood asked gently.

"Cy Greyling."

"And where does he come from?"

"He was born in Tangiers," Lalo said simply.

"Tangiers," Harewood repeated, clasping his hands together and staring at his feet. "Is he black?"

"Yes."

He sighed. "How old?"

"Thirty four."

Slowly he looked at his daughter. Harewood loved all his children, and although he was the closest to Deandra, he loved Lalo for her sweetness. She was sitting perfectly still in her velvet dress, her pale hair falling around her tiny face. A little elf, he thought lovingly, a good little urchin.

"This is a bit of a … surprise," he admitted at last. "How long have you known him?"

"Twenty-four hours."

Harewood laughed, then apologised when he saw the hurt look on her face. "Sorry, darling, but it is a bit sudden, isn't it?"

"I love him, Daddy."

"You can't. It's too soon."

"I know …" she admitted helplessly. "But it's real, not imagined. He feels the same way."

"He might say that."

"He's not a liar!" she snapped. "You haven't met him – how can you judge what he's like?"

"Ssh!" Harewood said kindly, "I'm not criticising him, I'm just don't want you to be hurt, Lalo." He stroked her cheek. "I don't want any man to hurt you."

"Cy won't hurt me, I know he won't."

"You think that now –"

"I'll always think so!" she said desperately. "He's the right person for me. There won't be anyone else, ever."

Harewood's voice was compassionate: "I know how you feel, believe me. I know what it's like to love someone blindly, knowing that you couldn't live without them; knowing that whatever they did, you would always want them – and only them."

"You mean Mum?"

"Yes," he admitted, glancing down at his hands, embarrassed by the admission. "I love her without logic, because I know she doesn't love me the same way. But that doesn't matter to me. I'd want her even if she hated me."

Lalo was touched by his confession. "Daddy, I feel about this man like you feel about Mum."

"But sweetheart, that's the point!" Harewood retorted. "I'm not happy. I don't regret marrying your mother, but I'm not happy – and I don't want you to be the same."

She moved over to him, laying her head on his shoulder. "But if he *could* make me happy – for all the drawbacks and all the problems – you'd back me up, wouldn't you?"

Harewood nodded. "I'd do anything to make you happy."

"So you'd support me whatever I decided to do?"

Harwood thought for a long moment. What did he want from life now? His own happiness, no, that was too much to ask, he could only hope that Leda's depressions were controlled and that he could curtail her extravagant spending. She would stay with him because she had no option; he would stay with her because he had no desire to leave. That was all he could expect for himself. But for his children? Deandra was sure to marry well, Tom was already the sportsman of the family, and Fraser was a down-at-heel teenage layabout, living on some other planet. Harewood smiled to himself – Lalo was born to be married; she had little interest in her artistic career and lacked the ambition to fight; she wanted happiness. And who had the right to deny her that?

"Lalo, think about this carefully –"

"I will, I will," she assured him.

"If you believe that you're right about this man, then go with your feelings." Harewood turned back to her. "You're twenty years old, not a baby, although you are to me," he smiled distantly and stood up. "Whatever you do I'll back you all the way."

"All the way?"

Harewood nodded. "All the way."

*

Cy was standing outside the hotel, waiting for her, Lalo getting out of the taxi and running over to him. It was nearly one o'clock in the morning, the moon white over the River Thames, the Embankment cold, without people. They held each other for a long moment and then began to walk, hand in hand, Cy almost a head taller, Lalo pulling the collar of her coat. Their communication was complete without words, Cy pausing by a lamp and then leaning over the parapet, his arm around Lalo.

"I love you," he said without preamble.

"I know," she replied, snuggling into his coat. "I love you too."

"We're mad."

She nodded. "But it's great, isn't it?"

"We have to talk," Cy said slowly, dreading the next words. "It can't work."

She stiffened. "NO!"

"Listen to me," he said, holding her tightly. "There are too many problems. My background, my age, my colour –

"It's because of Drago, isn't it?" Lalo replied, looking up into his face. "Alberto told me all about it – how he's taken you on and how he's put you up for Head of Surgery at the hospital in Rome." Her voice was disbelieving, "You think that if you want me, you're betraying him."

"I don't think that. But *he* would."

"And that's enough reason to run away?" Lalo asked, "Because of what Drago Razzio might say?" She pulled away from him, her voice wavering. "I've lived all my life with this feud – who said this, who said that. Bitterness, anger. How Drago blames Misia for Pila's death. The whole family's lived with the feud for generations. And to think that *you're* afraid of it. So afraid that you'd give us up just to avoid offending Drago Razzio."

"Lalo –"

Her pale eyes were hurt. "It's okay," she lied, "I understand. You're clever, you want to get on. You need his help … But Drago gave up everything for his career, and looks how wretched he is."

"But I owe him so much. I feel as though I'm betraying him –"

"By loving me?" Lalo sighed, her voice muffled. "It's your choice, Cy. I can't ask you to risk your future for me."

"It's not that simple!" he snapped, his frustration overwhelming. "It's not just Drago, I wish it were. There's more … Years ago I lived with a woman in New Orleans – I told Drago about it, but I didn't tell him the whole story. She was white. We were in love. She said it didn't matter about my colour: she said she could cope with racial discrimination. I think she even believed it. So she stood up to her family and came to live with me. But it got to her after a while, being parted from her parents, being talked about … In the end, she left me." He glanced over the dark water of the River Thames. "I knew she would, I told her she would, warned her at the start, but she was so *sure*," he sighed. "I couldn't work for nearly four months after she left. Couldn't sleep, couldn't think – couldn't stop my hands shaking. It took me years to recover. I never really wanted to fall in love again – and then I saw you." He touched her cheek tenderly. "I *can't* allow it to happen a second time. It would destroy both of us, and I love you too much for that. You'll find someone else. Someone similar background, age, colour –"

He stopped talking suddenly and caught hold of her, pressing his face against her shoulder, his head bowed. She could hear the muffled sobs and held onto him, her eyes filling. "I won't leave you."

"I can't risk it –"

"There *is* no risk," Lalo said firmly. "Wherever you go, I'll go. Whatever you do, I'll be with you … I'll never leave you. *Never.*"

And in reply Cy Greyling said nothing. Just held onto her as the moon swung higher and higher in the watching night.

# Fifty-Nine

Everything happened so quickly. The following morning Harewood woke to find a letter from his daughter on the hall table, whilst Alberto found a note posted through the letter box of the Holland Park house. Frowning, he read it and then passed it to Misia. They had gone, left in the early hours for Rome, Cy promising to tell Drago on his return, and swearing to take care of Lalo. I love her, he wrote, tell everyone that I love her and that I will do everything to make her happy ...

The letter was read by Misia then Portland, waking heavy with sleep and finding his wife sitting up in bed next to him, her hands cupped round a mug of tea.

"What is it?"

She laid the paper on his chest. "Read it and weep."

"Not another bill," he said, his eyes moving over the few lines rapidly. "Oh God, the power of love."

"It might be a good thing," Misia said suddenly. "I've been thinking – this might mean the end of the feud."

"How d'you make that out?"

"Well, if Drago takes to the idea of Cy marrying Lalo, it might reconcile the family. You know, bring the Bennings and the Razzios together."

"On the other hand, he might see it as a betrayal – his prodigy decamping to the other side."

She winced. "How *do* you think he'll take it?"

Portland groaned and got to his feet. "Badly," he said, padding into the bathroom. "Very badly."

*

Drago never thought that air could be so still; even winter air, bereft of bird song and chilled with cold. The marble floor seemed to seep through his shoes, clawing its way into his blood, his heart beating slower and slower as he listened. Cy had arrived on his doorstep that afternoon, a young woman sitting outside in his car, waiting. He had been hurried, his face anxious, worn from lack of sleep. How had his trip gone? Drago had asked, smiling and welcoming him in. It's so good to see you, tell me all about it ...

The pressure of the next words was unbearable; they dug into his ribcage, leaned on his skin, made indentations against his muscles, his breathing shallow. I don't want to hear anymore, Drago tried to say. Be quiet, stop it. Stop! ... But he couldn't speak, could only listen as Cy talked on, explaining, apologising, describing how he had fallen in love with one of the Benning offspring. One of the *Bennings*, Misia's granddaughter.

Drago was almost hysterical with disbelief. Of all the people in London, of all the woman he could have met – to pick a *Benning*. It was ridiculous, he wanted to say. Tell me it's a joke and we'll have a drink and a laugh about it. But it wasn't a joke, was it?

Drago thought. No, it was plotted, arranged so that the Bennings could steal the only person he had left. The person he cared most about. His prodigy, his successor.

They had taken him away, and he had gone willingly – walking into the enemy's camp without ever thinking of his mentor. Without giving thought to the debt he owed. I *made* you, Drago thought wildly, I took you in. You, a misfit, an outsider – I made you respectable, feted, I made you in my own image, to follow me. His breath caught in his throat. I loved you … and how did you repay me? Drago thought blindly. You betrayed me, like all the rest … His bitterness swung around him, it made an odour on his skin, it cloyed against his lips, it dragged on his clothes. I gave you everything, he thought madly. *I made you.*

And I can *destroy* you, he thought, turning away, his footsteps loud on the marble floor. Cy followed, pleading with him to understand, his voice reverberating in the vacuum of the silent house. Slowly Drago climbed the stairs, his eyes fixed ahead: I will bring you to your knees, he swore, I will ruin your life and beggar you. I will punish you – and I will have my revenge.

*

He was quick to strike, merciless, poisoned with anger. Within an hour Drago had telephone the Chairman of the Board of the Italian Hospital to tell him that he had withdrawn his support from Cy Greyling. He was not ready to be Head of Surgery, he explained; nor did he feel able to lend his backing to the proposal that he might be retained as a consultant. The Chairman was alarmed, but unable to resist the request; Drago Razzio had the money and influence to dictate terms. And so, when Cy reached the hospital later he was told that his services would no longer be needed.

There was no point in arguing, Cy knew that. So instead he drove out to Drago's house, a storm brewing overhead as he arrived. He knocked and was refused admittance, the first lightning strike coming down as he ran around the back of the house, calling Drago's name at the windows. There was no response, the clouds scuttling across the dark sky, the thunder rolling down the lawns from the sinister dark hump of the maze.

He was soon drenched, his hair matted with rain, his dark skin running with water, the lightning crashing overhead as he moved to the study window and looked in. Breathless with distress, Cy was frantic. Not just at the loss of his position – but at the sudden and ruthless withdrawal of love. He had thought of Drago as a father and his rejection was too cruel to bear. Wildly, Cy banged on the study window, his voice calling his mentor's name. Screaming, pleading, to be let in.

His fists hammered against the glass, his head thrown back, his voice hoarse with distress. Then suddenly he saw a movement inside, Drago's chair turning as the lightning struck again and illuminated his face. Startled, Cy stepped back, the rain plummeting against his body, the thunder crashing overhead, his eyes fixed disbelieving on the figure in front of him.

Drago sat in his chair, his hands clenched. He was staring out at the figure at the window, his eyes black, unblinking, his mouth rigid. In that instant he was possessed by the demons which had driven him all his life. Pride, malice, envy and hatred pouring like acid from his skin.

# Sixty

"No more," Misia said quietly. "No more." She was throwing clothes into a suitcase, her face drawn, thin lipped.

Portland stood by the bed, watching her; "I'll go with you –"

"No," she said firmly, "I'm going on my own. Thanks for the offer, love, but I'd rather do this alone." She snapped the case shut, looking at her watch. "Vincent's driving me to the airport, the flight's at nine."

"I don't see what you can do," Portland said, carrying her case downstairs. "You haven't seen your brother for years. What makes you think he'll listen to you?"

"Oh, he'll listen," Misia replied, drawing on her gloves. "This trip is long overdue."

She had taken the decision to go to Rome only minutes after talking to her granddaughter, Lalo tearful over the phone, her voice almost incoherent. "… he turned on him, Nana, just turned his back on him. All the things he'd promised Cy, all the things he'd said … he just rejected him. Oh God," she said helplessly. "You should see him, he's desperate … and it's all *my* fault."

"No," Misia said adamantly, "it's Drago's fault. It was his choice to do what he did. Where are you now?"

"At Cy's flat."

"And where is he?"

"He went out for a walk," Lalo blustered. "He said he'd be back soon. You should have seen his face, he was heartbroken."

"Stop panicking, I'll sort it out –"

"I should never have come to Rome!" Lalo cried. "I've ruined everything for him."

"STOP IT!" Misia snapped. "Stop it now! You've done nothing, you hear me? Drago's the guilty one: he's the one who has to answer for this." Her voice quietened. "Now, I'm coming over to Rome –"

"But –"

"Don't argue with me! I'll be over as soon as I can. Tell Cy not to worry. And don't you worry either … Have you had something to eat?"

Lalo laughed weakly. "Oh, Nana, what *are* you talking about?"

"Food," Misia replied. "Get some and eat it. It'll pass the time until I get back in touch."

As arranged, Vincent drove his mother to the airport, standing with Portland as they watched her walk to the plane. She was seventy one years old, moving quickly, her head erect, spoiling for a fight.

"Well," said Portland, "I don't fancy Drago's chances. If this was a match, how many rounds would you give it?"

"I wouldn't," Vincent said anxiously, watching his mother's figure move out of sight. "I reckon it could be a knock out."

"No bets on who gets knocked out?"

Vincent gave his father a wry look: "I never bet on a certainty."

They made light of it, but inside both of them were worried about the trip. They had tried to persuade her not to go, but Misia had been determined. The feud had gone on too long. She might have learned to live with it, but she was damned if it was going to ruin the lives of any more members of her family. If Drago Razzio wanted a fight, then he could have one. With her.

*

## Rome

Climbing into the taxi, Misia gave the address to the driver and settled back into her seat. She wasn't tired, wasn't afraid, she was just cold and bitterly angry. There had been a snowstorm, the soft unexpected whiteness clouding Rome, the streets dusted, the windows iced. It was dark, very dark, and colder than she expected, the city floodlights illuminating banks of statues and lighting the dark entrances of a hundred alleyways. The car hummed along, the radio playing an English tune – a pop song Misia had heard Lalo play only weeks before. Breathing in deeply, she glanced out of the window and watched the city disappear, the long stretch of the buildings dropping off one by one, the countryside coming into view, dark and empty.

She expected nothing; anticipated nothing; but when the driver paused at the entrance to the gates, Misia sat transfixed and looked at the palazzo before her. It was vast, bleak under floodlights, the windows unlit. Climbing out of the car, she paid the driver and refused his offer of help, picking up her case and walking towards the entrance alone. Dear God, she thought, this is an achievement, this is magnificent – and as inviting as the grave.

At the door she paused, then rang the bell, hearing footsteps coming from a long way away off before a man appeared.

"Si?"

"I want Dr. Razzio," she said simply, moving past him into the hall, the servant following her and gabbling angrily in Italian. Unconcerned, Misia laid down her case and looked about her, taking in the marble floor, the vast gilded staircase and the painted cupola above. She was composed, the man exasperated, hurrying off to find his master.

Come on, Drago, she willed him, come out and fight.

Silence. Stillness. No movement from anywhere.

Come on, she urged him, I've come a long way for this.

A fall of footsteps on the floor of the corridor above; urgent, heavy footsteps walking towards the stairs.

Misia glanced up, almost smiled. He was coming down, he was angry at being disturbed. Come on, Drago, come on.

His face was heavier than she expected, his hair white, his expression sour with bitterness as he approached, not recognising her, only annoyed at being interrupted.

"What is it?" he asked, then stopped suddenly. His eyes fixed on her face and then slowly he recognised her. "Misia?"

295

She nodded. "Yes, Misia."

He was wrong-footed. "What do you want?"

"I want to settle an old score."

He walked away, Misia following him into the study and watching as he closed the door. "You don't want us to be overheard? I understand, I doubt that you'll like what I have to say –"

"You weren't invited here."

"Don't try and intimidate me!" she hissed. "I'm not afraid of you, Drago. I never have been, and I never will be. You've always been a bastard, but this time you've excelled yourself." Misia walked towards her brother, leaning over the desk behind which he had seated himself. "I know what you've done to Cy –"

"It has nothing to do with you."

"IT HAS EVERYTHING TO DO WITH ME!" Misia shouted. "Lalo is my granddaughter, she loves Cy, she wants to marry him, and you're trying to ruin him, just because you think he betrayed you." Her voice was hard edged with fury. "You and I started this feud and you and I will end it, Drago. I don't care how you hate me, and God knows, I realise that if you could have done, you would have ruined me by now. I don't care what you think about me, but I *do* care about my children and my grandchildren – *and you won't harm them!*"

Drago's face was impassive: "I think you should leave."

She moved so quickly that he couldn't stop her, swinging back her arm and sweeping all the papers off his desk. They fluttered in the air momentarily then landed on the floor by her feet.

"Don't patronise me! I WON'T take it from you," she roared. "You must stop now, Drago, stop it before it goes any further. Cy Greyling has does nothing to injure you, he deserves his chance. Christ knows, you had yours! Our parents gave you every opportunity and you took everything from them without even a thank you." She paused, glancing round the room. "No photographs, Drago? No pictures of your wife, your children?"

"My wife and daughter are dead."

"But you have a son."

"Who hates me!" he spat the words out. "That must please you, Misia, to know how I've been cheated out of love. My wife and Pila dead, my son estranged from me. How you must gloat …"

"Don't judge me by your own standards."

He rose to his feet slowly, walking round the desk and standing in front of her. Tall, imposing, his voice low. "I know how you've sneered, laughed at me behind my back. Did Alberto tell you about Courtney? About my vile son?" His eyes were dilated with hatred. "I bet he did! He's been feeding you all the gossip for years. I can't operate now, did he tell you that?" Drago asked, waving his hands in front of his sister's face. "I'm crippled, finished. Or so I thought – and then I met Cy Greyling. My natural successor."

Misia stood her ground; Drago irrational, vicious as he continued: "I loved him like a son. He was the son I *should* have had. You have three sons, Misia, three healthy sons. What does that feel like, to have three heirs?"

"I'm not here to talk about my children –"

"Oh, but I *want* to hear about them," he said with mock interest. "I want to hear about how well they're doing, and about their children. I have two grandchildren, Misia. David and Lomond – did Alberto tell you about them? Did he tell you that Lomond was crippled? Well, *did he?*"

Misia refused to back down. "I know about Lomond, yes."

"But your grandchildren are all in perfect health, aren't they?"

"So are yours. Ahlia and Norton are both thriving."

"But I don't see them much," he said coldly. "Norton only visits when it suits him and Ahlia has become something of a recluse – with your son. Funny how everything seems to come back to you, isn't it? My sister, always there, always doing so well, always the one to whom the others run. Why? *Why!*" he howled suddenly, his face only inches from hers. "Why did you take Pila? And then her children? You had them all. All I had was Cy – and you took him too." His voice was rising, spiralling upwards into the shadowed ceiling. "For Jesus' Sake, tell me *why*. Why have you hounded me all my life, why have you stolen from me? *You* made me feel all this guilt," he said, banging his chest with his fist. "It was *you*. And I hate you for it."

He moved towards her. Startled, Misia stepped back, then straightened up again. "What do you want, Drago?" she asked, her eyes steady. "D'you want to kill me? D'you think that would change anything? D'you think that would make you feel less guilty?" She moved forward, her brother now stepping back. "I am not afraid of you. I've come to warn you, Drago, that's all. And I want you to listen to me. You're an evil man, and you deserve to be punished for what you've done. You were always selfish, arrogant, self-obsessed, you deserved to be miserable. You wanted to succeed, well, you did. Well done, Dr. Razzlo, you're a very lucky man."

"I want you to get out!"

"I know you do," Misia replied calmly, "but I'm not ready to go. I've made allowances for you for too long; I've excused your spite to our parents, I've learned to distance myself because I thought you were poisonous. And I was right!" she said violently. "But I won't let you destroy anyone else."

Drago glowered at her defiantly: "I do as I like –"

"No!" she retorted, striking out at him and catching the side of his cheek. "No! If you want to hurt someone, then hurt me. Take me on, Drago: fight *me*! But not the others, not my family. They've done nothing to you – neither has Cy Greyling. He didn't betray you, you betrayed yourself a long time ago." She slammed her hand against his chest fiercely. "What happened to you? I loved you once, I loved that handsome boy. You were so talented, and we were all *so* proud of you. We talked about you all the time. *You!*" she repeated, pushing him again, driving the words home. "Guido loved you. He said you would make your name. *His* name." She jabbed at him again. "*I loved you so much*. You were my brother, you should have been my confidant, the man I should have looked up to and turned to. But I never could, because you changed, you grew up and the boy went away … I miss him, Drago, and I miss the man you could have been."

He turned, unable to look at her, unable to speak, his body hunched over the desk.

"What happened to you?" Misia repeated. "I'd have had you back anytime, I'd have welcomed you home," she reached out and touched his arm. "I never gloated over you.

Never. I *missed* you … Drago, listen to me, stop this vendetta against Cy Greyling. If you don't you'll damn yourself." She rested her hand on his shoulder. "You'll die alone, is that what you want? All your success for nothing?" her voice softened. "We're getting old, time's passing. I want to help you."

"I don't want to die alone …" Drago said at last, "I don't want to die alone."

"I promise you, you won't."

"It's too late!" he said helplessly, "too late."

"No, it's not too late!" Misia insisted, "I want my brother back. Come back to me. Please."

Distraught, Drago slid to his knees, his head resting against the side of his desk; "I'm sorry, Oh God, I'm so sorry …"

"I know," Misia replied, kneeling beside him, "but it took you a hell of a long time to say it."

# Sixty-One

Pax. Peace – the quiet time coming after trauma. Stillness – each portion of each family settling, hostilities dissolving in the decade of the eighties, relationships shifting with deaths and births, and the coming of new blood. The feud had ended, Drago and Misia sharing an uneasy, but determined friendship; Drago making his peace with Cy and welcoming Lalo, seeing their marriage as his last chance and his final opportunity for redemption. Yet although Drago was relieved, almost optimistic, he was also shamed, finally seeing his actions for what they were – the behaviour of a malicious and spiteful man.

He accepted the salvation offered, but never fully recovered from the guilt of what he had done. In the vast house he wandered amongst his offspring, Nancy visiting with her children, Lomond handicapped, inheriting the dark red hair of her mother and the oblique eyes, David taking on the look of the Razzios – Italianate, heavy lidded, sombre. Lalo and Cy visited Drago too, constant and loving callers, Cy taking over the position of Head of Surgery at the Italian Hospital, his reputation increasing steadily. Drago's support reliable, unchallenged.

Contrary to what everyone expected, the Greylings had no children. Lalo had always longed for them and expected that life would follow its simplistic familial course – but it didn't. Some freak imbalance of the genes had made her sterile, cheating the most maternal of women out of her rightful role. She visited numerous specialists, but there was never any hope offered. There would be no children, there would be no heir … Cy accepted the news calmly to minimise his wife's distress, but Drago saw it as yet another peevish trick of Fate. His successor would have no successor. Cy Greyling was to be the end of the line.

Of course there was always Courtney, but he was never predictable and as the years passed he veered dangerously between periods of stability, and vengeful, unprovoked attacks. As Drago's bitterness faded, his son's increased: he was now jealous of the Bennings and resentful of their success. Had he applied himself, he could have been a major talent, but his character was too capricious to pursue any goal with conviction and as he aged he became idle. Not that Nancy didn't try to encourage him. After years of effort, her career had thrived. She was well known and travelled extensively, holding fashion shows all over Europe and later in her native America – but her husband remained stubbornly and wilfully resentful.

Long years spent struggling had prepared Nancy for the success and her natural optimism dictated that she enjoy it. Her home life might be insecure and unpredictable; but she adjusted. She had her children, and her purpose in life. She enjoyed them too, and whilst they were young Nancy took them with her everywhere, Lomond's condition treated as a minor inconvenience. It was largely due to her mother's attitude that Lomond never became bitter; she was treated normally – except for the fact she was in a wheelchair.

"Come on, hurry up," Nancy chided her. "I can't hang around all day."

Lomond came in, puffing with exertion, guiding her wheelchair down the hall. "I'm coming as fast as a can!"

"Well, make it faster, honey, or I'll have a have a motor fixed to the back of that thing."

She encouraged her daughter to do well, and when Lomond applied for University to study Design she bought her a specially adapted car to celebrate.

"But can she handle it?" David asked her, looking at his sister anxiously.

"Sure, she can handle it," Nancy said firmly, her American accent unchanged despite all her years spent in Rome. "Don't underestimate her. If she has confidence, she can do anything."

It helped that Lomond also had her mother's personality, whereas David was intense by nature; a doubting, uncertain young man. He was never malicious like his father, but he was a drifter, unsure of his role in life. It did not help that he had never really been close to Courtney. Not that anyone was – except his greasy coterie of friends, the jaded cronies with whom he mixed: the people who hung around him and flattered the money out of his wallet. Courtney knew they were worthless and in return, despised them and belittled them, watching as they all fell head long through the eighties, drunk, running on cocaine and moving miserably from bed to bed.

He was still promiscuous himself, until the Aids scare – and then Courtney reined in his sexual activities and began to find his pleasure elsewhere – in gambling and drugs. He was a frequent cocaine user, and when he was on one of his binges he would go away for weeks at a time, returning sour and haggard, sniffing and blowing his nose.

"What the fuck are you looking at?" he asked Nancy one night, leaning over her worktable and staring hard into her face.

"Go to hell, Courtney," she replied, turning back to her designs, her tone cheerfully dismissive.

She had learnt long ago not to expect her husband to change and was able to adjust to his moods. When Courtney was agreeable, she was; when he was foul mouthed and violent, she ignored him. Long ago she had made a deal, and she was prepared to stand by it. And, as the years passed, Drago watched her with open admiration. Just as he watched his son with ill-concealed loathing.

Their relationship was built on mutual dislike; Courtney never forgiving his father for his support of Cy Greyling.

"So how's your little prodigy doing?" he asked, his face ravaged, his nostrils reddened.

Drago flinched. "Cy's doing very well," adding cautiously: "I heard that your last designs were well received."

"My frocks …" Courtney said sourly, "… are universally adored. I have scores of moneyed ladies queuing to buy." His hand moved to his mouth; even in his forties, Courtney bit his nails. "I'm a success, Father – it must be galling for you to be proved wrong."

Drago turned in his chair to face his son. "Can't we be friends?" he asked wearily. "After so long, do we have to keep fighting?"

Courtney leaned over his father, the gesture threatening: "Are you ready to die now?" he queried. "Now that you've made your peace? Now that your sister loves you again and everything's sooooo delightful? I suppose it's hard for you, Father – being so old and so near death – I mean, you *must* be afraid, thinking of everything you have to answer for." His voice was goading. "Do you think there's an after life? I do hope so – then we can meet up again and spend Eternity together."

Distraught, Drago tried to push him away, but Courtney was surprising strong, and kept leaning over his father, his hands on the arms his chair.

"I'm sorry, but I don't think I can be friends with you," he said, his tone deadly, "You see, I don't think I can let you off the hook so easily. I think it's my duty to remind you of the past. My mother and Pila –"

Drago pushed him away, suddenly panicked. *"Get out!"* he shouted, struggling to his feet. "Get out!"

Courtney nodded, straightening his jacket sleeves, his tone cloying. "All right … but I'll come again soon. Don't worry, your son will keep an eye on you."

For a long time after Courtney had gone, Drago was unnerved. He was tired, longing to hear Nancy's voice, or Lalo's, longing for Courtney's words to be obliterated, buried. The feud was *over*, there was no more bitterness. Everything was all right now, he assured himself. He was forgiven, loved … and yet inside Drago was riven by guilt and the fear of death.

Struggling to his feet he picked up the phone, his arthritic hands clumsily dialling the London number.

"Hello?"

The voice soothed him immediately. "Misia?"

"Drago! How goes it?"

"Fine. How are you?"

"Portland's got flu and he's in bed, and Vincent's at the hospital waiting for Annabel to give birth."

Drago closed his eyes, smiling: "So soon?"

"So soon," Misia echoed. "You should see him, what a panic! I've never seen anyone so bloody jittery." She paused. "It's a girl apparently. They had one of those tests –"

"Amniocentesis."

"Yeah, that one," she agreed, "so they know the sex already. I don't agree with it myself, it takes away the element of surprise – like looking at the answers before sitting the exam."

Drago laughed; "Let me know when the baby's born."

"Of course I will," Misia replied, adding deftly; "… now tell me what's worrying you."

"Courtney came to see me."

She drew in her breath; Misia had met Drago's son a year before, and been shocked by his thin reptilian body and cadaverous face. Nothing had prepared her for the force of his malice. Be wary of him, she had warned her brother, please, be very wary of your son.

"I wouldn't see Courtney alone," Misia advised him. "When he comes, makes sure someone's with you."

"I can't, I never know when he's going to arrive."

"Then get your servants to tell him that you're out – unless there's someone else there."

Drago hesitated. "Do you think he's that dangerous?"

"I don't know," Misia replied honestly, "and that's what frightens me."

Drago put down the phone, then turned nervously as he heard the door open. But it wasn't his son, it was Cy, coming in smiling and throwing down a pile of case notes on his desk. He was distinguished now, his manner easy. Time and success had made him wealthy: Lalo had made him happy.

"Look at this," he said, passing Drago some case notes. "Tell me, what would you do?"

Drago took the papers clumsily, his fingers buckled, his movements awkward. He knew that Cy was perfectly able to manage without his help; he didn't need advice, he had come merely as a kindness, keeping his mentor informed, interested.

"... I'd do just as you suggested," Drago said, having looked through the notes. "... that procedure should work well."

He tried to sound enthusiastic but he was surprised as his limited interest. The work which had once consumed him had lost its magic: he might try to affect enthusiasm but he was old, beyond following the new innovations, his brain no longer as alert. A few years earlier his decline would have panicked him, but now Drago was interested in other matters. His life was closing down and he was eager to make amends; no longer proud, he was too lonely to be selfish.

"Tell Lalo to come and see me," he said to Cy. "Nancy's coming with the children tomorrow – will you ask her to join us?"

"Sure. She'd love to come," he bent to pick up his case and then paused, realising that the room had changed.

Then he saw them. The ranks of photographs which for years had been regulated to the storeroom were now newly displayed, row on row of faces replacing the old collection of surgical instruments. The human taking place of the inhuman. Cy walked over, mesmerised by the study of a blonde woman in white: and one of a girl laughing, sultry and fine boned, her smile showing the slight irregularity of her teeth. There were later pictures too – the dark girl holding a baby, then the same woman with two children – a son and daughter. She was older then, no longer smiling, her expression resigned.

So this was Pila, Cy thought, this was the daughter who had been killed ... Curiously he picked up her picture and stared into her eyes; dark, drowning eyes; eyes that caught the viewer and urged them not to look away.

"She was lovely," Drago said suddenly, looking over his shoulder.

Cy nodded. "Yes, she was." He turned and pointed to the blonde woman. "Was that your wife?"

"Catherine," Drago said quietly, almost as though she might hear her name and answer.

"Why did you put the pictures on display?"

Drago paused; why? To bring them home, to let them back into the house and his heart. "I want them with me," he answered, "It's important now."

Alerted by the one of his voice, Cy turned and studied the old man's face. Drago was in his eighties, the fierceness of his energy going out and a soft and limpid kindness coming in its place. He is preparing to die, Cy realised, he's surrounding himself with the past and making his peace, begging for forgiveness before the light fails.

# Sixty-Two

**France**

Ahlia had no thought of death, she was lying on her back on the bed in the farmhouse, breast feeding her son. The day was hazy, a June morning in St. Joryde de Chalais, the mist lifting under the sunlight, the smell of mown grass sweet, a blackbird calling from across the field. In the distance a church bell rang out from the hill, the cheap tin spire replaced long ago, a slow procession of figures moving. Black against the humming sky.

She dozed, her son falling asleep against her breast, his hair damp against her skin. Simeon had finished his book and had it published to blasting reviews. To the public he was now exposed as a crank, and worse, a fake. The response had crippled him, the migraines returning as he ran away from London back to the farmhouse. Back to Ahlia, back to the seclusion and the unjudgmental stillness.

"They're fools," Ahlia told him, her face the impassive Crivelli Madonna, "don't let them stop you."

"What did *you* think of the book?" Simeon asked.

He was very tanned, his eyes darkly shadowed, his hair thick and surprisingly grey. For years she had studied him, watching Simeon whilst he was working, sitting with him with the migraine attacks came, and listening. In time Ahlia had become the family chronicler, the holder of the past, and in time she came to know everything about Guido and Mary Razzio, about Fitting Billy, and about the time Simeon had had a vision of her running into the street as a child.

He had apologised to her many times over the years, explaining that he hadn't known what was going to happen or he would most certainly have helped her. They were premonitions, flashes: he went on helplessly: glimpses, no more … She always reassured him, her face still, impassive. It doesn't matter, she said, forget it, please …

After such talks, Simeon expected her to confide, to finally tell him what she had seen that night her mother died – but Ahlia never confessed. She never spoke about the accident. Or about her father. To her, Caryl de Solt was no more; she didn't speak to him or write to him. Only Norton was regularly in touch with Caryl. He was working in Holland as a physicist, and occasionally visited his father. After such occasions he would write to Ahlia, the letters read and then put away without comment, Simeon waiting for the confession he believed was certain to come.

But never did. The years glided past, the outside world with all its outside problems as distant as a dream. The farmhouse at St. Joryde de Chalais was remote physically and mentally from the world of other men; its two occupants seen as strange and somehow sad. No one knew that Simeon was a writer, although once he had had a vision of an accident concerning one of the village children. He had got up and dressed, hurrying over the fields whilst the morning was still coming to life, the long grass wet against the back of his hands. The woman had been wakened by his knocking, standing in her dressing gown, dull eyed from sleep as he explained what he had seen.

She had difficulty understanding but finally agreed to what Simeon suggested, listening at the dishevelled man on her doorstep, the reclusive Englishman who had seldom spoken to anyone in the village. *It's the car,* Simeon said fiercely, *look at the car …* She had nodded, pulling her dressing gown around her, watching as Simeon retraced his steps home across the fields, his eyes shaded with his hand, a migraine tearing into his skull.

He became a celebrity after that. The car *had* been faulty, the family outing postponed, tragedy averted. How had he known? they asked themselves, the woman taking food over to the farmhouse and leaving flowers by the back door. And so Simeon became their resident Magus, Ahlia his ethereal companion, and when her baby was born tributes arrived, the child welcomed. Who was the father? They asked, and they whispered about some man who had come to work nearby. It must be his child, they said. Surely it couldn't be Simeon's?

The same question was being repeated in England.

"Don't even think it," Portland warned his wife. "It won't be Simeon."

"But they won't say *who* it is!" Misia replied heatedly. "When I spoke to him he just said that Ahlia was keeping the father's name a secret. Can you imagine that!" she said, horrified. "Why does she have to hide everything?"

"It's her way," Portland said phlegmatically. "Ahlia never tells anybody anything. I wonder if the shock of Pila's death didn't change her more than we know –"

"She was *always* secretive," Misia countered. "Even as a child you never knew what she was thinking. Imagine having a baby out there in the wilds. God, what a life."

"She's with Simeon," Portland replied. "She's safer there than anywhere else."

"But it's not *normal* –"

Portland smiled. "For her, it is. If Ahlia chooses to come back into the world, she'll only do it in it her own time and in her own way – nothing we say will force her hand. You know that."

So whilst Ahlia bore her child in France, Vincent's wife, Annabel, gave birth to her daughter in the Portland Clinic in London, attended by most of the family, Vincent driven to paroxysms of anxiety. Doted on, Annabel was dizzily excited, their house – only streets from Misia and Portland's – filled with baby clothes, baby furniture, baby toys. The nursery decorated by the finest interior designer's, the nanny hired two months before the birth.

When she finally came into the world, Vincent's daughter was small, dark, with pointed ears and a heart shaped face; a mischievous baby, born to amuse.

"God, she's heavenly," he said, hanging for hours over the cot. "Look at her, look!"

Misia smiled wryly. "She's cute."

*"Cute!"* he exploded. "She's magnificent."

She was also born lucky. Grace, as she was called, was born smiling, like her father, her charm soon apparent. She would never be a beauty like Deandra, never as sweet as Lalo, or as secretive as Ahlia. She was her father's true child – as winning and precocious as he had been.

"So many babies," Misia said. "It's nice to be a great-grandmother."

"Grace is like you," Portland said, smiling. "You watch how she grows up, I tell you, that child is going to be a dead ringer for you."

Misia smiled at him, then wondered. The children had brought new life into the family, the feud over, the bitterness dissolving in a mess of new lives and new families. A steady peace had descended, the Razzios and the Bennings criss-crossing information. Misia was now in touch with Nancy; Deandra was in touch with Simeon; and – most surprising of all – Lalo had begun to visit Ahlia in France.

At first it had been a simple visit to view the new baby, Lalo coming on a whim, bearing gifts, Ahlia opening the door of the farmhouse with Michel in her arms. She paused, recognising Lalo and yet, for an instant, wondering why she had come – then she invited her in, laying her son in the wooden crib in the kitchen.

Warm in the June weather, Lalo's skin was flushed pink, her pale-lashed eyes fixing on the baby.

"He's handsome."

Ahlia smiled distantly, making coffee, the aroma filling the basic kitchen and drawing Simeon downstairs.

"Lalo!" he said delightedly, hugging her and then holding her at arms length. "You look happy."

"I am," she replied, "I also read your book – it was amazing."

"It was slaughtered."

"But you'll write more, won't you?"

"I haven't the sense to stop," Simeon replied, gesturing for her to sit down. "Can you stay?"

Ahlia paused, her hand holding the coffee pot.

"Well, I've booked a room – "

"You stay here!" he said, his dark eyes fixed on hers. Lalo smiled, wanting to remain.

"If it's no trouble …"

Ahlia turned and passed her a cup of coffee; her expression unreadable. "It's no trouble, Lalo, you're welcome."

They ate dinner with the front and back doors open to allow what little breeze there was to skitter through the house. The old beams over their heads seemed to trap the heat, the wooden floors warm under their bare feet. The night was loaded with the sound of crickets, the church bells peeling out over the listless air.

"They're practising," Simeon said, leaning back in his chair. "Every Thursday, they practice."

Lalo smiled drowsily, Ahlia's eyes fixed on her son, Simeon finishing his wine. "How's Cy?"

"Doing well," she said warmly.

"No regrets then?"

Lalo burst out laughing, the sound ringing out with the bells. "No, no regrets! We've had some problems, people are bigoted, but then people aren't just bigoted about colour, are they?"

He smiled at the remark. "Are you happy?"

"Yes …" Lalo replied, pushing her hair behind her ears.

"Except for?"

She laughed again, embarrassed, Ahlia keeping her head turned away.

"Go on," Simeon urged her, "tell me."

"I would have been really happy if I'd had children," she shrugged, as if it didn't matter, "but it didn't happen."

The bells were ringing out loudly, then they stopped, the echo plaintive as Simeon looked across the table and then took Lalo's hand. "You'll have a child," he said simply.

She shook her head, almost afraid to believe. "No, Simeon – I *can't*."

He was still holing her hand. "Don't you believe me?" he asked, "You should, I'm telling you the truth – I see you with a child."

She was distressed and took her hand away, turning to find Ahlia looking at her.

Her expression was as sphinx-like as it always was. "Believe him," she said evenly. "He's never wrong."

"But it's not possible!"

Ahlia was sure. "If Simeon sees you with a child, then it will happen," she said, rising to her feet and standing by the door.

Curious, Lalo turned to Simeon. He was peeling an orange, the smell pungent, acidic on the heated air. They are out of time, she realised suddenly, two people hiding, walking away from life. Her eyes moved to the walls, to the symbols painted on the whitewash; pentangles, crosses, images she didn't understand, and others she had only seen in Simeon's book. The family conscience, Misia had once called him. The mystic.

Aware of her scrutiny, Simeon looked up.

"I'm all right," he said quietly, reading into her thoughts. "This was what I chose." Far away the bells began to ring, their sound sweetly mournful as he spoke again. "You'll have a child, Lalo, I promise you."

# Sixty-Three

## Liverpool

"Vincent, she's not a pet!" Misia said hotly, as she watched her son carrying Grace in the crook of his arm. "She should be with Annabel."

"She needed a rest –"

"So she let you bring the baby *here*?" she asked, following him into the gym at the World's End.

He looked at his mother in amazement. "I seem to recall that your father toted you about with him everywhere. How come it was all right for you and not for her?"

"Things were different –"

"Like hell!" he said happily, watching Grace as she hiccupped.

"She's got wind now," Misia replied, taking the baby from her son and sitting down to pat Grace's back. "And another thing, that Terry Gibbs put up a good fight. You should let him go for the title."

"I can't, we're not ready. I need another trainer since Abbot died."

Misia looked down at the baby. Abbot dead; the last of the old school gone. "There must be someone else."

Vincent nodded. "There is, an Italian called Carlucci – Max Carlucci."

"He's with Norman Tort."

"Not any longer," Vincent replied. "I talked to him last night and he wants to change. I thought you might like a look at him."

Misia smiled. "What notice would you take over what an old woman thought?"

He leaned down towards her, smiling: "None – I just wanted a babysitter, that's all."

Grimacing, Misia changed the subject. "This Carlucci – why pick an Italian?"

"*Why pick an Italian!*" Vincent repeated laughing. "This business was *started* by an Italian – your father."

"I know that, but Guido was a one off – I'm not sure about Carlucci."

"You always say that," her son responded confidently, "but you should trust me, I know what I'm doing."

He did. Vincent had, in fact, made a fabulous success of the boxing and the casino. All Misia worst anxieties had been allayed; No. 100 Belington Row was exclusive, the rougher element of the gaming world barred from its luxurious doors. Membership was strict and the employees were all vetted by her or Vincent. Croupiers, pit bulls, managers and PR men were checked and re-checked, their references scrutinised.

From the first Vincent had been aware that his contacts with the boxing world might make some people suspicious about his opening a casino; he knew enough about the press to realise that his good luck invited envy and that some people would love to see him fail. He was aware that he had lead a charmed life. His career had been a luminous success and his marriage was a happy one. If any man had been lucky, he had. But Vincent was clever enough to know his advantages; and astute enough to avoid conceit. He might be easy going with the press and give nonchalant, charming performances on the television, but his brain was sharp and he was well aware of his competitors. In the past he had only had himself to protect, but now he had to defend his adored family and ensure that nothing tainted the Benning name.

Of all the Benning Brothers he had seemed the one least likely to the bothered by such matters, but as he became older, Vincent understood what his name meant and he was sufficiently proud of it to guard it fiercely. Harewood was as proud of his name as Vincent, but life had not been as easy for the elder brother. He had been unfortunate in his work: following Portland he had had to shoulder the formidable burden of his father's reputation, but he had, by dint of fearsome effort, made his own mark in the legal world. Complicated briefs became his forte, and after winning one particularly intricate fraud case, Harewood had the pleasure of seeing his name – temporarily – as well known as Vincent's.

His sudden prominence delighted Leda, who had suffered a severe set back after Lalo married Cy Greyling. It was of no use anyone telling her how successful Cy was, he remained, above all, a different race. In Leda's prejudiced eyes, his colour obliterated his acclaim and shamed her. Nothing anyone said could stop Leda believing that people were talking behind her back and every comment was misconstrued and twisted.

Her mental state, always precarious, fluttered unnaturally between stability and paranoia, her medication increased. Gradually, as Leda began to see a variety of specialists and psychiatrists, she mixed her drugs and once plummeted into unconsciousness, Deandra finding her and ringing for an ambulance. In hospital she received more counselling, but her malaise was too deep rooted and her depression was now fixed on the inescapable fact of her age and her children's growing independence.

Leda had always been a feckless mother; capricious, at times loving, at times dismissive; the children, for the most part, bringing themselves up. But now they had left home: Tom backpacking across Europe, and Fraser, untidy, monosyllabic Fraser, working as a maths teacher in Streatham. Only Deandra promised to live up to her mother's aspirations – her fabulous beauty enticing men and, hopefully, money. Avidly Leda watched her daughter's progress, cut out her clippings in the papers, framed her first headline – THE BENNING BEAUTY – and lavished attention on her. Deandra responded by being the only one of the children who still lived at home; her affection for her father unchanging.

In fact, she was the focal point of Harewood's life. He might love his wife to distraction – but it was to his daughter that he turned for companionship. Whilst Leda railed overhead, they sat together in the kitchen. When the bills came in betraying her ridiculous spending sprees, it was Deandra who calmed him. And when Harewood was exhausted by a case and desperate to talk, it was his daughter who listened. They treated Leda as they would a sickly child; she was bloated, getting fat, her hair bleached. Tiresome and tiring, pathetic and self absorbed – but she was needy and they nursed her.

Any mention of hospitalisation was dismissed. No, Harewood said emphatically, his wife was better at home. They could cope. Nurses came and left the house at St. John's Wood, staff staying for weeks and then handed in their notice, Deandra supervising the day to day running of the home. She saw her father as the perfect male, caring and constantly reliable, the men in her life forever held up to comparison and found wanting.

At times Harewood urged her to get away. "You should, it would be better for you. The atmosphere's not good here."

She shook her head, the Japanese doll haircut falling onto her shoulders. "No, Daddy, it's okay. I'm fine."

"But it's not right, it's *not*."

He was easy to persuade. "When the time's right, then I'll go, but not before," Deandra said, kissing him on the cheek. "You and I are in this together, remember?"

She kept in touch with her sister, Lalo, and relied on Vincent to provide her with amusement. He, in his turn, was delighted to have his niece's fantastic presence at the fights and knew that where Deandra Benning went – the press followed. In such a way they kept the status quo, and managed to hide the full truth of Leda's condition; only Harewood's sound legal career making the headlines.

But they were well aware of the tight rope they walked, and although Harewood loved his brother, he knew that Simeon could offer no help. He was too removed: the third Benning Brother's physic abilities fodder for the down-market papers, his peculiar home life gossiped about. Of the three brothers, only Vincent had nothing to hide; and so he became the one stolid core of the family.

But he had only one fear. Misia and Portland were old; their time short. He was pleased that the feud was over, that Drago and his mother had finally been reunited, but he knew that he was the one who carried the heaviest burden for the future. He was the man most likely to succeed, the steady hand who held the full cup. In time his parents would die; but that was a reality too wounding to contemplate. For the present the gods were being kind. The Razzios and the Bennings were at peace, and the days were long and full of promise.

It was a charmed time – an enchanted, tinkling moment of calm which portended change. They all felt it, for once the brothers in complete unison. There was a storm coming, a charge in the air. From where, none of them knew; from whom, none of them could guess; but each hung onto what happiness they had. And waited.

# Sixty-Four

**Two years later.**
**December**

Drago was dead.

"No," Misia said simply. "No …"

"I'm sorry," Lalo replied, her voice soft over the phone line.

Misia sat down in the hallway, her eyes unfocused. "Just tell me he didn't die alone."

"No, I was there," Lalo said quietly. "He didn't feel anything, he just said he was tired and wanted to go indoors." She had watched Drago walk into his study and begin to clean his collection of old surgical instruments. Surprised, Lalo had told him she would do it: but he hadn't seemed to hear her, his hands working away, polishing, cleaning.

"He was fine, talking about Cy, and then about you," Lalo paused, "he said he was thinking of surprising you – going over to England for Christmas."

"But he didn't die alone?" Misia repeated, wanting to be sure that the promise she had made had been kept.

"No," Lalo reassured her. "He finished work and then he sat by the window and began to talk … He asked me if I thought that he'd done anything important."

"Have I?" Drago had asked, "Would you say that my life was worthwhile?"

She had moved over to him, leaned on the back of his seat and looked out over the garden. The fountain was turned off, the water still.

"You've done more than any man could have hoped."

"I was cruel," Drago had replied, "Do you think that God forgives cruelty?"

Lalo frowned. "He forgives everything," she had said.

"No," Drago replied, "not everything. It's conceit to believe that … I want to thank you, Lalo, and I want you to tell Cy that he made me very happy. I was lucky in the end." He had paused, breathing in deeply. "Tell Misia first."

Lalo's voice was gentle. "Believe me, it was very peaceful."

"Thank you …" Misia said dully. "Thank you for being there."

Slowly she put down the phone and rose to her feet, walking into the study and then into the dining room. Portland was cutting into a slab of cheese, Vincent sitting with the baby on his lap, Annabel laughing. Without saying a word, Misia moved to her seat, her eyes fixed on Grace. Death, birth, it was so simple, so expected, and yet so horrible. Drago had been old, eighty six, ready to die … And she was eighty one, she realised suddenly, *eighty one years of age.* Misia looked at her son. Does Vincent expect me to die soon? Is he waiting for the phone call, or for the summons to come? She was suddenly panicked, and glanced at Portland. He was *eighty eight,* she thought helplessly. I never realised how old you were, darling. I never admitted that you might die.

311

Misia rose to her feet, stumbling over the chair, her hands thrown out in front of her. In that instant she was afraid of death; afraid of the indignity, of the long march her father had taken to the grave – and most of all she was afraid of losing her husband, the man who had been so much a part of her life. Struggling to her feet, Misia waved aside help and stood up, pulling on her coat and walking into the garden. It was a bitter night, offering no comfort as she moved briskly down the lawn and paused by the ruined summerhouse. There she leaned her head against the wood.

"Let me die first, please. Let *me* die before Portland," her voice was soft, for once wavering. "But if I can't go first, let him die easily. I don't care about me, but please don't let him suffer." Misia paused, her gaze turning upwards to the blank sky: "Drago, if you can hear me, then do this for me. You owe me that much."

There was silence. No sound, no indication that he had heard, and yet Misia felt suddenly comforted and a moment later walked back to the house.

\*

"What a first rate bastard," Vincent said simply, looking at his mother.

"But a good trainer," she replied. "I think you should take Carlucci on."

"On what – trial or trust?" he responded, nodding to Johnny Duncan and he moved into the ring and began to spar.

The gym was full, several new boxers coming in to work out for Vincent. Terry Gibbs had won the previous week, his face splashed over the tabloids, Vincent fielding interviews. They had a Champion again, Misia thought delightedly, after so long they had a World Champion again. The Benning Boxers were the best, she thought proudly. The best.

"Carlucci wants too big a percentage of the fight price," Vincent went on. "I don't like it."

"So talk to your lawyer," Misia retorted, turning at the sound of Annabel's voice.

She came in tiny, blonde, silly, carrying Grace aloft, the fighters gathering to take a look at the baby.

Vincent's scowl softened and his face assumed a goofy, soppy expression. Oh, boy, Misia thought grinning, will this kid run rings round him when she grows up.

"Look at her," Vincent said giddily. "Isn't she fantastic?"

"Fabulous," Misia agreed dryly then changed the subject. "I'm going over to Rome for the funeral on Friday."

He shook his head. "I wouldn't, it's a hell of a long way and –"

Misia's voice was sharp. "For God's Sake, Vincent, don't treat me like a baby!"

"But that's not what Vincent means," Annabel said guilelessly, "he's worried about you being too old."

Misia made a snorting sound and turned to her son, "Have you ever thought about a getting gag for her?"

He put up his hands in mock submission. "Annabel didn't mean it to come out that way," he explained. "But we both think –"

*"I'm too old!"*

"For long trips, yes!" he snapped back. "Listen, be reasonable, I don't want you pushing yourself."

Misia had risen to her feet, her face set: "I've pushed myself all my life, Vincent, and I won't have you telling me what to do."

"I'm doing it for your own good. You're not taking Father, are you?"

"No," she said, her tone softening. "He's got a cold coming, I don't want to risk it."

*Risk it* … the words hung between the two of them for a catching instant.

"Well, if you must go, I'll go with you," Vincent said at last.

"No, I'm fine," Misia replied. "Nancy's invited me to stay at the palazzo. I'll be fine, honest, stop worrying."

Vincent frowned. "I don't suppose Courtney's going to like the way the will was drawn up."

"No. I don't suppose he will."

Of all the vast fortune that Drago had amassed through his work and his investments, not one lira was to go directly to his son. Instead he had left the money to Nancy for her to control, and she alone had inherited the palazzo. Other sums of money were left to Drago's grandchildren, Norton, Ahlia, Lomond and David. Also included was Ahlia's child, his great-grandson, Michel; and lastly Cy and Lalo. He was generous to everyone – including Misia, to whom he left his paintings and a small collection of drawings, labelled Guernico.

When he heard the news Courtney screamed at the top of his lungs. The sound was animal, frightening. Then he stood in the hall of the palazzo and faced Nancy, his tone bitter.

"Well, you did very well out of your little arrangement," he said sourly. "I suppose you and Father had it all worked out before we got married?"

Nancy motioned for their son to leave and waited until David's footsteps faded overhead. "I never planned this – I knew nothing about it."

"Don't bullshit me!" Courtney snapped. "You're nothing but a bloody whore, no better than a prostitute."

"You should know," Nancy replied evenly, "you've spend enough time with them."

He struck her suddenly, knocking her off her feet, David running down the stairs towards her.

*"Go back!"* Nancy shouted to him. "I can look after myself." He hesitated. *"GO BACK!"* she repeated, watching him reluctantly turn away as she rose to her feet. "You can do what you like now, Courtney. You can screw around and stick cocaine up your nostrils until your brains bleed, I don't care. But I warn you now, *I am in control*. If you treat me well, we can all get along fine. But if you push me," she fixed her turquoise gaze on him, "and if you *ever* hit me again – I'll make your life hell."

She turned away, Courtney following her and watching her as she climbed up the stairs. "I'm glad you inherited the house, darling, it's just like old times again," he said, his tone acid. "It's never been a happy place and it never will be. You think you've got me over a barrel, but you're wrong. I'll get my own back, don't you worry – don't you fucking worry."

The funeral was quick, unemotional, Misia returning to the palazzo with Nancy. "I'm surprised that Drago had the details of the will made known before the funeral."

Nancy shrugged. "I think he did it deliberately to force Courtney to show his hand in public."

It did. His son never came to the funeral.

"So what happens now?" Misia asked her.

"Life goes on. Lomond's studying and David's coming into the business with me." Nancy paused and then drew up in front of the palazzo. "I can understand Courtney's bitterness – imagine seeing someone else take all this away from you."

"But you're not 'someone else'," Misia responded, "you're his wife."

She laughed, amused. "I've no special place in Courtney's heart. No one has. That's what makes him so dangerous." She walked into the magnificent hall. "But I'm glad I can protect this place and make sure his children inherit it."

Misia glanced over her shoulder. Lomond was being pushed by her brother, the nineteen year old girl laughing, the boy reserved, old for his years.

"Will you live here?" Misia asked Nancy, aware of the quiet crypt-like atmosphere.

"Yeah," Nancy replied easily. "The old place just needs cheering up," she said, "a few parties and few young people will soon liven it up." She stopped in front of Pila's portrait. "What was she like?"

Misia looked up at the painting. What was she like? "Pila was …" Exotic, sensual, sitting in a pub on Fleet Street with her and Portland. "She was …" A good mother. A woman who loved too deeply. Pila was … murdered. Killed by the man she thought had saved her. "Pila was unlike anyone else," Misia said at last. Her eyes moved towards the terrace, banked by snow, unfriendly, cold. "I have to go home now, Nancy,"

"Hey, so soon?" she asked surprised, "I was hoping you could stay with the others."

"No, you've got plenty to cope with …" Misia replied, "and I want to get home."

Vincent was waiting for her at Heathrow the following morning and drove her home, talking about Max Carlucci and the fight he had organised for the following January. It was December weather, wet with slush, the capital turned into a quagmire, the car wheels throwing up the melting snow as Vincent talked on about Grace and the presents he had bought her, and how Simeon said he might be coming over for Christmas.

"Simeon?" Misia said, surprised.

Vincent nodded. "Yes, he said that he and Ahlia might visit with the little boy."

A cold chill settled on Misia and she leaned forwards, turning up the heater. *Simeon was coming home.* Why was her son coming home *now*? Had he seen something, sensed something? … Uneasy, Misia sat in silence for the rest of the journey and when they arrived back at the house in Holland Park she hurried out of the car and up the steps, throwing open the front door and calling out:

"PORTLAND! PORTLAND!"

Nothing. No sign, no movement.

Terrified Misia ran down the hallway, looking into the dining room and the kitchen and then running into the study. He was lying perfectly still, the paper on his lap.

"Portland!" she said frantically, *"Portland!"*

His eyes opened and he focused on her blearily. "What's the panic?"

"I thought … I thought you were dead," she said, stupid with relief.

He pulled her onto his lap, flicking at her fringe. "Well, I'm sorry to disappoint you."

I'll try harder next time."

"It was just that Vincent said Simeon was coming for Christmas, and for some reason I thought …" she trailed off, looking into his eyes. "What is it?"

"Alberto died this morning."

So Simeon *had* seen something. The death of a friend who had been long loved. She shivered, it was cold, the count down to Christmas, the family time of year. Only this year some of the regulars wouldn't be attending; they had other pressing commitments in places no one could guess at.

"*Alberto* … Is he really dead?"

Portland nodded.

"It's a bad time of year," Misia said at last, "Winter, the killing season." Her voice dropped, "You know, Alberto was a good friend, the best. Without him, Drago and I would never have got together again."

"He was fun too. Good company."

Wearily Misia closed her eyes, seeing Alberto by the French windows in the Liverpool house, smoking, the moonlight on his glasses …

"I'll miss him."

"*We'll* miss him," Portland corrected her.

"Yes, *we'll* miss him," she agreed.

Misia would never have admitted it to anyone, but it was a relief that Alberto had died, and not Portland. Relieved, she set about the Christmas preparations with relish. She was, all agreed, full of renewed life, her wiry figure clad in its inevitable trousers, climbing up the ladder to put decorations on the Christmas tree. The family was going to enjoy a huge celebration at Holland Park, Misia having invited Vincent and his family and Harewood and his, Simeon expected on Christmas Eve. As she had already anticipated, Ahlia did not come and remained with her son in St. Joryde de Chalais, Lalo remaining in Italy with Cy. Otherwise the house was to be full, Teller pulled out of retirement and pressed into service.

"I could have helped," Deandra told Misia in the kitchen.

"But Teller loves it," Misia replied, "besides most of the stuff comes from Mark and Spencer ready-made." She paused, uncorking a bottle of port. "How's your mother?"

"Not well," Deandra replied carefully. "She wanted to come, but the doctor advised against it."

"So she's on her own?"

"She's got a nurse … it's the way she wants it."

"She's got away with murder for years," Misia retorted, flinging the corkscrew to the back of the drawer. "I know she's your mother, but Leda should be hospitalised for a while. It would stabilise her."

"She's fine," Deandra said flatly, laying out some mince pies. "We can cope."

"Well, just make sure that you get to live your own life," Misia warned her. "Don't lose out."

They walked back into the dining room, Misia chivvying Teller along as he carried the turkey, the table full, another pressed into service to accommodate everyone. The noise was impressive, adults talking, Grace sitting in a high chair like a toy elf. Satisfied, Misia looked around at her family and then opened the dining room door, bending down to flick on the electric switch. In an instant the Christmas tree was a blaze of lights, a huge glistening triangle throwing off colours and patterning the walls like stained glass. There was a spontaneous round of applause, each pair of eyes fixed on the tree and then on the woman who stood beside it: Misia Benning, mother, grandmother, wife. She stood startled for a moment, and then gratefully accepted their affection, before lifting up her hands and returning to her seat at the head of table.

Later that night, when everyone had gone to bed, Misia sat alone in the dining room, leaving the door open to look at the lighted Christmas tree.

"Are you all right?"

She glanced round. Simeon stood by the table, darkly shadowed.

"I'm fine," she replied easily. "I just wanted to spend a little while on my own."

He nodded and walked out, passing the tree, the lights making a sudden Harlequin out of him.

Above her she could hear Portland laughing with Teller, and then the sound of the cistern being flushed. She was unusually content; she had had her husband and her family with her, and around her: the day had been peaceful, without incident and now she was comfortably tired. Misia's eyes fixed on the coloured lights, her mind wandering to the first tree she had ever bought with Portland, a three foot spruce which they had put up in the first house they owned.

So many years ago, so many lives ago … She sighed, smiling to herself, the tree hypnotic. I should move, Misia thought, should go to bed. But she didn't, and for a while longer she sat alone before finally moving upstairs. Portland was snoring already, and she undressed quickly sliding into bed and spooning her body against his back. His breathing was deep, rhythmic, his dreams peaceful, and within moments, Misia fell asleep.

She woke at dawn, surprised to find herself so alert. Sitting up in bed she turned and glanced at Portland, at the ugly wonderful old head on the pillow, and then she froze, her hand going out slowly, hesitating before touching his cheek. His skin was cool – the life just gone.

Portland was dead.

For a time Misia didn't move; she simply talked to him and stroked his head – and then finally she dressed, walking downstairs and turning off the lights on the Christmas tree.

# Sixty-Five

"Disasters always come in threes," Harewood said to Vincent, Simeon standing at the foot of the stairs in Holland Park house. "God, what a bloody awful month – Drago and Alberto dying and now Father," he paused, taking off his glasses and polishing them frantically to hide his feelings.

"I can't believe the old man's gone," Vincent replied, "I keep thinking I'm going to see him walk out of the study any minute and come over and join us." He turned to Simeon, "You knew, didn't you? That's why you came home?"

He nodded: "Yes ... I knew he was going to die."

Harewood put his glasses back on and glanced up the stairwell: "How d'you think Mother will take it?"

"I don't know," Vincent said simply. "I asked her to come and live with us, but she wouldn't hear of it. I can't see how she can live here on her own."

"Give her time," Simeon said thoughtfully. "Let her come to terms in her own way. She'll be all right, I know that much."

Vincent was hoarse with distress: "She'll miss him so badly ..."

Simeon nodded. "We all will."

There were messages from all over the world, the papers generous in their obituaries, the church full for the memorial service. Little offers of comfort came from unexpected sources, the Hapsburg Harpies sending Misia flowers, the man at the newsagent writing her a letter, and neighbours telephoning trying to explain how they felt. Portland Benning was dead – and missed.

Alone, Misia fell into a long stillness. Her sons worried that the loss of Portland might send her into a decline from which none of them could rescue her; but they were wrong; Misia was too much the child of Guido and Mary Razzio to give up. But she was inhumanely bereft, and turned to Deandra for comfort, clearing out Portland's clothes and the pitiful accumulation of his long life.

"Are you sure you want to get rid of these?" Deandra asked her grandmother as she packed the clothes Portland would never wear again.

"I don't need his things to remind me of him," Misia replied. "Besides, it's what he would want me to do."

They worked for the whole week after Christmas and when the New Year began they brought in 1993 quietly, the one person loved above all, missing from their midst.

317

# Sixty-Six

"I need more money," Courtney said furiously, pacing Nancy's studio. She had converted one of the many upstairs bedrooms of the palazzo into a workroom, her designs arranged from a variety of free standing gondolas, a drawing board placed under the window where the light was good.

"What did you do with your allowance?" she asked him, pushing past her husband to arrange some material over a tailor's dummy.

"I spent it – that's what you're supposed to do with money," he said sourly. "And I don't see why I should have to come begging to you."

"Your father left me in charge," Nancy said simply. "You've had what was due to you this month –"

"But I'm skint!" Courtney hissed, glancing maliciously at her work. "Jesus, don't tell me people buy this crap."

"I don't see why they shouldn't," she replied evenly, "they buy yours."

He winced, then blew his nose, his nostrils reddened.

"D'you think I don't know what you're spending the money on?" Nancy asked him. "Do I look that bloody stupid? Listen, Courtney, I don't care if you want to blow your allowance on coke – fine by me – but I won't support your habit when you've run out of cash."

Her husband's voice was sour, "Why the hell did Father have to give his sister money? As if *she* needed it. The fucking Bennings have more than enough."

Nancy paused, a pair of scissors in her hand. "He wanted to make amends –"

"*He should have made amends to me!* Courtney shouted. "I was his son – but that never mattered, did it? Oh no, let everyone else have the money – you, Cy Greyling, Misia Benning – but not his son, not his flesh and blood."

As usual, Nancy refused to argue. "Courtney, give it a break. Next month you'll get your allowance again –"

"I WANT IT NOW!" he shouted, "I want what's mine." He paced the room frantically. "Those Bennings have been nothing but a thorn in my flesh for years," he said spitefully. "Everything they've touched has turned to gold – boxing, casinos, the law. They're all over the papers – the famous Benning Boxers." He paused, grabbed at a breath. "Why did that side of the family do so well? Why not *our* side? Why not the Razzios?"

"We *did* well," Nancy said, soothing him. "Your father achieved a lot –"

"My father achieved shit!" he replied, "Our family's gone down whilst the Bennings have risen like potentates. They never had any bad luck, we had that. I had that – my mother and sister died, my wife loathes me, and my daughter's crippled –"

"Stop it!" Nancy warned him. "You had everything, Courtney and *you* blew it. As for your children, it's not my fault that Lomond's handicapped. She's a wonderful kid. And you should thank God you've got a healthy son."

"*Who hates me!*"

*"With just cause!"* she shouted back. "You're repeating the past, Courtney, repeating the same mistakes over and over again. Your father never loved you – so you reject your own son. Your father envied the Bennings – and so do you." She laid down the scissors and looked at him, her eyes impatient. "You don't see it, do you? You can't hear yourself saying the same things he used to say – 'the bloody Bennings, it's their fault, they have all the luck'. They *made* their luck, Courtney, and they worked together as a family in order to keep it."

"I don't want to talk about them!" he replied angrily, chewing his thumb nail, his eyes quick with malice. "They should be brought down a peg or two – it would be interesting to see how well they coped if their bloody luck changed."

"Grow up!" Nancy ordered him. "The feud's over. I won't have a war begin again. I *won't* have my children suffer."

"You might have no option," Courtney said, picking up Nancy's scissors and moving over the tailor's dummy. "I need more money, and I need it now."

She watched him, saw him lift the scissors and then open the blades, waving them in front of the draped material. "Give me more money – give me *my* money."

Breathing rapidly, Nancy held her ground. "No."

He brought the blades of the scissors together, slicing into the fabric, the perfect line of the dress severed, the dun coloured dummy exposed underneath.

"I wish you were dead," she said simply.

Courtney smiled. "Fat chance, darling. Only the good die young."

He brooded for the remainder of the afternoon, gnawed on his anger, chewed over his bitterness. Nancy had been only partially accurate; he did need money for his cocaine habit, but also to invest in his design business. Against all the odds, Courtney had responded constructively to the humiliation of his father's will; since Drago's death he had worked secretly at his own studio in the centre of Rome, putting together a selection of designs which he believed might make his name. He wanted to succeed at all costs; wanted to crow to his wife, to show everyone that he could be someone in his own right. To that end he had worked as he had never worked before; running on coffee and coke, drawing, redrawing, designing, picking and rejecting materials, his days passing in a furore of activity. He was possessed, his whole energy concentrated on the one aim – to prove himself and restore his own pride.

But he had run out of money, his allowance – he baulked on the word – spent within days. Even refusing to tell his wife what he needed the money for, Courtney had been sure that she would give it to him. He had never considered her refusal and now he stood in his studio and brooded. Where could he get money? *Where?* He should have been a rich man, should have inherited a fortune. And yet at the age of fifty three he was begging for money like a ten year old.

Bile choked him, bitterness making him spiteful, cunning. There was a slim chance, he realised, only a slim one, but a chance nevertheless. He had been forced to eat humble pie so many times, why not once more? If it meant that he got the money he needed for his work, it was worth it. Once he was a success he would be free of the lot of them. Courtney stopped pacing, seeing himself as the toast of Rome, the son finally stepping out from his father's shadow. No one would remember the humiliations then; he could leave his wife and set up on his own with whoever he chose. The thought intoxicated him, and he trembled with pleasure.

All he had to do was to beg once more, only once more … and it would all be his.

*

"I can't help you," Misia said over the phone. "I'm sorry, I have my own family to think of, Courtney. Talk to Nancy, she'll help you."

In his Rome studio Courtney heard the words and felt his chest tighten. "It would just be a loan," he hurried on, trying to keep his voice even. "I'd pay you back."

Misia was adamant. She could imagine Drago's son and his expression – that feral look – and she could hear the wheedling, insincere tone in his voice. She had her own family to protect; she was not going to support the likes of Courtney Razzio. Not even her brother would have expected that.

"Please," Courtney pleaded, "It means so much, I need it for my work."

She didn't believe him; Misia knew about Courtney's drug habit and the life he led. Not one penny of hard earned money was going to support a man she disliked and mistrusted.

"I'm sorry, Courtney, no."

"You will be sorry!" he snapped, stung by the rejection. "You'll suffer for this –"

"You can't threaten me," Misia retorted furiously. "I've never been afraid of any man, and you won't be the first."

But he was blind to reason, malice pouring over the line. "My father hated all of you," Courtney hissed. "He was right to keep away from you. You think the feud's ended?" he paused, the words humming menace. "Well, you're wrong – it's only just begun."

He slammed down the phone, Misia sitting rigidly in her seat, still holding the receiver. After so much loss, she was numbed, an old lady in her eighties wanting to rest. Slowly, Courtney's words came back one by one, and she frowned, remembering them and thinking of her brother and the havoc his bitterness had caused. An unexpected vigour seemed to galvanise her, force her upright in her chair, her eyes losing the dead look of grief.

Courtney Razzio had *dared* to threaten her? she thought disbelieving. He had warned her, told *her* that the battle was on? Tried to cow her, to brow beat her into submission? How dare he! Misia thought, suddenly alert with fury, there wasn't a man born who could stand up to her. So Courtney Razzio wanted a fight – well, he had come to the right woman. If he started anything, or dared to harm any of her family, God help him … Misia's eyes sparked into life. Just let him try, she thought, just let him try, because he'd lose, and she would, without a second's thought, ruin him.

*

The trainer, Max Carlucci, was in The Roman House when the call came through. He was surprised to hear from Elina Succhi, he hadn't seen her for years since their affair had ended and she had gone into television reporting. He glanced over to the boxers, his thoughts running on as he listened to Elina's languid voice.

"I'm coming to England to do a programme on boxing …" she said, "and I heard you were with Vincent Benning now – d'you think he would give me an interview?"

Max hesitated, sensing that Elina was on the make. "He might – it depends."

"On what?"

"On whether I organise it or not."

"Max," she said laughing. "What do you want?"

He frowned bullishly. "It depends on what you're after."

"A story," she replied innocently. "What else?"

They met up the following week in the gym at the World's End, Elina walking in, her dark hair short, her eyes kohl rimmed. She looked good, he thought, wearing the years well.

"Hi," she said, kissing Max on both cheeks. "I'm glad you agreed to help me."

He pressed his hands into the small of her back and pulled her to him. "I was always very obliging …" he said softly. "You can interview Vincent this afternoon, and then maybe we can have dinner?"

She arrived deliberately late at the casino at No 100 Belington Row, walking in and smiling, her dress short, her fabulous legs lengthened in heels. Aware of the attention she provoked, Elina stood waiting for Vincent, seeing his approach in the mirror and turning slowly.

He smiled, looked at her small face and the boyish haircut – then noticed the long legs.

"Elina Succhi?"

She nodded; "Thank you for seeing me."

"No trouble," Vincent said amiably, taking her up to the restaurant above.

She was a fascinating companion; a woman who could talk about every subject with authority, a woman who knew a great deal about boxing and gaming. At first Vincent was suspicious of her, but as the evening wore on they had a few drinks and he found that he was enjoying himself, mesmerised by her the heady combination of beauty and intelligence.

"I don't feel that I'm interviewing you," Elina said smiling, "it's been such a pleasure."

Vincent could feel himself relaxing and then checked himself. She was good looking and desirable, but she was also a journalist. Be careful, he warned himself, be very careful … but she was so easy to talk to, fascinating company, her bolting laugh loud and unforced, and by midnight neither of them were willing to end the evening. Guiltily Vincent glanced at his watch – he should get back to work, and then home – he thought of Annabel and Grace, and suddenly altered his tone, becoming businesslike, professional.

"Well, I should be going –"

"Oh," Elina said simply, wiping her mouth on her napkin. "Well, perhaps I could talk to you again about the boxing. I haven't really got enough information."

They held each other's look for a long instant, Vincent scenting danger and backing off. "I'm very busy, perhaps Max could help?" The moment tingled electrically, Vincent hesitating, uncertain when Elina did not respond. "On the other hand" he said at last, "you could come to the gym tomorrow and we'll talk some more."

Simeon was glad that the first cold of the winter had passed and Spring was beginning again. In the farmhouse at St. Joryde de Chalais he sat by the window, reading, his gaze moving from his book to the garden outside where Ahlia played with her son. Content, he leaned back in his seat; he had been lucky to find such a sanctuary … Outside Michel laughed, running to his mother, Ahlia bending down and pretending to smack her son, Michel screaming with pleasure. She was unchanged, Simeon thought, her appearance, like her character, untouched by the years, her serenity awesome.

Yet she *had* been disturbed the previous day; a letter coming from Norton. He was still working in Holland and had married a woman called Penny; Ahlia smiled when she read the words; but he had some other news too, news which did not please her – about her father. Caryl de Solt was ill, Norton wrote, he was failing, hospitalised in London.

Ahlia had read the letter twice and then passed it over the table to Simeon.

He had read it and then looked at her. "Well?"

"I don't know, I don't know what I'll do."

Apparently Ahlia still didn't know – or appeared not to. But Simeon could never tell what she was thinking. She was the only person whose thoughts remained off limits – which was why they lived together so perfectly. Thoughtful, Simeon glanced out of the window again. He had heard her talking to Lalo over the phone that morning, her voice calm. Why Lalo? he wondered, expecting Ahlia to call her brother instead. The conversation had not been a long one, but when she finished the call Ahlia had been composed, almost resigned, as though a decision had finally been reached.

But she didn't explain.

It was also sunny in London, Elina walking with Vincent in Hyde's Park, pausing by the Serpentine, and then sitting down on a bench. The interviews were over; she had done her piece for the magazine and the television show was filmed. Time to go home, she said regretfully. He was detached, afraid to speak.

"I'm leaving tomorrow," Elina said, the sun shining on the top of her short hair.

"Can't you stay?"

She turned, fixing her eyes on his. "If I do, you know what will happen?"

He nodded, miserable and euphoric in the same instant. He loved his wife, he adored his child – and yet Elina fascinated him. Uncertain for the first time in his life, Vincent was childishly malleable.

"I care about you …" Elina whispered.

"Oh know. I care about you too."

She leaned her head on his shoulder. "If you want me to go, tell me. Tell me to go home." She knew he couldn't, knew that he would beg her to stay instead.

"No," Vincent said wretchedly, "stay with me … please."

That afternoon, they made love.

Caryl de Solt was dying, that much was obvious. Ahlia had left France and travelled to London, visiting her father at the Harley Street Clinic, sitting by his bedside as he slept. She had left a letter for Simeon with instructions that he should open it at the weekend. Silently, Ahlia watched her father, his face covered with an oxygen mask, his breathing laboured, drugged.

Emma Legg had seen her arrive and had left with her son, too nervous to face Ahlia, Norton leaving a message that he would come to London as soon as he could leave work. Ahlia was pleased with the arrangements – she had hoped to be alone with her father, had waited for the opportunity for many years. Caryl slept on, peaceful as a child, his daughter by his bedside, quiet, unmoving. The hours uncurled, unwound slowly, night coming down, and still he slept, Ahlia alert, watchful. There was little left of the father she remembered, little of the old charming de Solt. He had wizened, aged, his beard longer, untrimmed, his skin waxy.

Memories were easy to call back; the night her mother died, the sound of Pila's body hitting the hall floor and the cold … the horrible cold as Ahlia ran into the street. She remembered the court case too, remembered her confusion, her dumb inability to speak. Tell us what you know … tell us … but Ahlia hadn't told, had she? Never said a word, keep her counsel, as she always did.

Suddenly Caryl stirred, moved on the narrow bed and opened his eyes, seeing her. He blinked, panicked, trying to talk, his voice muffled under the mask. "Ahlia?"

She nodded, her eyes fixed on his face.

He watched her, tried to see something in that Madonna countenance, tried to read her thoughts – and failed. He had wondered about his daughter over the years, marvelled at the way she kept her distance, never writing, never phoning. No contact since the first few months after her mother's death. As always Caryl had succeeded in dismissing the past: had conveniently forgotten his first family and the night Pila died. Until now … Now he was looking into his daughter's face and wondering how much she knew.

She had looked at him the same way that night. Stared at him … and then later she had denied having memory of anything that had happened. Using silence, her best weapon, the one she had continued to use so skilfully over the years. Caryl might have run away from the past, but his daughter was always in the background, unspeaking, watching, remembering.

"Ahlia?" he said again, the question apparent in his voice. *Tell me, he urged her, tell me, console me, let me know …*

She kept staring at him; kept silent, letting him wonder, letting him suffer. *You want to know, Father, she seemed to ask. You really want to know? …*

He struggled to breathe, his focus blurring, sensing her rather than seeing her anymore, his thoughts clearing instead and another woman taking her place; a dark sensual woman standing at the top of the stairs in the Clapham house … Afraid, Caryl fought to regain consciousness, feeling the horrible sliding away, the slip into oblivion as he knocked away the oxygen mask, his voice frail.

"Ahlia. Ahlia."

*Speak, say you love me, forgive me; tell me you saw nothing, knew nothing. Lie to me, let me cheat my way out of the world, let me dodge the inevitable punishment.*

She saw him struggle and laid her hand on his forehead. Her touch was cool, remote, as controlled as her voice as she leaned towards him, her face impassive.

"I saw you …" she said chillingly. "I saw you do it."

He flinched and then suddenly began to fall, plummeting away from the world, his fear making him cry out, his hand reaching for his daughter, his fingers clawing to catch hold of her.

Unforgiving, Ahlia moved out of his reach and then rose to her feet … and Caryl de Solt kept falling, leaving reality, his breaths short, his eyes closing, his daughter's footsteps echoing in his head as he landed on the other side of the world.

*

The following day, the Saturday, Simeon opened the letter Ahlia had left. The directions were simple, but he had to read them twice to understand, and then looked at the sealed envelope marked simply – Lalo. Ahlia was entrusting Michel into her care, giving her child to the woman who had no children of her own. The premonition Simeon had had years earlier was to come true

*I see you with a child* he had said – never realising that the child would not be hers, but Ahlia's …

I could never read you, could I? he thought hopelessly, you were the only one off limits to me. The farmhouse was suddenly full of Ahlia; the scent of her skin, the sound of her voice, the little movements in the night when she rose and walked around the rooms alone. What were you ever thinking? he wondered, knowing then that she had planned for this moment, and waited a long time for it.

It was her way of taking revenge for her mother's death. A retribution plotted patiently, the moment saved until she chose to reveal what she knew. Not to him, not to Misia or Portland. Her father had been the guilty one, and it was he who would be punished. Quietly Simeon drew the curtains, closing out the sunshine, clouding every room in the house. In the bedroom upstairs, Michel slept on: soon Lalo would come for him, and his future would be with her.

Simeon realised that Ahlia would never come back. She had gone forever. No one would ever know where, or if she was living or dead. What damage had been done to her when she was a child had shattered her. Ahlia did not feel or act as others did, normality had gone the night her mother died. Simeon knew that few would understand her actions, he didn't fully understand them himself, but he knew she had gone and he would never see her again.

Not in this world anyway.

# Sixty-Seven

## London

Vincent was asleep, Elina beside him, her head in the crook of his arm. Slowly she rose to her feet and dressed, turning once when she heard him move: but he merely mumbled and then fell back to sleep, leaving her to work undisturbed. In the two months since they had begun the affair, Elina had carefully inveigled her way into his work; offering advice and suggestions, her intelligence making her a ready confidante. At first Vincent was resistant, but soon he found himself listening to her more readily, and, bit by bit, she undermined his confidence.

He had never been a snob, but she mocked him gently, laughing at his ignorance of the arts, at his admission that he had never visited a gallery. She seemed to be teasing him, and he laughed it off, but it hurt, the implication that he was boorish striking home. He wondered why it mattered; he had never been interested in such things – who needed paintings? Who cared about music? He was involved with his own business. It didn't matter, did it?

Of course not, she told him, then cleverly, artfully talked about other wealthy successful men, men who had invested their money wisely; men who had been seen as something more than Jack the Lad … Discomforted, Vincent found himself on the defensive, but was too besotted by her to realise what she was doing; and so he began to alter his life, taking more time off from work to visit exhibitions, going to the opera, and theatre with her, the press soon scenting a story. He was like a man bewitched. Soon little snippets found their way into the gossip columns, talk swapped in many bars, and snidely bandied about in the boxing world.

Deandra was the first to hear. She had met a man called Mark Lieberman, a Jewish impresario, their relationship touted as 'Beauty and the Beast.' He was an unlovely man, thin, balding, well known in the theatrical circles. That he should catch the lovely Deandra Benning was seen as a miracle, and when their photograph was splashed over the front of a tabloid when they attended one of Vincent's fights, Misia was baffled.

"Okay, so what do you see in him?" she asked her granddaughter.

"All the things no one else does," Deandra replied smoothly.

"He's old enough to be your father."

"So?" she replied "I never found another man who could match Harewood before."

Misia raised her eyebrows; "Oh no, not the father figure syndrome."

Deandra was quick to defend him. "Mark takes care of me -"

"A housekeeper could do that," Misia retorted cuttingly, then moderated her tone. "All right, just tell me one thing – is he good to you?"

Her granddaughter nodded, smiling with genuine pleasure. "He's what I wanted."

"Well, I reckon you'll get to keep him. I don't see you fighting off a queue of other women." She walked to the mirror and stared at her reflection, picking up a pair of scissors and snipping at her fringe whilst Deandra watched her.

"Have you spoken to Vincent lately?"

"No … now you mention it, he's been a bit busy lately."

"Yes," Deandra said thoughtfully, "he certainly has."

Alerted by the tone in her granddaughter's voice, Misia turned. "What does that mean?"

"You didn't see the paper this morning then?" Cautiously Deandra took it out of her handbag and passed it to her grandmother. "Who *is* she? That's what I want to know," she said, watching Misia's face harden. "When I saw Vincent the other night he was odd, not like himself at all. I was surprised, but I didn't think anything of it until I saw that."

Misia tossed the paper back to her. "God, what a bloody fool! I would never have thought my son could be such an idiot."

"I asked Mark about her," Deandra went on, "he said Elina Succhi's an Italian journalist with her own television show. Apparently she's well known – and not just for her work."

"Meaning?"

"Meaning that she's on the make," Deandra answered. "I don't like it, Nana, I don't like it at all. Does Vincent have full control of the business?"

"Yes. Why not? He's made a fortune for us."

"But he if he has full control, he could do what he liked?"

Misia sat down on the side and crossed her legs, one veined hand drumming on the bedspread. "What are you trying to say?"

"I think Elina Succhi's having a bad effect on him," Deandra responded. "She's making suggestions about the business. Terry Gibbs told me the other day that he overheard her telling Vincent that he should go into more respectable fields – and that she had friends who wanted to start up in the art world."

*Oh shit!*" Misia said violently, "What the hell does Vincent know about art?"

"Nothing," Deandra replied. "That's why she's dangerous."

"I don't like my son sleeping around."

"Especially if Annabel hears about it – and she will, everyone's talking. Vincent's acting like a lunatic, it's as though he wants everyone to find out about them."

"No wonder he hasn't been round to see me lately," Misia said bitterly. "I don't like this, I don't like this at all. My parents didn't set the business up to see some foreign tart ruin it, and I didn't work like a fool for years just to let my son make a fool of himself." She stood up, exasperated. "I just can't believe it of Vincent. Harewood, maybe – I mean, your father's got good cause to wander. But Vincent – no, it's not right, it just doesn't make sense."

"So what do we do about it?" Deandra asked her anxiously.

"This man of yours – Mark Lieberman – can he find out anything else about the Succhi woman?"

"I'll ask him."

"Yes, do that," Misia said thoughtfully, "and meanwhile, I'll pay my son a visit."

Vincent wasn't at the World's End gym, or up in Liverpool at The Roman House, which was where he was expected to be that night. Baffled, Misia phoned No 100 Belington Row, but was told the same thing – Mr. Benning hadn't been seen that day and had left no message. Frowning, Misia put down the phone and then reluctantly dialled her son's home number.

"Hello?"

"Hello, Annabel," she said nonchalantly. "Can I talk to Vincent?"

There was a long pause. "I thought he was with you."

"No."

"He's cheating on me!" she said without preamble. "He's with that bitch Succhi."

"I heard all about it –"

"How could he!" Annabel said, her voice high pitched, hysterical. "He's making a fool of me all over London. Everyone knows."

Misia drew in a deep breath: "Listen, Annabel, we'll sort it out –"

"What about his daughter? What about Grace, doesn't he give a damn about her?"

"We'll sort it out –"

*"He's a bastard!"* she shouted, her voice strident. "How could he?"

"Stop it!" Misia snapped, "We'll sort it out. Vincent's just gone off the rails – some men do in their fifties. He's at a funny age."

There was no consoling her. "I don't care, I just want him back."

"Oh, he'll come back," Misia assured her. "He'll come back."

*

Elina was lying on her stomach, naked, the light flattering the tanned smoothness of her flesh, her cropped head bent over a sheaf of papers, Vincent beside her. She had succeeded in getting him to invest money in a gallery, assuring him that there was no reason for him to talk to the other members of the family. They wouldn't understand, she told him, rolling over, her arms outstretched. He moved on top of her, her mouth avoiding his, her laughter teasing as he tried to kiss her.

He no longer made his daily visits to the World's End gym or his weekly jaunts up to The Roman House. At night he went to the casino still, but his interest was waning. He had worked all his life, he was entitled to some pleasure at last, some rest from all the paperwork … She agreed, soothed him, helped him with his decisions and skilfully drew him further and further away from his work. You need a holiday, Elina said, come away with me. Just for a while, no one will miss you for a while …

Utterly besotted, Vincent felt like a smitten teenager and was greedy for her. Their sex was explosive, urgent, their affair all the more potent for its sensationalism. He no longer cared who saw them, no longer worried if they were seen and photographed; he was consumed physically and mentally, sucked dry of resistance, tied and bound to her as though his life depended on her very presence. Adeptly, Elina played on his weaknesses, and daily pulled him further away from his family, finally asking him for a loan for her own business. She wanted to set up a magazine, she told him; just think of the prestige – you'll be a publisher.

He gave her the money; he paid the rental on her flat and invested in her friends schemes – cash pouring from him, Misia's calls unreturned, Deandra's visits ignored. He was caught, drowning, and he didn't even know it.

Mark Lieberman met Deandra at the Ritz, steering her to his table and then sitting down, his face concerned. "Darling, does anyone know about your mother?"

She winced; Leda had finally been hospitalised for treatment. Serious clinical depression was the diagnosis, Harewood bereft, beaten. Together they visited Leda, her mother having been admitted under a different name in order that the press wouldn't get to hear about it. Safely secreted away, Leda had been undergoing treatment for nearly three months and no one was any the wiser – or so her family thought.

"No one knows."

"They do now," Mark said softly, taking her hand and looking into her fantastic face. "I've heard that it's going to be in the papers tomorrow –"

"Oh God!" Deandra said simply, her hand moving to her mouth. "Not now, not with all this going on with Vincent." She was fighting tears. "How did they find out?"

Mark ordered drinks and made her sip her brandy, watching the colour come back to her cheeks before answering. "I think Elina Succhi's behind it."

"*What!* Why would she want to leak the news about my mother?"

"Why would she want to get her claws into Vincent?" he asked. "Think about it, Deandra – what's the reason for all of this? Why would she do it?" He fiddled with his desert spoon, thinking. "I can see that a woman on the make might want to get everything she could from someone as well known and wealthy as Vincent, but why expose your mother's illness? That makes no sense. It's spite, that's all, and who would behave that way? Who would want to destroy not only Vincent, but the family?"

Deandra face paled and she struggled to her feet hurriedly, Mark following her as she rushed out of the Ritz and hailed a taxi on Piccadilly.

"What is it?" he asked, out of breath.

She turned, her face rigid. "I think I know who's behind all of this," she said, climbing into the cab. "I'm going to my grandmother's, Mark. I'll phone you later."

They talked late into the night, Misia making coffee, her eyes shadowed from lack of sleep and worry. She's old, Deandra thought, too old for this kind of anxiety.

"We have to do something –"

"It's Courtney," Misia said, her voice flat with anger. "I should have known before. I should have recognised his hand in this. Oh, he's like his father," she said, smiling grimly. "The same savage streak."

"The family's falling apart," Deandra said, pushing her hair back from her face.

"Oh no," Misia replied, refilling their coffee cups. "This family's not going to fall. That's what he wants, that's what he's hoping for. He wants the Bennings as miserable as the Razzios. Well, he's going to be disappointed."

"But what can you do?"

"You set a thief to catch a thief," she replied enigmatically, "that's what you do."

*

The following morning Misia arrived at the World's End gym and looked at the books, then, stunned, she went to the No 100 Belington Row and repeated the procedure. Finally, she and Deandra drove up to The Roman House and there, for nearly three hours, Misia went through every account. The losses were substantial; Elina Succhi had, in the course of three and a half months, managed to relieve Vincent of a considerable amount of money. The Benning money.

Enraged, Misia and Deandra returned to the house by the park, Mary Razzio's portrait staring reproachfully down from the wall, the drawing room cold from neglect. Setting the fire herself, Misia had the housekeeper make them supper, then afterwards she sat for a long time by the French windows, thinking. Deandra did not disturb her; and could only guess at what her grandmother was thinking.

She would have been surprised to know that Misia was remembering Alberto de Brio, thinking of him sitting in that room with her, describing Courtney Razzio many years earlier. He is the barbarian within their midst he had said, talking of the Razzio family in Rome. And now, thought Misia, the barbarian has spread his coils and wants to destroys us too. The feud was not over. It was simply passed down, inherited by the next generation. She had been a fool to refuse Courtney the money, it might have been cheaper in the long run if she had given in … But surrender had never been Misia's strong suit and she was damned if she was going to be blackmailed. You set a thief to catch a thief she had said to Deandra – a thief to catch a thief.

You would have loved this, Portland, Misia thought, looking round the room. All the old familiar mementos were there, all the old remembered photographs, together with her father's watch and Tita's picture on the mantelpiece. She was bolstered by the spirits in that house and by the happiness she had known there. Oh no, Courtney, she thought, you won't spoil my life. She glanced over, Deandra had fallen asleep, her perfectly formed mouth open. No, you're not going to hurt my family. You've met your match, you bastard, and you're going to lose.

`*

The following afternoon, Vincent called at the rented flat in Chelsea and rang the bell, expecting Elina to answer – but she didn't. Puzzled, he unlocked the door and walked in, feeling a winding anxiety. The place was empty, stripped, the wardrobes left with their doors hanging open, the coat hangers swinging on the rail. He moved round frantically, searching for a sign of Elina Succhi or any message left for him – a letter, a note, anything – but there was nothing. She had gone without a word; she had left him.

Then, seeing a light burning under the door, he hurried towards the kitchen, a figure turning at the sink as he walked in.

"What the hell –"

"Hello, Vincent," Misia said calmly. "I'd sit down, if I were you … Whisky?"

He took the glass from her, his hands shaking, his shame perfect and crushing. "Listen –"

"No!" she said firmly. "*You* listen. You've been a bloody fool for months, you've embarrassed me and humiliated your wife, you've lost the business money – and worse of all, you've shown yourself up."

He glanced down at his hands, mortified, unable to speak.

"What the hell was it all about?" she asked her son. "Sex? Was that it? No one ever threatened the Bennings before. No one could hurt us. But you let some tart nearly destroy us. God, I'm glad your father can't see you now."

"I don't know how it happened."

"Middle age, vanity, conceit – that was *why* it happened. You forgot to keep your eyes open and your flies closed. Some clever bitch made you feel young again," Misia laughed shortly. "You are an ass! I thought you had more about you. I thought you were the smart one, the one no one could fool. If it had been Harewood I won't have been surprised, but *you* – Vincent Benning, running around like some smitten kid. Elina Succhi set you up, don't you realise that? She wasn't after your body, she was after your bloody wallet." Misia stood over her son. "And do you want to know why?"

"Go on."

"Because Courtney Razzio wanted to get his own back. He was angry because I wouldn't lend him money, so he sent one of his little cohorts over to undermine the family. And by God, if I hadn't stepped in, she'd have managed it in another few months."

Vincent face was incredulous, "It was a set up?"

"Think about it, Vincent – she had her hooks into you, but that wasn't enough – she was the one who broke the story about Leda."

He looked up at his mother, disbelievingly. "Why?"

"She was working for Courtney, that's why. She admitted it in the end. I'm sorry, love, but you've been sucker punched."

"All right, all right, you've made your point!" Vincent said hoarsely. "Where is she now?"

"Back where she should be, in Rome," Misia replied, "I set a thief to catch a thief – I upped the anti, paid her more than Courtney to back off, and I threatened to have her television show pulled off the air if she didn't release you from her 'friends' commitments."

"How could you pull her TV show?"

"I couldn't, but Mark Lieberman could – through his contacts." Misia sipped her whisky. "I like him. I think Deandra might have found herself quite a catch. If you forget what he looks like."

Vincent was silent. He felt foolish, his obsession seeming merely silly now, a school boy crush, nothing more. To have risked so much, to have been so easily duped. The truth was excruciating, the humiliation complete.

"I suppose saying sorry wouldn't help?"

Misia shook her head. "No, not a bit."

He nodded grimly. "What about suicide?"

"Yours or mine?"

He smiled wryly. "What about Courtney Razzio? He won't like being thwarted."

"You win a fight punch by punch," Misia said calmly. "We won this round –"

"But they'll be others."

"And we'll win them too," she said, her voice steady. "As a fighter, Courtney Razzio has no class and no style. He's mean, hungry, and vicious, but he's not disciplined. He's a street brawler – and they *never* stay the course."

"But he won't give up."

"Good," Misia replied, "neither will we."

The following day Vincent fired Max Carlucci, and hired another trainer. He heard the gossip and refused to rise to the jibes or the Mancunian jokes coming thick and fast from Terry Gibbs: he had undermined his own position and now he had to fight to regain respect. It was his own fault, and he knew it. He had been sucked into treacherous waters and was only grateful that he had escaped drowning.

So stillness settled again, and for a while nothing was heard from Rome. The family shifted on its axis and then righted itself; relationships settling again. Annabel forgave Vincent, Deandra became closer to Mark Lieberman, and Lalo took on the child who had been left in her keeping. Only Misia remained watchful, telling Nancy what had happened, growing steadily closer to the American woman as the months passed. They had a great deal in common; Misia was protecting her family and Nancy was shielding hers. She had no illusions about her husband, and was anxious that his malice did no further damage. Daily she watched the reserved David and looked for signs of his father's instability; but although the twenty year old was by nature pensive, he was protective of his mother and fiercely loyal.

Steadily Nancy worked on, as Misia had always done: worked to secure her name and her children's future, Courtney remaining secluded in his studio in Rome.

"No news from him?" Misia asked her over the phone.

"Nothing."

"What will he be doing?"

Nancy shrugged. "Who knows? He'll either be out wasting the money he has, or feeding his habit. Or he'll be plotting." She paused. "I can't stop him, Misia. If I could, I would."

"I know that. Catherine couldn't stop Drago either. Spite feeds them, it motivates them, keeps them alive. I don't know why he's like that, or why my brother was – my parents were good people," Misia sighed. "There must have been some bad blood somewhere, something that came down the generations. I don't from whom."

"Courtney looks ill," Nancy said suddenly. "I think he's drinking, and of course he's been taking coke for years …"

"He won't die," Misia replied, picking into her unspoken thoughts. "I've told you, malice will keep your husband alive – malice and the hope of revenge."

# Sixty-Eight

Courtney had destroyed every design, ripped into the materials with a knife, shredded the drawings and finally torn apart the two dummies, eviscerating them, the studio floor covered with horsehair stuffing. Finally he stopped, breathing heavily and wiping his mouth with the back of his hand before he fell to the floor on his knees. The bitch had stopped him! Misia Benning had ruined his dream; she had thwarted him again. Courtney was blind with fury, getting to his knees and then allowing himself to fall forwards, banging his head repeatedly on the wooden floor.

The sound echoed in the high ceiling, its shimmered against the skylight and rebounded off the metal framework, the slow thumping regular as a heartbeat. On and on he went, until finally, Courtney rolled onto his back and looked up through the skylight. He should have been famous; should have made his name; should have been admired and indulged. But instead he was cornered, caged, hounded by his wife and by Misia Benning … He thought of Vincent, remembered how carefully he had plotted his ruin; then he thought of Harewood, his wife's collapse made public, people mocking the Bennings as they had always mocked him.

It should have worked, his plan should have split the Benning family wide open. But another woman had betrayed him – Elina Succhi. Courtney was dry mouthed with spite. Women, bloody women! His mind ran on without order; Vincent Benning, back in favour; Harewood Benning, dignified, reserved; Cy Greyling, smoothly, sleekly successful. Courtney thought of the handsome Moroccan, and he burned with envy. They had *all* tried to destroy him . They all wanted him dead.

Courtney slowly got to his feet, his thoughts settling. There *had* to be another way, he decided, pulling open the drawer in his worktable and laying out a line of cocaine. He sniffed it up hungrily through a drinking straw then wiped his nose, his nostrils raw, cracked. His thoughts were steadying; there was no point losing control, he reasoned, no point at all. He had to remain calm and plan. The Bennings had to be vulnerable somewhere. The scandal with Elina Succhi and the exposure of Leda Benning's illness might not have brought the family to its knees, but they had been rocked out of their complacency and were now vulnerable.

All he needed was to find another way to strike. The Bennings had a soft under belly – everyone had – all Courtney had to do was to find it. His spirits soared, his enthusiasm restored, the drug punching adrenalin into him. He had gone for the strongest member of the family when he should have attacked the weakest. Courtney laughed softly to himself. Go for the weakest one, he told himself, focus on the runt of litter, the kindest and most trusting of them all.

*

Spring came heavy in St. Joryde de Chalais, Simeon sitting in the garden, laying out

332

a pack of Tarot and then writing the interpretations on the pad next to him. It was one of many experiments he had made, the results checked and re-checked, his hours long, unsociable since Ahlia left. He had no fears any more and was slowly sliding into seclusion and blissful neglect. His food was delivered by the village shopkeeper, his wine also, and post was left under his door. But otherwise he saw no one. He lived with the unseen, the spirits who walked the house with him. Sometimes, at night, he thought he saw his grandfather sitting in the rocking chair by his bed; other times he would turn, hearing a footfall on the stairs or the drumming sound of Fitting Billy's fists on the floor.

The dead made a place for him, and Simeon moved in, hanging suspended in some haze of life between living and dying. His migraines were now rare; the terrifying pain no longer a precursor to a vision because the visions were with him constantly. He moved around in time, amongst voices and people; he eavesdropped on the dead; and had flashes of the future. And he wrote up everything, put down every experience and dated and annotated every word – as Ahlia had done before him. His reason was simple, he was leaving a record. Of what? he was no judge, Simeon was quite prepared to let those who followed him decide. All he wished to do was to tell his story – and he had many tales to tell.

The dead rushed in on him – once he let them. He had nothing to protect any longer; Ahlia and Michel had gone, the only person he endangered was himself. So now the nights were patterned with voices and shadows moving lonely in the dark. Once Simeon had woken and turned over to see a woman standing by his bed; she had motioned to him, putting her finger to her lips and he had followed her into the garden. The moon was high, scudding clouds making ink shadows on the grass. She moved quickly, leading him on to the copse at the base of the hill, and then she faded.

Cold, he went back to bed, but in the morning Simeon returned to the same spot and found a wine glass lying there … Payment from the dead for believing in them? he didn't know, but was glad of the benign spirits, others coming more malevolently went the sun went down. Once he found a ghost dog barking at the head of the stairs and another time he saw a ghost child falling from the roof … He wrote everything down, and knew that no matter how menacing it became, he could never leave. This is my home, he told himself, this is where the dead come to me.

But sometimes, on the rare occasions when he was afraid, he sat up in bed with the sheets round him, shivering and waiting for morning – and then longed with all his heart for the rocking chair to move and the image of his grandfather to come in the night to comfort him.

"Are you there?"

Silence.

"Are you there?"

The clock ticked rhythmically, a wind nuzzling against the window and making little sighs down the chimney in his room. And then, in the dim light, the chair began rocking, its shadow moving darkly on the wall.

*

It was the first time Lalo had ever known perfect happiness. She had been content with Cy, but never fulfilled, and only after Michel came to her did she find a stillness of soul. At first her good fortune had been tempered by the loss of Ahlia. Her disappearance was complete; she was never heard from or seen again. The family tried to trace her, but she had gone, sunk into the earth or dissolved into the atmosphere, leaving no trace. She had wanted it that way; a suicide would have left a body, and questions, and grief.

As it was no one could mourn for her death, because she might still be alive, still out there somewhere, watching, the Madonna face impassive, secret, knowing. If she *was* alive, Lalo wondered, what was she doing? Was she living and working under another name? How could she survive, divorced from her family and her child?

But almost as she asked herself the questions, Lalo knew the answers: *if* Ahlia lived, she would exist alone, as she had always done. She had completed the task she set out to do, and had given her child to the one woman she could trust above all others … How long did you plan it? Lalo wondered. Was it that chance remark Simeon made years earlier when he said I would have a child? Is that what set everything in motion?

She looked over to Michel, watched him laughing, the nanny putting on his coat. What will I tell him about his remarkable mother? Lalo wondered. How will I ever be to able to explain? He would never even know who his father was. Lalo smiled to herself. So many questions, so few answers. She would watch him grow and see his expressions and never be able to match them to a known man, never be able to recognise a posture or the turn of a head.

How clever of you Ahlia, she thought suddenly, to leave me so little to go on. Without information how much more Michel can become my child and Cy's. Lalo studied the boy thoughtfully, feeling a swell of affection. I couldn't love him any more if I had given birth to him, she thought. You did well, Ahlia, you left him to the right woman and the right home.

*

"How's Leda?" Misia asked, yawning and stretching her arms above her head. She had had an indoor swimming pool installed at the back of the Holland Park house and swam daily to help her rheumatism, sometimes turning on the underwater lights and taking late dips, the London night dark against the skylights. She had just finished three lengths when Deandra arrived, Misia pulling off her swimming cap and yanking a towelling robe round her.

"Mother's okay … well, you know what it's like."

"Not without you telling me, I don't."

Wearily Deandra flopped into a wicker seat by the pool. "She's not going to get any better. I think she might have to stay in hospital for a while."

Misia frowned, rubbing her neck with a towel. Her skin was crêpe, paper fine. "How's your father?"

"He copes, as he's always done … he doesn't say much, just goes to visit her most days. He's very devoted," Deandra paused. "She looks hideous – I don't mean to be cruel – but she does. Her hair's grown out dark at the roots and without make up she looks bloated, unrecognisable. And now she doesn't talk or seem to understand anything around her …" Deandra paused, upset. "I keep wondering how long it will go on – I think my father should have his chance at happiness, should be able meet someone else before its too late."

"He won't," Misia said simply. "He loves your mother, always did. Harewood would never get involved with someone else … You should try to stop worrying about him so much, it doesn't help. Besides, you ought to get your brothers to do more."

Deandra laughed shortly. "Tom's still back-packing around America, and Fraser – well, Fraser's now living with a woman called Margot. She's twenty-one years older than him and she's got three grown up children."

"My God," Misia said incredulously. "I remember him when he was a scruffy kid, and dim as a Took H lamp."

"He's still is – he got fired from teaching, and now they've moved to Warwickshire and gone native. They live off the land apparently."

Misia changed the subject. "How's Mark?"

"Mark?" Deandra smiled, the exquisite face luminous. "He's well – really well."

"So it's serious?"

"He's talking about marriage."

"What does that mean? – he's 'talking' about marriage? – you can 'talk' about the Himalayas, but that doesn't mean you're going to climb them."

"He wants to marry me."

"Ah …" Misia said simply, throwing her towel onto the empty chair beside her, the lights puddling the pool in front of them. "Are you going to?"

"I'm thirty two years old, it's about time …" she smiled slyly, "and I adore him."

"Surely not for his looks."

"Looks don't matter!" Deandra retorted hotly.

"Not for males," Misia agreed, "But you don't see many men dating bald, pot-bellied women."

Laughing, Deandra shook her head in exasperation. "He'll make a good father."

"That's what you need," Misia replied, "You know, Portland was no oil painting, but I adored him, and he was a great father." She tapped her granddaughter's knee. "Marry Mark Lieberman – he's a solid as a rock, and you need a man like him. We all do."

"Do you miss him?"

Misia knew without asking who she meant. "I miss Portland every minute, every hour, every day. I wanted to die before him, but if I couldn't, I wanted him to go peacefully. I got one wish granted anyway." She pushed back her hair from her face, the fringe falling back into place immediately. "It's difficult being the one left – you have so much time to remember, and that's painful at first. Now it's not so bad. Now, simply remembering him is a happiness of a kind."

"You were lucky to find each other."

"No," Misia said shortly. "We weren't lucky, we were blessed."

*

The palazzo was cool inside, the marble floor soaking up the heat, the windows shuttered. The quietness was absolute, almost penetrating on the ear, an absence of sound more intense than sound itself. Noiselessly Courtney walked around the ground floor, keeping close to the walls, alerted for the sudden approach of a servant, or the return of his wife. But the stillness continued. He moved amongst the furniture touching the wood, running the curtain fabric through his hands, and weighing a pieta dura box in his palm. So much money, so much money … it hung around him like a miasma; his eyes smarted with it; his flesh sweated under the heat of opulence and his mouth dried from desire.

Be calm, he willed himself, be calm. Plot, plan, wait. The front doors opened suddenly, Nancy walking in to find her husband standing by the mantelpiece in the drawing room.

"Hi, Courtney," she said easily, covering her irritation.

"You don't seem surprised to see me."

"Why should I?" she asked, picking up her mail and flicking through it: "You always come back home in the end."

"I wanted to say sorry."

"Oh shit," she said simply, walking over to him. "What the hell are you up to now?" She studied his face, the gaunt expression, the deep indentation in the chin – and the giveaway signs around the nose. "You should cut back on your in-take, Courtney. I remember your father doing nose jobs to repair damage just like that." She stared at the raw skin around his nostrils. "Jesus, don't you know that coke rots the inside of the nose?"

Courtney moved his head away impatiently, then remembered why he had come and turned back to his wife. "I don't want us to fight anymore."

"We don't fight. We don't care enough to fight."

"All right, it's all my fault" Courtney said grudgingly. "But I'm sorry, I want to try and make things better around here. Make us into a family"

"Like the Bennings?" she asked. "I know what you tried to do to them, Courtney, so let's cut the crap. What are you up to now? Another plot? Another plea for money?" Her tone was light but firm. "I've told you, no more money yet. You'd only blow it, snuff it up your nose, or drink it." She paused. "I can smell it, Courtney, they say you can't smell vodka, but you can … Listen, if you want to kill yourself, fine, go ahead. But I won't let you waste the family's money making it the world's most expensive suicide." She shook her head. "I have our children to think about."

"Are you all right?"

Startled, Nancy spun round at the sound of her son's voice. David was standing at the door of the drawing room, his expression anxious, wary.

"I'm fine," she replied cheerfully. "Just having a chat with your father."

Openly hostile, David's eyes turned on Courtney, Nancy watching both of them. There was no similarity at all, the difference between them vast: unnatural, between father and son. Leaning against the mantelpiece, Courtney had a ruined and dissolute look, his slyness apparent even in his movements; whilst David stood erect in the doorway, his sombre face watchful, dignified.

"Should I stay?"

"I'm not going to bloody kill her!" Courtney snapped at his son.

David ignored him and turned to his mother. "Shall I stay?"

"Hell no!" she said lightly. "You go and pick up your girlfriend –"

*"Girlfriend?"* Courtney echoed spitefully. "I was wondering which way your inclinations lay."

Disgusted, David moved away, his father's voice calling after him. "Be sure and introduce her to me," he bellowed. "I'd like to see the kind of woman who sleeps with my son."

"You're despicable," Nancy said, closing the door and turning back to her husband, her loathing obvious. "I have to go out soon, so perhaps you could just tell me what you want. Then I can refuse and you can get the hell out of here."

Courtney was unruffled. "David's a good looking boy," he said thoughtfully. "You have to admit it, I did you a favour there, okay, so you weren't so lucky with the girl –"

Nancy slapped him hard, catching his cheek with the back of her hand. "She's called Lomond – *LOMOND!* – and she's your daughter too."

Startled by the blow, Courtney touched his cheek and then lifted a handkerchief to his nose. It had begun to bleed, marking the pure white of the linen.

Nancy looked at him. "So you have nose bleeds now, do you?" She turned away, exasperated. "Stop taking the bloody stuff, it's going to kill you."

"I hate to disappoint you," Courtney replied, tipping back his head, his voice cold, "but I intend to live at least as long as my father did. You'll have me for another thirty years. Quite a thought, isn't it?" His voice steadied. Remember what you're here for, be calm. "I said I was sorry, and I meant it. That's the only reason I came … "

Nancy hesitated, wanting, against logic, to believe him: *Is that the truth? No bullshit?"*

"No bullshit."

"Okay," she said simply. "Thanks for saying sorry – and take care of yourself."

An hour later David was standing on the terrace watching his girlfriend Francesca walk down the lawn. She was talking to one of the gardeners, asking for advice about a plant she was growing in her window box, her hands moving quickly, her face animated.

"She's full of life," Nancy said, coming over to her son and leaning on the balustrade next to him. "Quick witted, vivacious, pretty – and ordinary, Thank God. Are you keen on her?"

David ignored the question: "Why do you let him in the house?"

"Who?"

"You know who!" he snapped, his grey eyes impatient. "My father's plotting again, I can sense it – he's up to something."

"He came to apologise, that's all."

David's voice was incredulous. "You can't believe that! He's up to something."

"He might want to change –"

Her son put his hand over his mother's mouth to stop her. The gesture was tender, loving. "Stop lying to yourself. My father won't change, he'll never change. And I don't care anymore. I don't give a damn what happens to him. All I care about is you. You brought us up with no help and no support from that man, and I swore that when I was old enough I'd protect you from him." David moved a stray hair away from his mother's forehead. "Don't have my father here, don't trust him or pity him. Don't have anything to do with him. He's dangerous, believe me. Don't let down your guard."

Touched by his concern, Nancy smiled. "What would I do without you? I won't let him fool me. I promise."

"He'll keep trying," David went on. "He'll never *stop* trying – but let him turn his malice on someone else. Or even better, on himself." He paused, his expression implacable. "Someone's got to stop him. If he tries anything again –"

"He won't."

David was unconvinced. "He will. He keep going on and on until someone stops him."

# Sixty-Nine

It had been Cy's idea for Lalo to visit London; it would be a change, he said, a few days away from Rome. She had hesitated, thinking of Michel.

"... but he's got the nanny to look after him," Cy replied, "and besides, I'm here. Just go away for the weekend, Lalo. You've wanted to visit for months."

She was uncertain, wavering, "You don't think Michel will miss me?"

"We'll *both* miss you," Cy said easily, "but we can manage for a little while, you know."

It was true, Lalo needed a break. Her health, always fragile, had been undermined by Michel having a series of childhood illnesses the previous year. Devoted, she had stayed with him constantly, rationing her own sleep, sitting by his bed and tending to his every need. Despite her protestations, the nanny had been under-used, relegated to trivial domestic tasks, Lalo refusing to leave Michel's side.

He recovered fully, but Lalo had been weakened by events and was slow to regain her energy. Working long hours, Cy had offered what support he could, but his time was limited and after a while he urged his wife to accept Misia's invitation of a break in London. He had been alarmed by the loss of weight Lalo had suffered; her skin, always pale, was without colour, her eyes vast and listless. She had looked after Michel better than any mother could have done, but now she needed to restore herself – and she couldn't do that in Rome.

"Go on, go to Misia's and don't worry about us," Cy encouraged her. "After all, what can happen in a few days?"

So they made the arrangements and Lalo left within the week, before she could change her mind. Her bag was crammed with presents for the Bennings, photographs of Michel tucked in her purse, the perfume Deandra loved bought over from Rome. Lalo was alternately anxious and excited, and during the flight she slept fitfully, waking suddenly and wondering where she was as they put down at Heathrow in the late morning. Huddled into her coat, Lalo waited impatiently at Customs, her hands chilled, her collar turned up.

She was thinking of the house at Holland Park and searching for the sight of Vincent's face in the crowd when someone touched her arm.

"Mrs. Greyling, can you come with me?"

Lalo turned slowly, listlessly. "Pardon?"

"We need to search your luggage."

Her face was childishly astonished: *"What?"*

"Please, Mrs. Greyling, come this way."

She followed obediently, the Customs official showing her into an isolated room.

"You'll have to have a strip search – a female officer will be with you in a moment." The words jolted Lalo, and she coloured, suddenly afraid; "Why? What for?"

"We found drugs in your luggage, Mrs. Greyling," he answered. "We have to be sure that you've none on your person."

"Drugs …" she repeated stupidly. "No! Not my luggage. It *can't* be my luggage." Lalo frowned, rubbing her forehead, the full enormity of the situation coming into sharp and immediate focus. "I don't know what you're talking about!"

"Just come with me –"

"I won't!" she shouted, distressed and cornered. "I haven't done anything! *I haven't done anything wrong!*"

"Mrs. Greyling, please don't make this any harder on yourself," the official said flatly. "You have to be searched."

Dumbly, she allowed herself to be lead off, stripped and searched, her humiliation complete, tears pricking behind her eyes as she redressed. Nothing was found on her body, but Lalo was charged with smuggling four pounds of cocaine from Rome to London and a statement was taken from her. Catatonic with shock, Lalo was allowed to see Vincent for a few minutes before being lead away to the Customs detention cells where she would be held overnight.

She was incoherent, panicked, unable to explain clearly what was happening, Vincent listening incredulously.

"I didn't do it!" she said helplessly. "I didn't do anything. *I didn't! I didn't!*"

"I know."

"Someone planted those drugs on me! I packed that case, someone must have tampered with it –"

"Stay calm, we'll sort it," Vincent replied hurriedly, taking her hands. "We'll get it all sorted out. It was a mistake, that's all."

"But they're locking me up!" Lalo said plaintively. "God, Vincent, I can't stay here. *I can't.*"

"Lalo, we'll sort it out. I promise you."

Her voice was fading, shock settling in. "Tell Cy, phone him please …" she seemed to fail suddenly as though she was about to pass out. "Don't leave me here, don't. Please *don't* leave me here."

"We'll get you out, sweetheart, believe me, we'll get you out," he said firmly, holding her for a brief instant before she was lead away.

*

Having just returned from operating, Cy was sitting with Michel in the kitchen of the Rome flat, a patient's file open in front of him, his eyes still fixed on it as he lifted up the phone. He heard what Vincent said, but took a moment to respond.

"Lalo? But she's didn't … she *wouldn't* … what are they talking about? It's a mistake."

"We know that, but the cocaine was found on her –"

"I don't care!" Cy shouted vehemently. "It's a mistake, that's all … Where is she?"

Vincent paused. "In a Customs detention cell."

"She's locked up? Jesus, I don't believe it! She can't be locked up, she's can't take that kind of treatment."

"We can't get her out tonight. But I've got a solicitor going round to see her in the morning," Vincent hurried on. "I have to warn you, Cy, the papers have got hold of the story. It's going to be all over the news tonight. Someone tipped them off. I couldn't do anything to stop it … I'm sorry."

He paused, thinking of Harewood and how his brother would take the news. Dignified, private Harewood Benning, exposed to the glare of publicity again, a second blow coming after the revelation of his wife's illness. The scandal would beggar him, Vincent knew; his beloved daughter seen as a criminal, his career at the bar making him a sitting target for every mean blow.

"Lalo would never do anything like that. Everyone knows that," Cy said, distraught. "It's a joke, a mistake. I *can't* believe that they locked her up. She'll be lost!" he said wildly. "She can't cope. Oh God, not Lalo –"

The doorbell rang suddenly, Michel running to open it, a murmur of voices coming down the passageway as Cy turned to see David Razzio walk into the room.

"Vincent, I'll call you back," he said quickly. "Give me a minute and I'll call you back."

Preoccupied, he walked over to his visitor, his thoughts elsewhere as he ushered Michel out of the room with his nanny.

"What is it?" Cy asked, his tone disorientated as he looked at Lalo's nephew. "This isn't a good time, David. We've got trouble here."

"I know," he said calmly, "my father caused it."

"What?"

"My father did it."

Cy still didn't understand. "Did *what?*"

"Lalo's been arrested for smuggling drugs, hasn't she? They found drugs in her luggage?" Cy nodded. "Well, my father did it."

"*Your father?*" Cy repeated blindly. "Why? How?"

"He'll have paid one of his cronies or blackmailed someone into planting those drugs on Lalo –"

"But *why?*" Cy snapped. "I don't understand. Why would he do that to her?"

David Razzio was calm, in control. Impressive for a young man. "He did it for revenge."

Cy's voice was dangerous: "*Revenge?* Your father used my wife to get revenge? *He used my wife …*" he turned away, moving to the door and snatching up his coat, David following.

He was beyond reason, running to his car and starting the engine, David jumping into the passenger seat just as he drove off. The traffic was heavy, Cy's laying his palm flat on the horn as the car veered recklessly through the traffic. He drove without speaking, his eyes fixed ahead, his mouth set, his whole concentration focused on the road. They cleared the city quickly as he turned towards the isolated outskirts, the huge bulk of the palazzo coming into view as they swept through the gates.

The house seemed deserted, Cy ringing the bell and then hurrying past the servant as he answered the door. Bellowing out his name, he called for Courtney. His voice bounced off the walls and skimmed fiercely down the corridors, echoing in the emptiness. Nancy was out, David had told him as much, but somewhere, in amongst the bulk of rooms, was Courtney Razzio. His name skittered through the silence, but he didn't reply; the words carried through the passageways, searching him out.

341

Cy had expected him to hide and ran from room to room, throwing open doors and shouting for him.

"Courtney Razzio! RAZZIO! Where are you?" he howled. "Come out, you bastard. Get out here!"

Then, suddenly, unexpectedly, Courtney emerged. His face was malignant, his figure motionless against the far wall of the drawing room. He had opened the windows, the cold air coming in and dragging at the room, the curtains blowing, the terrace shaded by the fall of early evening.

Cy saw him, then lunged forward, striking out and catching him on the jaw. Courtney rocked back, but was surprisingly resilient and threw a punch, Cy jerking his head away from the blow, his voice hoarse with fury.

"She's my *wife*!" Cy shouted. "*MY WIFE*, you bastard!" he bawled, going for him again, his hands fixing around Courtney's throat, his eyes wild.

But he lost his grip when Courtney aimed a kick at his groin, and then stepped back, ducking out onto the terrace and into the shadows. He was darting about, urging Cy on, taunting him. Although smaller, he was a dirty fighter, and as Cy approached him again, Courtney stooped, gathering some gravel in his hand and then throwing it in Cy's face. He bellowed in shock, his hands going up to his eyes, but as he tried to clear his vision Courtney came out of the shadows again and struck him on the side of the head. Losing his balance, Cy went down heavily, his lip bleeding, Courtney kicking him in the ribs.

He was winning, and he knew it, putting all the years of malice into his blows, Cy staggering into the shadows, blundering after him as Courtney kept to the wall. He knew every inch of the terrace and his eyes were adjusted to the dark as he reined punches on the stooped figure of his hated rival, Cy defending himself blindly. The sounds of the blows were loud, the steady thumping and the gasping for breath coming from the shadows, Courtney grabbing one of the wrought iron chairs and lifting it over his head. He could imagine the sound as it made contact, the dull thud of the metal hitting bone, Cy Greyling crushed under the weight, the his head ground into the gravel.

Then suddenly the lights went on. All the floodlights at once, the terrace illuminated like an arena, Courtney exposed as he was about to strike. Cy saw him and reacted at once, rolling out of the way, the chair crashing down in an arc, Courtney screaming with fury and frustration as it missed its target. And in that instant Cy caught hold of him, jerking Courtney round and slamming his body against the brickwork, his hand fastening on Courtney's hair as he hammered his skull repeatedly against the wall. Then, when his skin was split along his forehead, his nose bleeding, his mouth hanging open, Cy finally let go of Courtney Razzio and he slid to the ground.

He glanced up to see David standing by the doorway, his hand still resting on the light switch.

"Can you help to get him inside?"

David nodded, both men carrying Courtney and dropping him into a chair in the study. Passing the phone over to the defeated man, Cy leaned towards him. "I want you to tell the police what you did …" Courtney's face was bloodied, but his expression was malevolent, Cy slapping him hard across the face. "You tell them, you bastard …

you tell you tell them everything." Courtney's nose was dripping blood, his white skirt mottled with red as Cy pushed the phone into his chest. *"Everything."*

He did. Aware that he had finally lost, Courtney made a statement, the details sent over to London to secure Lalo's release. Courtney was finished, and signed the papers without a murmur. He was peculiarly quiet, almost pliable, the blood now dried on his shirt, his cadaverous face puffy from the blows. The Italian police were in touch with their colleagues in London and after the details of Courtney's confession were Faxed over, Lalo was released into Misia's care; Vincent fending off reporters with a terse 'No Comment;' Harewood waiting at the Holland Park house for his daughter's return. She was silent from shock, hardly able to talk to Cy over the phone, her voice as bewildered as a child's.

And all the time, Courtney remained in the palazzo in Rome, never moving. He seemed even more threatening. It was uncanny, Cy thought, even when he's beaten he's dangerous. Apparently disinterested in what was going on around him, Courtney's was impassive, and yet, when his son came in, his eyes fixed on David. The lights had blinded him, had caused him to miss the final strike – and the lights had been turned on by his son. *His son.* Enraged, Courtney watched David, but his son refused to look at him. His had not been an act of betrayal, but one of reason; if he had not turned on the lights his father would have killed Cy Greyling. He could have backed his father, but his madness was his own, and as David had promised, he was the one who would stop him. It was a fitting judgement on the father from the son: David had made his decision and he would live with it.

The palazzo was silent, David watching as a police officer turned to Cy. "I still don't understand why Courtney Razzio went to such lengths to frame someone. What was the point of it all?"

Cy shook his head. "It goes back a long way, through several generations," he shrugged, "a feud based on envy, hatred – who knows? Once there must have been a reason, but how it came to this, I don't know. He would have killed me, if he could." He turned to David and touched his arm. "Thank you."

"Courtney will be jailed, you know," The policeman went on.

"I hope he dies in there …" Cy replied bitterly. "… because my wife would have done."

# Seventy

In London, Vincent turned to his mother. "He'll be back. I know it, Courtney Razzio will be back."

"No," she said firmly. "It's over."

He shook his head, listening for a sound from upstairs. Lalo was sedated, sleeping. "He'll get out. When he finishes his sentence, he'll start again." Vincent frowned. "Where did all that malice come from?"

"I don't know," Misia replied honestly. "Bad blood. But whose?" Her thoughts wandered. "I've often wondered about that; wondered why Drago was like his was, and then why Courtney turned out the way he did. He's not normal, Vincent, not just vindictive – that man could kill."

"So what made him that way?"

"*Or who*," Misia retorted thoughtfully. "I've been thinking about that for a while now. All I know for a fact is that my father left home when he was a young man. Which makes you wonder why. He would never tell us, but now I wonder if he was hiding something."

"Illness?"

"Or instability?" Misia answered. "Guido ran away. No son does that, leaves his home, his country, without having a good reason." She frowned. "I know everything about my mother's family, but nothing about my father's. Was Guido running away from something. Or *someone?*"

Vincent blew out his cheeks. "Can we find out?"

She shook her head. "Not now, it's too late. I know he told my mother what had happened, but she never confided in me. I suppose we'll never get to know the truth."

"So now we just wait until Courtney tries again?"

Misia was tired from the trauma, but her voice was steady. "I don't think he will, Vincent. I really believe it's over. The feud finishes with Courtney."

"Not until he's dead," her son replied. "Not until he's dead."

# Seventy-One

## France

Simeon paused, his pen in his hand, the sudden nausea overwhelming him, the pain breaking over his eyes and blurring his vision. He clenched the arms of his chair and breathed in, dragging air into his lungs. No, not now ... no ... But the pain continued, increased, burned into his brain and punched at his lungs, pictures appearing before his eyes. A man walking down a garden towards a gate ... running ... running in the heat. Hot ... hot ... Simeon jerked his head away, the smell of mimosa cloying, suffocating him. The man had his back to him, but he was familiar ...

Simeon tore at the shirt round his neck, ripping the material, his head forced downwards onto his chest ... there was a child in bed ... and a glass, the clear liquid shaking and throwing its shadow against the wall ... water, no, not water ... bitter smell, taste ... bitter ... Simeon gasped at the air, sweat trickling down his back, the muscles in his arms jerking ... There was a woman moving close to the walls, in a house, in the heat ... In a house, in the heat ... moving close to walls ... A dark woman, tall, carrying a glass ... Simeon reeled back in his seat, afraid of the woman suddenly, trying to turn his eyes away from hers.

She was killing him! ... No, *she was killing the child.* She was trying to kill the child ...

The image faded, turned on, the child grown in to a young man, a man walking towards a gate and passing through it. His grandfather, Dear God, it was Guido ... And now he was running away, away from the woman, Simeon realised ... He was running away from his *mother.*

The image changed once more. Guido Razzio was gone, in his place stood Courtney Razzio, walking across a marble hallway ... Simeon gasped at the air, the sinews in his legs juddering, his feet banging on the floor ... He was walking towards something ... What? what? Show me! Simeon shouted inside. Show me! Tell me what I should see ... Courtney was under red, under redness, under a ceiling of redness, fading, under red ...

Simeon threw himself forwards, his body blistered with pain, the images fading, leaving him, peeling back, his breathing returning slowly to normal. He slumped in the chair and opened his eyes, looking out over the field, trying to make sense of what he had seen. His grandfather had been trying to tell him about his past. That his mother had tried to kill him. *That* was why Guido had left Italy. She had been mad, and had tried to kill her own son.

Mad, Simeon thought. Bad blood.

Frantically he moved to the phone and dialled London, Misia picking it up on the third ring.

"It comes from Guido's mother," he said hurriedly.

345

Misia was alert, startled by the sound of Simeon's voice. "What does?"

"Mental illness," he paused. "Courtney inherited it from *her*. That was why my grandfather left Italy," he breathed in, steadying himself. "Guido came to tell me, he showed me what happened, and he showed me what's to come …"

*"What?"* Misia asked hoarsely.

"The worst is over, the family's safe –"

"But what about Courtney?"

"It ends with him," Simeon replied, his voice certain. "Courtney's going to die. I don't know how, or when, but he's going to die."

His hands shaking, Simeon put down the phone. He was sure he was right. Guido had shown him the truth, and his grandfather had never lied to him. Slowly Simeon moved upstairs to his bedroom and stood in the doorway, his eyes fixed ahead of him.

"Am I right? Did I get it right?"

He waited, watched for the sign.

"Guido, tell me. Was I right?"

A second later, the rocking chair began, very slowly, to move.

# Seventy-Two

## Rome

He wasn't going to jail. They might think he was, but he had a good lawyer, sly enough to get him of. Courtney smiled to himself, walking into the bathroom and turning on the taps. His head throbbed from the beating he had taken, his nose still blocked with dried blood as he thought of Cy Greyling. If his son hadn't intervened, he'd have finished Greyling off once and for all ... The water plummeted into the vast tub, hot water, filling the bath rapidly.

His head ached, his body stiff. The tub was vast, big enough for several people – he'd had several people in it before now, and he would again – no one was going to take him away, or lock him up. Carefully Courtney measured out a line of cocaine and then sniffed it up through a drinking straw, the water pounding into the tub behind him, the windows steaming. Clumsily he unscrewed the bottle of Smirnoff and took a drink, the vodka hitting his empty stomach and lifting his spirits immediately.

The bathroom was hot, the tub two thirds full as he turned off the taps and took off his clothes, wincing as he looked in the mirror and touched the bruising. A good soak would take away the pain, he thought, feeling euphoric as the drug began to take effect. Jail him, never! He wasn't going to fucking jail, no one would put him away ... Cautiously Courtney lowered himself into the water, his arms hanging over the side, his legs idling in the warmth. He was pleasantly drowsy as he reached for the vodka again and downed an inch, leaning forward to put it back on the edge of the bath within reach.

The fight had taken more out of him than he realised, his limbs ached and he felt suddenly exhausted. Around him, the steam rose up, his damp hair sticking to his head, his arms relaxing against the side of the bath. Feeling a trickle run down his top lip, Courtney cursed – his nose was bleeding again! Irritated, he wiped the blood away with his hand and then leaned his head back against the side of the bath. The water lapped around him, seemed to buoy him up, rocking him as his eyes closed.

The vodka was having its effect, mixing with the coke in his system and numbing his senses. Courtney relaxed more deeply, his breathing calming, the steady trickle from his nose dripping into the water around him and blooding it. Steam rose up in clouds, obliterating his figure in the tub, his mouth hanging open as he slid off to sleep.

He woke suddenly as the water closed over his head, gasping and struggling to raise himself, his hands scrabbling for purchase on the sides of the bath. But the porcelain was slippery and Courtney was too doped to haul himself upright. Under the water he went, his eyes open, staring in panic, his mouth taking in the hot liquid, blood seeping from his nose and blooding the bath. Terrified, he screamed underwater, air bubbles breaking on the reddening surface, his lungs filling with water, the haemorrhage from his nose turning the bath to a dark and malevolent red.

And he kept struggling; burning in the heat, sinking further underwater, his bladder relaxing in terror as he realised he was drowning. His legs scrabbled and kicked out uselessly, his eyes blistering, his ears filled with the roaring of the water, the bubbles finally dying away as Courtney's arms relaxed and his hands released their grip on the sides of the bath. Then – after all the splashing and the panic – there was silence, only an occasional drip from the taps breaking into the stillness as Courtney lay motionless under the bloodied water. His eyes were wide open, his flesh pink, the skin under his nose split, the nostrils raw and expanded in the heat.

It was a big bath. Big enough for several people to bathe in at once. Easily big enough to hide a body: Courtney lying, unseen, and unsaved, under the red water ceiling of blood.

# Seventy-Three

It had been Vincent's idea, a celebration of sorts, and a way of giving thanks. When the news reached England that Courtney was dead, the relief was universal. With his death, the feud was finally over; with his dying, the Razzios and the Bennings were at last united.

Almost one hundred years after Guido Razzio had first docked in Liverpool, his descendents were honouring his name and his achievements – and those of his wife. Putting all the violence and injury behind them, Vincent had laid on a boxing match at The Roman House, lining the walls with a pictorial history of the fighters. Bryn Davis was there, handsome, unchanged from the twenties; and poor Mick Leary, the eternal under-dog, was hung next to Jem Adler and the formidable Ron Poole. Posters from fights told of other days – Potter Doyle winning the Heavyweight Championship, Guido photographed with the Duke of Windsor, his dark eyes turned to the camera, his expression unreadable.

Not even the trainers were forgotten: bald Morrie Gilling was there and a print of Abbot looked out, his bowler hat resting on his jug ears, a cigar in his hand. Not one event was overlooked, the press invited to the match, cameras flashing and recording the fight, a selection of well known celebrities invited, Vincent resplendent in a dinner jacket, holding court in the centre of the ring. It was to be a bout in honour of his grandfather's memory, he explained to everyone's surprise, and in honour of his mother, who had kept that memory alive.

Taken aback, Misia was forced to her feet by the members of her family who surrounded her. Under the lights, recorded by a hundred cameras, she took an overdue bow, her thin, trouser-suited figure raising cheers from the audience. The Bennings surrounded her, her children, grandchildren and great grandchildren, all uniting together to pay their respects.

But only the immediate family – not the audience, or the press – knew that along with the Bennings came the other family. From Rome, Nancy came over with her children, Lomond and David, Norton attending with his new wife, the ghost of Ahlia seated somewhere amongst them. The feud was over at last; the next generation – the generation of David Razzio – would lay the acrimony finally to rest. With his father's death, both sides of the family had been unified. There was to be no fear of the future, and no overlap from the past.

Then the fight began, Misia looking around as the noise level increased, Vincent leaning towards her and taking her hand, Deandra beside him. The Benning Beauty had come into the hall last, a spontaneous round of applause greeting her as she took her seat. Of all the men you could have chosen, you picked him, Misia thought, looking over Mark Lieberman, and seeing, for one second, some shadow of the man she had loved.

"It's a great fight," Harewood said hesitantly.

Misia laughed. "You're *such* a liar – you know how you hate boxing."

He raised his eyebrows. "But I love you."

She hesitated, then nodded. "I love you too."

Ninety-five years; ninety-five years of work and struggle and children, and happiness. Misia thought of Portland, her eyes closing, then reopening suddenly as a roar went up from the crowd. The boxers were putting on a real show for them, fighting well, the lights burning down on the ring, the upturned faces of the spectators fixed on them.

It had been her father's dream, one which her mother had carried for a time and then passed down to her. A dream, which, in its turn, would be continued by her son. Misia gazed at the shouting man next to the ring, Vincent, lucky, happy Vincent. Take it on, she thought, enjoy it, live it. But who would continue *after* him? Misia wondered, suddenly anxious as she glanced round. Simeon saw her and nodded, his eyes as gentle as always. No, not you, she thought kindly, turning again, her gaze falling on Lalo. And not you. Or Cy – your futures are elsewhere. So who? Misia wondered, alarmed. After Vincent, who was there to carry on?

He was on his feet, calling out, caught up in the excitement of the fight. Misia saw him, then blinked, laughing outright.

Surprised, Harewood turned to her: "What is it?"

She jerked her head. "Look over there," she said happily. "I just got the answer to a prayer."

David Razzio was calling out, his hands cupped around his mouth, his usual reserve obliterated by a rush of energy. He was tall, she realised, and dark, like her father; the perfect inheritor of the dream. Over the shouts and whistles, she could hear David's voice, strong and clear, his expression animated, a fierce and solid vigour animating from him. David Razzio – *Razzio* – what a perfect heir. In the future the business would not be run solely by the Bennings; Razzio blood would mix with it, the two sides of the family coming together at last.

I like you, David Razzio, Misia thought. There's no part of your grandfather or your father in you, only the goodness of Pila and the strength of Guido ... Another roar went up from the audience and she smiled contentedly, glancing over and seeing Vincent punching the air and then grinning at David. He knows, she thought, he's seen what's to come, and he knows.

The fight ended shortly afterwards, Terry Gibbs coming over to Misia and taking a cocky bow, the press snapping pictures, the family moving to a restaurant nearby to celebrate. All of them were there; all the Bennings and the Razzios, and, on Vincent's orders, two seats had been left vacant at the head of the table. For the ones who had gone on before – Guido and Mary Razzio.

Then after the meal was finished, Vincent lifted his glass and looked at his mother. "To Misia Benning, nee Razzio – to a fighter in a class of her own."

Surprised, she looked around the table at her family. And then she caught Simeon's eye. Her son smiled, then glanced towards the two empty chairs at the table. Misia couldn't see what he could; she just understood what Simeon was telling her – Remember where you came from. And remember your mother, Mary. Remember as you sit here that she sat here once – at this very table – beginning the life journey which brought you here. As she began, we continue.

"Do you see her?" Misia whispered to her son.

In reply, Simeon said nothing. Just winked.

And then they all rose as one, hands held high, the candlelight blinking off the glasses: "To Misia Benning …" they said unison, "to the best and the bravest of them all."

# *Acknowledgement*

Many many thanks must go to my terrific agent, Sonia Land, at Sheil Land Associates, London, for her unwavering support and inspiring sense of humour. Also thanks to Gabrielle Hancock for all her help. And to both of them – as ever, thanks for your patience!

# About the Author

Alexandra Connor was born in Lancashire and educated in Yorkshire. She had a variety of careers including photographic model, cinema manager and personal assistant to a world famous heart surgeon. Yet, incredibly, it was only after being stalked and beaten up in London that she found her real forté. During her convalescence, Alexandra discovered an ability to paint. A further relapse resulted in her writing her first novel.

She has written one non-fiction and 28 fiction titles of which 9 are thrillers. *The Jeweller's Niece* (saga) was shortlisted for the Northern Booker Prize and more recently, *The Caravaggio Conspiracy* reached No 8 in the Kindle Chart and *The Rembrandt Secret* was a bestseller in the UK.

Her works have been featured in *The Times*, *The Telegraph*, *Observer*, *New Woman*, *Woman's Journal*, *Woman and Home*, *Hello!* *The Express*, *The Daily Mail*, and many foreign newspapers such as *Le Figaro* and *La Sicilia*. The BBC made a 40 minutes film on how she was stalked and beaten up and which is now on a University syllabus. She continues to be invited to give talks about her life experiences.

Alexandra Connor is listed in *Debrett's* 'People of Today'; is an entrant in the *Dictionary of International Biography*, and inaugural version of *The Cambridge Blue Book*. She is also a Fellow of the Royal Society of Arts.

Printed in Great Britain
by Amazon

39744296R00209